BLACK LYON

# BLACK LYON

THE ABI ACARDI SERIES

E.A. Stark

BURCH Publishing

"You can't blend in if you were born to stand out."

— *R.J Palacio*

Dedicated to all the young women who strive to be more.

E.A.Stark Books

For more information,

visit my website at www.EAStarkBooks.com

Printed in the United States of America

First Printing: July 2023

ISBN

ISBN Print- 978–1–7771124–8–6

EBook- 978-1-7771124-9-3

BLACK
LYON

# The Move

"American Airlines flight 338 with service to Los Angeles is now boarding at gate B9."

Upon hearing the announcement echoing through the terminal, Abi Acardi felt butterflies fluttering in her stomach.

*This is it*, she thought. *There's no going back now.*

Exhaling, she watched a few older passengers and those with young families gather their things and get in line. Not having a chance to think this far ahead, she wondered what living on the West Coast would be like. Concerned about whether she would fit in, the task of blending and starting over sparked unexpected anxiety and nervousness.

"Be brave, Abi. Focus on the positives," she whispered under her breath. "You'll be fine." Sighing, she repeated, "Everything will be just fine."

Having difficulty believing that statement, it hit her that they'd soon be flying high amongst the clouds and away from the city of Boston. Terrified, never having been on a plane before, she didn't know what to expect. Relying on her Mom, not knowing what to do, she saw her paying close attention to the second boarding announcement directed to all first-class passengers.

"That's us, Sweetie," the pretty, dark-haired woman said. Holding her passport and boarding pass, she stood confidently and slung her heavy tote onto her shoulder. "Let's go."

Abi was happy to see her mother more present. Alert, with abundant energy, it had been over three years since she'd seen her this way. Thankful to be a kid for a change, not having to think one step ahead and be the responsible one, Abi wondered if she knew how heartbroken she was to be leaving the East Coast. It's all she'd ever known.

Thinking back to the day her father accepted the once-in-a-lifetime position, a part of her wished it was just a bad dream - that she would wake up and everything would go back to normal. But sadly, it wasn't. Given little time to think, told that the life-altering decision was in her best interest, she felt forced to uproot her life permanently. So much had happened over the summer. It was mostly a blur. But today, the gravity of it all was slowly sinking in. They were leaving and never coming back.

Greeted at the gate and handed their documents, they walked through the tunnel to the door. It didn't take long to find their seats on the aircraft.

"Yours is by the window," her Mom pointed out. "That way, you can enjoy the beautiful view."

Settling in, Abi sat down, mimicked her mother, and tucked her backpack under the seat in front of her. While buckling up, she noticed all the activity on the ground below before scanning the number of affluent people around them. Aware of the many sights and sounds within the cabin, the teen took a deep breath. Once the plane filled to capacity, the attendants secured the doors for departure.

*Here we go,* she thought as they inched backward. A mix of feelings hit her. *This is it.*

Partially paying attention to the safety instructions mimed by the flight attendants, the plane turned and taxied toward the runway.

*The minute we leave the ground, everything changes.*

Hands clenched together, feeling every bump under the wheels, she recalled how she'd single-handedly sold their family home, all the furniture, and most of its contents, including the cars. Mentally exhausted and stressed, everything they owned was gone, erased. And briefly, she felt homeless. She'd only shipped a few precious items to the new house. Her father said he bought it fully furnished, so there was no need to salvage anything. A tear unexpectedly fell. Her childhood already felt like a distant memory.

Worried, Abi's mother found her deep in thought. "How are you holding up, Sweetie? Are you doing okay?"

Not knowing how to respond, Abi got overwhelmed by emotion. Confused by her Mom's sudden support and concern, she dried her tears and said, "Yeah, I'm okay."

"Just think, we will be in California in a few hours. I've always dreamed of living there, you know. Ever since I was a little girl."

Abi didn't say anything. All she could do was nod.

"This will be a new start for us," her Mom smiled excitedly.

The teen continued looking out the window, not feeling the same way. It seemed her mother wasn't worried about attending a new school, making new friends, or simply fitting in. Abi couldn't hide within four walls whenever she wanted. She had to venture out into this new place, rebuild her life, and hope it would all turn out better than the nightmares she'd had leading up to this day.

"Are you excited about starting at Gilderson? Your Dad said it is where the board sends their children. It must be good."

"I suppose so." Gathering her long, wavy brown hair to one side, Abi bent down to pull the registration package from her backpack.

Suddenly, the plane thrust forward, forcing her body into the seat. Dropping the folder, she grasped the armrests and held on tightly, afraid to peer out the window. Her mother bent down to pick everything up before securing it in the pouch on the seat in front. With the world whizzing by them at lightning speed, the wheels left the ground. Abi held her breath as the plane soared into the sky unsteadily at a sharp angle. Soon, they were flying amongst the clouds. Still clinging on, she slowly started to let go. Circling the New England area, never having seen it from the air before, it was a bittersweet goodbye. Some happy memories went with her, while others were best left behind. Feeling insignificant and alone, not having any friends who would miss her, she assumed that wouldn't change by moving to Los Angeles.

The fasten seat belt sign turned off, prompting people around them to go about their business. While a few grabbed their things from the upper compartments, others fired up their laptops to get some work done.

Figuring she'd do the same, Abi used this time to finish the paperwork required for the Gilderson Academy's orientation scheduled the next day.

Her mother tapped her on the arm. "Can I see?"

Handing her the welcome package, she perused the color brochure. "I know this school looks intimidating, but think of all the opportunities you will have because of your affiliation. I'm sure every college in the United States will accept your application after attending here."

"I haven't thought of anything past today," she muttered while answering the questions on the form.

Nodding, her Mom understood what she meant. "Don't worry, Sweetheart. I think you will do great in California. You're smart and athletic and have so much going for you. You're beautiful inside and out. I'm sure people will see that right away."

"Thanks, Mom." Abi wasn't at all convinced.

She forced a smile, knowing her daughter wasn't happy. "Well, tap my arm if you need me to help you. I am going to rest."

"All right."

It wasn't long before the middle-aged woman fell asleep, something that had become all too familiar over the past few months. She often faded in and out of Abi's life. Sadly, her daughter had gotten used to it now.

Slipping on her headphones to listen to music, the teen thoroughly examined the glossy Gilderson brochure, wanting to learn more about where she would spend most of her days. Until now, she hadn't had time to even peek at it. From what she could gather from the introductory letter, her first impression of the school was that it prided itself on a few main features. The first was the technologically advanced classrooms that housed a staff of highly experienced and knowledgeable professors. The second was the exclusivity of having the smallest student enrollment in the United States, and last but not least were the diverse, laser-focused classes that fell way outside the norm of a regular high school. Abi could tell that the place came by its reputation, honestly. It offered subjects like business strategies and analytics, marketing, branding, finance, and entrepreneurship to complement the modified Science, English, and Math classes. For a decade, it produced generations of competent, skilled heirs who'd become CEOs of numerous Fortune 500 companies worldwide. These strikingly attractive students excelled at many levels beyond the average adolescent. Long story short, it was an ultra-exclusive private school for the uber-rich. With only two hundred and ninety students in grades ten to twelve, Abi was concerned about blending into the niche environment. Bel-Air was a far cry from Boston.

*What if everyone hates me?* She thought rather destructively. Then something horrific dawned on her. *Great. There's nothing worse than being labeled the new girl.*

Thinking of a whole rash of challenges awaiting her, intimidation set in. It was the land of sandy beaches, palm trees, and Hollywood dreams. Being humble and straightforward by nature, uncomplicated and polite, Abi hoped that California's more vain society would appreciate the notable traits her mother forgot to point out. Never wearing designer labels or having driven fancy cars, she assumed she would still be considered poor among the students at Gilderson despite her father's seven-figure salary.

Flipping through the pamphlet again for the tenth time, studying every aspect of student life, picking out the finer details, Abi feared she would stand out. And not in a good way. Every girl in the booklet was blonde, blue-eyed, thin, and beyond pretty. Being a brunette, wearing little make-up, and more sporty than a fashionista, the teen briefly considered reinventing herself.

*This could be my chance to become someone else.*

Her Dad's voice internally intervened. He always reminded her that she encompassed this bright light that others would discover and gravitate to. It was something she had yet to experience for herself. Like most fathers, Abi assumed he had to say that. It was part of his job as a supportive parent. Sometimes, she thought it strange to be spoken of so positively all the time. Ever since she could remember, he'd always been her biggest fan. Knowing he believed and trusted in her, she, in turn, never wanted to let him down. This steered every decision she ever made.

*No. Abi, you must be yourself. If you change, Dad will be disappointed. You can't inflict any more stress on him. Not now. He has enough on his plate.* She encouraged while flying over a blanket of fluffy white clouds. *If they don't like you, then too bad. You have to say, Hi, my name is Abi Acardi. Here I am. Take it or leave it.*

2

# The Reunion

Approaching the City of Angels late that afternoon, Abi barely spoke with her Mother after waking from her nap. She recognized the look on her face and feared the woman might be experiencing the same anxiety she was. While staring forward into oblivion, having finished her small plastic glass of white wine, her Mom seemed scared and uncertain. Abi hoped and prayed this move wouldn't impede her progress in the past two weeks. It was nice to have her back.

In thinking about their new life in LA, she considered what her Mother's life might encompass. It wasn't easy being a surgeon's wife. She was sure they'd expect her to throw dinner parties, sit on charity boards, and do lunch with the other wives in the circle of friends her father had created since he arrived. It was always that way before her Mom got sick. Countless events and social gatherings were commonplace in their world. Then it all stopped.

*Perhaps I need to be more supportive of her, too.* She thought. It wasn't going to be easy for either of them.

Above Los Angeles, they only saw buildings, warehouses, and residential areas below. The mountain range ran as far as the eye could see, but the Pacific was nowhere in sight. Sadly, it made their arrival rather anti-climactic.

Before the wheels hit the tarmac, the aircraft jostled in the crosswinds, making Abi grasp the armrests with a white-knuckle grip.

Seconds later, they lightly touched the ground. Feeling the pilot apply the brakes, the plane slowed enough to taxi to the gate safely.

Prepared to disembark, Mother and daughter gathered their things while they got closer to the terminal. Anticipating her reunion with her Dad, Abi could hardly wait to hug him. It had been so long since they'd seen each other.

When they stopped, the engines turned off, and one attendant quickly unlocked the door to allow the passengers to depart at will.

Leaving the plane, they followed the crowd to the baggage claim. Her Mother grabbed their suitcases from the carousel and accounted for everything one by one. With luggage in tow, Abi searched for her Dad when they walked through the arrival doors. It wasn't hard to spot his smile amidst the crowd. Always happy and positive, she missed him immensely.

Dragging their luggage, Abi ran into his open arms as her Mother slowly followed.

"Hey, Abi Banannie," he said joyfully. "I've missed you!"

"Missed you too, Dad."

Sharing a group hug, the teen could feel that finally, after all this time, their family was together again.

Abi stepped aside to allow her Dad a moment with the love of his life.

Seeing him longingly gaze at her, he wrapped his arms around her waist and said, "Hello, my darling." Gently kissing her forehead, he knew her feelings about public displays of affection and respectfully abided by that.

With eyes closed, thankful to be near him, she whispered, "We made it."

"Yes, you did." He was proud of her.

Their bond always amazed Abi. Despite all the obstacles they'd overcome, their love was still deeply rooted. She prayed one day, she'd be just as lucky to find the same – someone who'd look into her eyes precisely like that.

Breaking from their reunion, her Dad said enthusiastically, "So, welcome to California, you two! I think you are going to love it here. The house is awesome, and the air is salty, just like Boston."

"I can hardly wait to see the house," Abi said. "I was disappointed that you didn't send pictures."

"Well, I wanted that to be a surprise. It's one of many," he hinted with a lot of pent-up energy. "With that said, we should get going. We don't want to get stuck in rush hour traffic."

Commandeering their baggage, one in each hand, her Dad proudly walked with his girls, excited to get the show on the road.

3

# Home Sweet Home

After an hour on the highway, suffering through stop-and-go traffic along the 405, they finally merged onto Sunset Boulevard.

"See, Banannie, the Gilderson Academy is on the hill to your left. It's not far from the house."

Abi peered out the window at the large white architectural building gracing the hillside.

"Excited about the orientation tomorrow?" her Dad questioned, looking back in the rearview mirror.

"I think I'm more nervous than excited."

"Understandably." Hearing the uncertainty in her voice, he said, "Don't worry, Sweetheart. Everything will be fine. Trust me." Not sure if his words helped, he added, "I don't think we say it enough, but we are so proud of you and who you've become. You are a driven young woman. We believe you're destined for great things."

"Thank you, but I feel you have to say that. You're my Dad."

"When have you ever heard me say anything that wasn't true?"

Abi nodded her head. "Yes, I realize. You always speak the truth."

"Precisely."

Driving along Sunset, they arrived at the iconic Bel Air West Gates. Quickly recognizing them from so many movies, she couldn't believe this place was about to become part of her reality. Staring out the window as they passed the many mansions nestled amongst the lush, manicured hedges and colorful foliage, the girl from Boston felt like a fish out of water.

Through so many twists and turns, only catching a glimpse of everything as they passed, her Dad soon slowed down. Inching towards a gate surrounded by trees, Abi leaned forward between the seats as he pressed the button on a remote. The gate slid to the left.

"Here we are—home sweet home. Abi, close your eyes. Quickly. No peeking. You too, honey."

Both ladies did what he asked while the SUV inched forward.

"Can we open them now?" Abi held her breath.

"One second. One second." Shifting the truck into park, he said, "Keep them closed." Getting out on his side, he rounded the vehicle and opened their doors. Offering each a hand, he escorted them to the center of the courtyard. "Okay. Open them."

Abi and her mother hesitantly peeked out one eye before opening both fully. There, parked in front of the modern home, were two vehicles with enormous red bows resting on the hoods.

"Wait a minute? Is one for me?" Abi was in utter disbelief.

"Yes. Do you like it?" her father questioned, analyzing her reaction.

Walking over to the black-on-black Mini Cooper convertible, her sights bounced between it and her Dad.

"Of course I do! I love it! Are you kidding me?" In disbelief, so thankful, she ran over to her parents and hugged them both. "Thank you! Thank you! Thank you! Wow! This is amazing. I can't believe it. I never thought I'd ever own a car." Teary-eyed, she was afraid to touch it.

"Well, in the past year, you've demonstrated that you are ready for the responsibility." Her father was so pleased to say it.

Lost for words, Abi didn't know what to say.

"So? Do you want me to show you its many features?" he asked.

She excitedly nodded while they walked toward the vehicle. Her mother looked on happily and took a peek at her new Mercedes, too.

"How is she?" her Dad whispered with heightened concern, careful his wife didn't hear them.

"She's been better the past couple of days."

"That's good to hear." While showing Abi her car, Dr. Acardi spotted his wife moving to the front door. "No, stop!" he shouted humorously.

Not moving an inch, she turned to him and asked, "Oh my goodness! Why?"

"Isn't it a tradition to carry you over the threshold?"

"Honey, really? That is so old-fashioned," she laughed playfully.

In a dramatic tone, he replied, "It might be bad luck otherwise. We can't risk it. I'm sorry," her husband said cheekily, sweeping her off her feet into his arms.

"Ooohh!" she giggled with delight.

Eyes affixed to hers, standing but a moment, he smiled and kissed her lips.

Shrieking with joy, she said, "Oh, Anthony. You don't have to do this."

"Yes, I do." While holding his wife, he turned to Abi. "Can you open it for us, Sweetie?"

"Sure can."

Swinging the white solid steel pivot door inward, Abi walked into the home with her parents close behind. She found a wall of windows to her left and a bench with artwork on the opposite side. Initially, from the exterior, the house was deceiving. It looked small and a bit cold – a typical modern design with only two windows visible. But inside, the floor-to-ceiling wall of glass framed the canyon views. Those windows extended the entire length of the home. It certainly made up for the exterior's lack of character.

Setting his wife's feet on the marble floor, her parents joined her in the bright, airy living room before moving onto the dining area, which had space for twelve. Upon rounding the corner, she found the kitchen and family room - both well suited for watching football on Sunday afternoons and cooking to their heart's content.

In disbelief at how beautiful the place was, Abi felt like she was dreaming.

Her Dad slid the Fleetwood doors to the side to give them access to the enormous backyard. The space consisted of an infinity pool, a contemporary pavilion with an outdoor kitchen, and a rooftop deck. The home looked out over a deep ravine with many mansions nestled amongst the mature trees on either side.

"Can I go and see my room?" Abi asked, hoping to give her parents some time alone.

"Absolutely. It's the first door at the top of the stairs."

Excited, the girl from Boston found the staircase and ascended the light wood steps alongside a stately twenty-foot-high window, intentionally framing the most majestic tree. Midway up the stairs, she paused to admire it.

"Well, this is a peaceful spot," she said, knowing it would be an excellent place to sit and think if and when she needed it.

Continuing to the second floor, she came across a library with two entire walls of bookshelves, comfortable seating, and reader-friendly lighting.

"First door at the top of the stairs," she whispered, repeating her dad's words.

Opposite the library, she timidly peered inside the room. Speechless, Abi was in shock. Professionally decorated and draped in white and grey tones, the space was so calming. With a fluffy king-sized bed as the focal point, crowded with pillows and accented by a pretty throw blanket along the footboard, she ran her hand along the raw silk comforter before noticing a new laptop, monitor, keyboard, and mouse already set up on the desk. On the chair were packages of pens and pencils, two binders, and stacks of paper, all stuffed in a new designer backpack. It was evident her Dad had been busy getting ready for her arrival.

"He is amazing," she said, feeling a bit spoiled.

Turning to find two more doors, she opened one leading to a walk-in closet housing a beach bag, flip-flops, sunscreen, and beach towels. The other led into a Carrera marble bathroom with a shower and a stand-alone tub, perfect for bubble baths. Scanning from floor to ceiling, she looked out into the bedroom as her eyes found the wall of glass and the view pictured beyond it.

"Knock knock," her father said as he brought in her suitcases and bag. "So? What do you think of your room?"

Startled, she said, "Oh, Dad. It's beautiful. Thank you so much."

"Don't thank me. You should thank the decorator who came to furnish it. I had no idea what to do. Candace did everything."

With outstretched arms, she hugged her father. "I absolutely love it."

He could tell it had been an emotional day for her. "Hey, are you okay?" he asked, holding her tightly.

Abi nodded. "I'm just happy to be together again."

"Me too." Knowing she was anxious and scared to embark on this new life, he leaned back to see her face. When she looked up at him, she somehow seemed so much older. "Don't worry," he said. "I'm here now."

"Okay," she replied.

"I'll let you get settled. Call if you need anything."

Happy to see his contented expression, she said, "I will. Thank you."

When he had gone, she didn't know where to start. Unzipping her suitcase on the floor, Abi slowly unpacked everything and neatly placed it flat on the bed.

"Well, Abi. You made it. Now what?"

4

# The Mansion Across the Canyon

Later that evening, after sharing a sushi platter with her parents, Abi said goodnight to them before climbing the stairs to her room. Over the next few hours, she continued unpacking. Neatly hanging her clothes in the closet, soon the space started to feel more like home.

Sitting on the edge of the bed, flopping backward to stare at the ceiling, she looked at her desk. Spying the new laptop, Abi decided to fire up all the new equipment and get it working. While configuring her settings and customizing her screens, the sun began to set in the western sky. An amber glow spread across the wall above her bed. It wasn't long until night fell upon the West Coast.

Leaning back in her chair while her email updated, Abi glanced out the window to find a large, brightly lit mansion on the opposite side of the canyon. Accented by blue neon piping, the spotlights at every corner helped boost its size. Curious, wanting to get a closer look, Abi repositioned the telescope sitting in the corner of the room. She realized her Dad remembered she'd sold hers and had thankfully replaced it for her. Carefully setting it in front of the window, she looked through the lens and lined up the tube to find the massive home. Swinging left and right, slightly moving up and down, she caught a glimpse and focused in. Able to see in the windows, it looked like a hotel versus someone's house. Each room had stunning modern chandeliers, marble floors, and furniture that was more for show than comfort. Abi scanned every floor of the place, not feeling guilty for peeking in on her neighbors across the way. When inspecting the rooftop terrace, she suddenly spotted a dark figure standing along the glass barrier. One man. By himself.

"Strange. He looks like a lonely king in such a large castle."

There wasn't another soul around. Unable to see his face in the shadows, Abi tried to bring him into focus more, but all she saw was him raising a glass in the air, somehow staring her way. After taking a sip, the man turned around and disappeared inside as all the lights illuminating the structure turned off simultaneously in sync with theirs.

"How odd," she whispered, wondering if the guy's timer was running on the same schedule as their pavilion lights.

Puzzled, wondering who he was making the toast to, Abi began to hit a wall with the time difference. On the East Coast, it was nearing midnight, and her body knew it. Getting ready for bed, she remembered what was on the agenda for tomorrow. With a sigh, she took a deep breath and had to gather the strength and courage to show up at her new school without fear - a tall order based on what she'd read in the welcome brochure.

Pulling back the covers, she tucked herself in and whispered, "Welcome home," before rolling over to get some much-needed sleep. Unfortunately, the next day would be a stressful one. She hoped being well-rested would help her survive it all.

# 5

# Orientation Day

With the time change, Abi was up bright and early. Disoriented not to be waking in her room in Boston, she sat up in bed and looked around. Scared to face the day, she prayed that the students at the new school would not be too critical of her, but somehow, she wasn't holding her breath.

Nervously changing clothes four times, thankful to be getting a school uniform to level the playing field from an exterior façade at least, Abi grabbed her crossbody bag and phone. Slipping the Gilderson Academy forms into it, she found the school's address and immediately entered it into her GPS app to search for nearby coffee shops. Locating one not far from her intended destination, she headed downstairs and found her Dad in the kitchen.

"Good morning, Sweetheart," he said with a pleasant smile. "How did you sleep?"

"Pretty well, considering. I'm still a bit tired, but not bad. I just want to get this orientation done and over with. The faster I get there, the faster I can come home."

He sensed his daughter's apprehension.

"Where's Mom? Is she up yet?"

"No, she's not. Don't worry. I've taken the day off today. I knew you would be out and didn't want to leave her alone."

Understanding what he was saying, she was thankful for the break.

"Take my credit card in case there are any incidentals you need to pay for. The pin is 3987. I've already paid the balance of the tuition. I'm not sure what the uniform pieces will cost and if there are any books you need. I think all of that gets handled today."

Abi could see her Dad was feeling a little down. To brighten his morning, she said, "Thank you. I'll tell you all about it when I get back."

Happy to hear that, he said, "Best of luck, Sweetie."

"Thank you. I'll see you later." She grabbed the keys to the Mini Cooper from the basket on the front entrance table.

"Remember! Be careful driving. This isn't Boston!" he shouted from the other end of the house as Abi opened the pivot door.

"Okay!" she shouted back before closing it behind her.

Excited, never having owned a vehicle, she found the jet-black convertible shining in the morning light. Getting behind the wheel, she picked up on the new car smell emanating from the leather seats. With her phone in the holder, she activated the GPS to get directions to the coffee shop. Ready to go, she stopped. There was a big problem. She had no idea how to start the car.

"When in doubt, YouTube it," she chuckled. Quickly finding a how-to video, she followed the step-by-step instructions and pressed the circular key fob into the slot until it clicked. The engine magically started when she pushed the smart button. "Hallelujah. Success," she whispered while fast-forwarding the video to find instructions on how to turn it off.

"Abi!" her father said, walking out the front door. "I forgot to show you the app needed to open the gate."

Proud to see she figured out how to start the car, his little girl suddenly looked so independent and grown-up. Showing her what she needed from the app store, she took it from there.

While the app was downloading, he said, "Press this button to retract the roof if you like."

Doing as he said, the roof peeled back and tucked away behind her. Testing the remote, she watched the large gate slide open. "It works," she said happily. Shifting gears, she slowly left the courtyard as her Dad looked on. "Bye!" she said, waving her hand above her head.

"Bye. Have fun!"

About to exit onto the narrow street, mindful of any oncoming cars that could fly around the hidden corner, she peered into the adjacent mirror. Making sure the coast was clear before carefully pulling out of the driveway, she listened to the GPS instructions, still craving her first coffee in California.

Safely maneuvering the narrow winding streets, lined by tall twelve-foot privacy hedges on either side, Abi battled the two-way stop at Bellagio Road. Thankfully, a man in a Rolls Royce graciously waved her into the gap ahead of him. On her way, she turned right on Sunset and was soon passing over the 405. Seeing the road that led to the school, she continued down South Barrington. There, she spotted the Starbucks in the plaza.

Space was limited in the parking lot. Pulling in slowly, she saw a person backing out as she approached.

"Perfect timing. Thank God. Maybe my luck is changing," she whispered.

Effortlessly recalling the shutdown instructions, she accomplished that step and got out. While locking up and paying the meter, she caught the heavenly aroma of freshly brewed coffee wafting through the doors. Before going inside, Abi spotted a group of girls in a fancy BMW convertible speeding recklessly into the plaza. Unable to find an open space, they swung around and left their car right outside the main entrance, blocking other patrons from leaving.

"That's so wrong," Abi whispered. "Who do they think they are?" She kept an eye on them while waiting in line.

When the girls came in, laughing and giggling, they were oblivious to the disturbance they were causing.

Shot a few dirty looks from people, the apparent posse's leader rudely asked one lady, "What's your problem?"

*Great. Here we go,* Abi thought as the girls stood behind her.

Not turning around, she stepped forward and politely placed her order with the woman behind the counter. Moving onto the pickup area, Abi kept her head down and glimpsed over occasionally.

"Yeah, just our usual," the mean girl said arrogantly, expecting the staff to know what that was.

Confused, the woman spoke up. "I'm sorry. I'm new here. You have to place an order."

"You're kidding, right?" the blonde leader said while rolling her eyes.

The group was completely annoyed and fuming. All blonde, thin, and well-dressed, they had matching designer backpacks slung on one shoulder.

The mean girl volunteered one of her friends to rattle off their long list of preferences. It seemed beneath her to do it herself.

While waiting for her coffee, Abi unintentionally eavesdropped on their conversation.

One of the girls asked, "Did you get your ticket for Black Lyon yet? It should be a hell of a party. I hear everybody is going next Saturday."

Another girl confirmed she'd received hers and flashed something on her phone screen as proof. The third girl did the same, while the fourth looked worried since she hadn't gotten one yet.

With little sympathy for their friend, the leader glanced over in Abi's direction and said rudely, "OMG. What color is her hair?"

"I don't know. How would you describe it?" another interjected.

"Mousy brown, maybe? What do you think?"

Abi's face went beet red as they stared her way. Her cheeks felt like they were on fire.

"Coffee for Abi," the barista announced at the most inopportune time.

Stepping forward to grab it, she heard one say to another, "Her name is Abi. What kind of name is that?"

"Maybe it's short for Abigale?" one questioned sarcastically.

"Wow, like from the 1900s?"

Needing to get out of there with her confidence disintegrating by the minute, Abi immediately felt sick to her stomach. Dashing out the door and rushing back to her car, thankful to escape the bullying, she started the engine and slid her cup into the holder. Quickly checking the GPS app, she carefully backed out of the space while the girls exited the coffee shop and loaded up in the BMW. Unable to get past them, she had no choice but to wait until they moved. Shot a series of snarly looks, the leader glimpsed in her rearview before stepping on the gas and squealing the tires. The others shouted while waving their hands wildly as they drove off.

Abi continued on her way, trying to calm down after the horrible experience. Upon making a right turn onto Sunset, she headed towards the Gilderson Academy, grateful the girls had gone in the opposite direction.

Instructed to take a left at North Church and a right on Beverly Park Drive, she drove around the winding corners and under a bridge. Following the tented parking signs with the Gilderson logo, she found herself at the entrance to the underground garage. Just outside, a man signaled for her to stop.

"Gilderson Academy?" he questioned, point blank with a clipboard in hand.

"Yes," Abi replied.

"Name?"

"Abi Acardi."

The man checked her off and found her parking pass inside an accordion file. "Hook this on your mirror when you park. Always have it visible. Your space is number eighty-two. It's the second aisle on the right. You'll be near the end of the row. To get to the registration area, take the elevators or stairs closest to me. From there, you can follow the signs."

"Thank you, Sir," Abi said with a smile.

Inching forward, the man suddenly raised his hand to stop her again. Slamming on her brakes and jolting the car, she looked at him.

"Appreciate the manners," he said.

Older, sporting white hair, slightly hunched over, he seemed nice.

"What is your name, Sir?" Abi asked politely.

"Gerald."

"Well, it's very nice to meet you, Gerald. I guess we will see each other often from here on out. Wish me luck. It's my first day."

Stunned by their conversation, the gentleman chuckled. "Good luck to you, Miss."

"Please, call me Abi, Sir."

"You're not from around here, are you?"

"Nope. I just moved from the East Coast." In that split second, she broke him from his stern exterior and got the man to crack a smile. "Guess I'll see you on my way out?"

"Yes, it seems you will," he said in disbelief.

Abi figured their conversation was something he wasn't used to having very often. That worried her. Did the students not have the same courtesy? What was she about to step into?

Allowing her to pass, Abi did as Gerald instructed and found parking spot number eight-two. Nervous, with her heart beating rapidly, she took a deep breath. Locking her car, she noticed the high-end vehicles in the garage. From Porsche to Lamborghini, Ferarri, BMW, and Mercedes —you name it—they were all there. Across from her was a custom Jeep Rubicon without doors or a roof.

"Don't tell me these cars belong to the students at this school. If they are, I'm in trouble."

Abi followed the signs to the steps that led to the next level. Arrows directed her toward another set of buildings north of the parking lot. Able to find her way, she opened the door to a large foyer dressed to welcome the Gilderson students back for another successful year. A bit over the top, with balloons and abundant swag, it wasn't but a minute before she heard a girl's voice.

"Excuse me. I can help you here."

Turning her attention away from the decorations and the many people, Abi found a pretty girl looking at her.

"Welcome to the Gilderson Academy. Do you have your paperwork?"

"Umm, yes." Abi pulled the forms from her crossbody bag and handed them to her. "My name is Abi Acardi. I'm new."

"Oh, good. I've got all the newbies on my list." Checking off her name on a piece of paper, the girl said, "I'm Jade. I'll be getting you set up today."

With a clipboard in hand and pencil in the other, Jade got serious. "All right. The first order of business is your uniform. It includes skirts, pants, tops, cardi, and gym clothes. I'm supposed to tell you about the school's brand of casual stuff, but...." Leaning in, she offered a word of advice. "Just FYI. Nobody buys anything but the uniform."

Abi got her drift. "Gotcha. Okay."

"Right this way, then." Led through a set of doors into the uniform shop, Jade turned to her and scanned her body from top to bottom. "I'd say you're a size six or eight on the bottom. Small or medium on top." She waited for an adverse reaction. Not hearing a rebuttal, she added, "All the girls usually get offended by that statement. Hmm, you didn't bat an eye."

"Why would they be offended?" Abi was confused.

"Well, the sizes fit small, so if you are a six regularly, I suggest you take an eight."

"Okay?"

"Most girls run zero or double-zero, so telling them to go up a size is like the kiss of death for most." Handing her two options of skirts and pants on hangers, Jade suggested, "Try these. See what fits better."

"Will do. Thanks."

Given a changeroom, Abi went to try on the skirts while Jade walked around the store and grabbed the other pieces she needed. Flopping them over the door, she asked, "How's everything fitting?"

"Think I like the eight better."

"Damn," Jade said under her breath.

Abi walked out of the changeroom and curiously asked, "What?"

"I thought for sure you were a six." Shrugging her shoulders, she said, "No matter – try on the rest."

Within fifteen minutes, Abi had an armful of Gilderson crested attire. Jade cashed her out. Folding everything neatly into a school logo-embossed cloth tote, she handed Abi her receipt after her credit card went through.

"Okay. Now to the school bookstore," Jade said, pointing across the hall.

While they walked through the crowd gathered in the foyer, everyone's eyes gravitated toward the front doors. As both flung open, a group of good-looking guys walked in, ready to soak up all the attention. Drawn to one in particular, she couldn't help but smile.

Jade caught the newbie fixated on the jocks.

For whatever reason, Abi couldn't stop staring.

"Word to the wise. Look away. Some of those guys are on the varsity football team, and three of them are the most famous students at Gilderson," Jade explained.

Abi tore herself from the scene unfolding. "Wow. They are really handsome."

"Don't even think about it," Jade firmly warned.

"Why not?"

Forced to give her some insight, she said, "See the ghostly, pale guy with the icy eyes?"

"Yeah."

"Well, that's Blu Brennan."

"Blue like the color?"

"Yes." Scanning the group, she said, "The two blondes with the same beach boy hairstyle are Alan Scott and Shawn O'Donnell. The dark-haired guy is the actor Aramis Knight. The shy one is Adrian Murphy, and Taizo is the tall Japanese American actor with rock-hard abs. He's from a billionaire family. You may have seen his helicopter landing on the helipad a while ago."

"Does he not have a last name?"

"No. A man that fine doesn't need one if you ask me."

Abi wholeheartedly agreed.

"Of course, my favorite is the dark-haired hottie with the dimples. That's Reggie Wilson. He is yummy, don't you think?"

"Yes, he's cute too." Fixated on the tall, sandy-haired guy with a kind smile, Abi queried, "What about him?"

"Oh, that's Shane Coppersmith. He's the captain of the team."

As the jocks gathered around, they greeted each other in a testosterone-infused display. Shoving and bumping chests, Shane turned and caught sight of Abi across the foyer. Mesmerized, he shot a curious look her way. Time seemed to stand still the moment he offered a partial smile. Abi timidly did the same.

Seeing this, Jade quickly shut it down. "Hey, Abi? FYI, Shane belongs to Emile Raven."

Reluctantly breaking away from the handsome football player, she asked, "What do you mean, belongs to?" before locking eyes with him again.

About to explain, whistles erupted from the crowd.

That is when Abi saw them. It was the girls from the coffee shop obnoxiously waltzing through the doors. Lowering her head, she muttered, "Oh, no. No. No. No..."

"What? What is it?" Jade asked, seeing the posse stop and look Abi's way.

"I ran into them at Starbucks this morning. They weren't exactly friendly."

"I'm sure they weren't." Attempting to save the new girl, Jade turned her back on Emile and physically did the same to Abi so they could make a run for it. Dipping into the uniform shop, they hid behind a clothing rack out of sight.

Hiding, Abi watched Shane look around. It seemed he was wondering where she went.

"That's Emile Raven and her posse. She's Shane Coppersmith's girlfriend and the cheerleading team captain."

"You're kidding?" Abi felt numb. "Wonderful...."

Seeing an opportunity to sneak away, Jade dragged the newbie into the storage room and out to the loading dock. A safe distance from the crowd, she said, "Come on. Let's see where your classes are. After that, we'll grab your textbooks and go shopping. No offense, but your wardrobe needs a serious update."

Peering down at her uber-casual attire, she said, "Why?"

"Girl, you look like you're from Idaho."

Successfully sneaking out a side door, Jade showed Abi around the school. They strolled through the spacious library, which had a peaceful feel. Abi recalled spending most lunch hours hiding in one, a quarter of the size back in Boston. It was a place where she could find peace and serenity amongst the crazy-loud teenage population buzzing the hallways. Part of her wondered if things would be any different here.

While walking through the outdoor bistro, Jade explained, "Unlike most schools, we are lucky enough to have an infusion restaurant. Chef Michael is a Michelin Star. He has something for everyone, no matter your dietary needs—dairy-free, keto, high-protein, nut-free, and gluten-free. You name it. We have it."

Not fussy, Abi knew she'd be happy to have anything nutritious.

Continuing their conversation, Jade asked, "So, do you play any sports?"

"Yes, a few?" Abi was afraid to rhyme them all off.

"Tennis, perhaps?" the girl questioned.

"Matter of fact, I do."

"Are you good?" She pointed and shot a serious look her way. "Cause if you are, the tennis team needs help."

"I would say I am." Abi didn't want to divulge more than that.

"Perfect, then it settled. Tryouts are on Tuesday after school. You're coming with me."

"Alright. I'm in." That excited Abi to the core.

Walking the grounds and locating all of her classrooms, Jade realized their schedule was the same. "Don't worry. We are together for every class. I'll protect you from the masses."

Abi was scared to ask why she needed protecting.

Having made a loop, they doubled back toward the bookstore.

"So, are you good? Feel comfortable here yet." She hoped the tour helped.

"Yeah. I'm sure I'll manage on Monday."

"Don't worry. We can meet up and walk in together if you want. The first day will be tough, and you'll need support."

Concerned, Abi fearfully agreed. "Thanks a bunch. Appreciate that."

Happy to take whatever help she could get and thankful to have found a friend, Abi followed Jade across the bridge connecting the north and south buildings. Along the way, they saw the football players and Emile's posse sitting on the lawn below them. Ducking down a little, they passed by unseen.

The front foyer was quieter now as Jade grabbed the textbooks Abi needed and quickly cashed her out. Stuffing everything into another crested cloth bag, the two girls left and headed to the garage.

"So, are you ready to go shopping now?" Full of confidence, she said, "Don't worry. I'll drive."

# 6

## Beverly Hills Style

Jade kept her eyes peeled for Emile Raven while crossing the courtyard. Out of all the girls in school, she was the one to avoid at all costs. Making it safely down the steps, she said, "Hurry. This way."

Abi did her best to keep up.

Approaching a black Rolls Royce SUV parked in the V.I.P zone, Jade asked, "Where do you like to shop on Rodeo?"

"Rodeo?" Abi didn't know what she meant.

A man dressed in dark clothing got out and opened the rear door.

Jade stopped dead in her tracks. "You don't know Rodeo Drive?"

Embarrassed, Abi said, "No, not really."

Rolling her eyes, the girl laughed. "Just get in."

Warned of things like this, Abi hesitated. "I thought you said you were driving."

"I am – well, indirectly, of course," she said before quickly making the introductions. "Abi, meet Tony and David. They're my drivers."

"You're what?"

"Don't you have a driver?" Jade was somewhat confused. "Like security?"

Thinking fast on her feet, she replied, "I just arrived here yesterday, so I don't know for sure."

"That's okay. I'm sure you'll meet your team soon."

Abi slipped into the bucket seat beside the confident girl. Surrounded by plush leather and wood accents, she didn't know how to act. Following Jade's lead, she held her head high and tried to blend. Watching the security guard close the door and get in on the passenger side in front, she saw him turn around and wait for instructions.

"Take us to Rodeo, boys."

"Very good, Miss," the man said obediently.

Winding down the hillside, waiting for the barrier arm to lift and release them from the school grounds, the luxury SUV maneuvered the circular driveway. After turning onto Sunset Boulevard, they linked with the highway and drove south.

Afraid to see what stores they'd be visiting, Abi was so nervous her hands were sweating.

Jade put her phone to her ear. "Hello, Lisa. Can you meet me in front of Ralph Lauren in five minutes?" Hearing a break in the conversation, she added, "Yes. I have a friend who needs your help."

That sent Abi into a panic. "No, it's okay. I think we'd be fine on our own. Don't you?"

"Hold on, Lisa." Muting the call, she curiously turned to Abi and asked, "What's up? Do your parents have you on a short leash or something?"

"Umm, no... Well, maybe? Can you elaborate?"

"Do they put a limit on you?"

For whatever reason, it seemed like Jade was speaking another language.

"Like, money-wise?"

"Yes," Jade said.

Abi realized that was her way out. "Sadly, it's a very tight leash," she replied dramatically. They don't like me spending any money— like at all."

"That's why you used your dad's credit card to pay for your uniform and books? You poor girl. Such a shame."

It was strange to see Jade unfazed by her statement.

"Don't worry. I get it. There are so many like you here."

"They make me account for every penny." Abi made sure to lay it on thick.

"But, regardless of all that, this is an emergency. You need clothes." Jade thought a second and said, "Hold on, guys. Change of plans. We're heading to Neiman Marcus on Wilshire." After they acknowledged her, Jade got back on the phone. "Lisa? Meet us at Neiman Marcus instead." When Jade ended the call, she turned to Abi. "If you go there, you can get more for less. Sound good?"

"Great...." Abi figured she might have gone from the frying pan into the fire.

Leaving Jade to scroll through her phone, Abi looked out the window. Captivated by the palm tree-lined streets, she felt like she was living in a movie. Marveling at all the upscale stores, lost for words, they soon slowed down and wrapped around to the rear of the large Neiman Marcus store before slowly stopping at the entrance.

Not skipping a beat, her new friend waited for the driver to open her door. Getting out, she instructed the men, "Wait here. We will be about an hour or two, tops."

A handsome young guy greeted her. "Good afternoon, Miss Webber."

"Hi, Jerry. My guys need to stay close by."

"No problem, Miss."

"Come on, Abi." Jade walked toward two other attendants who parted the doors like the Red Sea.

"Welcome to Neiman Marcus," they said in unison.

"Thank you," Abi replied politely on the way by.

Inside, Jade made eye contact with a woman in the aisle. She looked so regal, dressed in a tailored suit with a patterned blouse underneath and designer pumps. Despite her hair tied back in a tight bun, she looked a little flustered.

"Miss Webber! Hello!" the woman said, trying to pull herself together and seem presentable.

"Hey, Lisa. Good to see you. Hope this wasn't too last minute?" Not allowing her to respond, she turned and said, "Lisa, meet Abi Acardi. She's new."

The fashionable woman looked Abi up and down. "Spin," she instructed in a stern, monotone voice.

Doing what she asked, Abi was afraid not to.

"I can work with that," Lisa stated concretely. "This way."

Jade dragged her friend into the women's section while Lisa swiftly coordinated a few trendy, age-appropriate outfits.

Seeing what was happening, two Neiman Marcus salesgirls followed to assist the woman. Gathering the clothes handed to them at lightning speed, they started a changeroom, knowing the commission for the next hour would be enormous. Granting their every request, Jade left Lisa to do her thing.

"Come on, Abi. Time to play dress-up." The girl sat in the chair outside the changeroom. "Word to the wise. If you're gonna make it here, you must understand there is a difference between the rich and the wealthy. Lisa knows we hate in-your-face monogrammed labels. She finds me luxury brands that are understated. The one exception to that is Ralph Lauren. It's a legacy brand. For instance, if you flaunt the likes of Louis Vuitton or Prada, the wealthy think you're poor."

Shocked to hear it was the opposite of her perceptions, Abi stepped into the spacious room filled with clothes. All of it was understated, as she described, and boasted exceptional quality, style, and versatility. Most she hadn't heard of and would have never considered otherwise. Deciding to start with a more casual ensemble that wasn't too expensive, she emerged and showed Jade.

Sitting back in the chair, she said, "Spin," seemingly taking instructions from Lisa's playbook.

Abi swiveled around. "So what do you think?" The white Vince crochet-trimmed cardigan draped over a heather grey knit tank went well with the Veronica Beard denim shorts. It was comfortable, and she felt good. It was very California.

Jade took a photo of the look. "I love it. You can wear this to so many parties."

Returning inside the changeroom, she spotted a simple, royal blue eyelet summer dress. Afraid to look at the price, she was pleasantly surprised to see it marked down, assuming it was an end-of-season sale. About to try it on, she discovered that the dress had a built-in skort. Abi looked in the mirror and zipped it up.

"Love it," she said before happily stepping out to show her friend.

The girl's eyes opened wide. Taking another photo, she said, "Perfect. The color is awesome. It really pops. You've got to have this one. Where are the shoes Lisa paired with this?"

Returning to the room to find them, she didn't particularly like what the woman had selected. She wasn't a wedge kind of girl, and the designer Stuart Weitzman label meant they were at least four hundred, if not more. Scouring her options, Abi got an idea. Taking a chance, she stepped out. Pairing the dress with all-white Givenchy sneakers instead since they were now half-price, Jade was initially disappointed but changed her tune and smiled.

"I love it," she said. "You can dress it up or dress it down. Think the sneakers suit your style better."

Abi was relieved to hear it.

Moving on, having tried over twelve more outfits, the pile kept growing and growing as the salesgirls brought her what Lisa had chosen. Abi began to feel sick.

Almost at the two-hour mark, Abi was exhausted. She'd changed clothes at least thirty times. Stepping out in the last outfit, she looked in the mirror at the monochrome ensemble of Ponte leggings, a matching knit cropped tank, and a roomy cardi. Lisa paired a small Chloe crossbody saddle bag to top off the look. Before showing Jade, Abi looked at the tag.

"Thirteen hundred?" she whispered to herself. Unable to justify that, she left the bag on the chair and took the more understated Oryany neutral one instead.

"Love this too. Lisa did a good job. You look like you fit in now."

Completely spent, Abi said, "I think I'm ready to stop. I haven't tried on so many clothes, well, like ever," she laughed. "So," she paused, "how do I choose which outfits to buy?"

Jade looked confused. "What do you mean, choose? Aren't you taking all of it?"

A large lump developed in Abi's throat. "All of it?"

"Sure. We didn't spend all this time pulling these looks together just to put it back."

Abi smiled terrifyingly. "Right..." she said, returning to the room. She didn't want to come across as rude or ungrateful for what she did for her. From pants to tops, bathing suits, dresses, intimates, and shoes, Abi knew it was the nicest wardrobe she'd ever seen.

*Worst case scenario*, she thought. *I can always return it if I have to.*

Once Abi had changed back into her clothes, the two salesgirls gathered everything Abi handed them. She'd sneakily kept out a few items and left them behind. With the clothes neatly placed on the counter, one girl scanned the purchases while the other folded everything in tissue paper and packed it into the light grey, logoed bags.

Her heart beating a mile a minute, Abi pulled out her father's credit card and watched the total increase exponentially with every item of clothing added to the bill.

When the final piece got folded, the girl said, "So, your total for today is six thousand, five hundred, ten dollars and eighty-nine cents."

Fearful, Abi hoped her dad's card could handle the purchase. Slipping it into the machine, she entered the pin and waited. Time stood still before the word *Approved* appeared on the screen.

*Oh, thank God,* she silently thought, able to finally take a breath.

"Thank you so much, ladies," Jade told the sales girls.

"Make sure to come back soon. Here are our business cards. Call ahead, and we will be ready to assist you whenever you need," the pretty blonde sales associate confirmed.

Given all of the shopping bags, Jade helped carry some out while texting her guys.

Abi saw Lisa leaving. "Jade, aren't you going to say goodbye to your friend?"

Breaking from her device, she turned and shouted, "Thank you, Lisa!"

The woman stopped in her tracks. Not saying a word, she gave a subtle nod and walked out like royalty.

"Don't worry. I'll pay her fee when she sends me the invoice."

"Invoice?"

"Yes, she charges three hundred dollars an hour."

Abi almost choked while doing the math in her head.

When they exited, Jade's drivers were parked right outside the main doors. Coming to their aid, both men took the bags and carefully packed them in the back.

Polite as always, thanking them for their help, Abi got in beside her friend.

Before closing the passenger side door, Jerry, the valet, said, "Enjoy the rest of your day, Miss Webber."

Reaching across, she handed the guy a hundred-dollar bill. "Thanks, Jerry."

"Hope to see you again soon, Miss."

Exhausted, Jade waved but said nothing.

While driving away, only one thought troubled Abi to the core. How was she ever going to explain the staggering bill to her father? This was entirely out of character for her. She never went shopping - even when she did, she always looked for bargains.

*I must be honest with him and say I will return everything if he disapproves. Just tell him you didn't want to look like a fool in front of your new friend. Don't worry, he will understand.* She thought to herself.

It was a quiet drive to the Gilderson School. Upon arrival, Abi noticed Gerald sitting in the security booth when they entered the garage. Swinging the SUV around, the guys parked beside a white Porsche convertible.

Jade quickly got out. "Which one is yours?" she asked.

Abi pointed to the Mini Cooper. "That one."

"Really?"

"Yes, why?"

"No reason," she chuckled. "I don't know if it's all gonna fit." She smiled and turned around. "Okay, guys. Load the Cooper."

They transferred the bags from the SUV to Abi's car one by one.

Looking at the time, Jade said, "Oh! I'm going to be late to meet my mom. It's my weekend with her."

"That's okay. Just have them leave everything here. You go ahead. I'll pack the rest myself."

Genuinely apologetic, she said, "I'm so sorry."

"It's fine. No worries," Abi said as the men ran out of space. Gathering the last few bags, they left them beside her. "Thank you for helping me today. That was nice of you. I had fun."

Surprised by her appreciation, she smiled. "Yeah, me too. I'm so glad you like the clothes. You look fabulous in the outfits."

"Thanks."

"Well, I'm off." Feeling guilty for leaving the newbie behind, she asked, "You're sure you're okay here?"

"Yes, of course. Go! You don't want to be late. I guess I'll see you on Monday."

"I'll meet you here at eight-thirty."

"Great. Enjoy your weekend, then."

"You, too." Jade jumped into her car. As the roof peeled back, Abi watched her spread a silk scarf atop her head and tie it below her chin before slipping on sunglasses. It reminded her of old Hollywood glam. Starting the engine, the pretty girl waved to her and drove away – her security team was tight on her tail.

Abi leaned against the concrete pillar and gazed at all the packages, wondering how she would fit the rest. Deciding to condense a few bags, she packed the back seat with whatever she could and soon started filling the front passenger side. A bit shell-shocked by the afternoon with Jade, she took a deep breath and tried to relax.

"Do you need some help with those?" a voice said.

Looking up, Abi saw Shane Coppersmith standing there, towering over her with an athletic backpack slung over one shoulder.

Tongue-tied, she stumbled about. "Umm, yes. I mean, no." Flustered, she pulled herself together and rebounded. "I think I've got it. Thank you, though."

"No problem." Hesitant, he added, "My name's Shane. You're new, right?"

"Yes." Stretching to offer her hand, she said, "Nice to meet you, Shane. I'm Abi. Just moved here yesterday."

"Where ya from, Abi?" he asked confidently.

"Boston."

"Oh, so you're a Patriots fan?"

"Matter of fact, I am."

Caught off guard, the tall, handsome athlete said, "Wait? You know who the Patriots are?" He couldn't believe his ears.

"Well, you can't live in Boston and not see a game in Foxborough."

His eyebrows raised. Shane was impressed. He knew she was telling the truth since he'd been to a game at Gillette Stadium.

"I take it you follow Tom Brady?" Abi asked casually.

Shane laughed. "Wow, you know who that is?"

"Well, him and Phillips, Rodgers, Wilson, Brees, Ryan, Luck, Mahomes. The list goes on."

The football player looked away in disbelief. "Apologize. I've never heard a girl talk football before. Intelligently, I might add."

"Well, I'm not your average girl." A spark ignited inside her. Confident but not arrogant, she stood her ground and stared at him, not knowing what more to say.

"Apparently not." With an awkwardness looming, he added, "So, New England. It looks like you've got everything under control here. Guess I'll be seein' you around then?"

"Yes. Suppose so."

Fidgeting, he replied, "Okay. Have a good weekend." Shane turned and walked towards the custom Jeep Rubicon.

"You as well," she said, her heart still pumping uncontrollably in the aftermath.

Seated in his Jeep, having thrown his backpack in the trunk, Shane started the engine. While it rumbled, he slowly left, raising a hand to bid her goodbye - a gesture that gave her butterflies.

Stunned that Shane Coppersmith spoke to her, Abi got into her car feeling light as a feather. That was short-lived when reality hit her. About to head home, she now needed to explain her shopping spree to her father. Not sure how to do that exactly, she wondered if he would be okay with at least some of it. If not, she knew she'd be making a trip back tomorrow.

"Great... How embarrassing will that be?" she said, dreading the thought.

# 7

# Truthfulness

Climbing the hillside, rehearsing the pitch for her father, Abi tried to justify her actions, even though she had acted irresponsibly with his credit card.

"The best thing to do is own up to it and apologize right out of the gate," she said aloud. "I shouldn't have done it, but under the circumstances, I felt pressured after meeting a new friend." Her head bobbled around aimlessly. "I panicked, yeah, and failed to use my better judgment. Period."

Settled on what she would say, Abi pressed the remote for the gate. Driving through when it opened, she grabbed her school totes and left the Neiman Marcus bags in the car.

Walking inside, ready to present her spiel, she went straight to the kitchen, hoping to recite everything word for word. Rounding the corner, she found her Dad watching television while working on his laptop.

"Hi, Dad," she said. Her stomach fluttered nervously.

"Hi, Sweetie. So how did it go?"

"Good. I met a friend."

"That's wonderful. See, I said you'd do great."

She sat down adjacent to him. "Yes, her name is Jade. She helped me out at orientation."

"Is she nice?"

"Yes. Really nice. Umm..." Abi paused before confessing what she had done.

Her Dad stopped what he was doing and gave her his undivided attention. He could tell she had something to say. "What is it? What's wrong? Is everything okay?"

"Yeah, umm... I need to tell you something. Please don't be mad." She pulled out his credit card from her Burch bag. "Jade took me shopping today after I checked in at school. It seems my Boston style doesn't cut it here in LA."

"Okay..." He hung on her every word. "And...."

"We went to Neiman Marcus, and she got her stylist to help me. I, umm, was afraid to say no."

"How much?" He looked at her sternly.

Abi squinted before squeaking out the total. "About six thousand, five...hundred...."

Disappointed, he closed his eyes and looked away, trying to process the astronomical figure.

Waiting for him to yell, she bowed her head. "I know what I did was wrong, and I promise I will return all the clothes tomorrow."

Seeing her sitting there, with hands trembling, he couldn't believe what he was about to say. "That won't be necessary."

Abi stopped breathing, believing she'd heard him wrong. "Pardon?"

"Think of it as a thank you for dealing with all the stress of getting here. You looked after your Mom while I was away. You handled the sale of the house, packed up everything, and sold what needed to go. All of that, and you kept on the honor roll. You deserve the shopping experience you had today. The chance to be carefree and have a little fun for a change."

Speechless, she got emotional and teary-eyed. "Are you sure? I know it's a lot of money. I would never...."

"I know you wouldn't. You've just proved that. Look, I want you to go out and have fun. So, that said, you will need to dress the part. Sweetie, you have never asked for anything all these years. You are not spoiled or rude. You are always helpful and act beyond your age. I am so proud of you." He took a deep breath and added, "But you and I know we aren't out of the woods yet. We still need to tag team to get your Mom back on her feet here, okay?"

"Don't worry. I'll help whenever you need me."

He smiled. "Thank you." Changing the subject, he said, "So, I guess you're hungry after all this shopping?"

With a bright smile that melted his heart, she said, "Kind of."

"So, we can order Thai or wood-fired pizza? Maybe burgers? Thoughts?"

"Definitely burgers," she laughed.

"Okay, sounds good. I will get right on that."

Abi went to grab all her packages from the car. Fumbling about, she brought them upstairs in one trip. Tossing them on her bed, she received a text.

*Hey! How does everything look?* It read. Not knowing the number, she texted, *Sorry. But who is this?*

*It's Jade!*

"Jade? How did she get my number? I don't recall giving it to her." Before Abi could reply, she received another message.

*Hope you don't mind, but I copied your cell from your school data sheet and put it in my phone. Figured we would become friends before the end of the day.*

Abi smiled and typed, *Yes, that's fine. No worries. Glad you did. As for the clothes, I'm just about to hang them in the closet.*

All at once, she received photos of every outfit she tried on that day.

*Here are the reference pictures in case you forgot what goes with what. Group your clothes according to the outfits. It's easier that way.*

Laughing at her friend's organizational skills, Abi knew what she said made sense. *Will do,* Abi typed with a smiley face and thumbs-up emoji.

*Hey? What are you doing tomorrow?*

*Nothing, why?* Abi wondered what she had in mind.

*Well, you're coming with me to Venice Beach then. My friend Allie is having a get-together at her family's summer house. Lots of people from school will be there. We can introduce you to everyone. That way, you will see familiar faces on the first day of school. Are you in?*

Abi thought a moment. *That would be great. Thank you. I just have to check with my Dad. I'll confirm with you a bit later. Send me the details, okay?*

*For sure! Later Bestie!*

"Bestie?" Abi said aloud. "I've never been someone's Bestie before." Thinking about that, she said, "Well, maybe once upon a time."

Surrounded by shopping bags, excited to have plans for tomorrow, she started hanging up her new wardrobe piece by piece. Having done what Jade suggested, Abi stepped back and looked at her walk-in closet. Overwhelmed, she felt so fortunate to have such beautiful clothes. About to collapse on the bed, she heard the doorbell. Heading downstairs to join her Dad, she smelt the aroma of burgers and fries.

Saddened that her Mom decided to stay upstairs, they could see her slipping into the same state she'd been drifting in and out of for the past few years. Recalling everything her Mother had endured, Abi wondered how she'd made it this far. Believing she was often strong and courageous, times like this made her think she was giving up.

Aware of his daughter deep in thought, her Dad said, "Don't worry. She will be okay. We have to give her time to adjust."

"Yes," is all she could say.

Later that night, after sharing her highs and lows with him and giving the play-by-play of her shopping trip, Abi excused herself and went to get ready for bed. Walking into her room and over to the window, she looked at the mansion across the canyon. Checking the time, she wondered if the man would be standing on the roof again. The neon beams lit up the house. Tonight, it centered on a blue and white theme. Positioning her telescope just right, Abi scoured the rooftop for any movement. In minutes, right on schedule, the man appeared with a glass of champagne. Still unable to see his face, just a darkened silhouette, the man raised his glass, took a drink, and waited for the lights to turn off.

"Is he greeting the moon? Or ending the day in appreciation? It's so weird."

With impeccable timing, her home's pavilion lights turned off just as the mansion went dark for the second night in a row.

"This can't be a coincidence."

8 |

# Strength

Not needing to get up early that morning, thankful to have help with her Mom finally, Abi knew her Dad was in charge. Usually, she dreaded Saturdays. For the past two months, she'd have to be up before her Mom and be on watch. But not today. Today, her Dad told her to sleep in and enjoy being a kid. Thinking about her afternoon plans, she hoped he would allow her to go to Venice Beach with Jade. The invitation was both exciting and nerve-racking. Focusing on the positive, she could hardly wait to see the Pacific Ocean.

"What should I wear?" she whispered to herself. "You've gotta make a good impression if other students are going to be there." Believing she'd have a few more friends by the end of the day, Abi remembered she hadn't asked permission yet. Wrapped in a robe, she went downstairs to make her dad breakfast, hoping that would convince him to say yes.

Descending the stairs, smelling freshly brewed coffee, she knew he had beat her to it. Finding him in the same spot she'd left him last night, watching television with his laptop open on the coffee table and reading glasses perched on the end of his nose, she walked over with a smile.

"Morning, Dad."

"Morning, Sweetheart. Sleep well?"

"Yes, I did. Needed that. Yesterday was stressful."

"I wasn't expecting you for at least another hour or two. It's nine o'clock. Aren't kids your age supposed to sleep in until at least eleven on Saturdays?"

"Well, technically, it is way past eleven with the time change. I'm still on East Coast time."

"Oh yes, you're right."

"I'm feeling a bit anxious, so I felt the need to get moving." Wondering how to bring up the subject of Venice Beach, she asked, "How's mom?"

Her father removed his glasses and set them on the computer keys. Burying his face into his hands, he seemed frustrated and worried.

"She is the same," he said. "The trip took a lot out of her. I don't know what we are going to do come Monday. You will be in school, and I need to be at work. I've put in a call to medical services to get full-time help. I'm hoping they come through for us." The stress on his face was immense. "Listen, I don't want you to worry about your Mom. I've got this. You should focus on building your life here. Getting acquainted with things."

Filled with emotion, she nodded her head.

"Don't worry. She will be okay. I'm keeping a close eye on her." He leaned back against the sofa. "So, what's on the agenda today? Anything special?"

Abi felt terrible even bringing it up.

Her Dad could tell she had something on her mind. "What is it, Banannie?"

Liking the sound of the nickname that had followed her since childhood, she said, "Well, umm, Jade asked me to go to Venice Beach with her today. A bunch of Gilderson students will be there. She thought she could introduce me to everyone."

"So, then, you should go. No question." The guilt of leaving him at home on duty weighed on her. He knew it. "Sweetie, these first few days at the new school are important. Without social interaction, things could become difficult. I want you to enjoy the transition and not worry about your Mom and me, okay?"

"Are you sure? I feel bad."

"Don't. I want you to go and have fun."

Abi went into the kitchen and opened the fridge. Finding little there, she asked, "Do you need me to drop by the store this morning, you know, to stock up on a few staples? I can do that."

Thankful for his little girl, he got up from the sofa. Offering open arms, he hugged her. "No. I'll do that," he emphasized. "How about you watch Mom while I'm out? Then you can leave for the beach when I return. Deal?"

"Okay."

"Thank you for the offer, though. Love you," he said.

"Love you, Dad."

Breaking away, he was a bit teary-eyed. "I'm so happy both of you are here."

"Me too."

He headed toward the staircase. "I'll get going, so I'm back before eleven."

"No rush. It's fine."

When he made his way upstairs, she followed. Hearing the bathroom door shut and the shower running, Abi cautiously went to sit with her Mom. The room was dark as she passed through the doorway. Typically, when she wasn't feeling well, that was how she liked it. Walking to her side of the bed, the once lively woman who traveled with her to California now lay lifeless. It was like she had disappeared. Sound asleep, barely breathing, Abi recalled the past few months. Her behavior was much the same.

*Strange how she could muster the strength to get me here*, she thought.

Sitting quietly with her, she listened to the peacefulness of the space. When the shower turned off, she left the room to let her father get dressed. Sitting on the top step and seeing the wise old tree outside the window, she wondered what to wear to the beach party, so she texted Jade to ask her opinion.

*Hi Jade. My Dad says I can go with you to Venice Beach today. I'm kind of excited, but I don't know what to wear. Any suggestions?*

Within seconds, Jade began to type her reply.

"Well, that was fast," Abi said while the thinking bubbles cycled repeatedly.

*That's awesome. Wanna meet @ Starbucks in Brentwood @ 1?*

Abi answered, *Sure. Sounds good.*

*Just FYI - you'll have to follow me in your car. I'm heading to Malibu afterward. Gotta be at my Grandmother's for dinner @ 7.*

Not expecting to hear that, Abi's heart sank. She hoped she'd have enough courage to drive back home alone. To show her independence, she typed, *Yes, that's fine. No problem. I'll be okay. Now, what do I wear?*

*Oh, right. Wear a t-shirt, denim cutoff shorts, and those new Givenchy sneakers. Bring the slides, too. Wear your bikini underneath the clothes and bring an extra outfit just in case. Throw in a hoodie and a beach towel.*

Abi sent her a thumbs-up emoji. *Will do. See you then!*

*Lookin' forward to it, girl!*

Her Dad exited the bedroom and found Abi sitting on the stairs. "Everything all right?"

"Yes, just texting with Jade about our plans for later."

"Don't worry. I won't be long. Anything you'd like from the store?"

"Umm, maybe granola cereal and orange juice. Bread. Some fruit."

"Absolutely." He kissed her forehead and said, "I won't be long."

"Okay." She felt alone when her Dad left. It was the same feeling she got daily in Boston while he was gone. Shaking it off, she knew he would be back shortly.

Returning to her room, leaving her door wide open, Abi entered her closet to pull the outfit Jade suggested. She grabbed the royal blue Milly Cabana bikini she bought yesterday, the denim shorts, and a white t-shirt. Laying it on the bed, she retrieved her canvas beach bag and found a stack of pool towels in every color of the rainbow. Taking the turquoise one because it complimented her swimsuit best, she rolled it up and put it in the tote. With sunscreen, make-up, and a brush packed, she unplugged her charging cord and stuffed it in the bag. A whole list of things started to go through her mind.

"Hoodie. Can't forget that," she said. Taking one from her closet, she neatly folded it with another change of clothes similar to what she was wearing.

Ready to go, she decided to check on her Mother again. Still asleep, she wondered what had snapped her from this a week ago.

Recalling her meltdown before they left Boston, having done so many things to keep them afloat, Abi repeatedly begged her to help in the final days before the move despite her Mom not feeling well. Having packed their things and shipped them to the West Coast, Abi sold their furniture to some students from Boston College. During the broker's open house and every showing after that, she stood guard, ensuring nobody entered the guest room where her Mom was resting. For the most part, knowing their situation, their real estate agent worked within Abi's end-of-term exam schedule. Regardless, it wasn't easy. Under enormous pressure, she got desperate. Sitting at her Mother's bedside, she cried and begged her to return to her because she was afraid.

"That is what I said. Did that trigger her to wake up?" Wondering if it would work again, she thought she'd try it. Quietly moving to her side of the bed, she gently sat on the edge and held her Mother's hand. "Mom? Mom. It's Abi. Umm. I thought I'd let you know how my orientation went." Not receiving a response, she continued to tell her about the school, her classes, and that she got her uniform and books okay. She attributed that day's smooth transition to her new friend, Jade, before divulging that she had met the captain of the football team. Before telling her his name, she said, "Mom? Please wake up. I want to share these experiences with you."

Holding her hand tightly, Abi suddenly got a weak squeeze from her. "Mom?"

Her Mother's eyes fluttered and slowly opened. "I'm here, Abi," she whispered before looking around. "Where are we? What is this place?"

"It's our new house in California. Remember, you and I flew here on the plane two days ago. Daddy picked us up at the airport."

"Oh, yes, California. We are moving there." She seemed disoriented and confused.

Realizing her Mom wasn't coherent, she couldn't understand how she actively made it there, then faded away again. "Don't worry. You sleep. Dad just went to the store. He will be back soon."

Her Mom didn't say anything more.

9

# Life's a Beach

Within an hour and a half, her father returned carrying five cloth grocery bags full of food to stock the kitchen. Having lived alone for two months, constantly working and eating on the fly, he never needed to grocery shop.

While helping him unpack everything in the cupboards and the fridge, Abi explained what had happened with her Mom a few minutes earlier.

He was happy to hear that she got a response. "I will continue interacting with her while you're gone," he mumbled.

Abi felt he wasn't telling her something. "Maybe leaving her rest is not the answer. We have to keep her present and involved."

"Perhaps," he said as they folded the last empty bag. "Thank you for your help. Now, you go. Enjoy your day with your new friend – what's her name again?"

"Jade," Abi confirmed.

"Oh, yes. Jade. I have to remember that."

Not telling him she had to follow her to Venice Beach, she figured it was better he didn't know the details so he wouldn't worry. About to leave, Abi double-checked that she had everything. "Bye, Dad. I'll see you later."

"Have fun, Sweetheart. Keep your ringer on just in case," he advised.

"Will do. Love you."

"Love you too. Bye."

Abi left the house and closed the door behind her. Upon pressing her remote twice, the convertible top opened and tucked away automatically as the windows rolled down. Tossing her beach bag in the back, she was nervous about meeting new people today but excited to see the ocean. Carefully inching onto the street, she closed the gate behind her and started down the hill toward Sunset Boulevard.

Approaching the Bel Air two-way intersection, it was busy as usual. Stopping, waiting her turn to weave into traffic, a young woman in a Bentley graciously waved her in. Abi acknowledged with a smile before signaling right. Moving across Sunset, she drove over the 405 en route to Starbucks. Wondering how busy the plaza would be, she hoped they could find parking this time of day.

Partway there, she received a text from Jade.

*I'm at the Chevron across the street. Thought we should get some chips and drinks for Allie's.*

About to pull into Starbucks, Abi spotted Jade's Porsche at the gas station. Changing direction, she drove in and parked beside her.

*I'm here.* Abi texted before walking inside. Seeing Jade wandering about the store, she said, "Hi, I made it."

"Hey, girl!" Jade hugged her. Having picked up a few bottled water, chips, and soft drinks, she asked, "Ready to have some fun today?"

"Yes, definitely."

Arms full, she took everything to the cash. "This should be enough for the afternoon. Do you wanna grab an iced coffee or a berry drink for the road? Oooh! I could go for pineapple matcha."

"Sure. That sounds great."

Tapping her card on the reader to pay the bill, the two walked out. Jade set the bags in the back seat before they bolted across the busy street to grab a cold brew.

Abi opened the door and let her lead the way.

Waiting in line, Jade explained who she'd be meeting today. "So, from what I gathered, Allie said it would be a full house. It's kinda the last beach event before school starts."

Anxiety surfacing, Abi had a small request. "Please, for the love of God, don't leave me alone. I'm so nervous as it is. I hope everyone will like me."

"What do you mean? Of course, they'll like you. Anyone in their right mind would. Don't let Emile and her posse of bitches throw you off."

That reminded her of her run-in with them yesterday. Ironically, they were standing in the same spot. "All right," she said while trying to shake off the horrid memory.

"Oh, I'm praying Reggie shows up. I'm sure he's still jet-lagged, though. He only returned from Europe two days ago."

"Who's Reggie, again?" Abi asked while ordering two pineapple matchas and paying for them.

"He's Shane's best friend. You know, the guy I showed you - the one with rock-hard abs and muscles for days. Mr. tall, dark, and handsome. Just the way I like 'em." Jade's imagination went wild, wondering what Reggie would look like with his shirt off.

"Order for Abi?" the barista announced.

With a raised hand, Abi walked over. "That's me." Grabbing the drinks, she turned and found Jade still daydreaming.

"Earth to Jade?"

"Yeah... Sorry, I'm coming."

Ready to walk out the door, the girls heard someone call out, "Abi Acardi?"

The voice seemed faintly familiar. It didn't take long to find out who it belonged to.

Jade quickly took notice of the stunningly attractive man trying to get her friend's attention.

Surprised, Abi looked into the guy's eyes to confirm her suspicions. "Burton? Burton Lancaster? What are you doing here?"

His face brightened at the sight of her. "I was going to ask you the same thing."

Immediately recognizing her childhood friend, she reached out to him and offered a hug, which he greatly accepted. When she stood back, she couldn't get over how muscular he was. More manly and very well-dressed, Abi was stunned by his appearance. It was wild how much he'd changed. The only thing that stayed the same were his eyes. They were still as gentle as ever.

Jade nudged her repeatedly, unable to stop staring.

"Burton Lancaster, meet my friend Jade Webber."

"Nice to meet you, Jade." He shook her hand in the process.

Standing six feet three inches, with aviator sunglasses hanging from his Henley shirt, he wore cuffed joggers and white sneakers on his feet.

"So, what brings you to California, Abs?"

His ice-blue eyes and chiseled jawline were hard to ignore.

"My Dad started a new job here. Mom and I arrived on Thursday. How about you?"

"I attend UCLA. Com Sci degree."

"Oh, a college man," Jade whispered, still swooning.

"Wow, that's amazing." She was super impressed. "How are your parents?"

Burton hesitated before answering her. "Yeah, umm, they're good." Nervous, he asked, "Hey, can I get your number? Maybe we can hang out and catch up." He didn't want to elaborate with Jade there.

"Sure. Of course. I'd like that."

Burton handed her his phone. She easily entered her name and phone number in his contact list.

"Thanks. I'll text you." Before leaving, he thought he'd take a chance. "Hey? Are you free tomorrow?"

Surprised, Abi replied, "Suppose so."

"Good. Want to meet here at, say, two o'clock?" His eyes squinted, waiting to hear her answer.

"Okay. Two o'clock tomorrow. I'll be here."

"Great. See you then. It was a pleasure meeting you, Jade." He shot her a sexy smirk.

Jade giggled. "Nice meeting you, too." When Burton left, she asked, "Okay? Who the hell was that hunky man, and how do you know him? He is fine."

While the two girls walked across the street, Abi noticed Burton wave from a matte black McLaren sports car. It growled as he accelerated out of the plaza.

"You know that car is worth about four hundred thousand, right?" Jade pointed out.

Hearing that, she wondered how Burton could afford it. It wasn't like his family had money when they lived in Boston.

"I can't believe you've been in LA for only three days, and you've got boys asking for your number. That's unreal."

"It's not like that. We were neighbors for years. Before he left, I think I was in grade eight when he was in grade ten. We hung out all the time. Then, one morning, he was gone, and there was a for sale sign on the lawn of his house. No goodbye. Nothing."

"Very mysterious." Jade was intrigued.

Abi's mind was reeling. She had so many unanswered questions.

"Now that we've had a rather exciting start to the day, are you ready to go?" Her friend sipped her pineapple matcha before getting into the car.

"Yep. I'll follow you. Don't lose me. Okay?" Abi knew she might not find her bearings if she got lost.

"Don't worry. Just make sure you keep up." The girl flashed a devious grin.

When Jade pulled out of the gas station, Abi was right behind her. Heading back to the 405, they drove southwest to Venice Boulevard and backtracked to West Washington, which led straight into the parking lot at the beach. After paying for a four-hour pass, they found open spots on the far side.

The girls closed their convertible roofs. Jade divided the snacks and drinks she'd bought. Abi put half in her beach bag to share the load.

Walking toward the paved path, the two heard someone shout, "Hey! New England?"

Abi's heart dropped. Only one person called her that. Swiveling around, they found Shane and Reggie about thirty feet away.

"Wait up!" the handsome football player said.

With a smile, trying to play it cool, Abi simply said, "Hi. What are you doing here?"

Mere feet from them, he replied, "We're heading to Allie's place."

"Us too. Jade invited me," Abi divulged.

"Glad she did," he said with a slight tilt of his head.

Abi's heart fluttered upon hearing that.

Reggie approached with confidence. "Jade? How's it goin'?"

"I'm doing okay. How was your summer vaca?" she asked, despite having kept tabs on his Instagram with posts from Spain, Portugal, Greece, and France.

Not making a big deal of it, he said, "It was good. Nothing exciting."

While they walked along the path, Jade saw some Gilderson students hanging out at the beachfront home. As they got closer, everyone started shouting at Shane. Thrown a football and told to *Go Long,* the football captain dropped his backpack in the sand and jumped out of his slides to make the catch as everyone cheered and hollered.

Noticing the extent of Shane and Reggie's popularity, the team gathered around them while Jade and Abi headed inside to find Allie.

A stranger to everyone there, Abi felt out of place. The girls all had dark tans, making her look ghostly in comparison. It was hard to feel confident in that environment. Everyone in the kitchen was mostly blonde.

Spotting them, Allie shouted, "Jade! So happy you girls made it!"

"Thanks for the invite," she hugged her friend before making introductions. "This is Abi—the new girl I told you about."

The cheerleader pulled her hair into a high pony and secured it with an elastic. Sporting designer sunglasses and a killer body in a string bikini, she said in a bubbly tone, "Nice to meet you. Glad you could join us."

"Nice to meet you, too. Thank you for inviting me." Abi thought she seemed harmless enough. Not arrogant. Friendly, at least.

"Any friend of Jade's is a friend of mine."

Nervous, amidst so many perfect people, it was hard for Abi not to wonder what was in the water. Or was it the sunshine? Maybe DNA enhancers in the food?

"We brought snacks. Does anyone want any?" Jade asked, opening a bag of chips and tumbling them into an empty bowl.

"Thanks, girls. Appreciate that," Allie said. "Make yourselves at home. I think we're heading down to the shore soon. We will take that with us."

Jade gave her a thumbs up and walked with Abi onto the covered porch. She whispered, "I can't believe Reggie is here, and he talked to me. OMG. This is awesome." She grabbed Abi's arm excitedly.

"You really like him, huh?" she asked, staring at the boys. Shane and Reggie clearly stood out among the rest.

"I have liked him from the second he started at Gilderson. Technically, I've admired him from afar. Didn't think he knew I existed. We never spoke until today." She melted as he caught sight of her.

"Well, maybe that will change now."

"I hope so," Jade said, shrugging her shoulders, almost giddy.

Talking amongst their group, they noticed the guys keeping tabs on them. When Reg raised his hand to wave to Jade, she happily offered a flirty response.

"Come on," she said, "Let's go and join the party."

The two descended the steps and crossed the paved path, mindful of the constant string of pedestrians and bikers passing through.

"So, if Shane is here, does that mean Emile is coming?" Her guard went up as she scanned the beach for the girl.

"Oh, hell no. She wouldn't be caught dead here. There are too many people. She is a Malibu priss who only sits poolside."

Relieved, Abi started to relax.

Migrating to join the girls who'd merged with the loud partygoers, they communally overlapped their towels and beach blankets as the guys prepared for a flag football game.

Introduced to so many people, Abi was thankful to be accepted without having to try too hard. Adding Laney, Summer, Ming, and Mei to her friend list, each was curious about where Abi was from and why she'd moved there. A few had visited Boston before, making it easy to start a conversation. Slowly settling in, she stayed calm and tried to enjoy the day.

When some people returned to the house to escape the heat, Abi told Jade, "I'm going to go for a walk up the beach."

Sun worshipping, Jade replied, "Yeah, okay," without opening her eyes.

Standing to stretch her legs, Abi wandered to the water's edge and looked out over the vast ocean. The waves rolled in one right after another and hit the shore roughly. While soaking up the sun's warmth, she could feel the current tugging at her ankles.

About to begin her stroll, she heard, "Mind if I join you?"

Startled, knowing exactly who said it, Abi hesitated before turning to offer a quick recovery. "Umm, sure. If you'd like."

Shane was tall enough to cast a shadow over her. Seeing him standing there shirtless caused a flutter in her chest. But soon, that giddiness turned to a feeling of dread.

*What are you doing? If Emile gets wind of this, things will end badly.* Stopping the negative talk, she said, "I was just going to walk to the jetty over there. Stretch my legs a bit. I find it hard just sitting on the beach, doing nothing."

"Me too." He looked away and surveyed the crowd. "After you."

Abi took the first few steps and kept her head down most of the time.

"When we talked yesterday, I don't recall you mentioning why you moved to California?"

Knowing their brief meeting mainly consisted of football talk, she glanced up at him and said, "My Dad is a surgeon. He got a new job a couple of months ago. He moved here first and prepared everything for my Mom and me to arrive. What does your Dad do?"

"He's an entertainment lawyer. My Mom is a plastic surgeon. Maybe she knows your Dad if he is at UCLA med."

"I don't even know where he works. I haven't gotten that far yet. It's been a busy few days."

"So, what do you think of LA?"

Abi thought for a minute. "It's had its moments. Both good and bad."

"I'm Sorry to hear that. Maybe things will get better from here on out." His tone expressed genuine concern. You just have to find your groove."

"Possibly," she said while her brain formulated another topic of conversation. "Do you have any siblings?"

"Kind of. That is a complicated subject. My older sister died of a drug overdose six years ago. My parents divorced after that. It was messy."

Shocked by his statement, she said, "I'm sorry." This struck a chord with Abi.

"My Dad remarried, so I have a stepmom and a thirteen-year-old stepbrother. He'll be starting at Gilderson next year. It's hard. I don't have anything in common with him. He's a heavy gamer, not into sports. I kinda feel sorry for the kid. He spends a lot of time alone."

A large wave rolled in.

"Oh!" she said, falling off balance as her feet sank in the sand.

Quickly catching her, he said, "Steady. I gotcha," and propped her back up. "You're good." Almost in a trance, unable to look away, he waited for her to regain her footing. "The undertow here is pretty strong."

Embarrassed, she said, "Yes, I see that. Sorry, for ah...."

"Yeah, no worries." Reaching the boulders, he asked, "Other than following football, do you play any sports?"

"Back in Boston, I played badminton, tennis, volleyball, and basketball. I also did a lot of lane swimming, long-distance cycling, and downhill skiing."

He laughed at her lengthy list. "Impressive. Safe to say that you're a sporty girl, then?"

"Yes. I'm pretty competitive."

"Good to know."

Needing to put it out there, like ripping off a bandaid, she outright asked, "So, Emile is your girlfriend?"

Unsure how to answer that, he looked out over the water and said, "Sort of," and didn't elaborate further.

"I ran into her and her friends at the coffee shop yesterday morning. Let's just say it wasn't a good start on my first day here in LA."

"I'm not surprised. She isn't the friendliest of people."

"Yes, I found that out firsthand." Abi hated the thought of being bullied.

Shane could tell she was hurt by whatever his girlfriend had done. "Between you and me, she's been pushing my buttons for a while. She's mean to others and verbally beats me up every chance she gets. It's not a healthy environment."

"So why are you with her then?"

Shaking his head, he revealed, "I honestly don't know anymore." Cutting it off there, he asked, "Do you mind if we step away from that?"

"Sorry. It's none of my business. Didn't mean to pry." Thinking about what was happening, she said, "I'll be honest, I'm a bit concerned about someone at the party telling her we are talking. If word gets out, well…" Abi shook her head. She could see the girls looking their way periodically.

"Don't worry about it. I'll handle it if there's a problem."

"Thank you. I'll hold you to that."

"Sure thing."

A silence cloaked them.

"So, any plans after graduation?" Abi asked.

"I hope to get a scholarship to play NCAA football and earn a degree in business. How about you?"

"Me? I'm thinking of pursuing a political science degree. Maybe get into politics and change this crazy country for the better. Aspire to be governor of Massachusetts, perhaps."

Impressed by her aspirations, he said, "Wow, that's amazing."

"My parents are great. Whatever I choose, they'll support my decision one hundred and ten percent. Yours?"

Shane divulged, "My parents are too busy to be supportive. I've been on my own for a while now."

"I'm sure they're proud of you."

"Don't know for sure. They only talk to me if I accomplish something newsworthy. Then, they broadcast it to their friends to make them look good. Like when I made the NCAA recruiting watch list last spring, my Dad immediately hired an athletic agent to help promote me even further but never got involved otherwise. Last year, he didn't even watch one game."

Abi could see his frustration.

Shane scanned the horizon and moved his sights to their group. With so many eyes on them, he said, "Sorry for venting... Guess we should head back now."

"Never apologize for sharing your thoughts. If you like, I'm always here to listen if you need me."

"Really?"

"Of course. I happen to be a good listener," she said convincingly.

"I believe it." Walking down the beach, he said, "I've enjoyed our talk, New England."

"Me too."

"So, are you nervous about Monday? First day of school and all?"

"Truthfully, yes. I'm terrified. Everybody is so intimidating. I don't look like I fit in, either. I'm the brunette in a sea of blondes."

Shane thought he heard her wrong. "What? I beg to differ. Honestly, I think you add a bit of contrast to an otherwise cookie-cutter group of girls."

"I'm assuming that was a compliment?" she laughed unnervingly.

"You got great hair. Don't let anyone tell you differently." Standing straight and tall as they walked along, he did not look her way after that.

Abi blushed and tried to contain her smile. She knew associating with Shane would not be a good idea, but she couldn't help but like him. Jade had warned her that he was Emile's property. Technically, she didn't own him. He was free to make his own decisions. Or was he?

"If you want, I can meet you in the parking garage on Monday morning, and we can walk in together. If you're with me, nobody will bother you. You might have a better day."

"As much as I would like to accept your offer, I think I'd be setting myself up for social suicide. No offense, but Emile already hates me. The last thing I want to do is piss her off."

"Let me worry about her, okay?" he paused. "At least think about it."

It was tempting. "I will."

Reaching their spot on the beach, the two found every eye glued to them. Whispers and odd looks were flying everywhere. It was unnerving and made Abi feel uncomfortable.

Shane veered off and rejoined the flag football game while Abi went and sat beside Jade.

"Oh, girl. What are you doing?" she quietly muttered, having read the crowd's mood the past forty minutes. "Just a heads up, word has gotten out that you and Shane went for a long walk up the beach together. It's all over social."

"We just talked." Abi could barely breathe.

"That's all it takes. Remember, the rumor mill around here is not about the truth."

"He was the one that joined me. I didn't go after him. How is this my fault?"

"Sorry. You're the new girl. Everything is going to be your fault."

Abi cringed after recalling her run-in with Emile and her posse at the coffee shop. She feared the repercussions of what happened between her and Shane, no matter how innocent.

Suddenly, crazy shouts erupted as all the sweaty football players ran into the ocean simultaneously and plunged into the waves.

"They probably shouldn't go too far out."

"Why is that?" Abi was naïve.

"Word to the wise, it's almost the witching hour. The sharks swim closer to shore late afternoon," Jade confirmed with a straight face. "It's feeding time."

Noticing that the girls in the group kept looking at their phones, out of nowhere, she heard the name Black Lion.

Taking note of her watching them, Allie asked, "Hey, have you scored a ticket for next Saturday yet?"

Confused, she asked, "What is Black Lion? A band or something?"

The girls all chuckled at her.

Laney explained, "No, silly. He's a famous DJ who throws the most exclusive parties on the West Coast. They are epic."

Showing Abi the exclusive app, she immediately noticed the spelling of the word Lyon.

"He's so popular that he created a lottery for the tickets. When we enter our info into the app and request an event date, it will either accept or decline our admittance in a matter of days. Rumor has it that Black Lyon only invites the wealthiest and most popular at his raves. Apparently, algorithms search your platforms to compile your profile and see if you're worthy."

"What are these parties like?" Abi asked.

"The music is killer. It's always in a secret location. Nobody knows where it is. The ticket price includes access to the event, travel, beverages, and other stuff - if you know what I mean."

Abi played along. "Yeah, sure. I get it."

"Anyone who gets in, their social status skyrockets," Summer interjected.

"Hmm," Abi wasn't sure about it.

Ming overheard their conversation and came over to sit with them. "Nobody knows his identity either. He's a mystery - like the mythical black lion. There is not one photograph of his face. It's like he doesn't exist," the pretty Asian girl divulged.

Pulling up the app store, Abi searched for Black Lyon. Downloading it, unsure whether it was a good idea, Jade looked over at her.

"So, are you in?" she questioned.

Mildly pressured to participate, she said, "Yep. It's downloading as we speak."

While entering her contact information on the application, Abi assumed she wouldn't be selected. It wasn't like she fit the criteria Laney outlined. Strangely, it also asked what school they attended. Choosing Gilderson from a list provided, she looked it over before pressing submit.

"Now what?" Abi asked.

Jade smiled. "Now we wait."

There was nothing she could do. She'd taken the plunge, and there was no going back. Worried that some girls kept staring, Abi got nervous. It ignited a fight or flight response. Wanting to leave, she knew she couldn't. The last thing she wanted was to be rude or make the wrong impression. Lying down to soak up some sun, she closed her eyes and listened to the waves crashing against the shore.

Not long after, some students left and went back to Allie's place. Noticing a few were saying their goodbyes, Abi was secretly happy.

"I should get going, too. It's a long drive to my Grandmother's, and she doesn't like it when I'm late for family dinner," Jade said while folding her beach blanket.

Shane and Reggie were standing close by, talking.

"Are you sure you'll be okay driving home alone? Do you know where you're going?" She felt guilty, leaving the girl to fend for herself.

"Don't worry about me. I'll manage." Abi hoped she sounded confident.

Overhearing them, Shane said, "Hey, New England? Where do you live?"

Surprised, Abi replied, "Umm, I'm on Stradella, inside the Bel Air gates."

"You can follow me if you want. I'm going right past there."

"Are you sure? I don't want to be a bother," she said, relieved to hear he was willing to help.

"It's no problem," he smiled pleasantly. "Happy to do it."

The group made their way toward Allie's place. Inside the beach house, Abi went with Jade to get changed. Locating an empty bathroom on the upper floor, she slipped out of her bikini and into dry clothes before returning downstairs. Needing a peaceful moment, she went outside to sit and wait for Jade. While the sun was setting, the water sparkled like diamonds. It was mesmerizing. Soaking up the last of its warmth, she closed her eyes.

"Hey?" Shane said, sitting beside her after tossing his backpack in the sand.

Appreciating the view, she asked, "Isn't this just the most beautiful thing you've ever seen?"

"Possibly."

"Possibly? How can you say..." Abi stopped mid-sentence. Ready to refute his statement, she noticed Shane was not looking at the sunset. Immediately, her heart pounded dead center in her chest. Bashfully turning her head, the air seemingly seeped from her lungs.

With perfect timing, Jade walked out. Not saying a word, she saw them sitting together. With a shake of her head, she announced, "Okay, I'm off. Want to walk with me, Abi?"

She and Shane both turned around simultaneously.

"Sure. One second." Abi stood and folded her towel before packing it in her tote. Walking towards Allie, standing on the front porch, she said, "Thank you so much for including me today. I had fun. It was nice meeting you."

"Nice meeting you, too. I'll see you on Monday?"

"I'll be there," Abi waved. "Have a good rest of the weekend."

"Thank you. You too. Ciao, my friend," Allie said while hugging her.

Shane watched as Abi met up with Jade. He knew she was not like the other girls. There was an aura about her. It drew him in.

"I'm going to hit the road, too," Reggie said.

"Yeah, I'm doing the same." Turning to Abi, Shane asked, "Are you good to go?"

"Think so," she replied while walking alongside him.

Reggie and Jade were a few yards ahead.

Abi lightly pleaded, "Please don't lose me along the way. I don't want to get lost."

"Don't worry. I got you." The football player smiled from ear to ear. "Hey, maybe we should exchange cell numbers. You know, just in case we get separated."

"Umm, sure. Good idea."

He handed her his phone. She entered her contact info and handed it back. He immediately pulled it up and texted her, so she also had his number. "Perfect. Everything will be fine. Trust me."

Those words sent a shiver through her. "All right. Thanks again. I appreciate this."

"Like I said, all good."

Jade stopped in front of her Porche. Not seeing Reggie's car, she asked, "Did you and Shane drive together?"

"Nope. I gotta a new ride. Needed to test it out."

"Which one?" She swiveled left, then right.

The handsome football player took a key fob from his pocket and pressed the button. It triggered the lights to illuminate on a platinum Ferrari 488 Spyder. Proud of the new car, he admired it from afar.

Jade was shocked. "Are you kidding me?"

"I know. That's what I said when I saw it," Shane chimed in.

"Seriously, what did you do to deserve that?" She immediately assumed he'd done something uber-impressive.

"Well, if you should know, the entire summer, I day traded and paid for half. Dad said he'd match whatever I put in."

"That was a good deal." Jade approached the sports car. It was so clean and shiny that she could see herself in it.

"I told Reggie he'd have to teach me some of those skills. I need the money, too," Shane laughed. But he was serious.

"I'm impressed. Good job." Seeing him in a different light, Jade smiled while Reggie took a bow.

"Yeah, now I gotta work toward the Aston Martin."

Abi was stunned by their conversation. In front of her were three teens who had no idea how lucky they were. "I can't believe you drive a Ferrari," she said. "Do you know how many kids would kill just to have a car that starts? Never in their wildest dreams could any of them fathom owning a Ferrari or a Porsche in their lifetime. That is unreachable to most." Almost finished her rant, three sets of eyes stared her way. "Holy, and here I thought my Cooper was cool."

Turning to his friend, Shane explained, "Reggie just lives in a whole other tax bracket. To be clear, I'm not even in the same vicinity as either of these two."

"What do you mean?" Jade got a tad defensive. "Wait, Abi. Are you calling us spoiled?"

Afraid to have hurt her new friend's feelings, Abi tried to defuse the situation. "No, not at all. I just think you guys should appreciate your lives. So many aren't as fortunate." She was so sincere in her words it was hard for them to argue.

"You're right," Jade said. "I guess we do take it for granted sometimes. But in our defense, we can't help that we were born into this."

"I realize." Abi knew she'd created friction. "Look, I didn't mean any disrespect. Back in Boston, the kids at school had cars, just not near as nice as these. It's a bit of a culture shock for me. Impressive, nonetheless," she smiled, hoping to keep the peace.

Standing back, watching the conversation evolve, Shane witnessed how down-to-earth Abi truly was. Her observations were a refreshing change.

Intent on humorously getting a rise out of everyone, Reggie said, "Well, on that note, I am going to start my new Ferrari engine. Stick around. You'll want to feel how the sound reverbs off your chest." Opening the driver's side door, he slipped into the seat and pressed the ignition button. The bubbling growl echoed through the parking lot in seconds, causing all eyes to veer toward him, especially when he retracted the roof. It was a sight to see.

Jade clapped her hands excitedly. "Amazing. Love it."

Shane and Abi stood back while Reggie slowly inched out of the space, ready to drive away.

Waving to them, he reached out his hand to his best friend and offered a fist punch before leaving. "Later, man," he said.

"Yeah, later," Shane replied.

Jumping into her car, Jade departed right behind him. "See ya later, girl. I'll call you!" she said, waving goodbye.

Sad their day had come to an end, Abi turned to Shane.

"Guess it's just you and me." He adjusted his backpack on his shoulder. "Ready to head out?"

"Yes. Ready."

"I'm just parked over there," he pointed to his Jeep.

"Okay." Abi got into her car and started it up.

While waiting for him, she got worried. Assuming Emile had already gotten wind of her speaking to Shane today, the thought of it spread a chill down her spine. "You didn't do anything wrong," she told herself. "He came after you. Not the other way around." Entering her home address in the GPS in case the two of them got separated, Abi looked up as it calibrated. Shane had stopped in front of her. His Jeep still had no doors or a roof.

*How is it that he is so perfect?* Her thoughts started to run rampant.

Locking his eyes to hers, he gave a thumbs up. She, in turn, did the same, attempting to contain her eagerness. Watching him pull away, she followed.

Inching out the gates, Shane drove straight up Washington. Palm trees sparsely lined the route. Here and there, new construction was revitalizing the older parts of town. Some new condos had balconies dotted with colorful surfboards leaning against the walls. Being so close to the beach, it was definitely a surfer's haven.

When they turned at Lincoln, Shane then joined with the Marine Expressway. Reading the signs leading to the 405, he signaled and climbed the overpass ramp. Once on the freeway, he kept right except to pass.

As she watched him weave periodically in and out of traffic, Abi hoped she wouldn't lose sight of him. Happy to see him look in his rearview mirror often, he gave her plenty of notice before switching lanes. Concentrating, Abi could see on her GPS that it was now a straight shot to Sunset from there. She relaxed a bit and loosened her grip on the steering wheel.

Shane kept to the speed limit. His hair blew in the breeze while his white hoodie flapped with the gusts whizzing past.

Recalling their conversation today, she wondered what he thought of her. "Just be thankful he talks to you. Don't take it for granted," she told herself, believing nothing could ever happen between her and Shane anyway. He was with Emile, and she needed to respect that despite how horrible the girl was to her. "The past two days could have turned out quite differently," she whispered aloud, thinking she could be alone at home and doing nothing.

Shane suddenly signaled.

Happy to be in familiar territory, they climbed the off-ramp and slowed down while approaching the intersection. Abi noticed that he waited and did not turn until she could easily follow him. It was thoughtful.

While moving along Sunset, she knew where she was going now. Coming up to her street, she inched into the left turn lane and stopped beside Shane.

Looking down from his elevated seat, he said, "Told you I would get you here safe and sound."

"Yes, you did. Thank you so much."

"No problem." As the light turned green, Shane raised a steady hand. "Have a good night!" he said before departing.

She waved as he drove off and shouted, "You too!"

Slowly progressing up the hillside, having had the most memorable day of her life to date, she made a mental note to investigate the mysterious Black Lyon app she'd downloaded. Wondering what she had gotten roped into, she tried not to worry about it too much since, realistically, her chances of getting a ticket were slim to none.

"Time will tell, I suppose," she said aloud.

A flash of Shane smiling at her that afternoon gave her butterflies. That sparked a spontaneous flood of confidence. She figured Shane was a big boy. With Emile or not, he was at liberty to make his own decisions. "It's not like I'm stealing him from her. I've done nothing."

Waiting in the driveway for the gate to open, she tried to convince herself of that. She soon drove into the courtyard and parked the car. Closing the roof, she grabbed her tote bag from the back seat and got out to lock up. Upon opening the front door, she heard voices in the kitchen. A familiar laugh emanated through the entire house.

"Mom?" Abi whispered while swiftly heading toward the family room. Rounding the corner, she found her parents watching a movie on the couch. Dad had a glass of red wine, and her Mom had sparkling water.

"Hey, there she is. You're home." He put his wine on the coffee table.

With open arms, Abi stepped forward to greet her Mother, who was smiling so happily. In complete disbelief, the girl's sights bounced between them. "How are you feeling?" she asked her.

Her Dad gave a silent thumbs-up.

"I feel better. I think the move took a lot out of me. I'm sorry I've been missing in action the past few days."

"That's okay."

She walked into the kitchen. "Your Dad and I made lasagna. Would you like some?"

"Yes, that'd be awesome. Let me help you."

# 10

## Miracles

For the next hour, Abi's parents listened intently to their daughter as she shared the details of her afternoon at Venice Beach. They were slightly concerned about the football player's apparent interest in her. That is when Abi revealed the gloom of Emile Raven in the picture.

"It sounds like you were friendly and cordial," her Father said.

"Cordial? What is this? The late 1800's? Who says cordial anymore?" she laughed.

"Well, I do. Regardless, you did nothing wrong. What this Shane guy decides is his prerogative."

"That is what I thought, too, but I really don't want to get involved with her. I feel like she's unstable."

"For now, keep your distance and your head held high. Be the bigger person. Others will see how you handle things, and you want to be sure they don't fault you for it."

She valued his advice.

"I agree. Be yourself, Abi." Her Mom smiled. I bet this boy sees certain qualities in you—qualities that most girls in LA don't possess. To him, that is more attractive than money, clothes, and social stature."

Abi chuckled. "As my parents, you have to say stuff like that."

Both of them shrugged their shoulders. "It's the truth," they said simultaneously – laughing at the timing of it.

"Okay, on that note, do you mind if I take my lasagna to go?"

"Sure. Where are you off to?" her dad wondered if she was going out again.

"Just my room. By the way, you'll never guess who I ran into today?"

Intrigued, her Mom asked, "Who?"

"Burton Lancaster."

She raised her eyebrows. "Like Burton from Boston Lancaster?" She wasn't happy about how his parents handled their move many years ago, mainly because it affected her daughter for weeks and months on end.

"Yes. The one and only."

"Really? What is he doing in LA after falling off the face of the earth?" Her Father recalled the family's odd disappearance.

"He is attending UCLA. Computer science, I believe he said."

"Wow. That's good," he said, taking a bite of his lasagna. "They have a great program there."

"Anyway, he wants to get together tomorrow and catch up over coffee."

Taking a sip of his wine while her Mom sat beside him, he said, "You'll have to fill us in afterward."

"I will." About to walk away, Abi looked at the two of them sitting there eating together. It was like a miracle.

"I'm so happy you had a good day and that your life here seems to have started positively. It's important to be surrounded by good people."

"Yes. Thanks, Dad. So far, so good."

Abi went ahead upstairs. Hearing them laughing and talking was such a beautiful thing. Her Mom looked like her old self, but deep down, she wondered how long it would last.

Taking her damp bathing suit out of her tote, she washed it in the bathroom sink before draping it over the tub to dry. Hanging her beach towel over the door, she sat at her desk. Intent on finding out more about this DJ, Black Lyon, she typed the name into Google.

"Let's see who you are and what these parties look like." Abi pressed enter. To her surprise, there was nothing - not one picture from any of his events. "That's weird. If he were this popular, you'd think these things would be plastered across the internet everywhere." Reaching for her phone, she opened the BL app and looked at the messages. As expected, she did not find a response yet. "Guess I will check again tomorrow."

While finishing her lasagna, her phone chimed. She read the text and immediately realized who it was.

*Hey, New England. Wanted to make sure you got home okay.*

With her heart racing and hands shaking, she straightened up and began to type her reply with trembling fingers. *Thank you for thinking of me. Yes, I am home. All is well.* Abi watched his active thinking bubbles with butterflies in her stomach.

*Good to hear. Remember what I said about Monday morning? Let me know if you want to walk in with me.*

Desperate to say yes, she knew there was a price to pay for that decision. *Still thinking about it. But I'll let you know tomorrow night.* She waited to see what he'd say with anticipation.

*That's fine. No pressure. Enjoy the rest of your weekend.*

Happy to hear that she typed, *Thank you. You too.*

He signed off with a thumbs up, which ended their conversation there.

Setting her empty plate aside, she went to start the shower. Using this quiet time to think about the day, she tried to address some feelings that were hard to ignore. Shane was kind and thoughtful. It was refreshing to have a meaningful conversation, too. Most guys seemed hollow to her. They lacked substance. But Shane was different. There was just something about him. Beyond his good looks, he appeared humble. He was not flying somewhere high above everyone, arrogantly looking down on them. Strangely, she felt he was a lot like her.

Abi dried off and heard a chime come from her phone again. Wrapped in a towel, she read the text on the screen. This time, it was from Burton.

*Just confirming for tomorrow. Still on for 2:00?*

Answering him back, she typed – *Yes, for sure. See you @ two @ Starbucks.*

His thinking bubbles rambled on before a reply popped up. *Looking forward to catching up.*

*Me too,* Abi replied, *See you then.*

Ending things, he also used a thumbs-up emoji, a funny coincidence.

She set the phone on her nightstand and returned to the bathroom to brush her hair and put on pajamas. Wrapped in a cozy robe, she turned off the lights and noticed a glow from the window. Peering out across the canyon, the mansion's LEDs were dancing tonight. Slowly changing color, she watched the house turn from shades of purple and pink to blue and red. Positioning the telescope just right, she closed one eye and zeroed in on the roof. Standing there was the lonely man. He looked like a wolf howling at the moon.

"Who is this guy?" she said aloud. "Why does he do this ritual every night? It's odd."

In checking the time, she didn't want to wait another twenty minutes for the home's neon lights to turn off. She was tired and needed to get some sleep. Slipping under the covers, she couldn't help but think about Burton and reminisce about the good times they shared. It made her wonder what he'd say tomorrow. Still shocked by his appearance, it was hard to believe he was the same person. Frail and borderline geeky years ago, Burton was now far from it. He'd become a man.

"What an incredible transformation," she whispered.

Strangely not attracted to her former neighbor despite his hunky good looks, Abi figured it was because she always considered him like the big brother she never had. Through grade school, he was her protector. Her constant. The guy who watched out for her in the playground and safely walked her home from school every day. With memories of years past flooding her mind, she rolled over. Exhaling, her eyes drifted closed. Before long, she fell asleep.

11

# The Curve Ball

On Sunday morning, Abi heard the buzz of helicopters flying through the canyon. She assumed many elites didn't want to endure rush hour traffic, so they decided to fly instead.

Rolling over in bed, happy to see ribbons of light cascading through her window, she knew the day had promised to be bright and sunny based on the weather reports. With her skin still looking pale despite spending the afternoon at the beach yesterday, she figured she'd return home after seeing Burton and work on her tan. The last thing she wanted was to be the ghostly-looking new girl on Monday.

While stretching her arms above her head, she tried to motivate herself to get out of bed. Thinking more about her afternoon plans, she easily formulated a list of questions, hoping Burton would willingly provide the answers. From what she could gather, the boy from Boston had come a long way from his glasses and braces. Abi did the math. The last time they'd seen each other was at the end of her grade eight year before the summer break. That was a little over four years ago. Today, she hoped to find out why they suddenly left. It was sad. One day, they were laughing and joking. The next, there was a for sale sign standing in the front yard, and her friend was nowhere to be seen.

"Strange how he was once the poor kid on the street, now he's driving a four hundred-thousand-dollar sports car. I definitely need to ask about that, too." Wondering what the chances were of them finding each other, she said, "It's funny. When you least expect it, life throws a curve ball."

Quickly glancing at the time, seeing it was already eleven-thirty, Abi listened for her parents. No conversation emanated from the lower level, but she could smell the aroma of freshly brewed coffee.

"Maybe Mom went dark again?" She cringed at the thought. "Okay. Don't think negatively," she said, resting both feet flat on the floor. Standing up, she stretched and reached her hands toward the ceiling. Barely moving, she prepared for the day and selected an outfit from her closet. Referring to the pictures Jade sent, she picked the grey knitted tank with linen shorts and paired it with an oversized boho cardi and white sneakers. Her hair flowing freely across her shoulders, a bit wavey from doing damp braids before bed, she ran her fingers through to tussle her tresses. Applying some color to her cheeks, she ran gloss across her lips. Happy with the reflection staring back at her, she smiled.

Afraid to go downstairs, not sure what she'd find, Abi descended the main floor, taking her neutral Oryany crossbody bag with her. Upon entering the kitchen, she found her Mom and Dad wearing matching Bluetooth headphones and watching a movie. Intentionally standing to the side, out of sight, she was thankful to witness the two cuddled up on the couch like they used to years ago. Abi snapped a few pics before her Dad happened to turn and look her way.

He slipped the headphone off his right ear. Her Mother did the same.

"Morning, Banannie," he greeted happily. "How was your night?"

"Not bad. I feel like I'm slowly getting on California time."

"You've had a few busy days, so we wanted to keep things quiet for you."

Her Mother perked up. "I made Belgian waffles with mixed berries this morning if you're interested. I know they're your favorite."

"Thanks. I'd love some."

Walking into the kitchen, she found a waffle under a clear lid and placed it in the toaster to warm and crisp it. Taking the berry bowl from the fridge, she set it on the counter and dressed the waffle when it popped up. About to take a bite, she gazed at her parents, laughing and giggling at the movie. Their happiness gave way to a sigh of relief.

*Finally, some normalcy*, she thought.

Abi walked through the dining room and onto the pool deck to eat and get some sun. While staring out at the canyon, she could see the mansion in plain sight. Too far to focus on the intricate details without her telescope, she still couldn't fathom how one person could live in a place that size.

"Money does strange things to people, I guess," she said. The concept that had yet to make sense to her. Maybe the guy is compensating for something," she giggled.

The sun beat down with intensity. She could only stand it for fifteen minutes before returning inside. Inspecting the condition of her arms and face in the powder room mirror, she hoped she hadn't gotten burned. The last thing she wanted was to be peeling on her first day of school. Content with the sun-kissed color on her cheeks and shoulders, she went to put her plate in the dishwasher. It was already time to go.

"Well, I'm off to meet Burton," Abi told her parents.

Both removed their headphones.

Her Dad paused the movie.

"Have fun, Sweetheart. Say hello to him for us. Maybe you can invite him over for dinner sometime," her Mom suggested.

Not sure about that, she decided to go along with it anyway. "Yeah, maybe. I'll ask him. See you later."

"If you need some money, take it from my wallet," her Dad bellowed down the hall. "We still need to visit the bank and set up an account for you here."

"Thanks. Yes, I know. Maybe we will have time to do that this week."

"For sure. Have fun. Bye!"

Going out the door, Abi admired the Mini Cooper shining in the sunlight. Upon clicking the remote twice, the top folded back, and the windows rolled down.

"You are one lucky girl," she whispered to herself. "Don't ever forget that." Smiling ear to ear, she started the engine and opened the gate with the phone app. Slowly, the gigantic door slid open.

Carefully inching out of the blind corner, she took off down Stradella as the warm breeze swirled around her. Passing the freeway exit along Sunset Boulevard, she was nervous to see Burton again. Still unable to believe how much he'd changed, there was so much to catch up on.

Anxiously approaching the plaza, Abi mumbled, "Oh, please let there be a parking spot for me. Just one," she repeatedly begged, "Please. Please. Please."

Not knowing where else to park, she was afraid of getting towed. Holding her breath when she pulled in, a car happened to back out of a spot. Signaling, she was so relieved. "Awesome. Oh, thank goodness." She felt the Lord was watching over her right then. Maneuvering her car into the space, she muttered, "Hallelujah."

Locking up, she paid the meter for two hours in case they got carried away in conversation. About to go inside, she heard the rumbling of a finely tuned engine. Turning around, she found Burton's McLaren carefully inching across the slight incline on an angle, trying not to scratch the underbelly of the expensive car. He, too, got lucky and found a spot opposite her. When the butterfly door opened, her handsome friend emerged. Seeing her, he smiled and waved on his way over.

"Well, hello there," Abi said, tilting her head and squinting from the sun.

Sporting a nice pair of dark jeans and a long-sleeved henley with sleeves scrunched to his elbows, he replied in a deep voice, "Hey. You made it."

"Yes, I did." Abi found it hard to believe the guy was her, Burton Lancaster.

"After you," he said, allowing her to lead the way.

"Thank you." She took note of everyone staring at them.

Reaching to open the door for her, Abi went inside, feeling Burton's hand hovering in the middle of her back to guide her.

At the counter, he asked, "So, what will it be, my friend?"

"I think I'll have an iced coffee with a double shot of espresso, please."

"Hardcore. Okay, I like that."

Burton placed their orders before the two continued to the pick-up area.

"So, did you tell your parents you were meeting me today?"

Abi chuckled. "Of course, I told them. They said to say hello. My Mom wants to invite you for dinner."

"Oooh, a home-cooked meal. I mostly eat out now, so that sounds amazing."

"Well, I'll try and arrange it sooner than later."

"That would be awesome. Your Mom's cooking was always second to none."

The barista announced their names. Burton put up his hand to acknowledge the girl and grabbed their drinks. She greeted him with intrigued eyes, then flashed a scowl at Abi, who did her best to ignore it.

"Where would you like to sit?" he asked, scanning for open tables.

Pointing to some at the far side of the shop, Abi went and had a seat.

He set their drinks down and did the same. Leaning forward and resting his forearms on the table, he said, "So, Abi Acardi. What are the chances of two neighbors from Boston finding each other in LA?"

"I know, right? This is crazy."

"Yeah." His eyes zeroed in on hers. "It's really nice to see you." The sincerity in his voice was heartwarming.

"It's been a long time."

"A lot has happened since I left the East Coast." He looked down at his coffee cup and flipped the lid off. "I didn't say this yesterday, but you look great, by the way."

"Well, thank you. You look pretty good yourself. If it wasn't for those blue eyes, I don't think I would've recognized you."

"Guess I've changed quite a bit since you saw me last." He flashed a bashful look. "What has life been like for you the past few years in my absence?"

Believing she'd gotten the upgraded version of her childhood friend, she felt comfortable enough to spill a few details. "Not gonna lie, it's a long story. Might save that for another time. I only have two hours allotted on the meter outside."

"The good, bad, and the ugly. I want to hear it all." Burton took a sip of his coffee.

"Where to start? Umm, since you left, my life went downhill."

Burton listened intently.

"My Mom was sick for two more years after you'd gone. Dad worked all the time. So, I mostly went to school in the morning, spent lunch hours at home looking after her, and then returned to school for the afternoon." Reminded of her struggles, she paused. "When you avoid people, they start to talk. Rumors spread about me. Some not so nice. My Dad could see I was miserable. Mom was too sick to notice."

"Did she ever go into remission?"

"Yes. Only after struggling through two rounds of radiation and chemo. It took a couple of years, but she survived. We were all thankful for that. But, about a month later, my grandparents were in a car accident. Sadly, they didn't make it."

"Oh, wow... I'm sorry." Burton supported his chin with his hand and hung on her every word.

"The trauma of her parent's death caused her to fall into a depression. Grandma and Papa helped her a lot during the cancer treatments. They encouraged her when she wanted to give up. Then, suddenly, they were gone. My Mom changed in the aftermath. In the weeks that followed, she just went through the motions. From then on, she was never the same."

He didn't know what to say.

"My Dad thought that moving might help her start fresh in a new place. She'd always wanted to live in California. So, he searched for jobs here and secured one within a month. Unfortunately for me, it meant he had to leave Boston and move here within a week of accepting the position. That left me alone with my Mom to deal with the sale of the house, cars, furniture, and all the packing of what was coming with us. This past summer was a nightmare. But we made it. We are here. Mom has improved the past two days, so I'm glad."

"That was a lot for you to handle on your own."

"It seems like it is a distant memory now. But, yes, extreme stress. I felt like I was drowning in the thick of it." Abi began to tear up.

Reaching across the table, Burton placed his hand on her arm.

"Can we change the subject?" she asked.

"Sure," he paused as Abi looked on. "On a lighter note, tell me more about this beach party and the friends you met yesterday. What's your friend's name again?"

"Jade is the girl I introduced you to," Abi replied. "It was a good day. There was this guy there..." Immediately stopping mid-sentence, she realized he probably didn't want to hear about Shane.

"So, you've only been here a few days and met a guy already?" The thought of her with someone else brought out a little jealousy. "What's his name?"

Hesitant, remembering how long it had been since she'd poured her heart out to Burton, it felt like old times for some reason. Somehow, they had picked up exactly where they'd left off. "Umm..."

"Abi, you've gotta tell me now," he laughed. "Don't worry. I promise I won't hurt him."

"Burton!" She had a look of shock flash across her face.

"What? Just saying. No matter how much time has passed, I still feel like I need to protect you."

The endearing comment was nice to hear. "Look, long story short. He's shown interest in me, not the other way around. I'm hesitant because he has a cheerleader girlfriend, who is a mean girl. I've had one run-in with her already. So, despite liking him, it's not worth it."

"What's he like?"

She knew Burton would pounce on what she was about to say. "He's the captain of the football team—the quarterback," Abi winced.

I know—that's stupid. I shouldn't even consider going after a guy like that. What would he see in me anyway?"

"Wait? Hold on." He put up his hand between them to stop her. "What are you saying?"

She didn't understand.

"Don't ever think you are not worthy of someone – like ever. The question should be, is this football player worthy of you?"

She got sentimental. "You always know the right thing to say."

"Well, it's true."

"Can I ask you something?"

Burton's mind reeled, wondering what she would pose.

"Why didn't you say goodbye?" She couldn't look him in the eye.

Pausing, he rotated his coffee cup in a circle on the table. "I'm sorry for that. There is much to explain." He peered out the window to his left and sat back in his chair. "My Dad had worked for years on a secret project. Before we left, he found what he was searching for. After that, our life needed to include a certain level of discretion. My Mom and I left without notice at eleven o'clock at night, with just the clothes on our backs. Doing this, she told me to fill a duffle bag and leave everything else behind. Getting in the taxi, I looked up at your bedroom window and knew I'd probably never find another friend that would compare to you."

"Awww, Burton..." Abi was taken by what he said.

"I'm sorry I left that way. Life got complicated pretty fast. I didn't have time to think."

"Where did you go?"

Taking a deep breath, he continued. "We moved to the Northwest Territories. I can't elaborate on anything else, and for good reason. Please don't take offense."

"What's with the expensive car? The clothes?" she pointed, "The watch?"

He took note of everything she'd acknowledged.

"Well, you know my dad was a geological scientist?"

Abi nodded her head. "Yes. He worked at the university."

"Between you and me, let's just say he found a diamond deposit and leave it at that."

"Wait? Diamonds?" she whispered so those around them wouldn't hear.

Still harboring a secret or two, Burton nodded and remained tight-lipped. There was only one thing that needed to be said, though. "While living there, in the dead of winter, this land of ice and snow, I not only dreamt of warmer weather, beaches, and sunshine, I thought of you - what you'd be doing at any given minute of the day. I wondered if you were happy or sad." Hesitating, he added, "Or if you missed me too."

Afraid to address that part of her past, she recalled feeling abandoned by him. Despite that, she truly did miss the guy - especially when things were bad. "I thought of you every day and missed you so much. Why didn't you call or write?"

He laughed frustratingly. "No access to cell, mail, and no landline. We were off-grid. Eventually, I figured you'd forget about me anyway."

"Well, I never did."

"Now, I guess I'm no longer the poorest guy on the street."

A tear drifted down Abi's face, recalling their troubled past.

"My parents and I are worth about seven hundred and fifty million. Finally, after all this time, I feel worthy of spending time with you," he revealed nervously. "So, the question is. Do you want to spend more time with me?"

Unable to say no, she answered, "Of course I would. You should never have to ask."

Sitting across from her, he had this strange air of confidence.

"What are you doing next Saturday or Sunday afternoon?" he asked. "Maybe we can take a drive up PCH?"

Abi smiled. "Sunday works better. I am going to Black Lyon on Saturday night."

"Black Lyon?" he repeated in a questionable tone. "Why are you going there?"

"Do you know of it?"

"Yeah, it originated with the university crowd and has since drawn in the high school elites. Sometimes, the parties get out of hand. You have to be careful. It's not safe," he warned.

"It'll be fine, I'm sure. There's a group of us from Gilderson who applied for tickets. The app hasn't confirmed anything yet. We have to wait and see. Who knows? Maybe we won't get in after all."

"Well, if you do, be mindful. It's a far cry from parties in Boston." Intent on securing another face-to-face meeting, he suggested, "Getting back to next Sunday, how about coffee at around eleven and a drive up the coast to have lunch? With the first week of school done, you'll have lots to share. What do you say?"

"Sure. Let's do that." Abi felt her phone vibrate in her pocket. Glancing at the screen, she noticed Shane was texting her to ask about meeting up in the morning. Not wanting Burton to see, she put it away and said, "It's the parentals. Just wondering when I'll be home."

When Abi looked up, her face went white.

Noticing her sights gravitating to someone over his shoulder, Burton turned around to find three girls in the lineup for coffee. Facing Abi again, he found her trying to hide behind him.

"That's Shane's cheerleader girlfriend, isn't it?"

All she could do was nod. Burton saw her hands shaking as they clung to her iced coffee.

"Abi, you are with me. They will not bother us. If they do, I'll deal with it."

She flashed a fearful expression. "No, please don't. Don't say anything." Abi remembered that Emile probably got word of her walk with Shane yesterday. It was written all over her face. She looked pissed off.

When the girls placed their order, they spotted Abi and started whispering.

Her heart started racing. She found it hard to breathe.

Needing to do something, Burton reached across the table and lovingly held Abi's hand. Lifting it to his lips, he kissed the back of it. Confused, she didn't know what he was doing.

"Just go with it," he said sneakily. "This will throw them off."

Abi played along.

"Ready to go, Babe?" he asked, loud enough for the girls to hear.

She nodded and said, "Sure."

When the two stood up, Burton wrapped his arm around her and proudly walked by the girls, staring them down before leaving. They could hear their petty banter on the way out.

"You're coming with me," he said while walking toward his car. "I'm not leaving you here."

Reaching the McLaren, he opened the passenger-side door. Helping her get settled, he closed it and walked around to the driver's side. The girls watched their every move.

"What are we doing?" she asked.

"Just giving them a little show," he said, starting the car. The engine groaned, grabbing the attention of everyone in the plaza.

Abi realized that Burton was pulling out. Knowing they would have to drive right by them, Abi tensed up. "Burton?"

"Trust me. It'll be fine."

He smirked at the mean girls and revved the car several times, intent on causing a noise violation. It made the cheerleaders cover their ears because it was so loud. One of them recorded the whole thing.

When they pulled away, he looked in his rearview mirror. Emile Raven was sneering. In seconds, the girls got into their car and turned to follow them. Eventually catching up, Burton saw the freeway ramp ahead.

Abi looked in the side mirror. "Oh, no..."

"Don't worry. I've got a plan."

Driving along Sunset towards the 405, the posse was on their tail. Suddenly, Burton veered right on a dime. The girls did the same.

"Hold on," Burton said confidently, pedal-shifting to fly down the freeway ramp. Merging into traffic, he expertly zig-zagged in and out at high speed. Soon, they could no longer see Emile's car. Slowly blending with the flow, Burton turned to Abi and said, "Are you good?"

"I suppose so."

He kept driving. Abi didn't know where they were going.

"This was an unexpected detour," he laughed.

"Thank you for that."

Burton could tell by her somber tone that his stunt would only prolong the inevitable. "No matter what, Abs, you stand up to those girls. They have nothing on you. You hear me?"

"I'll try," she replied, hoping to gather the courage to do what he said. The thought of dealing with Emile Raven sickened her.

He was not at all convinced she would take his advice.

Approaching a tunnel, they emerged on the other side.

"Hey? We are at the beach?" Her face brightened.

"Thought I'd make a loop before dropping you off to get your car."

"All right," she said. "This is beautiful."

He looked out across the water. "Yes, it is."

Like old times, Burton had saved her again. His protective instinct was his most endearing quality. She knew he'd always cared. That was evident by the way he looked at her.

"I guess we got to take a short drive up PCH a week early."

Seeing him look at her with the biggest smile, she felt a few butter-flies in her chest.

"Yes, I don't mind. I love the ocean."

Confused, Abi didn't know what to make of these feelings. For years, she thought of him as a brother. But when he held her hand, she felt something. Walking out of the coffee shop together, she wondered if it was truly just for show.

Approaching a parking lot on the left, Burton signaled at the light and waited for a break in traffic before turning into Will Rogers Beach.

"Do you want to take a walk, or do you need to get home?" he asked, rolling down his window to pay for parking, assuming what she'd say.

Shaken by what happened, she said, "You know me too well."

Stopping beside the pay station, he tapped his credit card and processed a ticket while the attendant recorded his plate number. Placing the slip of paper on his dash, they continued toward the end of the lot, where ample parking space was available.

Turning off the engine, he opened his door and said, "Wait there."

He swung around to her side and opened the butterfly door. Offering his hand for her to get out, she took hold and stood up. Impressed that his gentlemanly nature stayed intact despite his wealth, she suddenly started to see Burton in another light. Well-dressed and mannered, not to mention a genius, she watched him put on a pair of aviators and turn her way.

"Shall we?" he asked, locking up.

"Yes." Feeling the salty breeze and the sun's warmth on her face, Abi looked up to the sky before scanning the horizon from left to right. She just loved being by the water. There was just something about it that calmed her nerves. Exhaling, she sighed.

Burton reached over and patted her back. "I can feel your stress. Don't worry. Everything will work out. It's a period of adjustment, and then this place will feel like home, too," he said. "I'm always here if you need me."

Abi stopped and turned to him. With arms open, she waited, hoping he would offer a hug without question.

Recognizing it, he smiled and bashfully did not hesitate. Holding tightly, he soaked up every second as his feelings for her deepened.

She felt so small compared to him now. Resting his chin atop her head, she could feel the strength in his arms. His body was solid as a rock, but it didn't stop him from gently coddling her. Offering compassion and comfort, he let go, making for an awkward moment.

"Want to go to the shore?" he asked.

"Sure," she said, crossing her arms in front of her.

They descended the path and strolled along the paved Ocean Front Walk. Every minute spent there recharged her soul. She felt connected to the ocean, like it was a piece of her.

Burton was concerned about her mental state of being. "Do you have to go to that private school?" he asked, wondering if she had another option.

"Gilderson? Yes. My tuition is paid. I have no choice."

He felt for her. Having been bullied years ago, he knew what she was feeling. "Anytime you need someone to talk to, or if you need help, please call me."

"Don't worry. I will."

Before sitting on a bench nearby, Abi said, "The shore seems very far away still." Looking at the time, she added, "I hate to say it, but we should head back now. My parents will be worried if I'm not home for dinner."

He seemed disappointed by her statement.

"Next Sunday, we'll have more time, and I'll be all yours. I promise," she giggled.

Laughing, he replied, "I think it's going to be a long week."

Upon hearing this, Abi knew she would have to tell him how she felt. The last thing she wanted to do was hurt his feelings.

When they'd returned to his car, he opened the door for her.

"Don't put your feet in yet," he said. Bending down, he raised one foot and removed her shoe. Dusting off the sand from it, he did the same with the other after she sat in the seat.

"What on earth are you doing?"

"One thing I can't stand is beach sand in my car."

She knew by the look on his face he was serious.

Allowing him to continue, he finally had her swing her legs inside. He did the same before getting ready to leave.

"I didn't know you were so particular?"

He glanced over. "This is my dream car. I never thought I'd ever own one in a million years. But here I am. So, I appreciate it every day."

Hearing that melted her heart. "I feel the same about my Mini Cooper."

He smiled. "See, you know what I mean."

"Yes, I do."

Starting the engine, they left the parking lot and crossed onto the highway. Heading up Temescal Canyon Road, Burton turned right onto Sunset Boulevard.

"This will bring us right back to the coffee shop."

"Okay. At least you know where you're going."

Easily maneuvering the twists and turns of the winding road, Abi prepared what she needed to say. Given everything that had happened today, she nervously grasped her hands together and rubbed them back and forth.

Burton assumed she was anxious about heading back to get her car. "I know this will be a tough week for you, Abs."

Hearing her nickname, she replied, "Yes. I'm not looking forward to it." She thought about how she wanted to phrase things. "Burton, thank you for helping me escape today. I'm so happy to have you in my life again. You're my best friend."

Abi noticed his body language change.

"Yeah?" He asked, reaching for her hand. Giving it a few gentle squeezes, he said, "I'm thankful to have you, too." After saying his piece, he left her hand on her lap and put his on the wheel. "Don't forget. I'm always here, day or night."

She nodded. "That means a lot."

When they arrived at the coffee shop, he carefully pulled in while Abi held her breath and scanned for Emile's convertible. Not seeing anything, she exhaled.

Pulling into a space close to her car, he got out and helped her with the door, offering his hand. Walking her to her car, she found a ticket on her windshield.

"Aww, man..." she said.

He took it from her and said, "Here, let me take care of that for you."

"No, I can't let you...."

"Yes, you can. It was my idea to take a drive."

About to speak, he raised his hand to stop her.

"Well, thank you," she whispered. Hugging him, he wrapped his arms around her lightly at first, then clung a little tighter, as did she. Parting ways, she got into her car.

Closing her door, he said, "So I'll see you next Sunday?"

"Yes, for sure," Abi replied with a smile. "I'm looking forward to it."

"Me too."

"Good luck with everything this week."

Starting the Cooper, she replied, "Thanks. I'm gonna need it."

"You'll be just fine."

Abi could tell he thought of her as more than just a friend. Girls have an instinct about these things. Not knowing what to do with that, she decided to keep the status quo, not wanting to complicate their friendship.

He stepped back from her vehicle and watched Abi drive away. Waving goodbye, he returned to his car and got in. For years, having suppressed his feelings for the girl, it all came rushing back like time had not passed.

"You've gotta give her space. Be patient and wait. Be there for her when she needs you - without fail. If it's meant to be, it'll be."

# 12

Worries

Driving along Sunset, Abi glanced down at her phone in the holder and noticed Shane's text awaiting a reply. Tomorrow was a big day. She knew she needed his help to get through it. How else would she manage after the run-in with Emile this afternoon?

"You have to meet him in the morning. There's no choice now."

Thoughts of Burton entered her mind at the same time. Their day together was effortless. She just felt safe with him. "He's the perfect guy who's always been there for you." Abi felt conflicted. Sandwiched between her feelings for Burton and the hope of what could develop with Shane, her mind started spinning.

Entering the courtyard at home, she parked the car and turned off the ignition before reading Shane's text.

*Hey, New England. Are we meeting up in the morning?*

Her heart went all aflutter. It was the second time he'd asked that today. Hands shaking, she texted him back.

*Hi, Shane. Thank you for checking in. If you don't mind, I'd like that. Are you okay if Jade tags along, too?*

She watched his thinking bubbles erupt immediately. Not sure what he would say, she hoped he would agree. Seeing his text pop up, it read, *Sure. I'll let Reggie know. Don't tell Jade, but he's kinda into her. See you at 8:30.*

Giggling a little, Abi smiled. "Well, Jade, I guess you will get your wish after all." Replying to him, she typed, *Okay. Mums the word. I won't say a thing. We will just let things play out naturally. I'll be there @ 8:30.* Signing off with a thumbs-up emoji, Abi pressed send.

*Good idea. He would never forgive me for sayin' that. BTW, don't worry. Everything will be fine tomorrow. I promise.*

The butterflies in her stomach took flight - a feeling she knew would appear if something were there. *Thank you for doing this. I owe you one.*

It seemed like it took forever to receive a text in return. Suddenly, it popped up. *No problem. Happy to help. Have a good night.*

Smiling, she wondered how things would go tomorrow before replying, *You too. Night.*

Happy to have made friends before school even started, she felt the dreadfulness of the first day subside slightly. Getting out of her car and locking up, she hoped it would be uneventful.

When she walked through the front door, she found her parents sitting in two lounge chairs by the pool, watching the sun midway in the sky. Holding hands, the two heard the door close behind her. Both waved.

Peeking her head out the door, she said, "Hello!"

"Hi, Sweetie. How did it go?" her Mom asked with a bright expression, ready to get the full scoop from her daughter.

Abi walked out to join them. "It was good. We talked the whole time. He is definitely the same Burton Lancaster, just the 2.0 version."

"Oh? What does that mean?" her Dad asked.

"Well, he's twenty-one. He's a man now—not the little boy that used to hang around the house. He's tall. Fairly built—like a linebacker, really," Abi laughed. And he is still the sweetest guy despite having millions of dollars to his name."

"Pardon? What do you mean millions?" her Mother asked. "Wasn't his dad a geology professor?"

"Yes, who found a diamond mine." Abi watched her Mom's jaw drop to the floor.

"You're kidding?"

"Nope. But that is just between us. No broadcasting – period."

Her Dad immediately chuckled and said, "We won't say anything, Sweetie."

"Good. Umm, I'm just going to go and freshen up."

"Hey, are you okay if we all go out for dinner?" He hoped she would agree. "We'd love to hear more about the excitement of the past few days."

Seeing both of them so happy, she said, "Sure, I'd like that. Give me a few minutes, and then we can go."

"Perfect." Her Dad smiled at her Mom.

"I guess I should go and change, too," the pretty woman said.

Getting up from the chaise, a little shakey, Abi saw her Dad unexpectedly reach out to steady her Mom as she wavered. Preventing her from falling, he helped her inside and locked the doors behind them.

Pretending she hadn't witnessed what just happened, Abi crept upstairs to get changed, knowing deep down something was wrong. Intent on keeping a close eye on her Mother from here on out, she prayed she would stay in remission. While getting dressed, so many scenarios flooded her mind. Not getting ahead of herself, she said, "Just think positively. Nothing more." With a spray of perfume and one last look in the mirror, she was good to go.

Meeting her parents in the upper hall, they descended the stairs together and walked out the door, ready to share a family night out.

That night, they celebrated their first weekend in Los Angeles and wished Abi good luck at her new school. With much laughter and happy banter surrounding the table, Abi looked at her Mother and wondered what they weren't telling her. True to the woman's character, she selflessly kept her focus on the two people she loved the most.

Upon returning home, Abi bid her parents goodnight and hugged and kissed them before going upstairs. Walking into her room and seeing her uniform hanging up on the hook outside her closet, she took a deep breath, hoping to get a good night's sleep. About to start the shower, she thought about texting Burton. With everything going on, she'd forgotten to send a thank you note to him - something he was probably expecting. Grabbing her phone, she typed, *Hi, Burton. I wanted to thank you for today. I really enjoyed our afternoon together. I'll text you tomorrow and tell you how my first day went. Enjoy your night.*

She waited to see if he would text back. Not seeing any activity, she started the shower and jumped in. About halfway through washing her hair, she noticed the phone screen light up and assumed he'd responded. Thinking about him, she felt like they had just scratched the surface today. Curious about what he was taking in college, she wondered what he hoped to do in the future. Making a mental note, she added it to the list of topics to discuss next Sunday.

Drying off, wrapping herself in a towel, she picked up her phone and confirmed it was him. His text read, *Hi, Abs. I should be thanking you for meeting me. It was nice to catch up. For sure, let me know what happens tomorrow. I'm interested to hear how it went. Looking forward to our Sunday drive. Ciao, B.*

Ready for bed, Abi pulled back the covers. Setting her phone on the charger, she checked on the mansion across the canyon. It was ablaze with lights once again. Positioning her telescope just right, she panned the roof for any sign of life. But there was nothing. Moving from room to room, she noticed a man walking around on the second floor dressed in grey joggers and a black hoodie. With a drink in hand, he moved around a bar surrounded by white furniture. Turning on the television, she watched him take a sip from the glass and set it on the edge of the pool table to play a game. All alone, there was no one else. Scanning the rest of the place, she suddenly stopped. There, in the corner of the most northeasterly room, was a telescope. But not just any telescope. Abi stepped back and looked at hers. Peering through the lens, she realized the guy had the same one, or so it appeared.

"Yeah, that is creepy." Hiding hers in the corner, out of sight, she turned off her lights and walked back to the window.

Oddly enough, the mansion across the canyon was now in darkness.

"Weird," she said before walking around the room and slipping under the covers.

Strategically setting five alarms to ensure she didn't sleep in, Abi finally got comfortable. Reminded of her morning plans with Shane, she texted Jade to confirm she could meet them, too. *Hi, Jade. Just wanted to ask if you still want to meet me in the morning. Maybe 8:30? I'm terrified to walk into school alone.*

Like her phone was an extension of her body, Jade started to reply within milliseconds of Abi sending the message.

*Yeah, girl. I got your back. No problem. See you then.*

Signing off with a heart, she did the same.

Abi set her phone on the side table and plugged it in. With so many things going through her mind, it was hard to stop it from spinning. She got up twice to check her uniform and shoes, then packed her backpack with binders, pens, and her laptop before getting up a third time to wrap her charging cable so she wouldn't forget it.

Grumbling, she said, "Okay. Go to bed – like now."

Forcing herself to fall asleep, she thought of both Shane and Burton. It helped her drift off and sparked a series of dreams she wished would come true someday.

# 13

## First Day

The first of many morning alarms woke Abi up in seconds. Not happy to leave her dreams behind, she focused and realized she had to be on the road in about an hour. Afraid to be late, she sat up and looked out the window at the sun shining brightly. The sky was clear and very blue over the canyon.

"Well, this is it. The big day," she whispered. Her heart pounded, and she felt nauseous. Thankful for Shane's offer, she figured the social hierarchy would accept or toss her aside within eight hours. The thought of it was terrifying.

Nervous, she texted Jade and confirmed they were meeting at 8:30.

Again, the girl replied within seconds of sending the text. *Yep. See you then.*

Dressed, with her hair cascading across her shoulders, Abi second-guessed how she looked in the uniform and took a step back. Adding two necklaces and a couple of braided bracelets, she left the room with her crossbody bag and backpack slung on one shoulder. Peeking in on her Mom, who was still sleeping soundly, she knew her Dad had already left for work two hours before.

Making it to the kitchen, she filled her water bottle and grabbed a granola bar, hoping to settle her stomach. Experiencing a high level of anxiety, she could barely breathe.

"Pull yourself together, Abi. Emile will smell your fear," she whispered, trying to gather the courage to face the day. Going out the door, she locked up and immediately noticed a post-it note on her windshield. Peeling it off the glass, she read it aloud. "Good luck, Sweetheart. Be yourself and smile. I'll see you later tonight. Love Dad." Abi clutched her chest. It was so thoughtful of him to do that. He was always her voice of reason and encouragement through thick and thin. Something she was eternally grateful for.

The gate of their family's compound opened with a push of a button. Starting her car, Abi opened the convertible top and moved her backpack and bag to the floor on the passenger side. Carefully pulling away, ensuring the gate fully closed behind her, she headed down Stradella. In desperate need of a coffee to help calm her nerves, that thought sparked the possibility of running into Emile. Cringing, she opted to drive directly to school.

When she stopped at the Bel Air west gate, she awaited the chance to merge onto Sunset Boulevard. It was so busy this early in the morning. Thankful to be let in by an elderly gentleman in a Mercedes, Abi waved courteously before occupying the space he provided her. Formally nodding to acknowledge her politeness, she focused on making the next turn.

Caught in stop-and-go traffic the whole way to the 405, Abi kept glancing at the time and knew, at this rate, she was running late. Her heart beat rapidly, causing her to feel on edge.

"Come on, come on," she said, peering ahead to see why no one was moving.

Suddenly, her phone rang. It was Jade.

Accepting the call on hands-free, she said, "Hello?"

"Abi? Where are you?"

"I know. I know. I'm in a conga line. I'm almost at the freeway. I should be there in five minutes. Please wait for me."

"Don't worry. I will."

"Thank you. I'll see you shortly."

Hanging up, Abi inched toward the intersection. Free to zip along North Church to Beverly Park Drive, she sped up the hill before making the left toward the parking garage. Slowing her speed, seeing Gerald standing watch, she stopped.

"Good morning, Sir!"

Gerald's face lit up. "Well, Miss Abi. Good morning. Cutting it a little close, aren't we?"

"Yes, I know. The traffic was horrible. I'll do better tomorrow."

Allowing her to pass, he waved and said, "Enjoy your day."

"Yes, I'll see you later."

Abi drove inside and turned down the aisle, where she found Shane, Reggie, and Jade standing around talking.

"Finally!" Jade shouted while Abi parked in her spot.

She got out and quickly gathered her things, looking flustered. "Please don't say it. I had no idea the roads would be that crazy."

Dressed smartly in his school uniform, Shane stepped forward with a smile. "I should have warned you about that. Sorry."

Immediately noticing the look Shane gave her friend, Jade knew something was happening there, but she didn't know for sure.

"So, Jade," Reggie nervously asked, "How was your dinner at your Grandmother's on Saturday?"

Mesmerized by the boy she liked, the girl turned and walked with him, leaving their friends behind almost as if they'd planned it.

"Shall we go? You ready?" Shane asked.

"Yeah, I guess. Let's just say I feel like I'm being thrown to the wolves."

"It won't be that bad," he laughed.

"I hope you're right."

Walking in silence, Shane cleared his throat, not knowing what to say to keep the conversation going. Pointing to his friend, he said, "You know, between you and me, that guy has wanted to talk to that girl for over a year. Finally, he's built up the courage to do it."

"Funny, she said the same thing to me."

"Really?" His eyebrows raised. "Well, this should be interesting."

Catching up with Reggie and Jade while ascending in the elevator, the doors opened to the courtyard. While walking along the path toward their building, all eyes suddenly were on them. It made Abi even more nervous. Lowering her head, not looking at anyone directly, she cowered.

Shane glanced over and whispered, "Hey. Hold your head up high. Don't show weakness."

She heard what he said and attempted to straighten her posture. Still feeling insignificant, it was hard to pretend she wasn't.

"Now smile and talk to me. Show that you fit in."

Abi turned and said, "Okay. What do I say?"

"Hey, did you see the latest on Jake Garcia? Think he's moving on to Miami after being in Georgia for a short time."

Having followed football with her Dad for years, she replied, "Yes, I did see that. The guy is determined and will do whatever it takes to prove himself worthy of earning a spot in the NFL."

Surprised by her response, he said, "That's right. I've been watching him and studying his plays."

Their conversation distracted Abi enough to make it through the main foyer, where the whispers of every student sounded like white noise. Heading down the hall to their first class, happy to make it to math unscathed, Jade and Reggie sat near the back, adjacent to each other, while Shane and Abi did the same in the row ahead of them.

Surrounded by other football players, Shane introduced Abi to a few of his friends. "Hey, guys. You remember Abi from Allie's beach party."

Introduced around, Abi recalled some of their names when Jade pointed them out at orientation.

"This guy here is Alan, and that's Shawn and Adrian," Shane said.

"Nice to meet you, guys."

Mr. Walker, their teacher, soon appeared and closed the door to the classroom. Scanning the students, he stopped when he saw an unfamiliar face. Greeting her, he said, "Miss Acardi, I assume?"

"Yes, that's right."

"Welcome to Gilderson. Happy to have you. Should you need anything, please let me know. In perusing your school records, I believe you will not have difficulty in my class." Tapping his knuckles on her desk, he went back to the front.

Jade and Reggie looked at each other.

Shane wondered what the guy meant. "So, what? You're a math genius or something?" he questioned.

Not wanting to air her past, she replied, "Something like that."

The classroom door opened just as the morning announcements began. Abi watched Emile and her friends walk in like they owned the place. Frozen, Emile scanned the room and only found the first row of seats open. Her eyes then zeroed in on Shane and, by association, Abi.

The blood drained from her face. *Oh, Lord. Here we* go, she thought. *I've got a target on my back now.*

"Quickly take your seats," Mr. Walker instructed them. "I don't have all day."

Embarrassed, the girls surprisingly did not make a scene.

Introducing grade twelve Finance and Business Analytics, Mr. Walker handed out a grade eleven assessment review. He got everyone to branch off, work in groups, and test their knowledge on what they learned last year.

Not wasting any time, Reggie moved his desk in line with Jade and Shane, then helped Abi move hers to combine a group of four. In seconds, Emile ventured over.

Angrily standing above them, with enormous hatred reflected on her face, she said to Shane, "I thought you'd save me a seat."

"Not today." He continued to peruse the questions. "Don't you have work to do?" he said, staring at her.

The jilted girlfriend peered down at Abi. If looks could kill, she'd be dead.

Ignored by them, Emile walked back to her friends at the front of the class.

"Move your desk this way so your back is to her," Shane said, sliding her closer. "Don't worry. Everything is fine."

While working through the questions, Abi taught her friends the ins and outs of every business-related problem, so much so that the other groups joined in to listen to what she was explaining, which caught Emile's attention.

Mr. Walker looked on, intrigued. Applauding at one point, he said, "You should pay attention to Miss Acardi. She's the East Coast's Mathletics Champion two years running."

That was a detail she wanted to keep secret. Abi bowed her head and kept working. The last thing she wanted was accolades.

With fifteen minutes left and their math review completed, the guys gathered around Shane and Reggie.

"So, you're the New England girl?" a voice whispered behind her.

"Yes, suppose so. I'm from Boston. Why?"

"No reason. Since you're new, we should give you the 411 on the classmates."

Turning around, Abi found Alan's sights glued to hers.

"See that guy there? The one with unnaturally whitish complexion and icy eyes?" he asked subtly.

"Yeah," she replied, remembering him from Friday.

"That's model, Blu Brennan. He's on every teen magazine cover right now."

"I don't know of him."

"He's pretty famous around here. Just FYI, nobody talks to him unless he allows it."

"What do you mean?" She could not fathom doing such a thing to anyone.

Shane pointed to the man standing in the far corner. "That's Blu's bodyguard. If anyone comes within five feet of him, he deals with it."

Squinting, Abi replied, "So, keep my distance. Five-foot rule?"

Adrian glanced across the aisle and joined their conversation. "Make it ten, just to be safe."

Another guy tapped Abi on the shoulder. "Ignore Brennan. He's a freak."

Adrian outwardly pounced on that statement. "Shawn, my man, you're just jealous 'cause he gets all the fame and an endless supply of chickitas."

"So what?"

Shane laughed. "Dude, the guy's your stepbrother. Give him a break."

"Whatever, man," Shawn replied, hating that Blu's Mom married his Dad.

"How about them?" Abi asked, subtly pointing to the two guys she'd recognized from Friday but couldn't remember their names.

Alan piped up, seemingly knowledgeable about everyone in the school. "That's Aramis Knight and Taizo. They are child stars."

"Child stars?" Abi repeated.

"They have been acting in Hollywood since they could walk. You may have seen them in after-school shows and movies the past few years."

She didn't recognize them in anything recently. "That's cool, I guess."

"If you see some big guys lurking around, don't worry. It's their security detail. At least they have the decency to wait out in the hall."

The banter between the team surrounding her got louder and louder. It made Mr. Walker step in and ask everyone to take their seats and put their desks back in alignment for the next class.

While doing this, Shane helped Abi out.

In the process, she noticed Emile looking her way with daggers.

Alan caught wind of it. "Not sure if you're aware, but Emile and her posse are spreading rumors about you."

Overhearing him, Shane turned and asked, "What? What are they saying?"

"Rather not repeat. I'm just being honest, man. She needs to be careful." Alan knew that ticked off his friend.

"Don't worry about Emile. I'll deal with her," Shane told Abi point blank.

He was confident, but it didn't make her feel any better. She knew her worst nightmares were about to come true.

The bell sounded, prompting all the students to move to their next class.

"What do you have next?" Shane asked while walking out the door.

Abi checked her schedule. "Environmental Systems and Societal Management."

"Science? Me too. Come on. Follow me."

Watching Shane command the hallway, many students parted to make way for the football quarterback. Nervous beyond words, Abi stayed alongside him, with Reggie and Jade tight behind. About to round the corner, they found a line of girls blocking their path. It was Emile and her friends.

Staring straight at Abi, she broke her deadly gaze, turned to Shane, and smiled. It was like she transformed from Dr. Jekyll to Mr. Hyde.

"There you are," she said playfully. "I've been looking for you."

Shane got annoyed.

Wrapping her arms around his waist, she tried to kiss him.

The guy took a step back and released her grip. "Knock it off, Em," he said bluntly, pushing her away.

The girl directed her fierce stare back at Abi and said, "My boyfriend is just playing hard to get." Looking her up and down, she added, "You're that girl? Aren't you?"

Abi didn't know how to respond.

"You're New England. The one who is trying to steal my man." She slithered toward her and stood mere inches away from her face. "Don't get too comfortable around here. I don't think you'll be staying long."

Immediately, Jade grabbed Abi's arm and got her out of there.

Shane stayed behind. "What the hell was that?" he asked.

"What?" Emile replied deviously.

"You're pathetic," he told her before running to catch up to Reggie.

His friend shouted to the girls as they were about to walk out the door. "Abi! Jade! Wait!"

When they caught up, the guys saw Abi still shaking from the confrontation.

"I'm sorry about that," Shane said. Focused on her, with his hands tucked in his pockets, he asked, "You okay?"

All Abi could do was nod.

"Come on. We gotta get to class," Jade said.

The four of them hurried along. Jade checked the seating chart posted inside the door and discovered that the professor had partnered her with Abi. The same went for Shane and Reggie. Thankfully, their desks were right beside each other. Having a seat, they waited while the rest of the grade twelves flooded in.

It wasn't hard to see that Abi was upset. Resting her hand on her arm, Jade said, "Don't worry. Everything's gonna be okay."

Abi shook her head and tried to refrain from crying.

Seeing New England look up at the ceiling, Shane silently asked Jade – *Is she all right?*

Jade shook her head - *No.*

He felt so bad. Not only did he break his promise to her, but he could have intervened sooner and didn't. *You idiot. You should have stepped between them.* He thought.

Alan sat down and waited for his lab partner to show up. Wanting to start a conversation, he asked, "So, who's going to Black Lyon on Saturday? Rumor has it that Gilderson is on the list."

Those sitting around them instantly checked their BL apps for a ticket notification.

Alan's face went blank when he found nothing. "Has anybody gotten anything yet?"

"No. Nothing," Jade revealed.

"Don't the tickets get issued Friday?" Shane asked.

Needing a distraction, Abi checked her phone. She was stunned to see a message. Clicking on it, she discovered her admission acceptance.

Hiding it, she figured she'd wait to see if everyone else got in before RSVPing. The last thing she wanted was to pay the four hundred dollars and not go.

"No, I got nothing," she said, keeping it to herself.

Amidst all that, their professor walked in and slammed the door. Placing his beaten-up brown leather satchel on his desk, he stood before the class, hoping to bring order to the masses. The students quickly put away their phones. They knew this teacher had a rep for confiscating them for an entire day if they got caught. Sporting a plaid jacket with elbow patches and a pocket protector full of pens, he adjusted the reading glasses perched upon his bald head before addressing everyone.

Jade waited for the man to turn his back and write his name on the board. Timing it to a tee, she whispered, covering her mouth with one hand, "That's Professor Grady. He also teaches Entrepreneurship."

"Right! Class! Let's get started! Turn your textbooks to page sixty-eight! Pronto people!" The man kept shouting orders.

"Why is he yelling?" Abi questioned quietly.

Shane leaned back and said, "Despite the prestige of winning a Nobel Prize, the guy's practically deaf. Rumor has it he conducts science experiments at home. Apparently, one exploded and burst his eardrums. He's never been the same since."

# 14

# The Divide

Abi easily understood what Professor Grady was teaching. She could tell that Shane was confused and frustrated while flipping through the pages. Reggie was the same.

Still shaken by her run-in with Emile, she was glad the girl was not in the period two class. She checked her schedule and remembered she had Graphic Design and Digital Art next.

"We have art together, right?" she asked Jade quietly.

Her friend nodded, hoping not to be called upon by Professor Grady. Abi gave her a thumbs-up.

When the bell rang, the guys packed their books into their backpacks.

Shane turned and said, "We have weight room now. Are you gonna be okay?"

Giving Shane the eye, Jade said, "Of course, everything will be fine. She'll be with me."

He raised his hands defensively. "Okay. Just askin'."

The football players walked with Jade and Abi toward the Art Studio.

"I'll see you at lunch," Shane said to her with a smile.

"Okay, see you then," Abi replied wearingly.

"Remember what I said. Head held high. Do not show weakness."

The guys took a right and split off from them. Bumping and shoving each other, the girls could hear their childish banter echoing down the hall.

Arriving at the state-of-the-art studio lab, Jade opened the door for Abi. The room was massive and bright, with cathedral windows flooding the space with natural light. Abi loved the vibe until Emile and her friends entered and sat at a table in the middle.

Assigned groups of six, Jade and her were thankful not to be near the cheerleaders. Taking their seats, it didn't take long for Emile to butt heads.

"So! New girl? What's your name again? Oh, yeah, my boyfriend nicknamed you New England. Isn't that right?"

Not paying attention to her, hoping the teacher would arrive soon, Abi could feel a heat spreading into her chest and neck. Her cheeks felt flush, and her ears were hot as hell.

Emile got nasty. "Do you think you can just waltz in here and be friends with everyone? Steal my boyfriend and not expect a fight?"

Focused straight ahead, Abi mumbled some choice words to herself.

"What did you say to me?" Realizing she was unwilling to play her little game, Emile snickered deviously. "You'd better watch your back, new girl. This school can turn ugly on a dime."

"Don't listen to her, Abi," Jade relayed.

"Oh, shut up, Webber!" Emile shouted at the top of her lungs.

"Miss Raven! I beg your pardon!" the art teacher sternly said while standing behind her. "Maybe you'd prefer spending the next ninety minutes in the office!" About to dispute the teacher, the woman interrupted, "Go! Now!"

She picked up her things and turned to her friends before stomping out the door.

Taking a deep breath, Abi sighed. Unable to smile just yet, she knew the girl's posse was still present and accounted for. Despite winning this round, she assumed there was more to come.

When the teacher took hold of the class, she assigned their first task. Abi settled in and felt more relaxed. She and Jade talked with the other girls in their group, most of whom she knew from Allie's party.

Abi and Laney got along well. Their artistic talents were similar. When they shared the details of their expressive masterpieces taking shape, Abi felt like she'd found another good friend.

"So, you said you're from Boston?" Laney asked.

"Yes, that's right."

"My family has a place in the Hamptons. We spend time there in the summer."

Another girl she'd met on Saturday, named Mei, joined their conversation. "Yes, my family does too. Have you gone there?" She looked at Abi for a response.

Knowing that area well, Abi said, "Unfortunately, my parents work a lot, so I only have a week's vacation with them each summer. They preferred the Outer Banks in North Carolina."

"Oh, like the Netflix show?" the girl named Summer asked.

"Yes, I believe so. It's pretty there." Abi kept drawing on her tablet as they talked.

"I've never been to North Carolina," Mei said disappointingly. "We always go to the Hamptons or cruise the Med. Our boat is in Palma. But I love Santorini the most. Have you been to Greece, Abi?"

Realizing the girls were well-traveled, she didn't know what to say. Having heard of the island from travel shows, she replied smartly, "No. My family has not made it there yet. I hear it is beautiful."

"Yes, I suppose it is," Ming replied.

Mei casually smirked. "My sister prefers Italy over Greece."

Finding out the two were related, she asked, "So, you're twins?"

"Yes, but not identical, obviously." Mei wanted to make that quite clear. "For years, our mother dressed us the same. We hated it, right Ming?"

"Totally," her sister agreed.

"One day, at age five, we teamed up and rebelled. Told her no more. From that moment, we were free to dress however we liked."

"Yes, the look on her face was priceless," Ming laughed. Our fashion choices are quite different, don't you think?"

Noting that one of the twins was more reserved and the other more outgoing, Abi agreed, "Yes. So different." Grateful to have a few warm bodies in her corner, she hoped the rest of the day would go as smoothly.

When the bell rang, the group got up from the table and headed down to the Bistro for lunch. Abi kept an eye out for the guys when they exited the building, happy to take in the fresh air during their sun-drenched three-minute walk.

Lining up, she gravitated to the turkey wrap and grabbed water. While they moved through the line, each girl paid with their school pass card and noticed Alan and Shawn had already pulled a few tables together.

About to sit down, Abi saw Aramis Knight doting on a beautiful girl. Jade caught her staring. "That's Aramis' girlfriend, Lexi Muller."

"The actress, right?"

"Yep. The two became an item during the summer holidays. I think they were working on a project together. The girl only attends school when she's not on location. I think she has a private tutor here. You won't find her in any of our classes. By the way, you're not the only one Emile doesn't like. That girl is on her hit list, too."

Somehow happy she wasn't alone in Emile Raven's vast vendetta, Abi spotted Shane and Reggie crossing the courtyard.

His eyes found her right away. Raising a steady hand, he walked over and sat down beside her.

"Hey. How was class?"

Overhearing, Jade answered, "Oh, it was peachy. Emile has a way with words, doesn't she, Abi?"

Shane turned to her. "What happened?"

"Yeah, no. I'd rather not relive it, thanks." Abi shot her friend a look. She hoped she wouldn't say anything. Forced to explain, she gave Shane the Cole's notes version. "Let's just say Emile took a trip to the Dean's office."

"Really? How'd you manage that?"

Jade chuckled. "It's not hard. All we need to do is get her to open her mouth when she's angry. The rest she does all by herself."

Reggie laughed before sitting down and setting his tray on the table.

Shane nodded, knowing too well what they said was true. "Hey, I'll be right back. I'm just going to grab some lunch."

"Okay," Abi replied.

"Make sure you save my seat," he said with a smile.

Seeing the two of them interact, Jade knew Shane was interested in her new friend. As much as she was happy for her, she was certain Emile would not go down without a fight.

Surrounded by the beauty of the outdoor gardens, hearing the sounds of waterfalls and the Pacific breeze whistling through the buildings, Abi opted to people-watch while eating. When Ming and Mei were about to sit at a table, she noticed the look on Mei's face. It wasn't hard to see what sparked her attention. Following her line of sight, Abi found Adrian. Standing with Shane, the guy snuck a glimpse at her. Producing a bashful grin, she, in turn, did the same.

*Hmm.* Abi thought to herself. *Something is brewing there.*

While watching the quarterback casually talking to groups of people on his way back to their table, Abi spotted Emile and her friends. "Great..." she said under her breath.

Hearing her, Jade turned around. So did Reggie.

Out of nowhere, the mean girl motioned for her boyfriend to go to her.

Ignoring the bossy requests, Shane continued his conversation, not paying her any mind.

Impatient and angry after multiple attempts, she shouted across the courtyard, "Shane!"

He didn't acknowledge her rudeness.

"Shane!" she shouted again. "Here! Now!"

Silence blanketed the crowd. All eyes were on the two of them.

Reggie could see his friend was beyond annoyed. "Fire and ice. Oh, this is going to be good. Pull up a chair. Sparks are gonna fly."

"What do you mean?" Abi whispered, with eyes peeled.

"You'll see…" he said, rubbing his palms together in anticipation.

After setting his tray on a nearby table, the quarterback calmly slipped his hands into his pockets and walked over to his girlfriend. He hated the devilish look on her face, believing she'd gotten her way.

"You know it's rude to interrupt a person's conversation," he said aloud, crossing his arms in front of him. "Especially by yelling at them."

Everyone could hear a pin drop while waiting for Emile's response.

She sauntered up to him and wrapped her arms around his waist. "I've missed you today," she said in an alluring tone, her eyes scanning the crowd, knowing the entire student body was watching.

"We need to talk." Releasing himself from her grip, he backed away and added, "In private."

"We can talk right here, Babe. What is it?" she asked, attempting to hug the athlete and kiss his neck.

Once again, tearing himself away, he said bluntly, "It's over."

Her fluffy expression turned downright evil - fire raged in her eyes. "What! What do you mean it's over?"

"I'm done. This…" Shane bounced his finger back and forth between them. "This is toxic."

His words shocked her. For once, Emile was speechless.

Swiveling around, Shane grabbed his food and sat at a table on the far side, away from Abi.

She was disappointed to see that.

With his now ex-girlfriend steaming at the public breakup, he intentionally kept his distance to avoid bringing Abi into the mix. Everyone around him whispered as he continued talking football with some guys at the table.

Then, in something resembling a drive-by shooting, Emile approached him and screamed, "I don't need you anyway! You don't interest me anymore! I'm bored of you!" With arms crossed, she stood there wondering what he'd say.

Not looking at her, about to take a bite from his sandwich, he said, "Whatever, Emile. It's been like that for me for a year, at least," he stated without remorse.

"Whoa," Shawn said shockingly.

Alan followed it up with a quiet "Oooh, burn" under his breath.

Emile stomped off with her friends close behind to comfort her.

With the diva gone, Shane made certain the coast was clear before returning to Abi's table. To her surprise, he sat beside her.

"Are you okay?" she said with concern.

"Yeah. It's been a long time coming. I'm so tired of the abuse." He seemed mentally exhausted by the confrontation.

She stayed quiet.

He leaned in and whispered, "Can we go for a walk?"

"Sure." Abi assumed he needed to escape.

When they got up to leave, everyone looked their way, making Abi feel uncomfortable. They knew she was the reason why Shane broke it off.

Taking their bags along with their lunch, the two left Reggie and Jade behind. With every eye glued to them, he led her down the ramp toward the botanical gardens. Hiding from view amongst the trees, he stopped and leaned against the concrete retaining wall.

"I'm sorry you've endured the same abuse today," he said sincerely.

"It just hasn't been today," she quietly said.

"What do you mean?"

"Well, I also ran into her at the coffee shop yesterday."

He exhaled. "Really?" He shook his head. "Again, I'm sorry. She's a loose cannon. Look, I can't promise Emile won't bother you still, but I will defend you every way I can." Pausing, he nervously asked, "Can I ask you something? No pressure."

"Sure." She didn't know what he would say.

"I've got football practice after school at UCLA field. I think Reggie is asking Jade to go and watch. Since you like football, I thought you might like to go. The rest of the week will be closed practices. No spectators."

Pleasantly surprised, she replied, "Yes, I'd love to."

"Really?"

"Yes. Absolutely.  That sounds amazing."

"Awesome." He seemed relieved to hear her answer. "Our first exhibition game is on Friday, so I was thinkin' maybe you'd wanna...." Shrugging his shoulders, not finishing the sentence, Abi got the drift.

With butterflies soaring, she nodded and said, "I'd like that." Unable to stop smiling, Abi liked the sweet, roundabout way he'd asked her out.

"When we finish study hall, you can drive to the field with me if you like. I'll bring you back afterward. Saves us taking two cars."

"Alright."

Despite his rugged exterior, he had a gentler side - something she hoped to see more of in the coming days.

To Shane, everything was easy with Abi—their conversations, interactions, and heightened maturity. It was all a breath of fresh air. Hearing the warning bell, he scoffed down the last of his sandwich and said, "Guess we should get going."

"Yes, we don't want to be late."

Emerging from the gardens, Abi followed him through the courtyard to the study hall library. Climbing the stairs together, they signed in and found a quiet cubical away from everyone.

Shane pulled out a chair for her.

"Thank you," she said, appreciating the gentlemanliness.

"No problem." Sitting beside her, he tried not to get wrapped up in his feelings. Watching her neatly set out her laptop and notebook, he asked, "Can we review finance analytics together? I, umm, kinda had difficulty with it this morning."

She noticed it was hard for him to voice that. Wanting to make light of it, she replied, "Absolutely. Let's start from the beginning."

Moving his chair closer, he rested his hand along the back of her chair and listened to how she explained the questions they'd done before moving to the rest of the homework. Thankful to have someone to help him, he wanted to tell her about his problem. Unable to gather the courage, believing she'd think he was a dumb jock, he decided against it for the time being.

They tackled the questions one by one over the next hour, and no one bothered them. It was the most peaceful part of their day.

Abi checked the time and noticed it was almost dismissal. "Do you have any more questions before we pack up?"

Locking eyes with her, he stammered, then asked, "Would you mind tutoring me this year?"

Concerned about the comment, recalling what athletes in Boston would do, she sternly said, "I don't mind helping you, but you've gotta do the work. I'm not doing it for you."

Shane knew what she was implying. "No, no. That's not what I meant. I just need extra help."

Seeing she'd misunderstood, Abi felt terrible for insinuating the negative. "I'm sorry. I didn't mean..."

"Look, I don't want special treatment or anything. And I certainly don't expect you to do my work for me. I gotta keep good grades to qualify for the NCAA."

"Don't worry. I'll help you."

"Can we keep this between us?" He seemed embarrassed. "I, umm..."

"I promise I won't tell anyone. It'll be our secret."

"Thanks. Appreciate that." Confirming the time, he said, "We should go." Standing up, he packed his backpack and waited for her to gather her things. Pulling out her chair when she stood up, he pushed both in and allowed her to lead.

On his way to the parking garage elevator, Shane received a text from Reggie. After reading it, he texted back. His friend was wondering where they were.

Seeing Gerald sitting quietly in his booth, Abi broke away from Shane. "Give me a second," she said.

The football player stopped and checked his messages. Watching Abi, he realized she'd gone to talk to the attendant.

"Gerald!" she smiled. "How was your day?"

His face lit up when he saw her in such good spirits. "Well, Miss Abi. It was fine. Same old, same old. How was your first day, dear?"

"It had its moments, but it's been pretty good overall." Abi turned and looked at Shane.

"That is wonderful to hear." He knew things turned out well because of the boy standing not far from them.

"Just wanted to wish you a nice evening. I'll see you in the morning, I suppose."

Amazed by Abi's actions, Shane walked over. "Hello, Sir. I'm Shane."

"Gerald. Nice to meet you, young man." He shook his hand.

"We met when I arrived for orientation. Gerald was my first friend here," Abi explained.

He was surprised to hear her speak so highly of the older gentleman.

Making eye contact with the strapping football player, Gerald said, "Take care of this polite young woman. Miss Abi is not like the other girls."

"I'm beginning to see that, too." A grin appeared on Shane's face.

Abi blushed.

"Hey, dude, you comin'? We gotta roll!" Reggie bellowed from inside the parking garage.

Not to be rude and interrupt their conversation, Shane didn't respond. He gave him a thumbs-up instead. "Nice to meet you, Gerald. We'll see you tomorrow?"

"Absolutely. I'll be here. You two have a good night." The man raised his hand to bid them goodbye.

"You as well."

"Yes, you too, Gerald," Abi replied while walking with Shane to the garage.

"You've kinda put me to shame," he pointed out.

"I don't understand."

"I've been at this school for three years, and I've never stopped to talk to that man. Technically, you've been here for what, two days, and you're on a first-name basis with the guy."

"Why not? He is sweet and made me feel welcome."

Shane smiled so much that it made him turn and look away. "You keep surprising me, New England, and that's hard to do."

"I guess that's a good thing?" She figured he thought so, too.

"Yes," he chuckled. "It's a good thing."

Meeting up with Reggie, Abi found Jade standing alongside him, ready to leave.

"You two doing okay after the lunch fiasco?" her new friend asked.

"We're fine," Abi said, despite Shane being worse for wear.

"Sure you're good, man?" Reggie could see he wasn't.

The quarterback nodded and walked with Abi to his Jeep.

Stopping, she fearfully inspected every inch of it. "Wait. You want me to go in that?"

Not understanding what she was insinuating, he questioned, "What's wrong?"

Scanning the vehicle from front to back, she said, "Well, for one, it doesn't have doors."

"Yes. That's correct."

Abi had a terrified look on her face. "Is it safe?"

He stood there, clearly offended. "I promise you'll be fine. We aren't goin' far." Shane tossed his bag in the lockbox. "You can put your stuff here." He reached out and took her backpack off her shoulder before carefully placing it in the secured space. Closing the tailgate, he guided her to the passenger side. Offering a hand, he said, "Jump in."

Abi grabbed hold and nervously climbed into the seat. Pulling the belt across her chest and fastening it with a click, she wanted to hold onto something, but there was nothing to grab.

He got in beside her. "Ready?"

Seeing Reggie's Ferrari slowly pull away, the engine's sound echoed through the building, gurgling and howling.

Shane pressed the ignition button. His, too, had a deep groan to it.

While leaving, they waved to Gerald, who bid them goodbye.

Unable to keep up with Reggie, who had sped off ahead of them, Shane drove along Sunset Boulevard with the flow of traffic.

The wind drifted through the vehicle from top to bottom, tossing Abi's hair freely. Feeling the warmth of the sun, she sat back and relaxed.

Occasionally glancing at her, he was happy she wasn't scared.

Signaling into the UCLA campus, making another right onto Charles E. Young Drive, they soon pulled into the parking lot. Slowly entering the structure, Shane flipped his visor down to display his parking pass. Not far away, they noticed Reggie waving at them. Both he and Jade were guarding an open spot.

Once parked, he turned to Abi and said, "See, we arrived safely. That wasn't so bad, was it?"

"No. Not really."

"You'll get used to it." Smiling, he jumped out and grabbed his athletic gear. Slinging the bag across his chest, he got Abi's backpack and helped her slip it on her shoulders.

Seeing Reggie and Jade walking hand in hand a few yards ahead. Abi thought, *Wow, they moved quickly*, unsure if Shane had noticed.

"Way to go, Reg," he whispered.

"What?" Abi hadn't fully heard what he'd said.

"Oh, nothing." He picked up the pace. "Hey, we've gotta get a move on."

Ascending the staircase, skipping every second step, they reached the top level. "Turn left. Down the ramp," he directed.

Abi saw their friends strolling along whimsically, with Jade resting her head on Reggie's shoulder. In comparison, Shane walked alongside her with a two-foot buffer between them.

*Perhaps he only wants to be friends. Maybe it's about the tutoring? Nothing else.* She felt disappointed but was not surprised. Given her inexperience, never having been in a relationship, she didn't know what to expect. Grateful for the attention, she took it for what it was, happy to have friends to hang around. That was something she never had in Boston after Burton left.

Upon entering the doors on the far end of the newly built facility, Abi was in awe of the state-of-the-art foyer. The guys registered their guests while the woman behind the reception directed Jade and Abi to the viewing area upstairs. With passes to wear, they wished the guys luck before heading up to the second floor.

"This facility is amazing," Abi said, admiring every square inch. "It is so professional."

Walking down the hallway, past a series of offices, they came across the observation deck and went outside.

"Did you see the tennis courts on the way here?" Jade asked.

Abi remembered. "Yes, I did."

"Tryouts are there tomorrow. You still in?"

"Yeah, sure am." Taking a seat in the shade, Abi seemed deflated. Her body language said it all.

Immediately, Jade had to know what was going on. "Okay, girl? Spill. What's the matter?"

"Nothing. I'm fine."

Jade tilted her head. "I don't believe you."

Abi was still processing the day's events.

"Instead of being on cloud nine, you seem sad when you should be the opposite. It's day one, and you've completely blown up the social order at Gilderson. I mean, wow, Shane Coopersmith broke up with Emile Raven today for a chance to be with you."

Abi was about to respond to that, but Jade interrupted.

"Wait, one more thing. Thank you, by the way, for bringing me along for the ride. Reg and I wouldn't be where we are now if you hadn't asked me to meet you this morning."

"Hold on. Let's clarify things. I didn't quote, unquote, 'blow up' the social order. And as for Shane and Emile, they were already on the rocks way before I showed up. It just so happened he chose today to break it off."

"No, honey, listen. You don't realize how you've interrupted the status quo. Everything would have remained the same this year without you here. Nothing would have changed." Jade pointed at the guys filtering out onto the football field below. "I guarantee none of this would be happening right now if it wasn't for you."

"Jade?"

Her friend was still reeling at how her life had suddenly flipped. "What is it?"

"I don't think Shane likes me in that way. Earlier, he asked me to tutor him. I think that's what this is about. I promised to help him, but I don't want to get suckered into doing his work for him."

"Whoa. Whoa. Where did you get that idea? I'm pretty sure you're mistaken. He wouldn't do that."

"Do what?"

"Sucker you into doing his work." She paused a second. "Okay. Listen. Driving here, Reggie told me what Shane told him."

That piqued Abi's interest. "Really?"

"The guy doesn't move fast on his own. When he started dating Emile, she steered the ship. He didn't. Reggie said he's nervous around you because you're different. He doesn't know how to act or what to say. He's intimidated and afraid of screwing it up. So, please have a little patience and see where it goes. At Allie's on Saturday, I noticed his eyes on you. You intrigue him."

"But, you and Reg are already holding hands, for crying out loud..."

"Yeah, but that was Reggie. Not me. He's a sweet, clingy kind of guy." Lost in her thoughts, she refocused and said, "Just give him a chance. Shane's not the sappy type, and that's okay. But don't count him out yet."

Seeing the team warming up on the field, the girls positioned their chairs along the glass to see better. Between plays, Shane and Reggie would often look up. As a football fanatic, Abi pointed two fingers to her eyes and then turned them on Shane to signal him to pay attention on the field. Laughing, he gave her a subtle thumbs-up.

Able to understand the significance of the drills they were doing, the brown-haired beauty grabbed her Burch notebook and recorded a few things while explaining the game to Jade, who was utterly green when it came to football. She was amazed by Abi's knowledge.

When the practice ended, the girls returned downstairs, handed in their passes, and waited in the foyer. Twenty minutes later, Shane and Reggie surfaced, looking exhausted.

Greeting them, Reggie held out his hand for Jade. Holding it tightly, he said, "Ready to head out? Maybe we can go grab a bite?"

"Yeah, sure. I'd like that," she replied, bumping his shoulder.

Shane didn't say much.

"Is everything okay?" Abi sensed something was up.

"The practice could have gone better."

"What do you mean?" Confused, Abi took out her notebook. "So, from what I saw, you completed thirty-six of forty-two passes during the scrimmage today. That's an eighty-six percent success rate. By my calculations, you advanced the ball three hundred and twenty-four yards, give or take—an average of about nine yards per throw. On top of that, two long ones came in at forty-seven and fifty-two yards, respectively. Despite those being incomplete, the bottom line is that you got them there. Impressive for the first day back, if you ask me."

"Wait?" He stopped, completely stunned by her accuracy. "Are you giving me stats?"

"Yes, why? Don't you want to know? Cause I think you did exceptionally well."

Shane stood in the middle of the path and looked at her.

"What?" Abi got nervous.

He chuckled. "Never in my lifetime has a girl ever understood football, let alone the stats that go with it. I'm mega impressed, New England. Wow. That's incredible."

"You're not mad?"

"Why on earth would I be mad?" He shook his head in disbelief. "I gotta say, I've never met a girl like you, Abs."

"Hey, you called me Abs." Her heart fluttered at the sound of it.

Peering into her eyes, he said, "Is that okay?"

"Sure. I don't mind."

"Okay. Abs, it is." Seeing their friends had disappeared into the garage, Shane said, "We should catch up."

Arriving at his truck, he opened the tailgate and tossed his bag inside before helping Abi with her backpack. Closing it, they got into the Jeep.

Before starting the engine, Shane turned to her and said, "Thanks for coming today."

"Well, thank you for the invitation. The facility is awesome. The team is so lucky to practice here."

"It's pretty nice."

Abi could tell he had something on his mind. "I can hardly wait to see the game on Friday. My first one in California."

"About that."

Abi wasn't sure what he would say.

"Aramis and Lexi are hosting an after-party in Malibu. Do you, umm, wanna go?"

"Like a date?" Abi taunted with eyebrows raised.

Shane smiled bashfully and lowered his head. "Is it too soon?" He stopped to analyze their situation. "Look, I want to reassure you that the Emile thing has been over for a while. It wasn't something that just surfaced today."

Not sure what to think, a little hesitant, Abi replied, "Okay."

"Okay, it's too soon, or okay, you want to go on Friday?"

"I'd love to go to the party with you."

Gripping the steering wheel, he said, "Good. Friday it is."

Confirming he was somewhat reserved, Abi remembered what Jade had said about being patient.

The Jeep rumbled when he started it. "Still scared of driving with the doors off?" he asked before departing.

"No. It's not so bad. Why?"

"Well, I thought, if you needed something to hold onto...." Shane offered her his hand. "You know, purely for safety reasons."

In disbelief, she timidly slipped her hand in his and replied, "Well, if it's for safety reasons, I guess I should."

His hand was warm and felt rough to the touch as he slowly intertwined their fingers. Feeling a fraction of its strength, Abi noticed her hand paled in comparison, sizewise. Gingerly pulling her closer, their elbows resting together on the center console, Shane let go for a split second to shift the truck into gear, then grabbed hold again.

While passing the tennis courts, she said, "By the way, that's where Jade and I'll be after school tomorrow. We have team tryouts."

"Really?" he said on their way toward Sunset Boulevard. Tennis is a complicated sport—it has a lot of working parts."

"It is, but did I fail to mention I was a state finalist in the U18s back home?"

He kept his eye on the road but glimpsed her way briefly. "Honestly, I'm not surprised."

"Why?"

"I figured you were smart and athletic."

"Don't get too excited. I haven't made the team yet."

He gave her hand a few gentle squeezes and said, "Don't worry. You will," then asked, "So does that mean I get to watch you practice?"

"If you have time."

"I'll make time."

The wind whistled past as they drove along. The sun was low on the horizon, occasionally blinding them. Despite the excitement of a budding relationship being foreign to her, Abi soaked up every second. Somehow, it felt like they'd known each other for years, not days. Maybe that is why she felt so calm around him. It seemed natural, not forced or pushed.

As the Jeep climbed the hill to the Gilderson School, Shane stopped at the intersection and turned left. Carefully inching inside the garage, noticing Gerald had left already, Shane turned down the aisle where Abi was parked. Pulling up alongside her Mini Cooper, he reluctantly let go of her hand to shift gears before turning off the engine.

"Here we are. Safe and sound."

"Yes, thank you for a fun afternoon."

"Glad you enjoyed it." Shane pondered whether to kiss her goodbye. Looking around, he realized the parking garage was not exactly the most romantic place for that and knew she deserved better.

"I should probably get going. My parents will wonder where I am," she said, unbuckling her seat belt.

"Right." He got out on his side and met her at the back. Opening the tailgate, he carried her bag to the car in a gentlemanly way and placed it in the front passenger seat.

Abi's heart pounded, not knowing how things would end.

He stood tall and towered over her, presenting both hands. Abi saw this and took hold of them.

"I guess I'll see you in the morning. Can I call you later?" he asked.

"Yes, I'll be home. No plans tonight."

Slowly pulling her in close, Abi wrapped her arms around his waist as he hugged her tightly.

"Goodnight," he said, releasing her from his embrace.

"Night."

Shane backed away as she got into her car and started it. For whatever reason, he felt intimidated by the intelligent girl from Boston. She was different from every other girl he'd ever dated. Waving to Abi as she pulled away, he got into his truck and followed her. Driving along, he knew a protective instinct had sparked inside him today - a fiery need to keep her safe from harm. It was unlike anything he'd ever experienced. Mimicking her every move, shadowing her Mini Cooper along Sunset Boulevard, they soon arrived at the gates of Bel Air. Seeing Abi signal left, he drove up alongside her. Stopped at the red light, he peered down at the girl who had captivated him from the moment their eyes met.

The opposing light turned yellow.

Ready to turn, Abi waved, "Bye!"

Lifting a steady hand, he couldn't help but smile. "See you later, Abs."

She melted to the core upon hearing that.

Suddenly, the cars behind her began honking. Abi realized she was missing the advanced green. Making the turn, she kept waving to Shane as he drove away.

Watching her leave his sights, he felt happy for the first time in a while. Despite all the drama Emile caused, the rest of the afternoon was easy and uncomplicated. Looking forward to the end of the week with anticipation, he wanted to do better and give Abi everything she needed.

"Still can't believe she recorded my stats," he said aloud. "That's incredible."

15

## Rumors

When she arrived home, Abi thought the house was too quiet after she walked in and locked the front door.

"Mom?" Abi said, moving room to room, looking for any sign of life. "Mom!" Not getting a response, she panicked and quickly started to scour every nook and cranny. "Mom? Are you here?"

Making her way upstairs, she cautiously entered her parent's bedroom, hoping to find her Mother asleep. There, she found the drapes open and the bed neatly made. Flinging open the bathroom door, she heard, "Aah!"

Water and bubbles flung everywhere from floor to ceiling! Taken off guard, Abi jolted backward.

"Oh, Abi!" Finding her Mom in the bath with headphones on her head, she slid one side off her ear. "You scared me half to death! Is everything okay?"

"Yes, all good," Abi said, so relieved. "I just didn't know where you were." Giggling, she said, "Sorry about that," recalling the terrified look on her Mother's face and the water exploding everywhere.

A few suds fell from the ceiling. It caused the two of them to erupt into full-on laughter.

"You should have seen your face," Abi teased.

"What? You were just as surprised." Putting away her phone and handing the headphones to Abi to put on the vanity, she asked her daughter, "So, tell me. How was the first day of school? Was it good? I want every detail."

On her hands and knees, mopping up the water with a dry towel, Abi cleaned up the mess. Thankful her Mom was coherent enough to listen, she counted her blessings. After telling her about Shane, Jade, and Reggie, she then shared information on Blu Brennan and Taizo being in her class and the actress Lexi Muller.

Glued to every word Abi shared, her Mother did not interrupt once.

After explaining how the school operated, she moved on to the confrontation with Emile Raven and the girl's very public breakup with Shane. Her Mother was all ears.

"When the smoke cleared, Shane asked me to take a walk with him through the gardens." Abi stared at the floor, unsure what she'd say to that.

Amidst the bubbles, her Mom inched closer and rested her arms along the edge of the soaker tub.

"He asked me out on Friday night," she squeaked out.

There was a blatant pause.

"The football team is playing an exhibition game, and Lexi and Aramis are hosting an after-party in Malibu. Can I go?" Holding her breath, she could tell her Mother was concerned. Attempting to smooth things over, she added, "I know what you're thinking. You believe I'm the rebound girl?"

"That thought did cross my mind," she said. "Look, the truth is, I just don't want you to get hurt." Reaching her hand out to her daughter, covered in bubbles, she said, "I trust you. I just don't trust everyone else."

Abi was disappointed.

"You can attend the party as long as other girls are going too," she said, knowing her seventeen-year-old deserved a normal high school experience after everything that's happened.

"From what I can gather, the entire senior class will be there—Jade and Reggie, for sure. Allie, the girl who invited me to Venice Beach on

Saturday, is going. I'll get a better idea as the week goes on. I'm sure most will not miss it."

"Remember, no drinking. No drugs."

Abi tilted her head in disbelief. "Really, Mom?"

"I realize. But this is LA, Sweetie. Peer pressure will be different than it was back home. Just be mindful, and don't drink from open cups. Take a water bottle with you, just in case."

"All right. I will."

For as long as she could remember, Abi knew her Mother was over-protective and meant well. "I should get to my homework." Seeing her Mom's shriveled fingers, she laughed, "And you need to get out of the bath. You look like a prune."

"I'll do that," the pretty woman giggled. "See you in a bit?"

"For sure."

Abi walked out of their room and down the hall. Taking out her books, she plugged in her laptop and started working on the math review before finishing her Enviro Systems notes. While thinking back to study hall today, she beamed inside and out. Recalling how close Shane was while listening to her, it didn't take long to start daydreaming. Yanked back to reality when her phone chimed, she wondered who it was. Picking up the device, she saw Burton's name.

His text read, *Hey, Abi. How was the first day? Did everything go okay?*

She thought about what she should say and opted to omit the social upheaval part. *It was good - better than expected. The teachers are nice. Class material seems easy enough. I even met a few more friends. So far, so good*, she typed before pressing send.

Hoping he wouldn't bring up Shane, she waited as his thinking bubbles cycled.

*Glad to hear you survived. Are you sure everything is okay?*

As much as she wanted to tell her best friend all the dramatic details, Abi refrained and kept things more general. *Yeah? Why?* She typed, feeling something was up.

*Well, there is a group of girls here at the coffee shop, and they're rambling on about a girl named Abi and an ex-boyfriend named Shane.*

The air expelled from her lungs. Now, she had no choice but to share everything. *Can you talk or not?* She texted.

Without hesitation, he typed, *Sure.* In seconds, Burton was calling her phone.

"Hello," she answered.

"Hey," is all he offered.

"So, Emile and her friends are there." She could feel her stomach churning.

"They're not sitting far. I've heard everything they've said." He muttered quietly with his hand over his mouth to ensure they didn't overhear their conversation.

"Then you know what happened?"

"Well, her version, I suppose. I'm sure it is very different from yours. She paints you in a very unbecoming way."

"I bet she does." Abi exhaled and groaned. "Arrgghh... What was said? Do I want to know?"

"Umm, I'm not sure if I can repeat it word for word, but I can paraphrase for you."

"Okay. Shoot. Give me the good, bad, and the ugly."

"Well, there's certainly a lot of the latter," Burton said bluntly.

"Oh, Lord."

He could tell how stressed she was. It confirmed most of what he overheard was true. "So, she said that Shane was hanging around you at the beach party on Saturday, and this morning, you walked into school together. Apparently, you acted like you owned the place, but I know that is a lie. It's completely out of character for you."

"Truth is, I was scared to death and mostly hid behind Shane, Jade, and Reggie the entire time."

"Figured as much." Recalling what else was said, he added, "She was angry she had to sit in the front of the class and said you guys whispered about her the entire time."

Abi pounced on that statement. "We didn't say a word about her. The teacher told us to work in groups. I explained the math to those around me. When class was about to end, some of the guys on the team gave me the inside scoop on some other students in class. That's all. Her name didn't come up once during that conversation."

"I believe you."

"Oh, I feel sick." Abi leaned over her desk and held her head in her hand. "What am I going to do, Burton? It's not like I didn't know this would happen. Remember, I told you on Sunday. I should have stayed far away. But..."

"But you like him."

She let out a whimsical sigh. "Yeah... Don't hate me."

"I could never hate you." His tone sounded incredibly sincere.

"Okay... What else? May as well know what I'm up against."

Burton thought a moment. "The Emile girl said that you have your claws in him. But you don't realize that Shane will always return to her."

"I can't see that happening. The girl is verbally abusive, and he knows being around me isn't like that. He realizes he doesn't have to take her BS." Abi huffed. "You know, she yelled across the courtyard for him to *come here*. It was like she was giving a command to a dog. He walked over and asked to speak to her privately. She declined, quite rudely, I might add. That is when he told her it was over and walked away without saying another word. To protect me, he went to sit with other friends to avoid bringing me into it. Emile stormed over to him and said some horrible things - like she was bored of him and didn't need him anymore. He flat-out told her he felt the same and was okay with it. Keep in mind the entire student body heard this. When she walked away, he came and sat beside me. Minutes later, he asked if I wanted to take a walk. I assumed he was desperate to escape the whispers and unwanted conversations."

"Wow. That's not how the girl told the story, but your version makes more sense."

"Believe me. Emile brought it on herself. She is horrid to people. That is something I can't even fathom. I could never say nasty things to anyone or point someone out in a crowd and say something mean. It's crazy."

"I know. That's not in your nature."

"Exactly." Abi took a deep breath. "I kind of feel sorry for the guy. I can see the scars she's left behind. Strangely, he is the most popular guy in school, yet his confidence was on shaky ground around her today."

Burton knew he had to be supportive. Abi needed him. Regardless of his feelings, the best thing he could do was be a sounding board. "So, what are you going to do?" he asked, believing she had a strategy.

"I plan to ignore it all. Rise above the pettiness and all the drama. Hopefully, avoid confrontation wherever necessary."

He saw one flaw in that approach. "You need to rehearse a response in case these girls taunt you. Something well thought out, more mature and irrefutable."

"Yes, you're right. But what?"

"That, I can't help you with. Just make sure you give it some thought. Maybe something along the lines of – I don't have anything against you, Emile. Not going to fight, or perhaps Shane made his choice."

"Oh, the first one is more me. Not the last one. It's too combative. I could never...."

"And that is why he likes you." He could tell how mentally shot she was from the drama that unfolded.

"Thank you for that."

"You're welcome."

"Look, I've gotta go. I need to finish up my homework and shower before dinner."

"Yeah, no problem. Sorry to be the bearer of bad news."

"No, I'm glad you told me. I'll be on the lookout for things to-morrow. Unfortunately, this won't be going away any time soon."

"Nope." Burton quietly chuckled. "I'm so glad I'm out of high school."

"Thanks..." she said, knowing their conversation was relatively trivial compared to his adult world. It made her feel like a whiny little girl - something she hated. Sitting straight in her chair, she fixed her posture. "You know what? I'm just going to be myself. If those girls don't like me, then so be it. I'll treat them with respect and not act the way they do. People will see them for who they are, and hopefully, I'll set a good example."

"That's a more mature way to look at it. In life, you'll always run into people who hate you and vice versa. It's inevitable. But how you react says a lot about your character."

"You're right."

"Yes, I am," he chuckled. "On that note, Abi Acardi, I'll bid you goodnight. I need to sneak out of here and get home."

"Speaking of which, where do you live anyway? Why do you study in a coffee shop?"

"That is a story for another time," he said, not elaborating. "Good night, my friend."

"One last thing before you go.... I have tennis team tryouts on campus at three o'clock."

"Well, I might have to stop by the courts and say hello."

Abi thought about it. "Just don't bellow at me from the stands or anything."

"Don't worry. I won't distract you."

"Okay," she replied, thinking perhaps this wasn't such a good idea. "Now, I'll say goodnight." Abi paused. "Hey, Burton?"

"Yeah?"

"Thanks for looking out for me."

He knew she was thankful for the heads up. "That's always been my job, Abs."

"Well," she replied, "I appreciate that."

"I know you do." He added with dead air between them, "Maybe I'll see you tomorrow if I can sneak out for twenty minutes."

"Okay. No pressure. Figured I'd mention it. Have a good night."

"You too. Night."

Burton ended the call on his end.

Abi put the phone down and thought about their conversation. She was so lucky to have him. He always made sense of things - especially in difficult situations. Perhaps it was because he was a good guy. Maybe it was because he was a genius. Regardless, she looked forward to their drive-up PCH on Sunday. She was sure their conversation would be non-stop.

Diving back into work, she barely picked up her pencil. A notification on her phone illuminated the screen. Peering down, she saw it was Shane.

*Hi. It's me. Just checking in.*

Abi felt all aflutter while texting back. *I'm good. Finishing some homework. You?*

Once again, she watched his thinking bubbles ramble on before his reply popped up.

*I'm stuck on math question number 14. Care to explain? But don't give me the answer.*

Abi referred to their review package and found that question. He was right. It was a hard one. Suddenly, her phone made a strange noise. Looking down, she noticed Shane was calling her on FaceTime. Nervous, unsure what to do, never having used it before, she slid her thumb across the screen to answer it. Suddenly, his face appeared in front of her.

"Hey, Abs."

"Umm, Hi..."

"Hope you don't mind. Less typing this way."

"No, it's fine." Abi thought about what she should say. "So, question fourteen? It's a hard one."

"Don't laugh, okay? I'm going to show you what I got. If it's wrong, just say something like *Good try* or *Back to the drawing board.*"

She laughed at his statement. "Okay."

He hovered his phone over his paper. Abi started to solve the equation herself and looked at his answer and the thought process of how he reached that conclusion.

"Well, done."

"Wait? You mean I got it right?"

"Yeah, look." Abi flipped her camera around and showed him her work. "Same."

With a subdued reaction, his eyebrows raised. "Wow. Okay. Good," he said humbly.

"Great. How about the next one." She could see that little success fueled him to keep going.

The two continued working through the questions for the next forty minutes. Shane kept doing the work himself, and Abi just checked it.

When they finished the last question, Abi said, "Great job."

"Thanks. I have an awesome tutor."

"You certainly do," Abi giggled. "Hate to cut this short, but I haven't had dinner yet."

"Me either." He waited for a second and said, "Thanks for your help today. I finally feel like I'm gettin' a handle on this stuff."

"All it takes is a little repetition and practice."

"Guess so."

"So, goodnight," she said bashfully. "I'll see you in the morning."

"Yes. I'll be there."

"Okay."

"Night, Abs."

Ending the call, having seen him sitting at his desk, looking so handsome, she embedded the image in her head and went to start the shower. While waiting for it to warm up, she walked to the window and found the lights turned on inside the mansion across the canyon. The man was walking around on the second floor. With a takeout container in hand, he sat on the sofa and turned on the television. He looked lonely. It made her wonder what his story could possibly be.

# 16

# Dissention

With strong wind gusts rustling the large palms below Abi's room, she woke to a calming shooshing sound. Opening her eyes before her alarm, she rolled over, excited to start the day. Mainly anticipating spending time with Shane, the thought sparked a bounce in her step as she made the bed.

Dressed and ready in record time, about to go downstairs, she peeked into her Mom's room and found her sleeping soundly. Not wanting to disturb her, Abi quietly headed to the kitchen. Intent on making a coffee to go, she noticed a note from her Dad on the counter.

*Morning, Sweetheart. Mom had a rough night. Please check on her before leaving and ensure the house is locked. I will be home early afternoon. Love Dad.* She silently read.

Taking her freshly brewed cup from the machine, Abi poured it into her insulated travel mug over the sink. After adding some cream and stirring it, she checked on her Mom again before leaving for school. Confident that she was okay, Abi headed back downstairs and walked out the door, locking it behind her.

While driving down Stradella, she tried to be patient while fighting rush hour traffic. It was a little heavier than yesterday. Paying attention to the activity around her, she turned onto Sunset minutes later, thankful she wasn't running late.

Climbing the hill to Gilderson, Abi turned left at the stop sign and saw Gerald in the security booth. It didn't take long for him to recognize her car.

"Well, Good Morning, Miss Abi. How are we doing this morning?" He could see she was happy but had a lot on her mind.

"I'm doing okay. It's day two," she said with less enthusiasm.

He sincerely replied, "Chin up, my dear."

"Thank you so much. I'll see you after, okay."

"Yes. Enjoy your day."

"You too."

Abi continued past him and pulled into the garage, where she saw Jade and Reggie. Shane's truck was there, but he wasn't. Her friend subtly got her attention and pointed to the far side. Following her line of sight, she located Shane. To her surprise, he was having a heated discussion with Emile and the mean girls.

"Oh, no," she said. "It's too early in the morning for this."

Shane locked eyes with Abi as she parked her car.

Emile shot her a venomous look in the process.

With a deep breath, hoping to gather some courage, she grabbed her backpack and prepared to join the mayhem. "I guess this is really round two," she said, her hands trembling uncontrollably. Rise above this petty behavior, Abi. Do not lash out in anger. Just stay calm."

Jade rushed over to her friend to offer support.

Seeing the worried look on her face, Abi asked, "What is it, Jade?"

"Ask her yourself!" Emile shouted at Shane combatively, determined for Abi to overhear. "Go ahead. Ask her!"

"Ask me what?" Abi walked up behind Shane. He did not look happy.

"Is it true?" he questioned.

"Is what true? Might need some clarification." She didn't know what was going on.

"We saw you on Sunday with another guy at the coffee shop," Maddy spouted, showing them the footage on her phone.

One of the twins chimed in. "Yeah, you two were hanging off each other when you left."

Emile stood firm and crossed her arms, wondering what the new girl would say.

Seeing the clip, Abi laughed. "You mean Burton?"

"So, it's true?" Shane looked deflated.

Jade stepped in. "That's what this is about? He's Abi's best friend from Boston. He attends UCLA. They used to be neighbors, not to mention childhood friends. I met him on Saturday. Nothing is going on between them." Jade laughed hysterically at Emile and her friends' epic fail.

"That's not what I saw?" Emile started to panic as her narrative crumbled.

"Abi, are you dating this guy or not?" Shane needed to know the truth.

"No, I am not seeing Burton. That would be like dating my brother. Eeww." Having addressed Shane, she turned to the mean girls. "I told Burton how badly you've bullied me since I arrived. When we saw you walk in, he wanted to get me out of there unscathed, so we decided to put on a show. It seems to have worked. You took the bait, hook, line, and sinker." Abi stood confidently in front of everyone despite her legs weakening.

"Arrghh!" The jilted girl huffed and stomped both feet, unable to contain her anger.

"I think we're done here," Shane said, unwilling to entertain the posse's antics. Joining Abi, Emile followed him, still furious.

Abi's heart rose into her throat as the jilted girl got closer. She didn't know what she would do or say next.

Inches away from her nemesis, she stared straight-faced at Abi and cautioned, "So you know, he always comes back to me."

"Yeah, Emile. Not this time," he interrupted without skipping a beat. "Don't listen to her, Abs."

The disgruntled cheerleader whisked around and took off.

Wanting to give their friends some space, Reggie and Jade started toward the elevator since the drama had passed.

Happy to see Emile leave, Shane asked Abi, "You okay?"

"Yeah." The truth was she felt verbally maimed.

"I'm sorry about...." Realizing he'd doubted her, he wanted to make amends. "If you say this Burton guy is just an old friend from Boston, then I believe you."

"There is absolutely nothing going on between Burton and me. He's two years older, for goodness sake. Besides, he has his pick of college girls. Like, really?"

Offering her his hand like it were an olive branch, Abi hesitated before taking hold. "Come on. We should get to class."

Having caught up to their friends, the elevator ride to the courtyard level was quiet. Reggie glanced at Jade and raised his eyebrows, then made eye contact with Shane, who shook his head, hoping he wouldn't rehash what just happened.

Once the doors opened, they walked out and moved toward the buildings on the north side. Hearing tires squealing, they saw Emile's BMW flying down the road while Taizo hovered above the school in the helicopter, preparing to land.

"I guess she decided to skip class," Jade said, looking up at the multi-million-dollar machine fighting the crosswinds.

"And now we can chill out," Reggie said, hating the drama.

Holding onto Abi, Shane hoped she'd have a better day with Emile gone. He knew all of this wasn't easy for her.

When they approached their building, they saw Taizo walking toward them, flanked by four men.

Reggie couldn't help but laugh. "Taizo! You've got a lot of excess baggage today!" he said to the actor from afar. Reggie could tell it wasn't his choice.

The handsome star smirked. "Let me know if you wanna share!" Annoyed by the men shadowing his every move, he hated that the studio was being so overprotective of him with the new movie coming out.

The guys laughed, but the girls felt sorry for him.

Noticing Alan and Shawn also taunting Taizo, the two stopped their captain.

"Shane. It looks like Emile strikes again," Alan whispered before Shawn interjected, "Thought you should know. She's started a rumor that Abi is cheating on you."

Shane turned to Abi. "We've been together one day, and all hell is breakin' loose."

Walking through the main doors in the foyer filled with students all glued to their phones, Shane decided to nip things in the bud publicly.

"Excuse me! Everyone! Hello!" He waited until he got the attention of every student there. "Do not believe the rumors spread by Emile Raven! They're completely false! End of story!"

The whispers got louder. Then, the crowd went about their business when the bell sounded.

"Well, that's one way of setting the record straight." Reggie patted his best friend on the back.

About to move to class, Abi pulled gently on Shane's arm.

Seeing him looking back at her, she said, "Thank you for that."

"Abs, I will always call it like it is. We had to put that to rest before things got out of hand."

Abi nodded. "I appreciate it."

He smiled. "I know you do."

# 17

## Social Matters

The rest of the morning went by smoothly. Life seemed almost normal. Focused on their studies, Shane kept close tabs on Abi's mood and often wondered what she was thinking when she stared out the window.

Midway through their second class, wanting one-on-one time with her, he quietly asked, "Do you want to go out for lunch today? Get outta here for a bit?"

Reggie overheard and said, "Sure. Where are we going?"

The comment piqued Jade's interest, too.

Turning to Abi, not knowing what to say, he shrugged his shoulders. "Umm, probably for pasta somewhere? Need energy for practice after school."

"I'm down," Reggie replied before anyone else could respond.

"Does that sound good, Abs?" Shane was worried. She was still so quiet.

"Yeah, that works for me. Sure."

"Okay. Good." He hoped the change of scenery would lift her spirits. The last thing he wanted was for her to be in a bad frame of mind for the tryouts.

Sneakily using his phone, keeping it out of sight under the desk, he sent his friend the website to pre-order their food before asking Abi, "What will it be?"

She looked up from her work and whispered, "What do you mean?"

"My treat. Whatever you want." His face brightened.

"A bolognese pasta would be good. Thank you, but..." Carefully reaching into her crossbody bag, making sure Professor Grady didn't see her, she handed him thirty dollars from her wallet. "It doesn't feel right, you paying for me. Here, this should cover it."

He waited for the teacher to turn his back. "I feel like it's my fault that today started off badly. Just trying to make it up to you."

"Shane, what happened was not your fault."

"But you're unhappy, and I feel to blame," he quietly explained before sneakily placing their food order online.

"I'll be honest. Dealing with Emile stresses me out. But I get why she's mad. Somehow, I don't blame her, really." Abi kept her eye on the teacher as he made the rounds.

About to respond, Shane heard the bell. It sidetracked their conversation.

Packing up, their group got a move on and headed to their next class.

Abi and Jade started to walk to the Art Studio while Reggie and Shane followed.

When they arrived outside the doors, the confident football player said, "You gonna be okay?" Peering into the studio, he searched for Emile and her posse.

"Yes, don't worry. I'll be fine." Abi said, standing beside Jade.

"Okay. I'll meet you in the courtyard after," he said.

Jade replied, "We'll be there."

The girls watched the boys continue down the hall. Not seeing Emile anywhere, they went to sit with the other girls. Everyone was relieved to see them. Without skipping a beat, each refuted the Emile rumors. Abi was glad to have their support. It meant a lot.

Before the teacher arrived, Allie walked in. "Hello, Ladies," she said while sitting down happily.

"Hey, Allie," Jade greeted while Abi waved to her. "You seem joyful."

"Read it and weep, girls! I got a ticket for Black Lyon!" The girl surveyed everyone's expressions, thrilled to spark a frenzy. Seeing them frantically checking their phones, she asked, "Anyone else get in?"

"No, nothing yet." Disappointed, Jade slumped in her chair.

"Me either," Abi replied, holding back the truth, waiting for the consensus on Friday.

Summer groaned and put her phone away. "Nothing," she said. "I don't get it. I have it on good authority that Gilderson is on the guest list this weekend. I'm not sure what's going on?"

"Maybe there will be something tomorrow?" Jade tried to keep their hopes up. "Let's take it as a good sign that Allie got in, though."

Their art teacher greeted the class before closing the door behind her.

"Let's get down to business people."

Abi opened her computer and prayed Emile wouldn't show up late. As the minutes passed, she realized she'd probably skipped the entire day. Thankful for the quiet morning, she looked forward to an uneventful afternoon. Focused on her project, Abi mostly listened to the banter flying about their table as they worked. The topic of Friday night surfaced.

"Who's going to Aramis and Lexi's?" Summer threw out the question for comment.

Voluntarily offering a show of hands, Abi noticed every girl was attending.

Their pretty blonde friend smiled excitedly. "Great! I'm so glad. It'll be fun. Has anyone been to his beach house before?"

"Nope," Jade said.

"Oh, it's awesome. Right on the water, like I mean steps from the ocean: a pool, hot tub, and multiple decks. Aramis and Lexi share the double-decker poolhouse. It's amazing."

Nervous about attending the party with Shane, Abi heard whispers from the table behind her. Someone asked if Shane was taking the new girl. Not about to turn around and see who said it, she ignored them to keep the peace. The last thing she wanted was another confrontation.

# 18

# High Noon

Thankful their class flew by, Abi and Jade rushed out the door when the bell sounded and quickly headed to the courtyard. There, they found the guys waiting for them.

"Hey. How was class?" Shane asked, reaching out to Abi.

Taking hold of his hand, she said, "It was good. Uneventful."

Overhearing her comment, Reggie said, "We got confirmation that Emile went home for the day."

"How?" Jade asked.

He showed her Emile's social media post. It was a picture of her at a Spa getting a massage. There was no caption.

Jade gave her two cents. "Guess she did that to save face."

Abi had mixed feelings despite Emile's rudeness. She could understand why she was upset. A new girl had waltzed into Shane's life and taken him from her in a matter of days. No wonder she was bitter. She had every right to be. No stranger to witnessing horrific bullying, she remembered the deadly end to one such incident in Boston. The thought made her shiver. Shaking it off, she tried to erase it from her mind.

Looking forward to the drive to the restaurant with Abi, Shane heard Reg suggest, "So, I guess we are goin' with you guys? No sense taking to vehicles."

Upon hearing that, Shane sighed. "Suppose so."

When they reached the Jeep, Abi noticed it looked very different. "Hey? It has doors and a roof?" she pointed out, surprised.

The football player chuckled, "Didn't you notice that this morning?"

She paused and tilted her head. "Nope. I was distracted by all the drama, I guess."

"Fair enough. Figured you'd feel more comfortable enclosed." Shane opened the tailgate for everyone to put their bags in the back. Rounding the vehicle, he opened the door for Abi and closed it behind her. Their friends slipped into the back seat when Shane got behind the wheel.

Starting the engine, he put it in gear and grasped hold of Abi's hand before driving away.

"Hope you're hungry," he said, glancing at her, then the road.

"Yes. I didn't have breakfast."

"This is the best pasta in Brentwood."

She raised her shoulders. "Mmm.  Now you got me excited."

He was happy to hear she liked carbs.

Passing by the coffee shop, continuing down South Barrington, Shane gently caressed Abi's fingers and seemed deep in thought as he pulled into a plaza on the left. Able to find a spot right in front, the group got out, knowing they had little time to spare.

Reggie was the first to the door of the place and reached out to open it for the girls.

Inside, the hostess greeted them with a smile. "Welcome to Rosti. Table for four?"

Shane spoke up. "Yes, we ordered online for noon pickup. Is it okay if we sit for a bit?"

"Oh, Shane! Hello! Absolutely. Please have a seat. I'll be right back. Everything is ready."

Jade and Abi sat on the slate blue bench along the back wall while the guys pulled out the wrought iron and wood chairs opposite them. The woman emerged moments later with everyone's food in hand. Presenting them with wrapped cutlery and sparkling water, she left them be.

Opening the take-out containers, each dug in.

"Are you ready for this afternoon?" Jade asked her friend. "Girl, you and I need to bring it at tryouts." She hoped to sway her attention away from the craziness that abounded earlier.

"Yes, I know. I'll be ready." Abi heard the door open. She turned to see who had walked in.

"Well, well, well. Who do we have here?" A tall young man said with a strikingly chiseled jawline. Surrounded by three tough-looking goons, he added, "If it isn't our buddy, Coop."

Shane lowered his head in disbelief. "What do you want, Eastwood?" He didn't give him the benefit of looking his way. Continuing to eat his food, Reggie kept a sharp eye on the troublemakers.

Knowing the rival quarterback all too well, Jade pulled out her phone and secretly recorded what was happening. Given their history, she didn't want to leave anything to chance.

Confused, Abi watched her friends' reactions.

Eastwood's sights gravitated toward her longingly. "So, Coop, I see you've got a new little tart."

"Knock it off." Shane confidently stood, pushing the chair back with his legs. Gripping his fist tightly in front of him, he towered over his nemesis.

The guy looked completely unfazed. "Sure you want to do that?"

Reggie joined his friend to create a united front.

"Hey! You, there! What are you doing?" A big man emerged from the kitchen. "Get out of here, or I'll call the cops!" The restaurant owner said with a phone in hand.

Jade intentionally pointed her camera at the goons to tick them off.

Seeing this, Eastwood said with piercing eyes, "You should delete that if you know what's good for you." The threat was a serious one.

Slowly lowering the device, Jade pretended to erase the footage. But she didn't.

"I said leave!" The owner moved closer and grabbed a baseball bat from behind the counter.

"Hey, Pops. Don't worry. We ain't gonna start somethin' – at least not here," Eastwood said in a cocky tone.

The mob turned around and walked out the door. Reggie kept his eye on them. With their reputation for vandalism, he hoped Eastwood would just go on his way without incident.

Shane turned to the man. "Sorry about that, Gary. Thanks for the backup."

The guy's face remained stoic. "Anytime."

"Who was that?" Abi questioned, needing to know more.

Returning to the table after confirming that the guys had left, Reggie replied, "That was Eastwood Korolev. He is part of the Korolev Oligarchs—the Russian mob in SoCal. He is the last guy you want to tangle with. He makes people disappear, if you know what I mean."

"That's insane. Shouldn't he be in jail or something?" Her eyes bounced back and forth between her friends in disbelief.

Shane answered, "No, not when you pay people to turn a blind eye."

"How does he know you?" Abi wanted to understand their connection.

"This past summer, we were invited to the same recruiting camp and competed for the top spot," he replied.

"Yeah, and Shane clinched the honors," Reggie confirmed proudly. "But now, because of that, we gotta watch our backs. Never know if Eastwood will take Shane out of the equation and steal the limelight."

"Take out?" Abi was afraid to know.

Reggie casually ran his finger across his throat.

The blood drained from her face. "You can't be serious?"

Point-blank, without hesitation, Shane warned, "If you ever, ever see that guy lingering around – if he follows you or anything – call 911 immediately. I mean it, Abs." There was a desperation to his voice. "He's dangerous. End of story."

"Okay," she said.

Shane sat down to eat the last of his pasta. "Come on. We need to finish up and get back."

Thanking Gary for his help, they paid their bills. In minutes, the group left. Abi noticed Shane and Reggie's heads on a swivel while approaching the truck. From there, it was a quiet drive back.

Abi thought about everything that had happened so far that day. She had an angry ex-girlfriend to contend with, and now, a crazy football player adding to the mix. It was only the first week of her new life in Bel Air, and she'd inherited a few enemies.

Returning to the school, parking in the garage, Shane got out and walked around to get Abi's door for her before opening the tailgate for everyone to get their stuff. He hoped Jade and Reggie would wander ahead so he and Abi could have a minute alone. Seeing them moving toward the elevator, Shane took Abi's hand and held her back.

Not sure what was wrong, she stopped and waited to hear what he wanted to say.

"Can we talk a second?"

Concerned by the look on his face, she replied, "Sure."

"I'm sorry I've pulled you into a mess of things. None of this was intentional. I hope you know that."

"You can't blame yourself for the actions of others."

"I know, but now you're being dragged into a lot because of me."

"Don't think of it that way."

"It's just...." Hesitating, he wasn't sure how to explain himself. He needed to share something but didn't want to frighten her.

Abi stood before him with eyes affixed to his.

The bell sounded while Shane was rethinking his last thought. "Umm, it's nothing. We'll talk later. Come on, let's get going. We're late."

The two walked to the elevators and waved to Gerald along the way. Reaching the courtyard, they hurried to the library, slipped through the doors, and checked in just in time.

# 19

# Study Hall

Scanning their student cards, Abi and Shane broke away from everyone and headed up the stairs to the same cubicle they had yesterday. It was the quietest spot and still unoccupied. For Shane, there were fewer distractions, allowing him to focus more.

Abi set her backpack on her chair and unloaded her laptop, notebook, and textbooks. Neatly placing everything on the desk, she sat down and prepared to finish the work assigned that day.

Shane followed her example. Setting up his laptop, turning the page in the text to the questions assigned, he looked over and saw Abi open a book.

Moving the ribbon marker aside, she recorded something.

"What are you writing?" he asked curiously.

She flipped the front cover upward to block him from seeing the page.

That is when he saw the ghostly tree logo on the front.

"This is my Burch Book. I need to get a few things on paper before I forget." Finishing her notes, she marked the page and closed the stylish Hermes orange journal. She bound the elastic around its edge and tucked her fine-tipped black pen into the attached holder. Setting it aside, she opened her textbook to the page Shane was on.

"Have to say, it's weird being around a smart girl. It's kinda intimidating."

"This isn't a competition."

"Yeah, I realize." He looked frustrated after glancing at the first question. Leaning back in his chair, running his hands through his hair, he said, "There is so much riding on this year. It's intense."

"I can't imagine," she whispered.

"I'm constantly under a microscope day in and day out. Sometimes it wears on me, you know?"

"You have to take one day at a time—not look too far in advance. Otherwise, you'll get overwhelmed. Live for today, not tomorrow."

"I guess," he paused. "The key word this year is performance. Academic success. Athletic excellence. Nothing short of perfect." Hunching forward, he rested both elbows on the desk to hold up his head.

"Don't worry. I'll help you manage the homework – but that means no secrets. If you're struggling with anything, you gotta tell me. That way, we can deal with it head-on and not let it get out of control. Do you know what I mean?"

"I get it. I promise I'll keep you in the loop and tell you if I'm overwhelmed—although I think you'll know before I do," he chuckled. Looking at the first question, he said, "Any idea what the hell I need to do for number five?"

Abi got a blank piece of paper while Shane pulled his chair closer. One by one, she explained the steps for the first two equations and then left him to answer six more on his own.

For the next half hour, he applied her strategies. With much hesitation, he asked, "Can you check these?" He handed her his work.

She could tell he was nervous about what she might say because he held his breath. Perusing his thought process and steps to get the answer, she said, "Not bad, Captain."

"Yeah?" Exhaling, his face brightened.

"You got four out of the six. On these two, you missed a step. Here, let me show you."

Shane watched as she neatly wrote the correction on the right-hand side of the page. In a bit of a daze, he suddenly felt a warmth inside his chest when she turned to him.

"See what I did there? You needed to recalculate this line and follow suit with the others."

He couldn't sway from staring into her eyes.

"What?" she giggled slightly.

"Umm, nothing." He smiled and lowered his head. "I think I got it."

"Okay. Try a couple more. We will go over it when you've finished."

"All right." He leaned forward and got to work.

In disbelief at the handsome boy sitting beside her, the flirty tension between them was hard to ignore.

Before the end of the work period, they covered the rest of the math questions. To Shane's surprise, he got a majority right.

"This is probably the most productive I've ever been in study hall. Kinda makes me feel like I will survive my last year of high school."

"Of course, you will. This is just the beginning of great things for you. You just have to believe in yourself enough to make it happen."

Impressed by the pep talk, he turned and said, "So, can you say things like that to me all the time?" He reached for her hands. "When you talk like that, it makes me feel like I can do anything."

"I'll try," she whispered while staring into his eyes.

Lost in silence, feeling the need to kiss her, Shane looked down at both of her hands in his. While caressing the tops of each with his thumbs, his sights suddenly bounced between her beautiful blue eyes and rosy lips. His heart hammered like never before. He could feel the spark between them had ignited an intense burning over the past few days – something that could neither be quantified nor described.

Abi froze despite the warmth radiating from head to toe. Barely able to breathe, she knew this was it. Her first.... Unable to finish that thought, seeing him mere inches away, her body trembled. Shane gently brushed his cheek against hers, causing her to shiver. In dangerous proximity, he watched her eyes sensually drift shut.

"Hey! There you guys are. We've been...." Reggie quickly realized they were interrupting something.

Veering off, Shane turned to his friend and shot him a disapproving look.

Shocked, Jade's eyebrows raised upon seeing the football player seconds away from kissing her best friend.

Abi felt uncomfortable and didn't know what to do. She nervously gathered her things and stayed quiet.

Disappointed that the moment had passed, Shane did the same.

Their friends walked towards the stairs to give the two a minute.

The awkwardness between them was almost unbearable. It made Shane think. Of all places, the library was not exactly the romantic spot he envisioned for something so memorable. Seeing her slugging her heavy bag, he slid his backpack straps over both shoulders.

Reaching out, he said, "Here, let me carry that for you." Carefully taking it from her, he slipped it on his left side.

"Are you sure?"

"Yeah. Absolutely." Offering her his free hand, he asked, "Shall we go?"

She nodded, knowing Shane did want to kiss her despite the mishap. Knowing he liked her that way, the realization made her heart bubble over. On top of that, the simple act of taking her heavy bag spoke volumes. In the aftermath, their connection was much stronger. Being close to him, feeling his cheek intimately rest against hers, was enough for now. It laid the foundation for what was to come and fueled her anticipation even more.

"So, it looks like you've got a pretty good handle on the math now," she said to break the ice.

He glanced down at her. "All thanks to you."

"I guess that means we don't have to study after hours?"

"Wait. Are you abandoning me already?"

Happy he still wanted to spend time with her, she humorously replied, "Never."

He smiled from ear to ear. "Good. 'Cause I really do need the help."

While walking along, she noticed how tall and straight Shane was. Confident, she knew he was proud to be holding her hand.

Meeting up with Jade and Reggie at the elevator, their friends felt terrible about interrupting their moment. Not bringing it up during the elevator ride, Jade figured she'd talk to Abi about it later.

Upon reaching the lower level, Abi noticed Gerald dealing with an elderly couple in a vehicle. They looked lost. Spotting Abi, he waved to her while trying to get them to back up and turn their car around. He looked like he was rangling cats.

"Looks like Gerald has his hands full," she said, making Shane turn to witness it.

"Yes. Poor guy."

Abi let go of Shane's hand and went to her car.

Not wanting her to leave, he said, "Hey, where are you going? Are you not drivin' with me?"

"Of course I am. I just need to get my tennis stuff."

He slipped her backpack off his shoulder and handed it to her.

Abi put it in the trunk.

That is when Shane saw her Wilson bag. "Wow, how many racquets do you have in there?"

"Six. You never know when you'll break a string." Locking up her car, about to swing the heavy bag onto her shoulder, Shane took it from her without hesitation while Reggie honked his horn and waved.

Leaving them alone, Shane scanned the dingy parking garage. Reminded of their missed moment, a part of him wanted to pick up where they'd left off. The other wanted to wait for when the time was right.

*No, this is not the place,* he thought to himself. *She deserves more.*

Opening the tailgate of his truck, he placed their bags inside before closing it behind him. Abi had already gotten in the front seat. Buckled up, he started the engine and shifted into gear before holding her hand.

While driving along, Abi leaned over and rested her head on his shoulder.

Sitting straight and tall, Shane peered down at her with a smitten smile. "So, any words of wisdom for me today?"

"Hmm. Words of wisdom, huh?" Abi thought of something insightful. "The best leaders in history lead by example. That is my advice. If you work hard and set a precedent, the rest of the team will follow. If you are confident – they will, in turn, be confident. If you give one hundred percent, they will too."

Shane was impressed.

"You're a talented QB. Don't let anyone tell you differently. You've got the mind for it. You can make split-second decisions and carry out your game plan without hesitation. The guys will follow you into battle anytime, anywhere. All you have to do is ask them."

"Thank you for that." He squeezed her hand sincerely. Bringing it to his lips, he kissed the back of it. Nobody had ever given him that kind of encouragement in life. He felt so close to her. It was almost addictive.

"Remember, keep your head in the game. I won't be there today to remind you of that," she giggled.

"Well, then, you won't be distracting me," he laughed.

"So, do you know the tennis coaches?" Abi sat up straight. "Any inside info for me?"

"All I know is the head coach likes aggressive players. Those who show no mercy."

Abi nodded. "I can do that."

"Yes, I feel you'll make a strong impression today."

"I hope so."

# 20

## Tennis Anyone?

Moving through the UCLA campus, the two maneuvered the winding road to the sports complex. Quickly finding a spot on the garage's upper level, Shane and Abi grabbed their bags. Seeing their friends hanging off each other about twenty yards ahead, they noticed they looked happy and carefree.

Following behind them, they were steps away from the front doors of the Wasserman facility. Abi witnessed Reggie kiss Jade goodbye. It made for an awkward moment between Shane and her. They both tried to pretend they hadn't seen it happen.

Not letting go of Abi's hand until the last second, he said, "Good luck today. I'll see you after."

"Thank you. You too." Abi waved as he walked through the doors.

When the guys had disappeared into the building, Jade looked like she was on cloud nine. Whimsically leading the way to the changerooms inside the adjacent Acosta Center, Abi walked in behind her.

A little jealous that the two were further ahead in their relationship, Abi thought about their failed attempt. *I guess the main thing was he tried.*

"This way, my friend," Jade said as they checked in at the main desk and continued down the corridor. "We can get changed here. I usually don't leave my stuff behind. I bring it with me to the courts."

"Okay. I'll do the same."

Ready to address the elephant in the room, Jade decided to fish for info. "So…" she said, giving Abi the eye. "Shane almost…you know… Care to share?"

"Well, he would have if it wasn't for you guys bursting in on us." Abi blushed.

"I know. I'm so sorry. We didn't mean to." Jade agonized over her comment. "It was an accident. Don't hate me." Almost begging, she pulled on Abi's arm.

"I don't hate you."

"Good. If it's any consolation, I think Shane will try again."

"I hope so." Embarrassed, Abi said, "So, you and Reg…."

While changing into their school's Lulu tennis skorts, athletic tops, and jackets, Jade said, "Not to kiss and tell, but our first was dreamy."

"Oh? How's that?"

Gathering their things, the two headed out to the courts.

Walking through the doors, Abi prompted a second time. "So? Details? Spill."

Jade giggled. "Okay. Okay, you pried it out of me." Leaning over to her, she whispered, "Last night, after we'd gone out for dinner, he followed me home. Before leaving, he kissed me goodnight as the sun was setting over the hillside," she swooned. "It was so romantic. I can't even tell you…"

Abi was happy for her.

While stepping onto the tennis court, she said, "Don't worry, girl. After what I just saw today, you're next."

They joined the coach and trainer in the middle of the stadium.

"Gather around, ladies, quickly," the blonde athletic coach announced. "Let's start with some stretching as I make introductions. I'm Coach Jenna Taylor, and this is our trainer and assistant, Coach Dave Williams. We will be heading up Gilderson women's tennis this season. Today and Thursday are assessment days. We hope to have a team selected by Friday."

The girls listened to their expectations and the governing rules of conduct the private school enforced.

Stretching arms, legs, and back with special attention on the rotator cuffs, hips, and ankles, Coach Taylor said, "Okay, grab a partner and start with a half-court warm-up."

Jade and Abi broke off and went to the far end.

They rallied the ball with precision, moving back and forth. Using split steps between every shot, they got into a rhythm that grabbed Coach Williams's attention. He nodded his head, happy with their agility.

Broken into groups, two courts had game-play, and one court had drills.

Assigned to the drills court, Jade and Abi listened to the coach's instructions. Multiple cones placed in the corners were their targets. The coach wanted them to hit down the line, then cross the court, aiming for the markers.

Abi smiled. It was right up her alley. "This should be fun," she said to Jade.

One after another, the girls completed the drill ahead of them. When it was Abi's turn, the coach hit the ball to her. Without hesitation, she nailed it down the line, making the cone fly up and flip three revolutions before landing on the court. The second shot came at her, allowing Abi to lightly maneuver her feet into position for the perfect cross-court angle. Hitting that cone, the coach ran over and reset the markers before continuing the drill. The line started again, but nobody hit anything. Most missed by mere inches.

Determined to do what Abi did, Jade aimed for the down-the-line shot and, subsequently, the cross-court but sadly missed both by a hair.

Frustrated as she took her place at the back of the line, she whispered, "Damn it."

Waiting her turn, Abi leaned forward, her feet bouncing off the court in anticipation, before Coach Williams hit a ball her way. Once again, she attacked it with great accuracy and hit the cone, knocking it to the back fence before doing the same to the other side.

"Wow, well done. What's your name?" Coach Williams asked.

"Abi Acardi, Sir."

"Hey, Coach Taylor!" he shouted to the Head Coach and pointed at Abi. "I've got a sub!"

"Okay!" The woman acknowledged, waving her over with her racquet.

"Abi, go to court two," Coach Williams instructed.

Doing just that, she left the drills line and walked to the court beside them as Jade looked on.

Joining a singles match rotation, Coach Taylor tossed a ball to her and said, "Your serve."

Abi secured a spare ball in the holder built into her skort. Setting up at the baseline, she bounced it three times before bending her knees and tossing it into the air. Firing it with a loud pop into the outside edge of the adjacent serving box, acing her competition, the sound echoed through the stadium. Not wasting time, she switched sides and prepared for the next point. Straight-faced, she went through her ritual and served down the middle for the ace. All eyes were on her, from the coaches to the spectators and their teammates. Everyone went quiet.

During the final push, Abi got immersed in the zone. Serving the ball to the girl, she finally got a piece of the return. It floated across the net to her side, mid-court. Abi locked onto the open spaces. Veering away from her opponent, not seeing anyone or hearing a sound other than the ball being hit from side to side in the rally, she soon saw her chance and fired the ball down the line for the winner. Laser-focused on her strings to control her peripheral, she served out the game with an ace to win the matchup.

Coach Taylor clapped. "Right on!" she said excitedly. "Super im-pressive! Let's go!"

Little did Abi know, the tennis coach from UCLA was also watching.

Over the next hour, she successfully executed everything thrown at her. Keeping her stats in her head, she lost count after winning all thirteen matchups.

Jade thought her friend had made it look easy.

Taking a water break and stepping out of the sun, Abi saw a big guy sitting on the steps lining the courts. It was Burton. With eyes on him, she subtly waved so as not to bring unwanted attention. He raised a steady hand and gave her a thumbs-up before presenting a tight fist. The signals gave her the courage to compete even harder.

Asked to see her serve and volley, Abi set up at the baseline, took a deep breath, and tossed the ball into the air. Hitting it with brute force, following up the serve, she executed a split-step mid-court, hoping for a return. But nothing came back.

Glancing at Burton, his fist clenched in front of him. She could see him mouth the words, *Yeah. Nice.* Focused on her strings while controlling her breathing, she waited her turn.

Sadly, after about ten minutes, Abi noticed Burton tap his watch. She knew he had to go. Nodding, she lifted her thumb and pinky finger to her ear to say she would call him later.

Acknowledging, he waved and continued onto the lecture hall.

With only ten minutes left, the coaches dismissed the girls and asked Jade and Abi to stay back for a few minutes. Waiting for the rest of the team to depart, Coach Taylor asked, "So, Abi. Where are you from?"

"Boston," she answered.

"Did you play tennis there?"

"Yes. I was in the U18 State Championships. Lost out in the finals."

Stunned to have a caliber of player like her try out, the Coaches were excited.

"Just want the two of you to hit a few extra points. No holds barred," Coach Williams instructed.

"Sure," Abi said. "Ready, my friend?"

Jade giggled. "You're mine, New England."

"Hey, nobody calls me that, but...."

"But who?" Jade laughed, trying to psych her out.

"Less talking and more tennis, please!" Coach Taylor reigned them in.

Jade served first. Abi bounced lightly on her feet, alternating her weight from side to side. Leaning forward with her racquet in front of her, she watched Jade set up. Serving the ball, it landed in the outside corner, making Abi stretch to her right to block the shot. Getting the return in deep, she shuffled swiftly to center court and prepared for the next ball. It sailed over with less power than she expected, allowing her to take advantage of it. With time to step round the shot, she brought her racket back halfway and fired an inside-out forehand cross-court, catching Jade flat-footed.

Point after point, Abi annihilated her, so much so that she could tell her friend was getting angry. Lightening up on her aggression, she let Jade win a few points, trying not to make it obvious. After twenty minutes, the coaches had seen enough.

"Okay! We want to see you both back here on Thursday. Great effort today. You are my top two."

"Thank you. We'll see you then." Abi left the court and slugged back some water. Jade joined her. Seeing the guys sitting on the steps, Abi pointed. "They're here."

"Yeah." Picking up her stuff, Jade angrily walked off the court.

Leaving her behind, Abi exhaled, knowing she'd have to apologize to her. When she played, it seemed the world would disappear, and her judgment blurred. To her, it wasn't just a game—it was survival.

Stomping past Shane, Reggie went after her.

Approaching the handsome football player, Abi said, "I guess I was too hard on her today."

"Never apologize for being competitive," he said. "She'll come around. It's not a bad thing to get beat once in a while. It builds character and resilience. I'm sure you two will be fine." He sounded so sure of himself. "We know there's always a winner and a loser when it comes to sports. It's the way it is. I wouldn't worry."

They walked toward the Acosta building.

Abi said, "I'll make it quick."

"Take your time."

She dreaded going inside and wondered what to say to make things right. Opening the door of the changeroom, she searched the aisles for Jade. Finding her sitting on the bench, hunched over, Abi stopped and said, "Please don't be mad at me."

Jade turned around and did not say a word.

Moving closer, Abi stayed a safe distance. "You were my first friend here. Well, other than Gerald, the security guard. But that's here nor there." She humorously ended on a tangent. "I am so thankful to have you as a friend and never want anything to come between us."

The girl said nothing.

"I am prepared to quit the team if it means we can still be friends."

Her head jolted upward. "What do you mean quit? You can't quit. We finally have a fighting chance with you here," she huffed before exhaling.

Abi stayed quiet.

"You aren't quitting. That's final." She rolled her eyes. "I'm sorry I got mad. I'm super competitive. Guess I need to bring my A-game on Thursday and kick your ass." Laughing, Jade slid down the bench. "Don't you let me win either? You and I are going to fight to the death, you hear me?"

Abi nodded. "Deal."

"I'm kind of excited about our first tournament now. I think we'll wipe out our competition—like, destroy 'em!" she giggled.

"I think I'm down for that." Abi hugged her.

The girls quickly showered and changed. Exiting the building, arm in arm, hair tied up in messy buns, dressed in cropped joggers and tees, their light jackets draped across their shoulders, they met up with the guys sitting in the shade.

"Hey, baby." Jade greeted Reggie with a hug and a kiss.

"You guys good?" He was thankful to see the two had seemingly worked things out.

"Yeah, all good," she replied with a smile.

He put his arm around her. "See you guys later," Reg said as they left.

"Later, man," Shane said, turning to Abi. "Ready to head out?"

"Yes. Ready." On their way to the parking garage, she asked him, "How was practice?"

Only a few yards ahead, Reggie overheard her. Raising his voice, he said, "You should have seen it! He threw sixty-seven yards for a touchdown! Damn, it was spot on! The team went wild!" Turning to the QB, walking backward, he pointed at him and said, "Now, we need you to do that in the game on Friday."

"Thanks," Shane said to him. "You just added to all the pressure."

Abi grabbed hold of his arm. "That's awesome. Don't worry. You'll do great."

"Lead by example, right?" Shane recalled the advice she gave.

"Yes. See, I told you."

Shane looked at her and felt so supported. It was such a different dynamic compared to being with Emile, who would bitch and complain, even call him down to the lowest for the smallest mistakes. She often destroyed his confidence, making him crawl from the ashes every time. With Abi, it was just easy. Wrapping his arm around her as they walked, he smiled uncontrollably. "Your positivity is borderline addictive," he said.

"So, do you consider that good or bad?"

"Oh, it's definitely good."

# 21

# The Plan

Lightheartedly driving back to the Gilderson school, seeing the sun descending toward the horizon, Shane had an idea. Nervous, he hoped it would pan out. Inching along Sunset to North Church, they passed through the Gilderson School gates.

Pulling into the garage, he turned off the engine and asked, "Do you want to take a walk before you head home?"

Abi knew what he was doing. "Sure, I think I have time for a quick stroll."

He locked his truck and waited for Abi to put her tennis gear in her car.

Reaching his arm above her shoulders, he wrapped her tightly in his arms.

She, in turn, clung to his waist.

Moving past the reflecting pool in the southern courtyard, he led her towards the stairs to the upper viewing level. The place was devoid of people. Peaceful and quiet.

Abi heard her phone. Knowing the ringtone, she stopped in her tracks and said, "So sorry. It's my Dad. One second." Answering it, she said, "Hey, Dad. Is everything okay?"

Shane listened intently to her conversation.

"Don't worry. I'm just leaving school now. I'll be home shortly. Maybe fifteen minutes." She looked up at Shane and silently mouthed the words, *I gotta go.* "Okay. Okay. No problem. For sure. I promise. Love you, too. Bye." Ending the call, she felt terrible. "I'm so sorry. He needs me to go home."

"That's okay. I understand."

"Rain check?"

Shane smiled and said, "Yes. For sure."

While walking back to the elevator, Shane hoped everything was alright. Having deciphered very little of Abi's telephone conversation, he asked, "Do you want me to go with you? Need any help?"

Pressing the button to take them down to the garage, not ready to share details of her home life, she quickly replied, "No, no. It's okay. We'll be fine." When the elevator doors opened, she said, "I'll call you later tonight, if that's okay?"

"Yeah, for sure."

Shane walked Abi to her car.

After opening the driver's side, she said, "Thank you for the encouragement today."

"I didn't do much. Besides, I should be thanking you for the pep talk."

Needing to leave, Abi bravely placed her hands on his shoulders and raised on her tiptoes to kiss Shane's cheek boldly.

Caught off guard, it struck a chord with the strong athlete. His face beamed.

"Bye," she said before sliding in behind the wheel.

"Bye," he replied, closing her door. Before walking to the truck, he watched as she waved.

Getting into his Jeep, he sat there a minute. Bashfully lowering his head, he started the engine, intent on following her. He hoped to see her turn at the Bel Air intersection.

Pulling onto Sunset Boulevard amidst bumper-to-bumper traffic, sadly, he was unable to reach her in time. With his eye on her Mini Cooper from afar, he watched the pretty girl make the left on the advanced green. By the time he passed, she'd already disappeared.

22

# Banter

When Abi got home, she pulled into the courtyard and texted her Dad. Telling him not to worry, she received an *OK* in return, assuming he was super busy. Opening the front door and closing the gate, she locked her car with a beep.

The house was dark inside. Not one light was on. Eerily turning on a few switches to brighten the main floor, Abi went upstairs to check on her mother. Peering into her parents' bedroom, she found her fast asleep. With a deep breath, she went to her room and settled in. Sprawling across the bed in a heap, exhausted beyond measure, she took a minute to rest. Recalling the day and everything that happened, she mustered the energy to change and remembered Burton's visit. Texting him, she asked if he could talk.

Within seconds, he responded with one word - *Sure.*

Selecting his number, she heard it ring.

"Hey, how's the queen of the courts?"

"Oh, I'm doing all right. Had a lot going on."

He could tell by her voice something was up. She sounded exhausted. "Do tell."

"Today started with a rumor spreading about us."

"Is that right?" he said.

"Remember on Sunday when we evaded Emile and...."

He interrupted, "Oh, I remember."

"This morning, she and her friends told Shane I was dating you. He didn't take too kindly to that."

"I would say not." He couldn't wait to hear more. "So, just for the record, are you really seeing this football player?"

"Possibly. Why? Jealous?"

He hesitated and answered, "Maybe."

Abi knew what he was getting at. "Burton, you could seriously have any girl you want. They would throw themselves at your feet if you let them. Have you looked in the mirror recently? You're hot."

"Yeah, money does that."

"Do you not realize how handsome you are?"

"Not in the slightest. But you can keep the compliments coming. Kinda like it."

"I'm being serious."

"So am I," he laughed. "Look, Abs, I'm still your neighbor from Boston, no matter how much money I have or what I look like." He wanted to change the subject. "Tell me more about this guy."

"I like Shane. There's just something about him. It's like our souls are aligned."

Burton's thoughts ran wild while she rambled on. He couldn't believe she was so invested in him already. Knowing what he needed to do, he stepped up to be the best friend she needed - the guy she could count on when things went wrong - the guy who would offer support through thick and thin, without excuses. The guy who'd help her pick up the pieces when this relationship crashed and burned.

"Burton? You still there?"

Shaking from his thoughts, he said, "Umm, yeah. I'm here." Having to say the right thing, he added, "I think he's the luckiest guy on the planet."

She gasped and replied sincerely, "Thank you."

"You're welcome – but don't think I won't kick his ass if he screws this up – I swear if he hurts you...."

"No, you won't. Well, unless I say to, of course," she laughed. "But seriously, I'm happy right now."

"Well, then, I'm happy for you." Circling back to the morning's drama, he said, "Tell me about this rumor."

"Emile told Shane she witnessed me hanging off you."

"Well, in all fairness, you were."

"Hey, that's here nor there."

"Just wanted to clarify that."

"I know, but...." Abi blushed.

"Okay, continue..."

"While the other girls corroborated Emile's story, Jade stepped in and said we knew each other from Boston. To save face, I added – and don't hate me – but I think of you as a big brother." Abi scrunched up her face, believing she should not have said that. The last thing she wanted to do was hurt his feelings.

"Ouch..."

"I explained how Emile was bullying me and that you wanted to get me out of there. So you decided to give them a show in the process."

"Very true. So, what did Shane say to that?"

"He believed me over them, and Emile and her friends stomped off. But the rumor had already spread. All the students in the halls were whispering and looking at me strangely. Wanting to nip it in the bud, Shane got everyone's attention and quickly cleared things up. Life returned to normal after that, but Emile's credibility fell beyond repair, so she decided to leave for the day."

"Just so you know, if that girl has been the number one forever and has suddenly fallen from grace, I would be careful. You don't want to be responsible for her demise. Many elitist kids here are emotionally unstable. Just saying."

"I kinda thought the same thing," Abi recalled. "In all fairness, though, she's brought it upon herself."

"I realize. Just telling you to see things from her perspective. She's lost a lot in two days."

"Yes, you're right."

With a slight pause, he asked, "So, how was the rest of the day?"

"It was not bad until we went out for lunch and ran into this guy named Eastwood Korolev. Apparently, he has a vendetta against Shane. They are battling for the number one NCAA prospect spot."

"Wait? Oligarch Korolev?"

"Yeah? How did you know?"

"Abi, word to the wise. If you see that guy again…"

"I know. I know. Call 911. That's what Shane said, too. From what he and Reggie say, the guy is trouble."

"Umm, Abi, listen to me. He is more than trouble. He's…."

"Dangerous? Shane said the same thing."

He thought she was acting too cavalier about it. "The guy is used to getting whatever he wants – like anything. Mostly by force, I might add."

"I didn't like the way he looked at me today. It was weird. Borderline creepy."

Hearing this, Burton knew Eastwood had marked her. "You call 911 and text me immediately if you see the guy lurking around. Even better, give me access to your location services. Text me 911 instead, and I will find you faster than the cops."

"Burton? Is that necessary?"

"I'm serious, Abi. The guy's last girlfriend disappeared. This isn't a joke."

A bit scared now, Abi said, "Fine." She shared her location with him. "There. Do you see me?"

Making sure it connected, he said, "Yeah. Be sure it's not time-regulated. Select indefinitely."

She did just that. "Okay, done."

"I wouldn't ask you to do this unless it was for your safety."

"I'm sure nothing will happen. But we should cover all the bases, right? "Concerned about his tone, Abi got a bad feeling.

"Always be aware of your surroundings if you're alone."

Scared, she said, "All right, I get it. Can we change the subject?"

Believing he got through to her, he replied, "Sure."

"On a lighter note. I scored a ticket for Black Lyon on Saturday night."

"What the hell, Abs!" He flung himself back in his desk chair.

"What? All the seniors from Gilderson are hoping to go. An insider said we are on the list."

"I thought you decided against it?"

"A few people got tickets. Everyone else thinks theirs will arrive tomorrow. So I'll see who else is going before I accept it."

*Sucker for punishment,* Burton thought to himself. "Guess you're going with Shane?"

"Hopefully. He hasn't got a ticket yet."

"Just – for the love of God – stick close to your friends and him. It's not your scene, Abs."

"If anything, it'll be an experience, I guess. I won't go a second time. Promise."

"Friggin..." Burton was frustrated.

"Don't be so dramatic." She laughed at his reaction to it all. Smiling, she said, "I've missed this."

"What?"

"The banter back and forth between you and me."

"I'm glad we reconnected too." His voice sounded a bit deeper when he said that.

"Look, I'd better go. I'm looking after my Mom. Dad needed to return to work. So, I'm here."

"Everything okay? Need any help?" He knew Abi would never ask.

"No, I'm good. Thanks, though. I'm just going to use this time to finish homework and chill out a bit. I'm pretty tired."

"Hey, if you get bored, call me."

"I will. Thanks for the chat and for stopping by the courts today."

"I'm always happy to see you dominate and crush the competition. I'm sorry I couldn't stay longer. I had to get to class."

"I figured. No problem. I'm looking forward to the drive along PCH on Sunday. Can hardly wait to see the ocean views."

"You'll love it. I promise."

"Sounds great. Night, my friend."

"Night Abs."

Ending their call, she went to check on her mother. Sitting by her bedside, she noticed her breathing was shallow. The past few days had been short-lived like she thought they would be. A flood of guilt passed over her. She felt like she should have been home more to enjoy it. Covering her mother up, she let her rest.

Upon returning to her room, she walked over to the window. The sunset had painted the sky in a fiery orange glow. Spying on the mansion across the canyon, she set up her telescope and looked into the eyepiece. She saw the big guy in a black sweatshirt with a hood over his head walk into the kitchen area. Disappearing from view, unable to see the details clearly, she knew she had to finish her work.

Unable to focus, she felt like she'd run a marathon the past few days. Life had been nonstop. Mustering the energy, she cuddled with the pillows on her bed to finish her math and the unit module assigned for their first biology task. Checking social media, in between, she found sixty-two new followers on her Insta account despite not having posted anything yet.

"Guess I gotta get with the program." She never used social while living in Boston, so she had no idea what she was doing.

Hearing the security notification, Abi found her Dad at the front door. She got up and went to greet him.

Descending the stairs and rounding the corner, she said, "Hi, Dad. How was your day?"

"It was good. Many crises averted, thankfully." Tired beyond words, he handed her three take-out bags, looking a bit weathered. "How is Mom?"

"Still sleeping."

"That's good," he divulged, not knowing how to tell her, "I'm bringing in twenty-four-hour nursing care. They start tomorrow. I will be here for the transition, and hopefully, by Monday, we will be able to attend work and school without worrying. She will be in good hands."

"As long as she doesn't have to go to the hospital again. She hates being there."

"Agreed." Barely able to string a sentence together, he was about to head upstairs with some soup for his wife. "I am going to try and get Mom to eat. Then, I've got to get some sleep. You should, too. Thank you for getting home quickly. Appreciate that."

"No matter what, I am here to help." She walked over and hugged him.

All he could do it nod and produce a half smile.

Parting ways, she watched him drag himself up the stairs.

Walking around the main floor, she turned off most of the lights. It wasn't hard to notice the mansion across the canyon standing out in the dimness of dusk. Lit up beautifully, she wondered if the lonely man would be on the rooftop again tonight. Skipping steps, with food in hand, not wasting time, she repositioned her telescope by the window. Focusing in, she noticed two bright rooms in the left wing of the large home - the kitchen and family room. She spied the dark figure walking around the white sectional furniture while another man in a black jacket fluttered around the kitchen.

"That must be the guy's chef?" she whispered. "What a lonely existence. You'd think that with a house that size, he'd be having parties with loads of people around."

Leaving the guy be, she returned the telescope to its rightful place in the corner of the room. Determined to get to bed early tonight, she ate her dinner and surfed the web to catch up on the news.

When she finished, she went to wash her face. Gathering her hair, she secured it in a messy bun. Slipping on her Patriots nightgown, which reminded her of home, she heard a strange ringtone from her phone.

"What is that?" Recognizing the sound, having only heard it one other time before, she knew someone was calling her on FaceTime.

Picking up the device, she found Shane's name and picture.

"Oh, crap," she muttered.

Quickly dimming the lights, she jumped into bed and buried herself under the covers. Upon sliding her finger across the screen, Shane's face instantly appeared in front of her. Dressed in a white t-shirt, it made his tan seem much darker.

"Hey, Abs," he said with a smile. "Is this a good time to chat or not?"

"Hi. Yes, it's good. I'm just getting ready for bed."

"I see that."

Holding the phone higher to get the best angle of her face, she didn't know why she was so nervous. "I know. I look horrible."

"Horrible? You're kidding, right?"

Abi's heart melted. She smiled and tilted her head slightly.

"I think you look amazing."

"Well, thank you."

He reached up and placed his hand behind his head. The muscle in his arm bulged. Slouched under his comforter, he looked tired.

"So, can I ask you something?"

Not sure what he would say, she replied, "Sure. Shoot."

"I kinda struggled with two questions in math tonight. Hate to admit that, but as you said, no secrets. Is there any way we could meet after practice tomorrow and review more of the equations stuff?"

"Sure. I don't have tennis until Thursday."

"Maybe I can sneak you in to watch the practice, and afterward, we could grab some dinner. Maybe come back to my house."

"I'll have to check with my Dad first. Make sure he doesn't need me home. If I'm free, then, sure, we can do that."

"Okay, let me know. There's this great wood-fired pizza place close to my house. Would you like to try it? They also have pasta and different types of salad, too, if you prefer that."

"It sounds wonderful," she said. "But remember, the main reason for doing this is to study for the test," Abi giggled.

"Yeah, yeah, I know. Think of it as a balance of business and leisure. Just thought we could make an evening of it."

"Well, it sounds nice, despite the math part."

Shane ran his hand through his hair. "I'll be honest. I hate the subject."

"I know it's hard for me, too, but you just have to break it down piece by piece. I'll help you along."

"Thanks. I don't know what I would do without you."

"I think you'd survive."

"Maybe." He didn't sound convinced.

Abi suspected he had an undiagnosed learning disability—a subject that wasn't easy to discuss. He had difficulty with multi-step problems—a common issue with students suffering from this. "As for the math, it'll get easier the more you ask questions and learn by repetition."

"But that is easier said than done."

"I know. Hang in there. Have patience," she said.

"I'll try." He exhaled.

"On that note, I should go. Tomorrow is going to be another long day. Gotta recharge," he said.

"Well, goodnight, then."

"Goodnight, Abi."

Waving to him, she said, "See you in the morning."

"Yeah, for sure."

"Night." Ending the call, Abi burrowed further under her blankets. Even though the day was not the best, she felt like it ended on a high note. Amidst her thoughts, she took a deep breath and said, "Don't worry, Abi. You got this. One day at a time."

# 23

# Decisions

Up earlier than usual, having had a solid night's sleep, Abi said goodbye to her Dad after checking on her Mom. Not eager to battle traffic, she walked out the door, craving an icy matcha brew. Prepared to risk going to Starbucks, she hoped the detour wouldn't take too long. Emile Raven crossed her mind. Believing the girl wouldn't be there that early, Abi tried not to psych herself out. Leaving home, she wondered if she should surprise Gerald with something.

"Maybe I should get him a breakfast wrap and a coffee," she decided while focusing on the intersection coming into view. "I hate this part." Waiting for someone to let her into the conga line, she was offered a spot and inched closer to Sunset Boulevard before turning right. Moving slowly across the 405 overpass, she prayed things would soon speed up. Thankfully, it did.

Just before eight o'clock, she pulled into the plaza and noticed a familiar car. It was hard to miss. The matte black McLaren stood out from the rest. Sleek and sophisticated, Abi thought it fit Burton to a tee. Surprised he was already there, she spotted him in the corner by the window.

With books sprawled out in an orderly way and two coffees on the go, Abi walked over and said, "Hey. Good morning."

"Abi. Hi. Good morning. You're here early."

"I was going to say the same for you."

Standing up, he offered her a seat. "Would you like to join me?"

"Thank you, but sadly, I can't stay. Just here to grab a few things before school."

"What do you want? I can get it for you."

"No, don't be silly. Appreciate it, though."

Seeing that the line had died down, Abi placed her order. While she waited for it to come up in the queue, she returned to Burton.

"So, why are you studying here?"

Stressed, he said, "I have a big test today - Cyber Security informatics."

"I'm not even going to pretend to know what that involves," she laughed.

"Well, it studies the concepts of information security necessary to understand risks and mitigation associated with protecting systems and data." Seeing her with a blank stare, knowing he'd lost her, he said, "Long story short, it's about keeping data safe."

"Well, okay then. It sounds super complex and out of my scope."

"Lucky me."

"Order for Abi?" the Barista announced from behind the counter.

"One second." Abi went to grab her order. Balancing the drink tray and two small bags, she returned to him.

"Wow, are you feeding an army this morning?"

"No, not really. The coffee and matcha are for me. The extra coffee, breakfast sandwich, and muffin are for the parking attendant at school."

"Oh? That's awfully kind of you."

"Yeah, he's a sweet older man. When I arrived for orientation, he was the first to welcome me. Just wanted to do something nice in return."

"Well, I would not expect anything less."

Abi could tell Burton seemed down. "Are you okay?" she asked, getting concerned. "Do you want to talk about it?"

"No," he laughed. "I don't want to bore you with my problems. I'll be fine. Got a lot going on this week, that's all. I'll get through. I always do."

Silence fell upon them. Abi sipped her matcha and noticed the time on the clock behind the counter. "Guess I should head out," she said.

"Okay. Enjoy your day. Maybe we can talk later?"

"For sure. Good luck with the test. I'm sure you'll pass with flying colors."

"Thanks," he sighed, giving her a thumbs up.

She walked toward the door while juggling her drink tray and food bags. Waving, she saw him do the same before continuing his work.

When Abi got settled in her car, she couldn't help but feel something was wrong with her friend. "On Sunday, you'll just have to pry it out of him," she said aloud, knowing she'd eventually have him singing like a canary.

Carefully pulling out of the plaza, thankful not to see Emile anywhere, Abi headed north in stop-and-go traffic. Anxiously glancing at the time, she muttered, "Oh no, it's 8:20. Come on. Come on...."

In a matter of minutes, things opened up. In record time, she turned onto North Church before making the left on Beverly Park. "Okay. Now you're golden." Able to breathe, her body relaxed behind the wheel.

Arriving on time, she found Gerald reading the morning paper in the booth. Seeing her, he folded it neatly in half and walked out to say hello.

"Good morning, Gerald!"

He stood tall, hands on his hips. "Morning, Miss Abi! How are you this fine day?"

"Feeling pretty good." Handing him the coffee and the food, she said, "This is for you."

"What is this?" he asked, surprised to see her hand it to him.

"Just a little coffee break. I didn't know what you'd like, so I got you a coffee, a breakfast sandwich, and a lemon blueberry muffin. Can't go wrong with that, I think. And there's cream and sugar inside the bag if you need some."

"This is so very thoughtful. Thank you." He was beaming.

"Well, enjoy! I'm going to tackle another six hours of learning." Her voice took on an overly sarcastic tone.

He laughed, "Best of luck with that."

Abi noticed Shane coming up behind her. "I should get moving before I hold up traffic."

"Yes, I suppose so." With a grateful smile, he said, "Thanks again. Enjoy your day!"

"You as well. I will see you after."

As she drove inside the garage, Shane waved to the man and greeted him before heading inside.

After reversing into her space and locking up, she got out to meet Shane. "So sorry I'm late," she said.

"Why are you apologizing? You're not late." Outstretching one arm to her, holding her tightly, he asked, "How'd you sleep?"

"Not bad. Somehow, mornings on the West Coast come quite early." Abi was having difficulty managing her drinks and her backpack. "I mean, it feels like I just put my head down, and it's time to wake up again."

"I know the feeling." Seeing her struggling, he said, "Need a hand? What is all this?" He took her backpack from her and effortlessly slipped it onto his shoulder.

"Fuel," she said with a giggle. "Never thought to ask. Do you drink coffee?"

"No, never touch the stuff." He smiled as she took a sip of her matcha. Raising his protein drink, he said, "Now, this is fuel." About to cross the driveway, they noticed Emile entering the garage. Ignoring her as she drove past, Shane said, "What did you give Gerald?"

"Thought I would surprise him with a coffee and a couple of snacks. I'm sure it's a long day for him."

On their way to the elevator, they noticed the mean girl heading there, too.

"That was nice of you to think of the guy," Shane said. Wanting to avoid another diva confrontation, he suggested, "Let's take the stairs."

"I believe it's important to thank those who don't get any credit. Show people they're appreciated and that their presence does not go unnoticed."

"Couldn't agree more."

Once they reached the top, they spotted Jade and Reggie waiting on the artisan steps.

"Hey, good morning," Shane said.

His best friend looked up. "Hey! Mornin'."

Jade watched Emile walk across the courtyard. "Look who came to school today?" she quietly announced.

"Yes, we saw her." Abi could feel her stomach doing flips. "It's fine. What am I going to do? Just have to make the best of it."

The comment made Shane feel guilty. All of this started because of their breakup. Abi was innocent. It wasn't her fault.

The group walked along and ascended the stone steps to the next level. About to pass through the main door, they met Emile on her way out. Shane held it open for her while the rest stood back to let her through.

Noticing a yellow slip in her hand, Abi whispered to Jade, "What does the yellow piece of paper mean?" She was unfamiliar with office protocols.

"She signed herself out because she's sick," Jade replied, "Which is odd since she just got here."

"Why would she bother driving to school and then leave?"

Her friend turned and shrugged her shoulders. "I don't know."

Listening to their conversation, Shane watched his ex walk away, knowing her life was far from easy. In a way, her actions concerned him. He knew there were times when she wasn't mentally stable, especially when her parents were in town. Regardless of how things ended, he wondered if she was okay.

They continued up the staircase and down the hallway to class. Finding their seats, Abi felt the vibe was less scary and intimidating without Emile around. The blonde bombshell twins, Shiresse and Shiri, were seated near the front. Mandy glanced back at them a few times, almost like she was spying.

When Mr. Walker arrived, he immediately began handing out another review package. "Break off into small groups of four," he said. "Work on the questions, and we will convene near the end to discuss the answers. This review will be the basis for the quiz tomorrow. I guarantee you'll do well if you can answer these."

Leafing through it, Shane tensed up. He leaned over to Abi and quietly asked, "I really need help studying for this. It's the first mark of the semester. I want to start strong." He seemed nervous but determined to work hard.

"Don't worry. I'll help you prep. It'll be okay."

He was happy to hear it.

Reggie and Shane moved the girls' desks together with theirs to form a group. For the next hour, Abi explained each equation step by step. Finally, understanding the concepts introduced, Shane showed more confidence.

With a half hour left, Mr. Walker asked volunteers to show their work on the smart board. Abi represented their group.

Shane watched as she single-handedly tackled the problems, making it look easy. Not only was she pretty, kind, and athletic, but Abi was also super intelligent. He knew then that she was one of a kind—a diamond you only find once in a lifetime. Smiling at her, proud of what she could do, Abi glanced over at him when she'd finished.

Mr. Walker was so impressed by her delivery that he asked her to continue solving the problems on the last page. Exceptionally delivering the material, the bell rang when she completed the final question.

About to return to her seat, Mr. Walker said, "Ms. Acardi. Please, see me after class, if you will."

"All right," she replied. Joining her friends, she packed her bag and helped Shane return the desks to their original position. "Give me one second," she said. "Mr. Walker wants a word."

Shane followed Reggie and Jade out into the hallway. Curious about what the teacher wanted, the football player eavesdropped on their conversation.

"The work you did today was impressive. I expected as much from a Mathletics state champ such as yourself."

"Thank you, Mr. Walker."

"I was hoping you'd consider joining the team here at Gilderson. We certainly could use you."

Not wanting to get overwhelmed, especially with her Mom not well, she graciously said, "Thank you. I'll have to think about it."

"Certainly. Given the level of commitment we would require, I understand. Let me know by the end of the week."

"Yes, I will." Exiting the room, she found her new friends shamelessly listening.

"So?" Shane wanted to know what she would decide. "Are you gonna do it?"

"Do what?"

"Join the math team?" he asked. "Cause I think you should. You're good at it."

Abi looked up at him. "Shane…"

While walking down the hall, he said, "What? What did I say?"

"Come on. We gotta move."

"So, that's a no?" He kept pressing her.

"Will you stop, please?" Frustrated, she sped up and left him a few steps behind.

Arriving in the science lab, just before Professor Grady closed the door, Abi and Shane took their seats and looked at the paper in front of them explaining the requirements for the day. Each student put their safety glasses on while Professor Grady loudly explained what he expected. Earning a biology component was compulsory for the Environmental Systems and Societies credit. A very different curriculum than what she was used to, but interesting nonetheless.

Throughout the class, Abi stayed quiet.

Aware that their teacher read lips, Shane waited for him to face the board before he whispered, "Hey?" Seeing her look his way, he presented open hands to ask what was up.

Understanding his mannerisms, she was afraid to cause a scene, so she wrote down her response on a blank page inside her Burch book and showed him. *It's nothing. Let's talk after. I'll explain then.*

Somewhat relieved, Shane nodded as the first task started. Wondering what Abi would share, he had difficulty focusing on his work.

A majority of the class went by at a snail's pace. With ten minutes remaining, Shane helped his classmates tidy and reset the room for the next group coming in.

Moving out the door, Abi noticed Shane's attention on her. "Look, I know you've gotta get to the weight room, so this is the thing... In Boston, I did well in athletics and academics. As an only child, my parents wanted me to interact with other kids and always kept me busy. Long story short, it caused a bit of burnout. When we moved here, I promised to balance my life as much as possible – not take on too much. I know the commitment required to be on the math team. I've been there and done that. It's not something I want to revisit."

"Sorry, Abs. I didn't know."

"Well, now you do. Look, I'm not mad - just a little frazzled. That's all. Just FYI, I'm not accepting the spot on the team."

Shane raised his hands between them. "Okay. But you're still able to tutor me, right?"

"Yes, it seems I have my work cut out for me, huh?" she smiled.

"Yes, you do." He brushed his shoulder against hers playfully, making her blush.

"Okay. You're going to be late if you keep dilly-daddling." Abi melted. The way he looked at her gave her goosebumps.

"What the hell is diddy datting?" Knowingly mispronouncing her words, he laughed. "I know you're trying to speak to me, but I have no clue what you said."

Realizing he didn't understand one of her mother's old sayings, she quickly gave up. "Oh, it's nothing. Just go! I'll see you at lunch."

"Yeah. I'm going."

"Bye," she said. Standing outside the Art Studio, she felt as light as a feather.

About to round the corner, he met up with Reggie and waved to her before disappearing.

"How did you get so lucky?" she whispered faintly.

"What? Lucky to meet me?" Jade humorously stated.

Shocked to see her there, Abi smiled. "Yes, Jade. I'm lucky to have you as a best friend."

"Awwww. You're so sweet."

"I know."

# 24

# Girl Talk

Amidst the chaos as their classmates socialized before the teacher arrived, Jade led the way into the Art Studio. Abi followed. Happy that Emile was still absent, she figured the next hour and a half would be uneventful.

Barely through the door, Mei frantically waved them both over with urgency.

"What's going on?" Jade asked.

Laney, Ming, and Allie quickly took their seats and leaned in to hear what she was about to share.

At first, she whispered, "I just got my ticket for Black Lyon!" The girl ended the sentence squealing in a high-pitched tone, unable to contain herself.

Everyone quickly checked their apps. Abi counted each surprised face erupting around the table. She knew they we all going on Saturday night.

"Abi? Did you get one too?" Allie asked with anticipation.

Checking her app, not letting on that she'd known for a few days already, Abi confirmed with fake enthusiasm, "Yep! Me too!" A part of her wondered why she'd gotten accepted before all of them. It was odd.

"This is gonna be epic. I've never been to a Black Lyon rave yet," Allie said.

"You haven't?" Laney chuckled.

"Well, how many have you been to?" Ming interrupted.

Laney sat tall in her chair and said proudly, "Twelve."

"What? How is that even possible?" Mei wondered how she managed that.

"Don't judge me. I can't help if I have connections who think I'm beautiful."

"What's it like?" Allie questioned, ready to hang on Laney's every word.

The confident girl said, "The night starts pretty calm. People hang around talking and networking while some are up dancing and partying. But, by midnight, the place is rockin' out of control. Everyone has had a few drinks in them by then, so it's bound to happen."

"Have you met Black Lyon?" Jade asked.

Laney frowned. "Sadly, no. But it's because nobody can get close to him. He's got a dense layer of security surrounding him at all times. Besides, to most, he's a myth anyway. So, everyone just respects that. You should hear his original tracks. The music is amazing. I don't know why he doesn't produce an album." Thinking a second, she added, "Oh, and sometimes he incorporates crazy things like 7D holograms and pyrotechnics and sometimes offers guest spots to international DJs. It's an experience you won't forget. You'll love it."

Their teacher arrived soon after and closed the door right on time.

Opening her laptop, Laney got ready to work.

Catching sight of Mandy, Shiri, and Shiresse glancing at their table and giggling, Abi thought, *Here we go again.* She exhaled deeply. No stranger to rumors running rampant, she tried to ignore them. But that was easier said than done.

Enduring all the whispers for nearly a half hour, she heard her name pop up more than once. Abi asked the other girls what Emile's friends could be going on about.

"Yeah, how do we find out?" Mei naively stated, having picked up on the chatter. She, too, was bothered by their behavior.

Laney pulled out her phone. "One second. One second." They saw her madly scrolling before she quickly recorded her screen. "One more second. Gotcha." Not sure if she should show Abi, she turned her phone around, mindful of their teacher's proximity, and quietly said, "This is probably the reason."

Shown the video of Abi and Burton leaving the coffee shop, Abi's heart raced. She'd never been a target like this before. Assuming this was Emile's way of getting back at her for their confrontation, she watched the entire video and saw the word cheater plastered across it like graffiti.

"How did you find it so fast?" Ming was impressed by the pretty blonde's skills.

Laughing proudly, Laney revealed, "I have seven hundred and eighty thousand followers. Emile is one of them."

"Never mind that. Who is that incredibly handsome hunk of a man, Abi?" Allie was drooling.

Jade stepped in. "That's Burton. Abi's old neighbor from Boston."

"Wow," Allie started daydreaming. "He is sooo good-looking," Allie repeated the clip and took a pic of him off Laney's phone. Staring at it, she said, "He's dreamy."

"Okay. Okay. Relax," Abi said.

"Is he single? Please tell me he's single." Allie hoped she'd say yes.

"He hasn't said." Abi felt strange answering that question.

The girls at the table spotted Emile's friends videoing Abi's reaction to the post. Each devilishly smirked while keeping an eye on the teacher.

"She can't get away with this. We need to do something." Jade was angry. "There is a zero-tolerance policy for bullying."

Sadly, everyone knew that policy wouldn't stop most from inflicting pain on others.

Abi stayed calm and did not let the posse see her react rashly. "Yeah, I guess it's par for the course."

"What do you mean?" Jade asked, not understanding the analogy.

"The captain of the football team likes me. That's bound to cause unrest amongst the ranks." Abi kept her composure and turned to Jade.

"I don't want Shane to get wind of this. He has enough to worry about. It's the last thing he needs to see."

Jade nodded. "Agreed. Mum's the word."

"Thanks," Abi said, getting the girls' attention. "Look, if we show interest in these posts, Emile will win. So, please, let it go. Let's not make a big deal of it."

Hearing the bell a while later, they quickly packed up and walked out. The entire way to the courtyard, Abi and Jade listened to the girls whispering behind them. It made Abi's blood boil.

The second they joined the guys, Reggie asked, "Wanna go out for lunch?"

Jade quickly replied, "I'm in."

His friend looked over at the quarterback. "So, man? Gonna join us?"

Shane turned to Abi and asked, "Want to go?"

"Sure. Why not?" At this point, she wanted to escape the craziness.

"I have a craving for sushi. Everybody okay with that?" Jade wasn't thinking of the guys' dietary needs.

Reg said, "I'm sure Shane and I can get rice, veggies, and fish or something. Sushi won't sit well for practice later."

"Sorry. I forgot about that. We can go somewhere else. What are you in the mood for?" About to respond to her, she put up her hand and said, "Let me guess? Pasta."

"What? Allegro is pretty close," Reg suggested.

Jade was not happy about the added carbs. "I will be a million pounds if I keep eating lunch with you," she joked.

Shane turned to Abi. "What do you think?" he said.

"I'm game."

With that decided, the four of them hurried down to the garage.

"Shane, you're drivin'," Reggie said, volunteering his best friend for the task.

"I guess I am. You know, Reg, you've gotta get a car that fits more than two people."

"Why?" He looked perplexed. "They don't make a four-seater Ferrari."

"Sure they do," Abi interjected. "The Purosangue."

Shane's eyebrows raised at Abi's knowledge. "Yeah, Reg. What she said."

Reggie pulled out his phone to see if she was right. Spotting the car that Abi had mentioned, Reggie scoffed. "What? That?" he said. "It's a family car. I can't drive that."

Immediately, laughter erupted at the level of Reggie's vainness.

# 25

# Pressure

After a hearty lunch and a productive study hall session, Shane and Abi packed their bags and left the library. Hand in hand, they walked across the courtyard as the sun's rays beat down on them.

Having avoided telling Shane about Emile's social media fiasco thus far, she was thankful nobody else showed him. Wanting to keep his head clear for practice, she could see he looked stressed.

"Hey," she nudged him. "What are you thinking about?"

He forced a smile and said, "Nothing."

"You're quiet today."

"I'm thinking of the big game this week."

"Don't worry. I have faith in you, and so does everyone else."

He didn't want to tell her about the one person who didn't. "Thank you," he said humbly, knowing his Dad would be super-critical of his performance.

"Is your schedule this hectic all the time?"

"This is nothing. We haven't even started traveling yet."

"Traveling?"

"Right now, we are in the pre-season - mostly exhibition games. Once we hit late September, we go into the regular season. To kick it off, I will be gone for two or three days before our first home game."

"Homecoming, right?"

"Yeah," he said. Wanting to ask her to the dance officially, he swayed from the subject, hoping to give Abi a memorable proposal later.

Disappointed that he side-stepped that conversation, she assumed he didn't want to go. Jumping into his Jeep, they left school and headed out to practice.

Turning onto Sunset, he asked, "So, for tonight, as I said, I usually pick up woodfired pizzas for dinner. What kind do you like?"

"Hmm, do they have tomato, buffalo mozzarella, and basil?"

"Like a Margherita? I assume so."

"Okay, good. What do you usually get?"

"The works," he laughed. "Everything imaginable piled high on top."

"So, a fully loaded pizza," she giggled.

"Yeah, sort of."

Arriving at the Wasserman Center, Abi could see Shane did not have the same energy as yesterday.

"You must be tired trying to keep up with school, games, and practice."

"It does weigh on me sometimes, but I try to stay in a good frame of mind and get sleep when I can." He knew university would be much worse.

"Spending time with me must add extra stress," she said, wondering what he'd say.

"Are you kidding? If anything, you are giving me more energy. Don't even think you're causing me grief because you're not. You're kinda my bright light in life right now."

"What about football?"

"Football is becoming more of a job. I knew it would at this point. Still love it, though. Don't get me wrong. But this year is make-or-break. It's a lot of pressure."

"You will do great. You're destined for this."

"When you say things like that, I feel there's some truth to it."

Abi smiled at him. "I'm happy to hear that."

While walking over to the Wasserman entrance, Shane could hardly wait for practice to be over because it meant he would have time alone with Abi. When they arrived, he held the door open for her and went to the main desk to sign her in. The woman working there didn't have a problem with him having a guest today.

Before saying goodbye, he watched her meet up with Jade, who was sitting on the sofa glued to her phone. Waving to Abi, he watched them climb the stairs to the next level.

"Oh, Abs..." she whispered as Shane walked through the door.

She turned to her friend. "What?"

"That boy has it bad for you," she giggled.

On their way to the viewing area, she hesitated. "Jade, can I ask you something?"

"Sure." She swung open the glass door for her friend and walked onto the balcony.

"I have very little relationship experience," she divulged. "Let me rephrase that. Truthfully, I have no relationship experience. I have nothing to compare to."

"So?"

"So, my question is, do you think Shane is moving slowly for a reason? Like he is not sure about me?"

Jade thought about it. "Like I said before, you, my dear, are different than what he's used to. To me, he's taking things slow because he respects you. I could tell that right away."

"How?"

"He's being careful about what he does and says. He always looks at you for approval and includes you in decisions. I believe he considers you a couple."

"Even though we haven't...."

"Well, he was about to yesterday in study hall. That must account for something," Jade chuckled, tilting her head.

"No thanks to you guys," Abi laughed embarrassingly.

"I said I was sorry," she grumbled. "We didn't know we'd be walkin' in on anything."

Abi stayed quiet and analyzed what she said.

Jade could tell she was bothered by it all. "Look, tonight Reggie said Shane is taking you to his house. He nevvverr does that - like eeevverr. Hell, no one has ever seen the guy's place. That must be a sign. He's letting you into his life. You get to see behind the curtain, Abs."

"But we are just going there to study for the math test."

"Sure, you are." Giggling, she added, "Tell me how that studying went afterward."

Abi got nervous. Was this a ploy to get her alone? Not knowing him overly well, she got scared. "Hey, Jade?"

"Yeah." Her friend watched the guys filter out onto the field.

"Should I be worried? I mean..." She peered down at Shane, practicing below. Throwing the ball to a receiver, he seemed laser-focused.

"What? You're kidding?"

"No, I'm not. Can I trust him if we're alone?" Right then, he looked up at her and smiled.

"Abi, Shane Coppersmith is the nicest guy you will ever meet. There is nothing to be worried about. Period. I would warn you otherwise."

"Okay. I trust you."

"And you should. I'm your best friend."

# 26

# Study Date

Once practice ended, the girls wandered back to the lobby to wait for the guys. It didn't take long for them to emerge from the locker room looking freshly showered.

Abi remembered her friend's comment about her study plans with Shane that evening.

Reggie hugged Jade before kissing her lovingly without reservation. "Ready?" he asked with loving eyes.

Jade's face beamed. "Yeah, ready."

Never having parents around to make them dinner, he suggested, "Up to getting something to eat?"

"Sure," she said.

Turning to Shane, his friend held out his fist to say goodbye. Tapping his knuckles with his, he said, "Later, my man."

"Later, Reg."

Following the two as they playfully left the building, Shane was excited about spending time with Abi. "I can hardly wait for you to try this pizza. It's awesome. I think you'll love it."

"That sounds great."

Walking into the parking lot, they heard Reggie's Ferrari growling as it echoed through the structure. Shane tossed his bag in the back of the Jeep and got in beside Abi. Putting in his earbuds, he said, "Give me a second."

Abi texted her Dad and said she was going out to eat with her friends. He texted back and told her to have fun.

"Hey, Drago. It's Shane. How's it goin' today?" The football player smiled as he spoke to the man on the phone.

Abi figured he was like family to him.

"Yeah. All good on the field, Sir."

Abi assumed he asked Shane how practice went.

"I need a Margherita pizza, a Coppersmith special, and some pasta pomodoro. And, can you add three tiramisus to that?"

"Special occasion?" Shane repeated what the man said. Looking at Abi, he said, "Maybe." Pausing, he added, "Thanks, man. I'll be there in twenty minutes. Perfect." He listened intently to the person on the line. "For sure. See you shortly. Bye."

Watching him pull the buds from his ears and put them back in their case, Abi said, "A Coppersmith Special?"

He started the Jeep and put it in gear. While exiting the garage, he laughed and said, "I eat there a lot. That pizza has become a staple for me, I guess. My stepmom doesn't cook, and the chef is only here from Friday to Sunday. The rest of the time, my stepbrother and I fend for ourselves or eat what little the nanny makes."

His home life didn't seem all that different from hers. Recalling when her Mom was sick, she'd eat dinner alone every night when her Dad was at work. Making something from whatever was available, Abi would take food to her Mom's room, hoping she'd eat something. Hating that memory, she shook it from her head.

"So, where do you live?" Abi casually asked while they merged with 405 North.

"Umm, I'm just a few canyons over from you. If I remember correctly, you're on Stradella, right?"

"Yes. That's right."

"I'm on Beverly Park Circle."

Not familiar with the area, Abi didn't bat an eye at the prestigious address. Shane wasn't surprised.

"I don't know where that is," she giggled.

"You'll see shortly."

Driving up the busy highway, thankful that rush hour wasn't too bad today, Shane veered to the right and climbed the off-ramp.

Turning left at the intersection, they continued up the hillside to the next street. Abi read the sign. "Mulholland Drive? This is a famous road, isn't it? Sounds familiar."

"Yes. It has some incredible views."

With every twist and turn, the vista captivated her. Down to one lane now, surrounded by gated homes, she got small glimpses of the scenery on their left. They were really high above the city. Soon, the view opened up on both sides.

"Wow. Look at that. It's amazing," she said, moving around in her seat to get a better look. It felt like they were driving along the edge of the world.

Shane found her excitement entertaining. When he turned on Beverly Glen Boulevard, the canyon was a panorama from left to right.

"We will pick up the food here and then drive to my place. I don't live far. Just live over there," he pointed toward the cliff on the driver's side.

Pulling into Beverly Glen Center, Shane parked in an angled space in front of the plaza.

"Here we are – il Segrato.  My second home."

Getting out of the Jeep, he reached out his hand and proudly walked alongside her toward the restaurant tucked in the corner. Entering the airy space through the glass doors, Shane moved to the point of sale beside the open kitchen. There, a man in a white coat greeted them.

"Mr. Coppersmith. Good to see you, my boy!" he said cheerfully.

"Hey, Drago. How are you, Sir? Havin' a good day?"

The man nodded and said, "Yes. Busy as usual." His sights gravitated to Abi. "Who is this beautiful young lady?"

"I'd like you to meet my, umm, girlfriend, Abi Acardi." He hoped she'd be okay with the title.

"Oh Meraviglioso. Lei parla italiano, signorina Acardi?"

"What did he say?" Shane asked.

Having caught a few words, Abi translated, "He asked if I speak Italian." She replied shakily to the man, "Sono un po' arrugginito," hoping she pronounced it right.

The man laughed.

Shane's eyebrows raised. "I didn't know you spoke Italian."

"When my grandparents were alive, they taught me, but sadly, I haven't kept up with it since they passed."

"My condolences, dear," Drago sincerely expressed.

Abi nodded.

"Your pizzas are coming out now. Two minutes, okay?"

"Sure. No problem, Sir. Thank you," Shane replied.

Reaching into her bag, Abi pulled out money to help pay the bill.

He looked down at it. "I'm not taking that," he chuckled. "You are my guest tonight. It's the least I can do for all the help you're giving me."

Drago listened in with a sparkle in his eye.

"But..." Abi raised her hand. "Please let me pay my share."

"Absolutely not."

The chef interrupted their admirable banter. "Mr. Coppersmith is a true gentleman, Miss."

"Yeah, what he said," Shane smiled.

Putting away her money, she could tell she wouldn't be able to win that battle. It was two against one.

"Here we go! Two pizzas, a Pomodoro, and three tiramisu. Enjoy!"

Handed the pizza boxes and bags with their desserts and pasta, Shane slid his card into the point-of-sale reader and added the tip before punching in his pin. "Thanks so much, Sir."

"You are so welcome," he turned to Abi. "It was nice to meet you, Miss Acardi. I hope to see you again soon." Winking, he patted Shane on the back. "This young man is here often; he is like family."

"I look forward to seeing you again, too. Have a good night," Abi said.

"Graziosa ed educata," he said.

Abi smiled. "Thank you. You're too kind."

"What did he say?" Shane asked.

"I think he said pretty and polite." She confirmed that with Drago. "Am I right?"

"Yes, Miss. Perfetto." Waving to them, he said, "Arrivederci."

"Arrivederci," Abi replied.

On their way out the door, Shane said, "Wow, you are full of surprises. I can't believe it. On top of everything, you speak Italian."

"Well, in all fairness, you didn't ask," she chuckled while getting in the front seat. "And, for the record,  I would never say I speak Italian – I dabble." About to drive away, Abi recalled what Shane had said. "So, girlfriend, huh?"

He wasn't sure if she had caught on. "Thought it fit. Am I wrong?" He shot her a charming look.

Staying calm, she said, "I'll entertain it."

"Oh, you will. That's good. I'm glad." Content, he reached and took hold of her hand before getting settled in the Jeep again, leaving the plaza and continuing to his house.

Back on Mulholland Drive, the views returned. Abi was in awe. It felt like they were in another world. It wasn't long until Shane signaled and turned into an upscale gated community with beautifully manicured grass and foliage with flowers everywhere. Passing slowly through the gates, a security guard acknowledged them. Descending the hill, Shane purposefully didn't reveal his celebrity neighbors. Making a left, turning down Beverly Park Circle, they approached a large wrought iron gate with two enormous coach lights on either side. Peering through the iron mesh as the door slid open, Shane proceeded inside and over the wood-planked bridge with a moat underneath. The light-colored stone mansion was stunning.

Abi's jaw dropped. Realizing her expression, she quickly composed herself. "This is your house?"

"Yes," he said, not making a big deal of it.

"Shane. It's beautiful."

Happy with her appreciation of the home and that she didn't make any derogatory remarks, he pulled up to the side and turned off the engine. "Well, I'm hungry. Let's eat before it gets cold."

Abi got out and scanned the grounds. Flowers were bursting from the gardens. Everything was lush and tranquil. She turned to admire the sheer size and each intricate detail, like the family crest above the front entrance and the lightning rods lining the rooftop. It was all so regal.

Slinging his backpack and athletic bag over his shoulder, Shane grabbed the pizza boxes while Abi took the bags and her backpack. Timidly following him toward the wood artisan doors, he opened one side and held it for her before closing it behind them. The sound echoed through the huge halls with high ceilings. Standing in the foyer with an ornate marble and iron staircase sweeping to the second floor, Abi didn't know where to look first. It was unlike anything she'd ever seen before. Her house looked minimal in comparison.

Setting his athletic bag and backpack on the chaise by the stairs, he said, "The kitchen is this way," before rounding the corner with pizza boxes in hand.

Abi left her backpack with his and followed him down the long corridor. Room after room, she was surprised by the traditional décor. It reflected that of a castle or French chateau, with crystal chandeliers, custom silk draperies, curved barrel ceilings, and matching upholstered furniture.

Walking into the enormous ivory kitchen overlooking the back garden, Shane set the food on the counter. Taking out his phone, he texted someone. "In a minute, you will meet my stepbrother, Jacob."

With perfect timing, they could hear the boy bounding down the stairs and running toward them. Bursting into the kitchen with abundant energy, the lanky, blonde-haired boy with dark brown eyes suddenly stopped dead in his tracks at the sight of Abi.

He glanced at Shane and rudely asked, "Who's she?"

"This is Abi."

With a partial smile, he replied, "Hey."

"Nice to meet you, Jacob." Abi hoped he'd like her.

"Yeah. You too." Grabbing his pasta Pomodoro, he whispered, "She's nicer than the other one," before disappearing around the corner.

Left alone once again, Shane laughed. "And there he goes."

"He's cute."

"You wouldn't say that if you had to live with him. Kids of his generation are troublemakers." Shane grabbed two plates, placemats, and napkins. Setting the table by the windows, he walked to the beverage fridge and asked, "What will it be?" Scanning their selection, he said, "Soda, sparkling water, iced tea, or juice?"

"Sparkling water would be great."

"Sparkling it is. Please have a seat."

Sitting on a cushioned chair while Shane moved the orchid from the center, he opened her pizza box and said, "Tomato, buffalo mozzarella, and basil for you."

"Thank you." Abi couldn't wait to see the Coppersmith special. Upon flipping the lid, she spotted the ingredients heaped on top. "Wow. That is definitely loaded."

He grabbed a slice and took a bite. "Oh. It's so good."

Abi noticed the large house was devoid of people. "Where are your Dad and stepmom? Don't they come home for dinner?"

"Most nights during the week, they are in the city. Jacob and I rarely see them."

A man dressed in a grey jacket and black pants entered. Taken aback, he straightened up. "Master, Shane. I'm sorry to intrude," he said in a stiff English accent. "I did not know you had company. May I help you with anything?"

"No, Alfred. We are good." Making eye contact with her, he said, "Abi. Meet Alfred, our butler extraordinaire."

The man blushed. "Thank you for the glowing introduction." Approaching them, he said, "Very nice to meet you, Miss Abi."

"Good to meet you."

"She came over to help me study for our math test tomorrow."

"Very good. I will leave you both. Ring if you need me," the man said formally.

"No. We'll be fine. Thanks, though."

"Enjoy."

Left alone, the two continued eating. Shane even took two slices of pizza and folded them over. Devouring half of it in one bite, he finished chewing and said, "How's yours?"

"Really good. Thank you," then asked, "Is your house always so perfect?"

"Yes, unless my parents have a party. Then, the cleanup crew arrives early the following morning. It's back to normal in a matter of hours. But that rarely happens anymore. They are too busy with work." Not afraid to let her into his world, he asked, "I'll show you around after if you'd like?"

"I'd love that."

Jacob carefully entered the room with this empty pasta take-out bowl.

Taking notice, Shane said, "Wow, buddy. That didn't take long."

"You know that's my favorite." Rinsing the container out in the sink, Jacob tossed it in the recycling and put his glass in one of the two dishwashers before taking off again.

"I try to change it up each week, but when I get il Segreto, he eats all of it."

Abi saw Shane in a different light. The fact that he thought of his stepbrother was so sweet. It made her like him even more. About to ask how Jacob knew Emile, she quickly decided against it.

When they finished, they tidied up and left the kitchen like they were never there. Returning the orchid to the table's center, he neatly pushed in the chairs. "Our bedrooms are our domain. Everywhere else is my stepmom's. She likes things neat." Stepping back, he scanned the space and made sure everything was good. "Want the tour now?"

"Sure," she smiled.

Following Shane around the house, up and down the many corridors and exquisitely decorated rooms, he showed her the indoor pool, theatre, and games room, even his Dad's library with a glass floor exposing the fully stocked custom wine cellar below. Meandering back the way they came, Shane walked out onto the covered patio through French doors. Abi found many sitting areas, including a living room with a television and bar and an outdoor dining room with seating for fourteen guests. Beyond that was the beautiful pool surrounded by pencil Cyprus cedars towering above them. Passing through the wispy drapes swaying in the breeze, they stood on the edge and watched the many jet spouts cascading into the crystal clear water, creating calming bubbling sounds. With lounge chairs perfectly spaced to one side, Abi eyed up the two circular covered cabanas anchored in each corner.

"I've never brought anyone here before."

"Why wouldn't you? It's beautiful."

"That's just it. Most would trash the place, and I'd have to take the heat. Not worth the trouble."

"Thank you for trusting me," she said.

He took her hand. "I knew you'd appreciate it." Leading her to the far end, they had a seat on the circular lounger.

She felt Shane's place was more like a prison in a way. Believing that anyone gifted such luxury was fortunate, she realized the truth was hidden behind closed doors. For him, the opulent façade was hiding a broken, unstable home.

"It's so peaceful here." Abi closed her eyes and listened to the breeze and the birds chirping nearby.

Shane admired her love for nature. To him, she fit in well with the beauty of his surroundings. Sitting back in the chair and putting his head on the pillow, he crossed his arms atop his chest. Exhausted, he closed his eyes.

Seeing him lying there, she nudged him playfully.

Opening one eye, he raised his arm to invite her to join him. Hesitant, she timidly rested her head on his shoulder before he wrapped his arm around her. Not sure how to react, she noticed him close his eyes again. Hearing the water trickling into the pool, Abi felt like a princess living in an enchanted castle. Enjoying the views of the chateau while Shane napped, she couldn't believe this was her life now. It was beyond anything she could ever imagine.

A while later, startling himself, Shane turned to find Abi cuddled beside him. "I'm sorry. Must have drifted off."

"Only for a few minutes. Don't worry. I've been enjoying the Zen environment, and you clearly needed a minute."

"Yeah, umm. I can never catch up on sleep during the week." He rolled onto his side and wrapped his other arm around her.

With their heads on the pillows, inches between them, their eyes met briefly in a longing stare, making Abi think he might...just.... With anticipation, she held her breath and waited.

Shane broke the silence between them. "I guess we should get studying?" Sitting up beside her, Abi did the same while he checked the time on his phone. "We only have about an hour or two at most."

Getting mixed signals, Abi was disappointed and wondered if it was something she'd done. Had he seen Emile's post from earlier today? She hoped he hadn't.

Standing up slowly, Shane stretched his hands above his head. Abi could see he was sore. He turned to her and said, "Shall we?"

"Sure." She followed him back inside.

When they returned to the foyer, he grabbed their bags. "My room is upstairs. We can study there."

Nervous, she followed him.

About to pass a large laundry room with three washers and three dryers in a row, Shane stopped. "Wait one second." Taking his dirty athletic clothes out of his bag, he tossed them in a free machine and started it. "Follow me."

They walked down the hall to a set of double doors at the end. While rounding the corner, the lights automatically illuminated the room when they entered. Abi found it had a very different vibe. The masculine space with dark hardwood floors, a grey area rug, and light walls was the opposite of the rest of the house. A more modern space, the sprawling floor-to-ceiling black upholstered headboard framed the kingsize bed to one side. A sectional sitting area and TV were on the other. Shane walked into an alcove with a circular desk, two chairs, and an impressive state-of-the-art computer system with three monitors.

"Have a seat," he offered, wheeling the ergonomic chair over to her.

She sat down and pulled the chair closer to the desk. "I wish my room had this much space," she said.

"Yes, it's a nice place to escape to."

Not knowing what he meant, she assumed he avoided the rest of the house at all costs. From her vantage point, she could also see his walk-in closet with black built-ins and a fully tiled ensuite. "It's like you have your own apartment."

He laughed. "Guess so." Humble, he didn't flaunt his family's wealth—a rare trait in this part of the country where keeping up with the Joneses took on a whole new meaning.

For the next hour, Abi willfully explained the answers to their review questions once Shane had a crack at them on his own. Within the first twenty minutes, she started to see improvement. But Abi knew something was up. In recent years, she worked with young kids with learning disabilities in the summers. Not letting on that she had seen signs of this, Abi continued encouraging him and showed patience as he struggled a bit. Knowing repetitive strategies helped students with LDs, she incorporated a few things and noticed him tackling all the problems, just not the easy ones.

He leaned back in his chair. "Wow, I can't believe I'm actually getting it."

"See, practice makes perfect."

He looked at her from across the table. "How can I ever thank you for all your help?"

"I'm just glad that you feel more confident." Surprised to see the time, she said, "It's getting late. I need to be back by eight-thirty."

"Do you want me just to drive you straight there? I can pick you up in the morning if you want."

Abi remembered her car was still at school, and they locked the garage down at nine.

"It will take at least twenty minutes to get back to Gilderson. We might not make it. Even if you did, you'd be pretty late getting home then."

Believing her car would be safe overnight, she said, "Maybe it's better to go straight there. Are you sure you don't mind picking me up in the morning?"

"No, I don't mind. Besides, it'll incentivize me to get moving bright and early."

Putting her books in her backpack, Shane grabbed his car keys off the table behind the sofa.

"Will Jacob be okay on his own?"

"Yes, Alfred lives here, and Gillian's room is beside his," he said.

"Who's Gillian?"

"She's the nanny. They are on the opposite wing of the house." Shane took Abi's bag from her shoulder. "Here, I'll carry that."

Leaving his room, they walked down the hallway to the marble staircase. Shane opened the front door, and they jumped in the Jeep seconds later. Starting the engine, he turned around, crossed the moat bridge, and waited for the gates to open. Holding her hand, Shane was quiet.

"Hey?" she said, "Penny for your thoughts."

He turned to her. "I forgot to tell you I got a ticket for Black Lyon."

"Oh, good. Me too."

"Do you still want to go with me?" He held his breath after asking the question.

"Yes, I'd love to."

She could still tell something was off. Needing to know, she asked, "Is there something wrong?"

"I feel you might be looking at me differently after being here," he said with a low tone.

"How so?"

"Now you know what my life is like after hours. My friends don't see this side of me, but I thought it was important to show you."

She was relieved to hear what he said didn't involve Emile's social media post. "I'm glad you did. And for the record, I know you're life is far from perfect. But mine isn't either."

Guiding Shane to her house on Stradella, she pressed the button on the gate app. As the barrier slid open, they slowly moved into the courtyard. Surprised by the ultra-modern structure uplit at every corner, he stopped in front of the tall pivot door.

"I'd invite you in to meet my parents, but it's a bit late."

"Totally understand," he paused awkwardly. "Thanks again for your help."

"Well, thank you for dinner. I think you're ready for tomorrow."

"Yes, I think so too." Fidgeting with one hand on the steering wheel and holding her hand with the other, he opened his door and got out. Getting her backpack, he carried it to the front porch. "I'll swing by at eight to pick you up."

"I'll be ready."

Reaching out, he hugged her with one arm before carefully placing her backpack onto her shoulder. With eyes latched onto hers, he inched closer.

Body shivering from the chill of the evening air, she felt his fingers gently slide behind her right ear.

Resting his forehead against hers, he tried to understand why he was so nervous.

Anticipation building, the lights suddenly turned on inside the foyer.

Startled, thinking her parents were coming, Shane stepped back and ran his hand through his hair.

Mortified, Abi peeked in the side window. "I guess I should go," she said.

"Umm, yeah. I'll see you tomorrow."

"Okay."

Shane turned and walked to the Jeep. Looking at her before getting in, he waved and started the engine.

Abi watched him leave, then closed the gate when he'd gone.

Taking a deep breath, she walked into the house, afraid of what awaited her.

When her Dad emerged from the kitchen, he said, "Abi, who was that boy, and where's your car?"

"That was Shane Coppersmith, and my car is still at school. But don't worry, the garage closes at nine, so it's safe."

"That's not the point," he barked. "I didn't buy a car for it to sit in an underground parking garage while you get boys to drive you home."

Realizing her Dad was angry, she wondered what had happened. This was out of character for him.

"I'm sorry, Dad. I was just helping him study for our math test tomorrow. He's trying to secure a scholarship."

"Wait. That was the football player?" A look of concern flashed across his face.

Abi couldn't lie. "Yes." She lowered her head, knowing he must have seen them on the porch. "You were watching?"

"It's hard when the motion sensors keep sending me movement notifications. Imagine my surprise when I see my daughter about to kiss a guy in full view."

"I'm sorry, Dad." She knew she needed to concede. "No matter what you think, I know he is different. He has goals and drive and determination."

The frustration on his face escalated.

"Where's Mom?"

Her father looked up at the ceiling before running his hand down his face. "She's resting upstairs." Almost in agony, he said, "There's something I must tell you."

"What? What is it?" Abi got scared.

"Your Mom wanted us to do this together, but...I think it's best if I, umm..."

Abi felt the air leave her lungs.

"The cancer is back, Abi." He exhaled, having said it.

"No..." She felt her feet falling through the floor.

"It moved into her blood and her bones. That's why she hasn't been well."

Crushed, Abi didn't know what to say. A lump developed in her throat. "Well, we will fight like we did before. Do everything it takes to get her better."

He shook his head. "Not this time, Sweetie."

"What are you saying?"

"I'm saying Mom is terminal. We need to keep her as comfortable as possible. I will keep her at home for as long as I can."

She nodded, understanding her Dad knew what he was talking about. Timidly, reaching out, she hugged him tightly.

"I thought this move would be good for her. You know, fulfill the lifelong dream she had."

"She told me about that on the flight here."

Emotionally drained, he said, "You'd better get to bed. It's a school night. I'm working from home tomorrow. The nursing staff will visit in the morning. After that, they'll be here around the clock."

"Alright."

Seeing her walk away, shell-shocked, he felt horrible for how he had acted. He'd taken out his emotions on her, which wasn't fair. "Abi?" He stopped her before she got too far.

She turned around. "Yeah."

"I'm sorry for getting upset. I shouldn't have..."

"It's okay, Dad. I understand."

She went upstairs and stopped at the top. Peering down the hall at her parent's room, seeing the door open a crack, she wanted to go in and see her, but she just couldn't.

Going to get ready for bed, she thought about everything that had occurred that day and how much she would have loved to share some of it with her. Abi sighed while daydreaming about what it would be like to sit on her bed with her Mom, laughing and talking about boys. But as of now, that would never happen.

Setting her alarm for seven, she thought her Dad would be awake when Shane arrived. Pulling out her phone, she figured she'd give him a heads-up. Sadly, he did not text her back.

# 27

# Dad?

Morning came too early. Not having had the best sleep, Abi rolled over upon hearing the sound of her alarm filling the room. Over the past twenty-four hours, she didn't know if she was coming or going. On the one hand, she found out her mother was dying; on the other, she was slowly building a new life and finding happiness. Despite her walls crumbling, her relationship with Shane was the silver lining. He was the reason she got out of bed every morning.

Dressed and downstairs by seven-fifty, Abi raced into the kitchen to grab a coffee. Hearing a notification on her phone, she opened the gate and said, "Damn. He's early."

Her father descended the stairs. "Is there someone here for you?"

"Yes! Don't worry. I got it!" Abi bolted toward the foyer, making sure she didn't spill her hot drink. Opening the door, she waved to Shane.

"What? I can't meet him?" her father said, peering out the window.

"After last night, no, not today."

Standing in the doorway as Abi walked over to Shane, her dad saw the football player respectfully turn off the engine and get out with a smile.

"Oh, bloody hell," Abi muttered.

Presenting an outstretched hand, Shane greeted, "Good morning, Sir. I'm Shane Coppersmith."

Surprised by his demeanor, Dr. Acardi shook it. "Nice to meet you, Shane."

Abi awkwardly looked at them and cringed. "Dad, he and I will be late if we don't get going."

Ignoring her plea, he asked the young man, "So, I hear you play football."

"Yes, Sir. Quarterback." Shane stood tall with his hands positioned militarily behind him.

"Impressive. A leader, then?"

"I try to lead by example, Sir."

"That's good."

"Dad? We need to go." Abi was freaking out.

"Any plans for university?"

"Yes, twenty-four scholarship offers to Division One schools to date."

"Dad!" she shouted, so embarrassed.

"Okay, I'm sorry!" Dr. Acardi chuckled at her. "You two go ahead. It was nice meeting you, Shane. Hope you see you around more often."

"I'd like that as well. Enjoy your day."

"Thank you." Her father waved and said, "Bye, Abi!"

She did the same while Shane slipped behind the wheel and started the Jeep. "Thank goodness. I'm glad you got my text last night."

"What text?"

She swung around and looked at him as he inched onto Stradella, mindful of the blind corner.

He laughed. "Relax. I'm kidding. Yes, I got your text."

Abi leaned back and rested her head. She seemed stressed and on the verge of tears.

Shane picked up on it right away. "What's up, New England?"

"Hey, you can't call me that anymore," she snapped, unable to look him in the eye.

"Seriously, what is it?"

Abi looked sorrowfully out the side window.

Thinking it was bad, he offered what he could. "If you ever need a shoulder, I have one you can borrow anytime."

"Thank you," she said, slumping down in the seat. Not liking how the day started, she knew surviving the rest would be much harder than anticipated.

# 28

## Weighed Down

Arriving at school on time with only a few minutes to spare, they rushed to class. Both found their seats and got ready to take the math quiz. As Mr. Walker handed out the test, Shane glanced at Abi and gave her a thumbs up. She gathered a half smile and did the same. Emile walked in and shot her a disturbing look. Suddenly, she felt pain in her chest. Weighed down, overwhelmed by everything, her walls began caving in. Forcing herself to focus on the questions, she tried to regulate her breathing to offset the anxiety that set in.

Within the hour, having finished in record time, Abi turned to Shane. He looked to be struggling. She prayed he'd calm down and implement the strategies they'd practiced the night before. Soon, she saw him pause and do just that. Taking a breath, she believed he'd be fine. Antsy, unable to sit in class any longer, Abi asked the teacher to use the washroom.

On her way out, Shane watched her leave. He looked concerned when he noticed she'd taken her bag.

Proceeding to the office with her backpack in tow, Abi signed herself out, sighting she was sick, before heading home. Given the news her dad shared, she needed a day to think. Not telling anyone where she was going, she just left. Passing by Gerald, she stopped briefly.

"Where are you off to, Miss Abi? Shouldn't you still be in class?" He could see something was wrong.

"I'm dealing with some family troubles. I'm just going to head home. I kind of need a mental break."

"I'm sorry to hear that. You take care."

"Thank you."

Before she stepped on the gas, he stopped her. "A piece of advice, Miss?"

She gave him her undivided attention.

"Sometimes we bottle up our emotions and feelings to avoid causing others grief or burdening them. But the truth is, the only person that is hurting is ourselves. If I may, Miss Abi. You've got some kind-hearted people to call friends. You might want to confide in them. When you open up, things won't seem so bad."

Hearing his wise words, she said, "I'll try. Thank you, Gerald."

"Anytime. Drive safe."

"I will."

Pulling away from the garage, Abi thought about what he said. She turned and looked at the building her friends were in, knowing she'd abandoned them. Especially Shane. She hoped her departure didn't cause him to lose his focus.

"You're so selfish, Abi. You shouldn't have left. What were you thinking?" A level of guilt washed over her. She stopped the car and texted him.

*Sorry. I had to leave for the day. There is stuff going on at home. Don't worry about me, okay?*

Not waiting to see his reply, she continued down the road. Feeling out of control, she started to cry as the gravity of what was happening became more real. Her life had gone from bright and promising to dark and sorrowful overnight. It was then it hit her. She was going to lose her Mom, and instantly, the tears flowed.

# 29

# Torrent

Minutes before ten o'clock, Abi returned home to find a strange car parked in the courtyard. Looking in the rearview mirror, she fixed her face before going inside. Blotting her tears away, she was afraid of what she'd find. With a deep breath, she got out and walked to the front door. Standing there a second with her hand on the handle, Abi exhaled and said, "Be brave, Abs."

Walking in, she saw her Dad sitting in the living room, speaking to two nurses. He was hunched over this laptop on the coffee table in front of him with multiple file folders stacked on either side, each over an inch thick. The nurses were taking notes and offering advice. Hearing the door, he looked up.

"Abi? What are you doing here? You're supposed to be in school."

"I know... I..." Abi started to cry.

He immediately stood up and went over to her. "What is it?" Turning to the women, he said, "I'm sorry. Please give us a minute."

Sliding open the Fleetwood door, her Dad led her to the patio. Sitting on the sofa, he asked, "What's going on, Sweetheart?"

"I just...umm... I couldn't..." Bursting into tears, she could barely form a sentence.

Seeing her in such distress, he clung to his daughter. "Oh, Sweets. Everything is going to be okay."

They sat there as Abi expelled a torrent of emotion. Unable to catch her breath, her chest heaving between sobs - the flood kept coming.

Holding her, wondering what he might say to help her through the turmoil, he waited until she was ready to talk.

Sitting back, drying her tears, chest still heaving intermittently in the aftermath, Abi said, "I just need a day to regroup. It's too much."

"I understand. Don't worry. If the school calls, I'll explain. You go to your room and relax. I will check on you after my meeting."

Abi nodded and got up from the sofa. Walking inside together, she veered toward the staircase while her Dad returned to the living room. On her way upstairs, she looked at her phone and noticed multiple texts from Shane. He was worried. She texted back and told him she was okay – that she would talk to him later.

About to walk into her room, she stopped and stared at the door down the hall. Slowly inching toward it, she peeked in and found her mom hooked up to an IV and heart monitor. As much as she wanted to go in, she couldn't bring herself to.

Distraught, she left and went to change into the coziest clothes she had. Slipping under the covers, she curled up in bed and fell asleep.

# 30

# Settled

A couple of hours later, she heard a knock at her door. Disoriented and unsure of what was happening, she rolled over. A second knock followed and spread across the room.

"Come in," she said sleepily.

Her Dad stood in the doorway. "Is it okay if we talk for a minute?"

Nodding, she said, "Sure."

He walked over and sat on the edge of the bed. "How are you holding up, Sweetie?"

Abi didn't know how to respond to that. "Okay, I guess."

Unable to look her in the eye, he held onto her hand. "I know this is hard. You've been under a lot of stress for months, and the move was challenging enough. I can only imagine how bad it got when I was gone. I'm sorry for that." He pondered that thought. "It's your grade twelve year. I hate to say it, but you need to be in school. You've got university applications coming up, and I need you to focus on the future. That said, I also don't want you to miss out on having a social life. In Boston, you shut everyone out. You can't live your life like that. From what I can tell, you've made some good friends. Please lean on them during this time. I promise, if they are who you say they are, they'll be there for you through thick and thin. Of course, I am always here too, but you will need more than just me."

Tears rolled down her cheeks.

"I've arranged the in-house nursing help. It'll be a little intrusive, but I'm sure we'll manage. We will keep Mom here for as long as we can."

Abi silently agreed.

"So, as for you playing hooky today? I vouched for you when the school called. But as of tomorrow, it's business as usual, Capiche?"

"Okay," she said.

He hugged her and said, "On that note, are you hungry?"

"Maybe a little."

"Okay, I will order some food, and we can eat together. Deal?"

"Deal."

That evening, Abi took the night off to spend with her Dad. Seeing that Jade had texted her, she put her phone away and did not respond. Given his undivided attention, they talked through quite a few things. Afterward,  Abi felt a little better.

An hour before bed, she went to sit with her Mom. The night nurse allowed them time alone. Initially silent, she soon started to ramble on. Giving her an update on everything happening in her life, she pretended her Mom was listening. Running out of things to say, not receiving a response, she kissed her forehead and said goodnight before the nurse silently returned to take her place.

While getting ready for bed, she noticed Shane had messaged her. He was checking in to make sure she was all right. Abi recalled what her Dad and Gerald said about letting her friends in and sharing her struggles. Debating it, she figured if the moment presented itself, she would.

Texting Shane, she typed, *Hi. So sorry. I just got your text now. It's been a rough day. I will see you in the morning. Goodnight.*

Seeing his thinking bubbles go into action, she waited to see what he'd say.

*I'm sorry for whatever you're going through. I am here if you need me. I'll see you tomorrow. Night.*

Abi noticed he signed off with a heart this time. Of all people, she knew he would understand and would support her no matter what. As scary as it was to let him in, it wasn't fair not to. Rolling over in bed, she tucked her arm under the pillow. Snuggled in, she tried to get some sleep. Tomorrow would be a busy day, and she needed the strength to get through it.

| 214 |

# 31

## Confide

Unable to sleep past five o'clock, Abi reluctantly got up and went to school early. Arriving before anyone else, even Gerald, she slowly walked into the class and prayed she'd survive the next six hours or more. Sitting by herself, the room was empty and cold. She took advantage of the silence and recorded her thoughts in her Burch book to pass the time. So much had happened in the past twenty-four hours - an emotional rollercoaster that tested her faith. Trying to stop the tears from flooding, she tilted her head periodically and looked at the ceiling. Composing herself, she continued writing until the students began to trickle in. Each seemed confused to see her sitting alone.

Getting a text from Jade, she read it. *Where are you? Are you coming to school today?*

Abi exhaled and typed her reply. *Yes, I'm here. I'm already in class.*

When her friends arrived, they all paused before walking to their desks. They could tell something was very wrong. Abi didn't look like herself.

Jade was the first to sit down. Treading carefully, she asked, "What happened to you yesterday? You missed tennis practice. The Coach was wondering where you were."

Barely able to gather the energy to respond, she said, "Umm, there was a family emergency." Seeing that her friend was about to fish for more information, Abi added, "Jade, look. I'm sorry. Can we leave it at that for now?"

Seeing tears develop in the girl's eyes, she replied, "Yeah...umm, sure." Pausing a second, she rested her hand on Abi's arm. Looking past her, seeing Shane, she gave him the eye, not knowing what could have happened.

Shane tapped Abi on the shoulder.

It caused her to exhale and turn around almost rudely.

"Hey, umm, I was worried when you didn't meet me this morning."

"Sorry. I got here early."

Throwing it out there, he said, "If you need to talk, we can leave. Just say the word."

As tempting as that was, Abi shook her head and turned back around. Her reaction concerned Shane even more. Seeing their teacher enter the class and close the door, he knew there was no escape for the next ninety minutes.

Keeping to herself the entire time, Abi half-focused on the work assigned to them. Her friends noticed her gazing out the window, deep in thought. Bouncing glances between them, trying to figure out what was wrong, each tried to finish their assignment as their teacher roamed the room.

Given their graded quizzes ten minutes before class ended, Shane held his breath when the teacher passed him his paper. Seeing an A- in the top right-hand corner, he smiled and tapped Abi's arm.

When she turned around to see what he wanted, she found him holding up the test with a big smile. He looked happy and quite proud of the accomplishment.

Her face slightly brightened as she gave him a thumbs-up.

Reggie was sitting across the aisle from them and saw her reaction. He turned to his friend and shrugged his shoulders, puzzled.

When the bell rang, Abi gathered her books and slipped them into her backpack. Shane stayed by her side and motioned for Jade and Reggie to go ahead of them.

"Can I walk with you?" he asked, hoping she would open up.

"Sure."

Quietly leaving the room, Shane followed on her left. Knowing he deserved an explanation, she said, "I'm sorry I'm not myself this morning."

Surprised to get some information, he replied, "That's okay." Pausing, he added, "I don't know what happened, but I'm here if you...."

"Thanks," she interrupted, knowing what he would say.

Afraid to press further to discover what was bothering her, he took a deep breath and offered his hand.

Abi noticed and waited for a second before taking hold. He was glad she accepted.

On their way to the science lab, they saw Jade and Reggie standing outside in the hall, waiting.

Happy to see their friends walking hand in hand, Jade whispered, "Well, that's a good sign."

Reggie quickly agreed. "Yep."

Taking their seats, Professor Grady plopped his briefcase on the desk. In that instant, Abi regretted not taking Shane up on his offer to leave early, but the last thing she wanted was for her Dad to receive another call from the school.

The old white-haired teacher requested they turn to a page in their textbook. Doing just that, she thought, *Hang in there, Abi. You can do this. Just one more class after this, then you can go home.*

Remembering that Shane had a football game tonight, she didn't know what to do. Her Dad's words echoed in her head.

*You have to go tonight,* she thought. *He needs you there.*

Confused, she glanced at Shane and found him listening intently to Professor Grady. Abi admired his facial profile, wondering how she got so lucky to have met him.

*You can't screw this up,* she said silently. Her thoughts then drifted back to her Mom. *Come on, Abi. Focus.*

While following their teacher pacing the aisles as he talked, she attempted to look interested in the information he was presenting. Thankful to be given group work to complete, Shane and Reggie joined the girls at their lab desk. Switching seats because Jade wanted to sit beside Reggie, Shane hoped Abi would be okay with him nearby. Everyone allowed her to work independently but hoped she'd join the discussion. The three of them conversed amongst themselves to answer the questions. Sadly, Abi didn't have anything to add.

Glimpsing over periodically, Shane offered his left hand. As it brushed against her hip, she reached across to grab hold. Feeling his touch helped her cope. It was like he'd thrown a lifeline.

About to wrap up the class, Professor Grady wrote their homework on the smart board.

"Oh, man. Who assigns homework on the weekend?" Reggie whispered while closing his books and snapping a pic of the page numbers and questions due the following Wednesday.

When the bell sounded, Jade walked out with Reggie to give Shane and Abi time together.

As the two strolled down the hall, Abi saw how attentive he was. Silently trying to be supportive and not putting pressure on her, she grabbed his arm and rested her head upon it.

Looking down at her, seeing this, he pulled her aside in a doorway. Not saying a word, he hugged her. Hoping she'd embrace him, he felt her arms encircle his waist. Pulling her in tightly, they just stood there for a second. Offering reassurance, he kissed her forehead before they let go and continued to her classroom.

Stopping outside the studio door, Shane said, "I'll see you at lunch?"

She nodded. About to let go of Shane's hand, she suddenly pulled him toward her.

Surprised, he looked into her eyes and hugged her goodbye. It was all she needed to get through the last class of the day.

Jade waited just inside with eyes peeled for Emile Raven. When Shane left, she took over for him and stayed by Abi's side. Sitting down at their desks, the teacher arrived at the same time as Emile and her friends.

Ready for tonight, the girls had used the first three hours of the morning for glam. Sporting perfect ponytails and freshly painted manis and pedis, they glared at Abi on the way by.

Seeing this, Jade kept a close eye, knowing Abi couldn't take their drama today.

Working independently on their assignments, Abi found it easier to breathe. The sunlight cascading through the windows made the day a little brighter despite the darkness lingering inside her. The time went by faster than she expected.

Near the end of class, they handed in their work.

"I'll be right back. Just have to ask the teacher about something. Wait for me," her friend said.

Abi nodded. But when Emile shot her a look, the pain and heaviness in her chest suddenly returned. Bolting out the door, with her heart racing, she dreaded another confrontation. Fleeing toward the gardens, Abi tried to calm down. Feeling faint, she raised her hand to her forehead and sat beside the waterfall. The sound of it cascading was tranquil. It wasn't long before her talk with her Dad the night before replayed through her mind. Realizing her Mom would eventually go into palliative care, she thought about having to say goodbye to her. The tears flowed. Burying her face in her hands, she sobbed.

*Pull yourself together, Abi,* she said, chest heaving.

Her phone vibrated in her pocket. She knew her friends were wondering where she was. After the scare she gave them yesterday, she felt obligated to respond. It wasn't their fault. She needed to let them in.

Blotting the tears, she focused on the blurred screen. Shane had texted twice and Jade three times. Forced to reply, she heard people talking. Abi turned around and found them frantically scouring the grounds.

Abi texted Shane. *I'm at the reflecting pool.*

It only took seconds for him to find her. Hiding her eyes as he sat down, Abi felt him graze her shoulder with his.

"Hey," he said, resting his elbows on his knees and grasping his hands together.

Trusting him, she removed one hand from her face, exposing her bloodshot eyes. Seeing this, Shane reached his arm around her and pulled her in tightly. The emotion behind it made her cry. Holding her head against his chest, he comforted Abi as best he could.

"Please tell me what's wrong."

She finally squeaked out the words, "My Mom is sick."

He didn't know what to say. But hearing that explained a lot. Shane noticed Reggie and Jade standing to the side, watching what was transpiring between them. Waving the two over, they sat one riser below. Jade supportively reached out and rested her hand on Abi's knee upon seeing the condition of her face. Reggie stayed quiet and turned to his friend. Shane subtly shook his head for him not to talk. He, of all people, wasn't good in a crisis. Empathy was not his thing.

"I'm sorry I've not been myself," Abi whispered. "There's stuff going on at home." Breaking down again, Shane held onto her.

"We are worried about you," Jade replied. "What can we do to help?"

"Nothing." Knowing that wasn't a good enough answer, Abi had no choice but to reveal the truth to them, too. "I just told Shane..umm, my Mom is sick."

Afraid to set her off again, Jade tried to stay positive. "Oh, Sweetie. I'm so sorry. We are here for you, okay?"

Abi nodded.

Reggie looked at the time on his phone and subtly showed Shane. He silently acknowledged him, knowing they had to get going, but he didn't want to leave her.

With a breath, he said, "Umm, Abs. Reggie and I have to get moving. Coach scheduled a team meeting in ten minutes."

"That's okay. You go," she said.

Jade interjected. "Don't worry. I'll take good care of her."

Offering Abi a tight side hug and a kiss on the forehead, he said, "Okay." Before leaving, he wondered about the game. "You know, Abs, if you want to go home and rest, don't worry about tonight. I can drop by your place afterward if you want."

Not wanting him to go into it distracted, Abi straightened up and put on a brave face. "Umm, no, I want to go. It's the first of the season. I will be there."

"Are you sure? No pressure." He rested his hand on the middle of her back.

"Yeah."

"I'll drive her. That way, she won't have to worry about a thing," Jade encouraged, taking Shane's place when he stood up.

"Okay. I'll see you after, then." Shane smiled before waving goodbye. She said, "Bye."

The guys walked up the path toward the main building. Abi noticed Shane look her way a few times before he disappeared.

"What am I doing? I am so stupid. I hope I didn't ruin his focus."

"I'm sure it would be better if you go tonight. If you went home, he'd worry more."

"You're right." Abi looked to the sky and patted her eyes with her sleeves. "Damn it."

"Gotta take one day at a time." She could see how frustrated her friend was.

"I know. It's just so hard."

When she broke down again, Jade hugged her. "It'll be okay."

Even though she knew it wouldn't be, she inhaled deeply and said, "I probably look like hell now."

Tilting her head sympathetically, Jade said, "Not gonna lie. We need to fix that face." With a smirk, she hoped to get her laughing.

Abi cracked a smile.

Texting someone, Jade said, "Come on. Allie is going to meet us in the bathroom. She says she's got a bag full of makeup. You'll look like a million bucks in no time."

Standing on her feet, she slid her backpack onto her shoulder and slipped on sunglasses to hide her swollen eyes. Arm and arm, the girls climbed the zig-zagged pathway to the main building. Reaching the bathroom, they met Allie, who quickly fixed her makeup, no questions asked. Abi was thankful not to have to explain. She knew Jade had probably warned her ahead of time.

In minutes, the girls joined the pep rally in the quad. Almost every student had gathered around. Waiting for the coaches and team to surface, they found a spot amongst their group and saw the cheerleaders arrive. Emile led the charge.

Jade noticed Abi's reaction. "Don't pay her any mind," she said.

The girls started the music and filtered out onto the lawn to begin their cheer routine before the Dean introduced the Coach and the players one by one. Of course, when they announced Shane as the QB, the cheerleaders went crazy and whistled at him.

To Emile's dismay, Shane's gaze did not sway one ounce from Abi's the whole time. Jade could see the girl huffing and puffing in anger. It made her wonder if she would plot something against her friend. She knew she'd have to remain on high alert for the next several hours.

Making it through the rally, Shane and Reg went to see them before having to board the bus.

Abi did her best to keep a brave face so Shane could focus on winning tonight.

With arms outstretched, he hugged her tightly. "Okay. Wish me luck."

"Good luck—but you won't need it. You're talented and fast, and you can make decisions on a dime. Look for your teammates. Keep your head in the game. Reggie has your back—all the guys do. We will be there to cheer you on for the win."

Shane smiled and said, "Thank you." He couldn't believe she was dealing with so much, yet she thought of him. Giving her one last squeeze, he replied, "I'll see you later."

"Okay."

Reluctantly walking away, he met up with the team to head to the Wasserman Center.

Jade asked, "So, are we still dropping your car off? That way, you can go with me, then hitch a ride with Shane to the afterparty." She stopped herself upon saying that. "That is if you want to go. It's okay if you don't. Either way."

"Thank you. I think dropping it off is a good idea." Abi could tell her friend was walking on eggshells. "I'll go to the party. Shane needs to make an appearance, I'm sure. So, yeah... Might call it an early night, though."

"For sure. Sounds good." Jade prompted, "Shall we go? We have two hours to kill before the game. Maybe you want to grab something to eat?"

"Sure."

"Perfect," Jade smiled.

Before entering the garage, the girls noticed Emile and her friends glaring at them. Steering clear, they veered toward Gerald, sitting in the security box.

"Well, hello, Miss Abi," he said with a smile.

"Hey, Gerald. How's your day going?"

"Pretty slow, but I'm glad it's Friday." He could tell the girl he met a week ago was not the same person. "How are you doing now? Better than yesterday?"

"It's had its moments," she said with a sigh.

Jade nudged her.

"Oh, Gerald, this is Jade Webber."

Happy to be introduced to the older gentleman, she said, "Hello, Gerald. Nice to meet you."

"It's a pleasure," he said. "So, any big plans for the weekend?"

Jade interjected. "There's a football game tonight and an afterparty. Tomorrow, we are going to, umm, a concert." She caught herself before she revealed that they were going to Black Lyon.

"Yes. It should be fun," Abi added.

"Well, enjoy. I'm looking forward to reading a book in my garden tomorrow."

"That sounds wonderful. We will see you on Monday." Abi waved to the gracious man.

"Yes, I will be here."

"Nice to meet you, Sir."

"Lovely to meet you too, Miss Webber."

Suddenly, they saw Emile and her friends fly past with pompoms flying in the air, hooting and hollering loudly. If looks could kill, they'd both be dead. Emile had a way of stabbing people with her stare.

Rolling her eyes, Jade said, "Don't worry about it. Ignore them."

"Yeah, I know."

When they reached the cars, the girls went their separate ways. Abi waited for Jade to pull out behind her. They waved goodbye to Gerald as they passed. Heading south, arriving at Sunset Boulevard, Abi turned and slowly made her way toward the gates of Bel Air in rush hour. Finally, making it to the intersection, she signaled left. Getting the advanced green, she drove up the hill with the white Porsche a car length away.

Wondering if she should invite Jade in while she changed clothes, Abi thought the last thing she wanted was for her Dad to grill her with fifty million questions. Then, there was the issue of the nursing staff moving about inside her Mom's room. That said, at some point, Abi knew she'd eventually have to let someone into her life. She would need her friends to help her through the inevitable. This helped her make the decision.

Abi pulled up to the house and waited for the gate to open. Inching her way inside, she stopped and got out to join her friend.

Parked beside her, Jade looked at the typical modern white box. "Wow. Nice place," she said.

"Thanks. It doesn't feel like home yet." Abi walked to the front door. Hesitantly, she asked, "Do you want to come in?"

"Do you mind? That way, I can change clothes, too."

"No. Not at all."

Jade grabbed her clothes and followed Abi inside. Looking around at the minimalist design, she complimented, "This is cool."

"I like how open it is." Leading her friend up the stairs, seeing her eyeing up the ancient tree outside the big window, Abi reached the top and looked down the hall. Her parent's room door was partially closed.

"Umm, this is my room. You go ahead in. I'll be there in a minute."

"Sure."

Continuing down the hall, Abi peeked inside. Seeing the nurse sitting in the chair, quietly reading, the woman spotted her and got up.

"How is she?" Abi asked, remaining a few feet away.

"She's been asleep a better part of the day. But resting comfortably."

Happy to hear that, she replied, "Thank you."

"You're very welcome, Miss." The woman nodded and returned to her post.

Able to take a breath, Abi went back to her room. Walking in, she saw Jade had already changed out of her uniform into more comfortable clothes. Not only that, but she'd also coordinated an outfit for Abi to wear.

"What do you think of this?" she asked.

Smiling, Abi was thankful to have her there. "It looks great."

"Tonight, you'll need to dress a bit warmer. The nights are much cooler by the water."

"Okay."

While Abi got dressed, Jade sat on the bed and waited.

When she returned, she asked, "Is this good?"

"Perfect," Jade replied. She focused on keeping things light and positive.

"Thank you for being a supportive friend. I'm so happy we met."

Sympathetically tilting her head, Jade said with a rush of emotion, "Awww. Me too." Hugging her, she suddenly let go. "Ready to head out?"

"Guess so."

"I don't know about you, girl, but I'm starving."

Her dramatics made Abi laugh. "I could eat, too."

The two left the room and descended the stairs. Noticing the nurse glance out her mother's room door, she smiled at her as a rush of guilt flooded Abi's soul.

*Should I stay home with Mom? Maybe I shouldn't go out tonight.* She thought on her way to the front door.

Having told Shane she'd be there, the last thing Abi wanted was for him to see she wasn't. That would ultimately throw him off and possibly cause the team to lose the game. She had no choice but to go.

Jade started the engine the second her friend got in and closed her door. As it purred, she backed up before shifting the Porsche into drive. Inching her way onto the road, watching for cars to whiz around the blind corner, she slowly left.

Abi made sure the gate closed behind her.

Driving down Stradella, heading south on Veteran not long after, they soon pulled into a public parking lot. Looking around, not knowing their location, she trusted her friend.

"You are going to love this place. It's the best oven-fired pizza around," Jade said while paying for parking.

Abi got out and closed the door. Not to hurt the girl's feelings, but to her, the best pizza she'd had was at il Segreto's. Hearing the vehicle lock remotely, she followed her down the street.

"California Pizza," Abi said, reading the sign.

Opening the bright yellow doors, Jade got Abi to enter first.

Taking charge, her friend approached the hostess and asked, "Table for two, please."

The woman behind the counter grabbed menus and said without hesitation, "Follow me."

Seated by the window, Abi was happy. She loved to people-watch.

"Your waiter will be right with you," the woman said before leaving them.

"Thanks so much." Jade flipped open the folder and did not waste any time. "I'm grabbing a Margherita pizza with a dash of arugula."

"Arugula?" Abi thought that was a weird option.

"What?" she laughed. "I need to get my greens in somehow."

Laughing, the girls fell silent. Jade closed her menu and rested her hands on the table. Debating whether she should ask Abi what was wrong with her Mom, she decided against it, hoping she'd bring the subject up herself.

"I'm sorry you've had a rough day."

Abi knew Jade wanted her to share what was going on. Sitting quietly for a minute, watching the pedestrians walk by, Abi took a deep breath and said, "My Mom is terminal."

A sorrowful expression flashed across Jade's face as she reached to grab hold of her hands. "Oh, Abi...."

Choking up, she tried holding back the tears. Looking to the ceiling to keep the droplets from falling, she composed herself. "My Dad's known for a while and didn't tell me."

"I'm sure it was hard for him to process, too. Maybe he had to deal with it first to be strong enough to tell you?"

"Perhaps," she said, not having thought of it that way.

"I won't pretend to know what you're going through. Truthfully, I can't even imagine how difficult it must be. But we will be there for you. Whatever you need, okay?" Jade squeezed her hands to show support.

Interrupted by their waiter requesting their orders, Abi hadn't even decided what she wanted. "You go ahead, Jade."

"Yeah, I'll grab the Margherita pizza. Can you throw a good dash of arugula on that?"

The guy looked at her weirdly. "Umm, sure."

"And I'll have a Perrier."

"Very good." The young man turned to Abi.

"I'll have what she's having. Make it two."

When the guy left the table, Jade laughed. "Living on the edge, huh, New England?"

"Suppose so," she laughed. "Truth is, I couldn't be bothered looking at the menu."

"I figured as much." Concerned her friend had reduced to a shell, Jade knew she needed a distraction.

Hoping to change the vibe, Jade looked out the window and said, "Okay. Let's see who's walking by this joint. Maybe we'll spot some fine-looking men – not like I'm in the market or anything," she giggled.

"Yeah, me either."

Over the next hour, they ate their arugula-sprinkled pizza and commented on the people passing by. Keeping an eye on the time, Jade paid the bill and got them moving so they wouldn't be late for the game.

# 32

# Friday Night Lights

With twilight fast approaching, the sun descended in the western sky. Never having been to a high school football game before, only seeing the scenes depicted in the vintage show Friday Night Lights and the nineties movie Varsity Blues, Abi wondered what it would be like. She knew private schools functioned differently. They relied heavily on order and discipline, so she figured it would be fairly civilized. Or at least, that is what she hoped.

Reaching the stadium parking lot, Jade punched the button for a ticket before the barrier raised to allow them access. She found an open spot not far from the field. There were loads of people there already. Blue sun shelters lined the track for VIPS attending. Parents sat in folding chairs along the sidelines with designer cooler bags filled with drinks and snacks.

Jade only brought a blanket with her. Finding space on the concrete bleachers, she doubled it over to create a comfy seat for them. It wasn't long before they saw the Gilderson coach bus pulling up on the private road behind the field. Abi took note of the ratio of fans cheering for either side. Brentwood certainly had the home-crowd advantage.

While the Gilderson team filed out onto the field, the coaching staff set up their bench and prepared to play. Seeing Shane and a few other players gathered around, Abi watched as they listened to the coach's final words. She couldn't imagine the amount of pressure Shane was under tonight. The weight of the world was on his shoulders. Reggie spotted Jade in the stands and hit Shane's chest with his hand to get his attention. He pointed to them. Shane looked at Abi and smiled before putting on his helmet. That is when she was happy she came. She knew he needed her there.

Over the next ninety minutes, the plays were intense. One by one, Shane threw strong, precise passes, bringing Alan and Shawn in for touchdowns. While cheering for the guys, Abi noticed him making eye contact with her as often as possible. She suspected it might energize him – perhaps give him the strength to soldier through.

In the final minutes of the fourth quarter, tied at fourteen, their offensive spread across the forty-yard line. After the snap, Reggie bolted down the field. He was wide open.

Jade stood up. Her nerves got the best of her. Clenching her hands tightly, she watched Shane launch the ball at his best friend. The talented wide receiver kept his eye on the bullet aimed at him. Catching it, he crossed into the end zone for a touchdown!

"Yeah! Baby!" Jade shouted to Reggie. "That's my man!"

Abi lifted her praying hands to her lips and caught Shane's reaction. Raising his fist in victory, he took a knee before crossing himself and getting up to celebrate their win.

Punting the ball through the uprights, Gilderson won against Brentwood 21 to 14.

The home team dispersed quickly. The Gilderson players gathered around the coaches before heading back to Wasserman. Abi and Jade got as close as they could to the team.

Their Coach, Shane, Reggie, Alan, and Shawn, walked over to speak to the press set up under a few tents. Abi witnessed how each confidently gave interviews. She saw Shane in a different light that night. Not only did he have the stress of winning the game, but he also needed to impress every scout watching the live stream.

Once released from their media duties, Shane made his way over.

"Hey, you," he said.

Abi blushed. "You played great."

Humbly unable to contain himself, he looked at her and smiled. "Well, thank you." Leaning in, he whispered in her ear, "Don't tell anyone, but I wanted that win for you."

"Is that right?" she said, her chest fluttering slightly.

"I was happy to see you perk up at the half." Peering down at the girl who had stolen his heart, he wished he could hug her. Hot and sweaty, he figured he would wait until after he showered. "Look, we are heading back to Wasserman. Can you guys meet us there?"

"For sure," she replied.

Attached at the hip, Jade was clinging to Reggie.

"Reg?" Shane said, trying to get his attention. "Come on, dude. We gotta move."

Reluctantly letting go of his girl, Reggie jogged off the field with Shane toward the coach bus while the girls climbed the stairs toward the parking lot.

"So, what did you think?"

"About what?"

"The game silly. Was it what you expected?"

"It was intense. They played really well." Abi went quiet again.

Reaching out to her, Jade didn't know how to cheer her up.

When they returned to the car, Abi got in while her friend started the engine. Carefully leaving in the conga line of spectators departing the field, they soon broke free.

Abi barely said a word on the way to UCLA.

Hoping to spark conversation, Jade said, "I'm excited about the after-party. It should be fun."

"Yeah, my second beach party in Cali."

"So that you know, this one may be very different than Allie's at Venice Beach."

Abi turned to her. "Oh? Why's that?"

"Let's just say Allie follows the rules, but Aramis and Lexi tend to break them."

Unsure what to expect, she replied, "Thanks for the heads up."

Parking in the garage adjacent to the facility, they walked to the building's front entrance before sitting on a bench to wait for the guys.

"I think Reggie will follow me to my house so I can drop my car off. That way, he and I can drive together. You guys can go ahead. We will meet you there."

She needed to be honest. "I don't know how long we will stay. Not sure if I want to be surrounded by a bunch of drunken teens tonight."

Jade laughed. "Yes, that sounds about right. You do what you need to. I'm sure Shane will be okay with whatever you decide."

She nodded.

"Hey, ladies!" A female voice said.

They spotted Allie and Laney walking down the path.

"Ooooh. Who are you here to see?" Jade asked, intrigued to know who was pairing up this year.

The first to spill was Allie. "Alan asked me out. I'm kinda nervous. But he's just so darn sweet. I couldn't say no."

"How about you, Laney?" Abi inquired, catching the pretty blonde girl eyeing the Wasserman exit doors.

"Well, after our date Wednesday night, Shawn asked me to go to the party with him." She seemed a bit off.

"And?" Jade's spidey senses were tingling.

"I don't know. He's quiet. I need to bring him out of his shell. Maybe spark some confidence in that boy," she laughed slyly.

"Okay, I'm not sure if Shawn is ready for that. But best of luck," Allie giggled.

"Your guys got tickets to Black Lyon, right?" Laney questioned. "I know Shawn did."

Each girl confirmed they were going.

"Good. So far, I think most of our class got in. Should be a hell of a party."

Alan was the first to emerge. Spotting his date hanging out with Jade, Abi, and Laney, he walked over, looking sharp. With a straight face, he approached, exuding extreme confidence.

Stopping a few feet from her, he said, "Hey, Allie. Ready to go?"

Mesmerized by the smile on his face, the girl melted. "Yeeahh," she replied, lovestruck, as he offered her his hand. Flustered, she hesitantly took hold before waving goodbye to the girls. "See you later!"

"You two have fun!" Jade said loudly.

Amidst their departure, they saw Shawn walk out. Meeting up with Laney, his dark blonde hair flowed freely in the wind.

The girl found his baby face and dimple irresistible, even though she'd never admit it.

"You look great," he said, hoping the compliment would break the ice.

"Thanks. You too."

Lost for words, he took a chance, pointed, and said, "I'm parked that way."

"Okay. I bummed a ride with Allie, so...."

Despite her tough exterior, the girls could see Laney was smitten with the dreamboat wide receiver.

"Good. You can ride with me, then." He offered his arm. "Umm, shall we? Maybe we can grab dinner first?"

Cracking a smile, she replied, "Yeah. I'd like that."

Before heading out, Shawn turned around and said, "Oh, Shane and Reggie were right behind me."

"Thanks, Shawn," Jade said as the two slowly walked away. "I don't think he knows what he's in for with that girl." Giggling, she added, "She is far too experienced for him – if you know what I mean."

About to reply, Abi spotted the guys. Tapping her friend's arm to get her attention, Jade turned and locked eyes with her boo. Immediately, she forgot about everyone else and focused on him.

Watching her friend run and jump into Reggie's arms, Abi stood and went to join Shane. This was the moment he'd waited for all day.

Reaching out to her, Abi slipped her arms around his waist as he pulled her in tightly.

Bothered to find Jade and Reggie already locking lips, Shane taunted, "Dude, get a room."

Ignoring him, Reg draped his arm around Jade's shoulders. "Hey, we're droppin' Jade's car at her house, so we'll be a little late."

"No problem. See you there, man."

Watching them walk ahead to the garage, Shane let them get a head start. "So, New England…"

"Hey…"

"What? I'm just kidding." Holding her tightly, he said, "Are you doing okay?"

"Better than this morning."

"Look, it's fine if you wanna pass on the party."

"No, I'm good."

"You're sure?" He expressed a heightened level of concern.

"Yeah. We can go for a bit."

"Whenever you want to leave, tell me, and we'll hit the road."

Abi nodded. "Thank you."

"Absolutely."

Holding her hand, she clung to his arm and rested her head on it as they walked along. Reaching the Jeep, he threw his stuff in the back and opened the door for her. Abi buckled up before he got in on his side. Taking out his phone, he found the address of Aramis' house in Malibu. While the GPS calibrated, he secured his seat belt and pressed the ignition button. Putting the Jeep in gear, he rested his elbow on the center console and intertwined his fingers with hers.

"Ready?" he asked.

"Yep."

"It looks like his place is about an hour out. Sure you still wanna go?"

"You're the quarterback. What would that say to everyone if you didn't?"

Shane stopped the truck and said sincerely, "Don't ever worry about that, okay? Just say the word, and we will do something else. For me, my main concern is you."

Nodding, Abi replied, "I'm fine. Really. Let's go."

"Okay. We'll make a brief appearance, then take off. Deal?"

"Deal."

Releasing his foot from the break, they continued south to Wilshire. It was a quiet drive across San Vincente to the Pacific Coast Highway. Only on the road for twenty minutes, Shane looked down to find Abi had drifted off with her head lovingly resting against his shoulder. Clinging to his arm, he felt this overwhelming need to protect her. That is when he knew how much she meant to him.

With a hint of color left on the horizon, the ocean looked dark, almost black. Thinking about his life and the future ahead, it seemed Shane wanted to succeed more than ever. Except it wasn't just for him. He wanted this for Abi, too. Peering down at her sleeping peacefully, he felt like she came into his life for a reason. The timing was impeccable. The past week was nothing short of perfect.

Turning the radio on low, he listened to music while driving past Zuma Beach. It wasn't long before Abi started to stir.

Startling herself, she sat up and said, "Oh, Shane. I'm sorry." She was panicked.

"Abs, it's okay."

She ran her fingers through her hair. "You've had to drive all this way on your own," she said.

"Abs?"

She was borderline frantic.

"Abi?"

"Yeah?" she said, getting her bearings.

"It's fine. I take it you hardly slept last night."

Sitting silently, she replied, "Less than three hours."

"Well, then, you needed to recharge. It's all good." Needing to state the obvious, based on everything that's happened, he said, "I think we should skip Black Lyon tomorrow."

Deep down, Abi wasn't one hundred percent sure either way. Knowing she'd paid a lot for the ticket, she replied, "This is probably our only shot at going, and we've already paid." Scared and unsure what to expect, she added, "Truthfully, I'm a bit worried about it. I've never been to anything like that before."

"If you still want to go, don't worry. I'll stay by your side the whole time." Giving her hand a few gentle squeezes, he looked at her and smiled before returning his eyes to the road. "Do you know they send the location info about an hour before the event? The whole thing is pretty secretive."

"Guess it adds to the allure."

Hearing the GPS guiding them to turn left onto Broad Beach Road, Shane slowed down and let go of her hand to signal. "Looks like we're here."

Upon veering left at the lights, he followed the narrow roadway and searched for what looked to be a private lane coming up on their left. He knew they were close by the number of cars parked along the side of the road ahead. A guy with a flashlight waved to them. Shane rolled down his window.

"Hey, Shane! We got you a spot right in front."

"Thanks, Dan. Appreciate it."

Abi heard the humbleness in his tone.

"No problem, man! Right, this way." Dan walked down the road, removed the orange traffic cones from the driveway, and guided them in. Arriving safely, Shane got out and went around to Abi's side. Opening her door, he said, "Ready?"

"Yeah." Nervous, not knowing what people would think, unsure if anyone would remember Emile's post earlier in the week, Abi took a deep breath and clung to Shane.

He could tell by the tightness of her grip that she was scared.

"Do you think Emile is going to be here?"

"Not sure, but I'm assuming not. She hates the beach," he said.

Still not reassured, Abi's heart raced as they moved through the wooden slat gate and down a set of stairs. They could hear the music blasting and voices yelling back and forth. Before going any further, Shane said, "We'll just stay a few minutes, then we'll head out."

"Okay."

When they rounded the corner, the DJ caught sight of Shane. "Hey! It's QBeeee!" Like a wave of energy, the guy started a chain reaction, causing everyone to chant, "QB! QB! QB!"

Handed a drink from one of the two bars set up, Shane passed it to Abi before getting one for himself.

Immediately taken off guard, she didn't know what to do.

Walking through the crowd, drink in hand, everyone patted Shane on the back.

Completely out of her element, she could see some girls giving her the eye. Unsure if they were friends of Emile's, she lowered her head and allowed Shane to lead. Reaching the second beach house, the two climbed the steps to a balcony overlooking the ocean.

"Have a seat," he said.

Taking the drink from her, she watched him walk to the balcony's edge and pour the alcohol out before leaving the empty cups on the wicker table.

"By the way, I don't drink—I never have. Just want them to think I do."

Abi was relieved.

"I've got a lot riding on this year. Can't afford to screw it up." About to walk away, he said, "I'll be right back." He disappeared into the beach house.

Left alone, Abi wondered where he'd gone.

Returning seconds later, he handed her a bottle of water. "Would you like one?"

"Yes, that would be great. Thank you."

"You're welcome." Sitting beside her on the lounge chair, he said, "Mind if we, umm...." Lifting his arm, inviting her to move closer, she slipped her arm around his waist and cuddled beside him. Dangerously close, resting her head upon his chest, she said nothing while his heart beat rapidly.

"Are you comfortable? Is this okay?" he asked. His tone was questioning it all.

"It's nice." Tightly clinging to him, he wrapped her in his arms. "We will sneak out in a few minutes."

"Okay."

Sadly, the loud music drowned out the tranquil sound of the waves below.

*What I would give to be in a peaceful place,* she thought.

Not hearing a word from Shane, she looked up and found his eyes closed. She couldn't believe he could sleep with all the yelling and screaming around them.

Given a few minutes to think, she felt guilty about being out and having fun while her Dad struggled with everything at home. Reminded of her life in Boston, she never went out. Ostracizing herself after Burton left, she mostly avoided people at all costs. Trying to justify her decision tonight, she thought, *This is the life you've been missing out on. You're just making up for lost time.*

BANG! BANG! BANG BANG!

Startled, Abi jumped up.

Shane lept to his feet to instinctively shield her. Scanning their surroundings, realizing what was happening, he asked, "Are you okay?"

A series of sparkles lit up the night sky.

BANG! BANG! BANG-BANG! BANG!

"Fireworks," Abi said, pointing up as Shane sat on the end of the chaise and buried his head in his hands, still disoriented.

"I think we need to go." Grabbing her hand, he said, "Come with me. This way." He flipped his hood over his head so nobody would see them leave. Abi did the same.

Walking behind the DJ's set-up, Shane made a b-line for the exit stairs before escaping through the gate. Closing it behind them, he unlocked his truck with a click of the fob. In seconds, they were gone.

Thankful to be out of there, he said, "I'm sorry about all that. I know it's a waste of time."

She kinda laughed. "They certainly don't think so."

"Most of them cut loose at parties like this because of the pressure they're under at home. For a few hours, they forget about how miserable they are. Once they inherit their family's company, it's game over. They will be under a microscope their whole life. Luckily, I have the freedom to choose what I want to do. Carve my own path, you know."

"Yes. I'm in the same vote."

Disappointed for the night to end this way, he noticed they were passing Zuma Beach. "Hey? How about a detour?"

Seeing him point to the sign, she said, "Sure."

# 33

# Alone

Approaching Zuma Beach along the Malibu coastline, Shane recalled seeing that the pay station entrance was closed on the way to the party. Bypassing the beach's main gate, he pulled onto Westwood Beach Road and drove into the darkness.

"Where are we going?"

"You'll see in a minute," he said.

Inching along, he flicked on his high beams, and there, to the right of them, was a beach about twenty yards from the water. Shane parked curbside near the streetlight.

Not seeing anyone around, Abi knew it was just the two of them. Away from the busy highway, she could see the moon sparkling on the waves crashing against the shore.

"So, we have a few options." He opened his door and said, "We can sit on the lifeguard tower right there, or I have a blanket to sit on the beach. If you feel safer, I can open the tailgate, and we can sit in the back of the truck. Figured you might want to look up at the stars, though. I sometimes come here when I need to get away from everything. You know, clear my head."

Abi opened the door. The cool breeze off the ocean made her wrap her jacket tightly around her. Meeting Shane at the rear of the truck, she surveyed their options. The lifeguard stand was less than ten feet from them. Tucking her hands under her arms, Shane could see she was cold.

Disappearing for a second, she heard him open the door and unzip a duffle bag before reappearing with a warm hoodie in hand.

"Here. Put this on. It'll keep you warm," he said.

"Thank you."

Shane helped her slip on his sweatshirt and thread her arms through the sleeves. The hood stayed on top of her head.

"Better?"

"Much." A bit big, she could smell the scent of Shane's cologne on it.

"It's clean, by the way."

She chuckled, "Good to know."

"So?" He waited for her to decide what to do.

Looking up at the clear sky, she said, "Definitely want to star-gaze from the beach."

Taking his hand, they trudged through the sand to a spot not far from the surf. Shane spread out the blanket while it flapped in the breeze.

She was the first to have a seat. Peering up at the heavens, she lay flat on her back. "This is so beautiful."

The view was captivating. So many twinkling specks were overhead, and the crescent moon looked magical.

Lying down beside her, he said, "Yes. Most never take the time to appreciate it."

"No, they don't." She felt lucky to have someone who felt the same. The little things in life meant a lot to her.

He inched closer and got her to lift her head.

She cuddled beside him while he encircled her tightly in his arms.

"You know, this is the first time we are totally alone," he whispered.

"What about at your house?"

Shane smirked. "There were cameras everywhere - eyes on us the entire time. It's another reason why I don't bring friends over."

He lifted his hand off his chest. Seeing it, Abi intertwined her fingers with his.

"Do you ever wonder what is out there?"

"Where? In the universe?"

"Yeah. You know, other planets, maybe countless other civilizations. Looking at the sky makes you feel pretty insignificant."

She loved the depth of his observation. "I often think of my place in the world - how to make a difference. Sometimes, it seems like an unreachable task. As for the universe, I guess we won't discover its secrets until that fateful day when we leave here."

"You think about that?"

"Sometimes. Especially now with my Mom..." Abi unexpectedly cowered into him.

Shane held onto her, hating to see her cry. "I will help you through this."

Tears streamed down her cheeks as she sobbed.

"It's okay. I got you."

Lying there in silence, he let her release the sadness in her heart.

Abi soon realized what she was doing. Abruptly drying her tears, she sat up. "I'm sorry. I guess this is the saddest date you've ever been on."

Sitting beside her, their shoulders touching, he replied, "No. It's the best date I've ever had."

"How can you say that?" She turned to him. "I fell asleep while we were driving here."

He interjected. "So, you needed a nap."

"We left the party super early because of me."

"I hate those things anyway. Nothing worse than being around drunk people and loud music."

"Now I'm here crying my eyes out."

"And for good reason. Why are you being so hard on yourself?"

She could feel her heart hammering, and the sound reached her eardrums. "In my mind, I wanted tonight to be perfect."

Lowering his head, he then turned to her. Seeing Abi's pretty face tucked inside the hood, he slowly slid it back, allowing her hair to blow freely in the breeze. Reaching to tuck a few strands behind her ear, he asked, "What makes you think it's not perfect?" Resting his right hand on the blanket behind her, propping himself up, he leaned in close. Looking into her eyes, he asked, "Where did you come from, Abi Acardi? It seems you showed up when I least expected." He gravitated to her, unable to defy the hold she had on him.

Abi watched his gaze bouncing between her eyes and lips as he inched even closer. Hearing nothing but the waves crashing along the shoreline, he lovingly brushed his cheek against hers.

The scent of her perfume along her neckline brought back memories of their week together. Waiting, drawing out the special moment with anticipation, Shane watched her eyes drift shut just before he kissed her.

As his lips washed across hers, she discovered his gentler side - a piece of him hidden behind the rugged exterior. A warmth spread through her from head to toe, causing her to shiver nervously. Never having been kissed, she relied on instinct, hoping it would not let her down. Barely able to catch her breath, she felt this bond - something she could never describe or explain. She trusted him wholeheartedly at that moment and believed he would never hurt her.

Reluctantly parting, Shane pressed his forehead to hers. Taken by a flood of emotions, he felt the need to save her from the grief engulfing her soul.

Hit by a gust of wind, she instinctively clung to him.

Now cheek to cheek, he quietly whispered, "I've wanted to do that all week."

"Why didn't you?" she blushed.

He leaned back. "Because I wanted it to be memorable. Not in a dingy parking garage, a library, or at my place," he paused. "I don't know if you are aware, but you are very different from other girls."

"Oh? How's that?" Her face brightened.

"You're the once-in-a-lifetime kind. The one you don't let get away."

Abi was speechless. What he said made her shyly burrow her face into the crease of his neck. Staying there for a second, she moved her sights to the sand below. "I can't believe you like me."

He inhaled and tried to contain himself. "I gotta say, I've fallen hard for you, Abs."

"You have?" Her heart lept.

"From the moment I saw you in the foyer at orientation, I knew I needed to meet you. So when I heard you'd be at Allie's party, I made sure I was there."

Surprised to hear that, she asked, "So, that wasn't by accident?"

"No. As soon as Reggie knew Jade was going, he was in too."

She grinned from ear to ear.

"Guess things worked out how they were supposed to."

Never having heard compliments like that from anyone, she replied, "I'm sorry. Umm, it's kinda strange to hear you say such nice things."

"Why? I'm sure you've had other guys try and sweep you off your feet?"

She subtly laughed and shook her head. "No. Not at all."

"What do you mean?" he questioned.

"Well, there haven't been any others."

"You never had a boyfriend back in Boston?"

"No."

"Ever?"

"No." She was nervous to admit it.

Shane looked out over the ocean, wondering how a pretty girl like her could go unnoticed. "Wait? So does that mean you've never, umm, kissed..."

She interjected. "Nope," feeling quite uncomfortable about the subject. Afraid to hear his thoughts, she focused on the stars overhead.

Clearing his throat, he cautiously asked, "So, you've never, umm, you know?"

Frozen, it took a second for her to respond. Fixated on her feet, sifting through the sand, she confirmed quietly, "No," before looking away.

"Hey." He took her hand in his. Weaving their fingers together, he said, "Abs, it's a good thing."

She innocently smiled. "Glad you think so."

Wanting to lighten the mood, he said, "Is there any chance that was your last first kiss?" Shane watched for her reaction.

Recalling the line from the movie Hitch, she raised her eyebrows. "Depends," she playfully countered.

"On what?"

"If you play your cards right."

"I'll make sure of it." Hugging her tightly, he lightly kissed her again.

She felt light as a feather. "I'm glad you know now. It's been weighing on me."

"Why? It shouldn't."

Abi nodded and rested her head on his shoulder.

While sitting in silence, Shane heard his phone ringing. Checking who it was, seeing Reggie's name, he answered on speakerphone. "Hey, man. What's up?"

"Hey, where are you?" There was an urgency to his tone. In the background, they could hear a commotion.

"I'm with Abi at the beach. We left the party a while ago. Why?"

"Eastwood is here. He said he has a score to settle with you. Apparently, the draft list came out. You've officially beaten him for the number one spot, and he's ticked off. Jade and I are leaving. Aramis called security. They are breakin' up the party and escorting Eastwood out as we speak. It's a crazy scene, man."

"Thanks for the heads-up."

"Just wanted to make sure you weren't gonna walk into this. I'll call you later."

"Sounds good." Shane had a million thoughts rolling through his head. He knew what Eastwood was capable of. "I think we should stay for a few more minutes, then get moving. I don't wanna run into him on the PCH."

Abi looked at the time. It was almost midnight. "I'm going to be severely late for curfew."

"I know. I'm sorry. If your Dad gets mad, say it's my fault. I'll take the heat for it."

"No, I'll tell him the truth. He'll understand," she said, recalling what Reggie had mentioned. "Congrats on the number one spot."

"Thanks," he replied. "Appreciate that."

"It's a big deal."

"Yes, but nothing is set in stone."

"It will open a lot of doors."

"Hope so." Overwhelmed, he checked the website and found his name at the top. To him, from that moment, the pressure was on. In need of a distraction, he said, "We'd better go back to the truck. We'll wait another fifteen minutes before leaving." Shane got up and offered his hand to help her to her feet. Carefully flapping the blanket to rid the sand, he rolled it up into a ball and walked with her hand in hand. Tossing it in the back, Shane closed the tailgate and jumped in beside her. He started the engine and put on a bit of heat to take the chill off the air.

"You probably want your hoodie back," Abi stated.

About to take it off, he stopped her.

"No. I want you to keep it."

"Are you sure?"

"Absolutely." Resting his elbow on the center console, he looked at her. Meeting him halfway this time, she placed her hand lovingly on his face and ran her thumb along his cheekbone. Confident enough to kiss him first, Abi felt Shane surrender to her touch. It wasn't hard to see she had become his only weakness.

When they parted, he said, "Guess we should get you home."

Under cover of night, he made a U-turn and drove back down Westward Beach Road to merge onto PCH, keeping his eyes peeled for Eastwood's custom Land Rover. Like his Jeep, it, too, was easy to spot.

"So, what did you think of the game today?"

"Truth?"

"Hit me. I can take it."

"I think you played pretty well, but...."

"But what?"

"You could've thrown a hail Mary to Alan in the first, then Reggie in the third. They were both wide open."

"I wish it was that simple. The coach calls the plays. I execute what he needs."

"Then I guess you have to go by what he says." Abi hesitated, then said, "You know what makes Tom Brady exceptional?"

"Precision, dedication, Football IQ?"

"Yes, that, and his ability to pick apart defenses to turn up the heat. His ability to perform in the pocket under an enormous amount of pressure. He's the hardest working guy out there." Abi tried to remember a quote of Brady's. "He says if you're going to compete against me...."

Shane nodded, knowing what she was about to say.

"You'd better be willing to give up your life because I'm giving up mine," they said simultaneously.

"Wow. Can't believe you know that." He was impressed.

"Brady is a natural-born leader who knows how to maximize the strength of his teammates. I see that quality in you. You've got Alan, Shawn, and Reggie out there. Today, Reg and Alan were open. But, in the clutch, you played it safe and went with what Coach said versus relying on instincts. Which I totally get, by the way. It's a tough thing to defy authority. I know. I'm not saying go against the plays given, but if you see an opportunity and it looks like a sure thing, you should have enough faith in your guys to execute. If it works out, the coach will praise you. If it doesn't, you work harder to gain the confidence to make that play again when it counts."

She could see Shane's mind reeling.

He was in awe of her knowledge.

"Look, I've obviously never been part of a football team. I don't know the coach/player relationship and where you stand with him. It's a big year for you. You have to impress the scouts at every game. The last thing you should do is ruffle feathers."

He took a deep breath. Expelling it, he replied, "Yeah. But you're right."

Giving his hand a few squeezes, she said, "You can do this. I believe in you."

"I think I mentioned before my parents have never been to one of my games. They don't even ask what the score was or how I did. Nothing. What you've just said, no one has ever told me." He glanced over and gave her this look. Picking up her hand, he brought it to his lips and kissed the back of it. "Thank you for believing in me."

"You're welcome," she said, looking straight ahead. "Without a doubt, you'll make it to the NFL, Shane Coppersmith."

"If that's the case, I want you by my side the whole way there."

"Well, then, I would be honored."

Approaching Sunset Boulevard, deciding to take it versus Highway 10, assuming it would be safer, he turned left. With every twist and turn, they climbed the hills.

Passing through the cutest shopping district, Abi said, "I wouldn't mind coming here during the day."

"This area is called the Palisades Village. It has a ton of shops and restaurants. Maybe we can visit on Sunday?"

Abi paused, knowing she was meeting Burton for their drive along PCH that day. Not wanting to ruin the date, she said, "Sure. Umm, I'll have to see how things go with my Mom. Not sure if Dad will need my help."

Almost forgetting about her situation, Shane replied, "No problem."

When stopping at the red light in front of the gates of Bel Air, Shane didn't want the night to end. In strange territory, he found himself not only cared for but highly motivated after his conversations with Abi.

Slowly rounding the corner to her house, he veered into her driveway as the gate remotely opened. Looking down at the clock on the dash, it read 1:10 am. Parking the truck, Shane turned off the engine. Getting out, they walked toward the door, hand in hand.

"Well, despite the party, I had an amazing time." Her eyes sparkled when she said it.

Standing there, he fiddled with her hands in his, but the words weren't coming to him. "Abi, there is so much I want to say." He took a deep breath and looked away before returning to her. "Tonight, I meant everything I said. I feel so lucky to have met you. You came into my life at the perfect time - it's like the universe knew when I'd need you the most." He leaned in to kiss her goodnight.

Out of nowhere, the pivot door swung open. Her Father stood there silently, flashing a stern expression.

"Dad?"

"You're late... Say goodnight." Not saying another word, he walked back into the house.

Stunned, Abi turned to Shane. "Umm, I'd better go," she said before mouthing the words, *Sorry. I will call you later.* She didn't want her Dad to hear.

The football player nodded, wishing he would have intervened and said something before her Father disappeared. "Night, Abs."

She stayed to watch him walk back to the Jeep. Waving, she waited until he turned left before closing the gate behind him. Abi took a deep breath, realizing she must now defuse her Father. While walking into the living room, she found him sitting on the sofa in the dark.

"You know you need to be home by midnight. It's after one o'clock." He still used a stern tone. "I've been sitting here wondering where you are and what you are doing."

"I wasn't doing anything wrong."

"I beg to differ."

"Look, I know you can always see where I am. I agreed to share my location in case something happens and I need you. I hope it's not because you don't trust me." She waited a moment, determined to tell him the truth. "Tonight, the football team won their game, and there was an afterparty out in Malibu hosted by Aramis and Lexi. Mom said I could go when I told her about it on Tuesday."

"Well, Mom's not...." He stopped himself.

"Regardless, the drive there was almost an hour. We only stayed twenty minutes. Shane just needed to make an appearance. He is not a fan of parties and crowds."

"Really?" Her Father found that hard to believe. An abundance of sarcasm in his tone reflected that. "That's not where I saw you."

Quite sure he didn't believe her, she said, "Afterward, we left and stopped at Zuma Beach to talk. He's a good guy with goals and a plan for the future. He just made the NCAA prospect list – the number one spot. He comes from a good family, even though they are not supportive or present. We have this strange connection. It's actually an intellectual one–I mean..." Abi's face brightened. "I can't explain it," she said before whimsically plopping herself on the sofa.

After what had transpired the past twenty-four hours, he was secretly thankful to see her so happy.

"I'm sorry that I got home late. It won't happen again. I know you're under enormous stress with Mom and don't need me complicating things. It's just...." Abi giggled subtly. "I can't believe this is my life right now. Despite everything going on," she said with tears developing, "It's like a fairy tale, Dad."

He lowered his head, knowing he trusted his daughter and her judgment. She had never given him a reason not to.

Calming down, he said, "I'm glad to have you home safe. Let's get some sleep. We can talk about this more tomorrow."

"Alright." Hugging him tightly, she said, "I love you."

His heart melted upon hearing her say that. "Love you too, Sweetheart. Goodnight."

"Night."

Abi walked away and ascended the stairs to her room while her Dad made the rounds and checked all the doors. Quickly slipping into her bathroom and locking it behind her, she went into the water closet and closed that door. Calling Shane, she heard the phone ring. Suddenly, he picked up.

"Abs? Hey, is everything okay?"

"Yes. Everything's fine. He's disappointed in me. Kinda feel awful."

"I'm sorry. We should've come back sooner."

She paused. "But then our night would have turned out differently."

"True." There was silence on his end.

"What is it?" she asked.

"It's just...the moment I drove away, I kinda missed you already."

What he said took her breath away. "I miss you too. Hopefully, we will get to see each other tomorrow."

"So, at this point, will he even let you go out?"

Thinking about it, she said, "I don't have to convince him to trust me. He just does." Abi exhaled. "I'll have to see how things go in the morning. I will let you know."

"If we don't make it to Black Lyon, it's not the end of the world."

"I know, but I paid a lot for the ticket." Abi knew she'd have to come up with a plan. "It's late. You should get to bed. We will talk about this more tomorrow. Thank you for tonight. You lifted my spirits and helped me think about something else. I really had fun."

"Me too." He was pulling up to his house.

"Night, Shane. I'll text you in the morning."

"Sounds good. Night, Abs. Sweet dreams."

Saying goodbye, with her heart all aflutter, Abi ended the call and left her bathroom. Getting ready for bed, having changed into her pajamas, she walked over to the window. The mansion across the canyon was all ablaze. Turning off her desk light, she looked out the window again, only to see the mansion lights go off simultaneously.

Tired, Abi slipped under the covers and closed her eyes. Recalling her night with Shane, she relived the special moments they shared.

While clutching her pillow, she couldn't contain her smile. Despite the rough few days, it was the happiest she'd ever been.

# 34

# Permission

By eleven that morning, Abi had electronically received her QR code on the Black Lyon App, dated for one night only. Lying in bed, she read the instant message. It mentioned she'd receive another notification divulging the pickup coordinates by seven o'clock. Not sure what that meant, she texted Shane, assuming he'd be up. *Morning! Hope you slept well!  Received my BLyon QR. Did you?* She watched and waited.

It took a minute for his response bubbles to activate before a message suddenly popped up. *Yes, I got mine, too.*

With a million questions running through her head, she asked, *So what's so special about these parties, anyway?*

Waiting and waiting for his response, she figured he was typing a long list of reasons. Then, he replied, *Well, for one, they are usually 'the' party to be at. The guest list is pretty exclusive. Getting a ticket is rare unless you've made it into certain social circles. Not just anyone gets in. Some of those who attend use it as a social networking tool.*

This new world she found herself in was confusing and unfamiliar. Why would anyone have to attend a party to enhance their social net-working? *What do you mean by - made it? Aren't most just a bunch of rich kids wanting to party?*

Awaiting a response, she thought about what she should wear tonight. In the process, his repetitive bubbles stopped, and her phone rang.

Answering it, she said, "Hello."

"Hey. I thought it would be easier to talk than type." He sounded tired. Pausing a second, he referred to her last text. "So, networking? Rich kids? Yeah." Gathering his thoughts, he said, "It's much more than that. They aren't just a bunch of entitled heirs. Elites have power, influence, and money. Those who attend Gilderson will eventually carry the torch and their family's legacy. It's a lot of pressure. Why do you think we have a different curriculum than other high schools? The skills we're learning will carry us further than basic math, science, and literature. We are acquiring what's needed to survive in the corporate world. Eventually, after our time there, most students will not attend university. They are placed with a mentor chairman and assigned a title within the company. That is when the real studying begins – hands-on, in-the-trenches kinda stuff. They will learn from the best of the best. It's a different path than the brainwashed worker ants toiling nine to five to make someone else wealthy."

Abi analyzed what he said. "But you and I aren't part of that realm. Your parents and mine don't own companies on that scale."

"My Dad is an entertainment lawyer. He's a major shareholder in the firm. If he had his way, he would prefer I join him than play NFL football."

"I see..." she said. "My Dad always told me he would consider his parenting a success if I grew up happy and settled in a fulfilling career."

"That kind of parent is incredibly rare."

Thinking more about the Black Lyon rave, Abi recalled how the girls fawned over the idea of going. "So, why are all the girls excited to attend this thing?"

"Because they need to solidify their place in this society. Some are assigned tasks to merge with other families and expand the family business."

"Merge? What do you mean merge?"

He chuckled at her naivety. "It means marrying into a family whose business would benefit their corporation. You know, merge or collaborate with other companies to build a major conglomerate."

"But they are just kids. What do they know about conglomerates?"

"Oh, Abs…" he laughed. "Reggie's parents are a good example. They've incorporated him into the family's twenty-year forecast. They want him to merge with this one girl's family eventually, so their relationship will open the door for his father to launch a subsidiary in a new and innovative space. But you didn't hear that from me."

"So, this girl is not Jade?"

Shane stayed quiet. "Seriously, Abs… If he knew I told you… Let's just say it would be the worst betrayal ever."

"Don't worry. I won't say a word."

"The thing is, he really, really likes Jade. He has for a while. He isn't interested in that other girl and secretly hopes this ridiculous expectation blows over. But none of his life's decisions are his own."

"That's terrible. So, he's not free to love whom he wants to love?" Abi heard Shane sigh.

"Correct. It sucks."

"So, what should I expect tonight?"

"It's best to go into it without expecting anything and roll with the punches. If you stick with me, you'll be fine. If your Dad lets you go out, I'll pick you up around seven. We will head to Reggie's first and pick up Jade along the way."

Abi rolled over on her side. "Once I speak to him, I'll text you."

"Sounds good. We'll chat soon, then," he replied. "Bye."

"Bye." Putting down the phone, she had no idea what to wear. Remembering she'd bought a few dresses when shopping with Jade, she texted for advice. *Can you talk?* In seconds, the phone rang. "Hello?" she said.

"Hey, how are you doing today? Any better?"

Abi had mixed feelings. "Yes and no."

"Oh… What's wrong?"

"Last night, I kinda got home really late."

"Does that mean you have news to share?" she giggled.

Knowing her friend was fishing, she replied, "Maybe...."

"Woohoo!" Jade assumed she had her first kiss finally.

"No, not woohoo."

"What!" She was borderline frantic. "He didn't kiss you?"

"Yes, he did."

"Amazing! I'm so happy! And?"

"And we had an incredible night. I can't even tell you how much fun it was."

"Awww, that's great."

"Then I came home and dealt with the repercussions."

"Was your Dad mad?"

"That's an understatement," Abi said frustratingly.

"Oh no...How bad? Like mediocre or raise the roof?"

"I was an hour and ten minutes past curfew."

"Okay, I would say that is mediocre." She tried to play it down.

"Long story short, I don't know if I can go out tonight."

"Nooo...are you kidding me?" she whined before backtracking to ask the obvious question. "But, you feel up to going out, right? No tears today?"

"So far, no. But it's still early. I cried so much yesterday - don't think I have anything left."

Thinking about her Mom down the hall and her Dad, who was probably downstairs, Abi wasn't a hundred percent sure what to do. She felt pulled in two directions and needed to strike a balance somewhere.

"I guess I'll be home most of the day with them. Maybe it'll be okay to see all of you later tonight for a couple of hours?"

"Well, if you don't go, I'm not going. And if that happens, Reg and I are expected to attend my Dad's housewarming party in Calabasas with his live-in girlfriend. Not exactly how I want to spend my Saturday night."

"I get it." Looking in her closet, she asked, "So, I called because I need your help. If I get permission to go out, what do I wear?"

Jade immediately scrolled through the pictures of Abi's outfits. Sending her a photo, she said, "It's a high-end crowd, so you need to flaunt without overstating. Definitely wear this plain LBD with the Burberry belt. Maybe the Maje cropped tweed jacket. And because you don't need to impress anyone, no offense, I don't think you need a heel. Pretty sure you can get away with the sneakers. I think that would be cute, but I'd have to see a picture when you get dressed. I'm concerned that the ivory jacket will clash with the white on your feet. Wearing the neutral flats and matching crossbody bag might be better."

Seeing what she picked out for her, Abi pulled each piece. "Okay. Got it."

"Remember to send me a pic. I want to see."

With a deep breath, Abi exhaled and said, "For sure. Will do. Have to see if I can get permission first."

"Well, you'd better go figure that out. Call me back."

"Yeah, I'll talk to you soon."

The girls ended their call. After hanging the clothes on the hook, Abi walked to her bed and fell back into it. Not sure what she was getting herself into tonight, she thought, worst case scenario, if she went, she hoped to have fun and return home unscathed.

Hearing activity downstairs, Abi left her room, stopped, and walked down the hall. Peeking in, she saw the nurse taking her Mom's vitals. Standing there quietly, the lady changed the IV bag.

*If she's getting fluids, it's not a good sign.* She thought.

Finding her father downstairs in the kitchen brewing a cup of coffee, he turned when he heard footsteps. Upon seeing her there, he smiled. "Good morning. Sleep well?"

"Yes. I suppose."

Taking the coffee from the machine, he opened the fridge to get the cream. After pouring some, he raised it silently, wondering if she wanted it.

"Umm, yeah. I'll have one. But you go ahead." Abi got a mug from the cupboard and put a coffee pod in the machine. Pressing the brew button, she wasn't sure where things stood between them. "I saw they've got Mom on a steady IV."

Her Dad stopped. "Yes. We didn't want her getting dehydrated. It's also easier to administer her pain medication intravenously."

"Has she gotten up at all? It seems like days since she's been out of bed."

"The nurse usually got her to the bathroom every few hours, but now we are contemplating other measures."

"Is she talking? I mean, is she still in there somewhere?"

He knew she was scared. "When you sit with her, ask a question. She'll squeeze your hand. I've seen her sometimes nod or shake her head."

Abi turned her back to him. "How long?" she asked, dropping her sights to the floor, dreading the answer.

"It could be a few weeks, maybe a month or two. It's progressing." He hated to be so blunt. "She will have to go into palliative soon. They will be able to provide better care."

Tears developed in Abi's eyes as she tried to compose herself.

"You aren't alone in this, Abi. I'm here. We must be strong for her. Give her every ounce of love we can give. And when the time comes, we need to let her go."

Droplets flooded her face. Turning around abruptly, she clung to her father.

He held her tight and courageously comforted her despite his world crumbling, too.

Composing herself, she looked away. "Sorry…"

"Don't ever be sorry. You can't keep things bottled up inside. You need to expel these feelings, or they'll fester and consume you."

She knew he was right.

To distract her, he asked, "So, what is on the agenda today?"

Unable to tell him the truth, she said, "I plan to be home most of the day. I was supposed to attend my friend Jade's housewarming party. You know, her parents got a divorce, and now she lives in two places. Her Dad and his girlfriend moved into a new house in Calabasas. It's a dressy thing." She hated herself for lying.

"Well, you should go then. Better you get out of the house versus wallowing around here."

"Are you sure? 'Cause I can stay." The guilt she was feeling was overwhelming.

"No. No. You go. I'm catching up on work, anyway."

"Okay."

Before sitting in the family room, he turned and asked, "So... Is that football player picking you up?"

She tilted her head. "Dad, that football player has a name."

"Right... What is it again?"

"Shane Coppersmith."

"Oh, yes, hmm." Careful of how he should say it, he questioned, "I assume he will have you home on time this evening?"

"We will, Dad."

"That's good. I'm trusting him - and you."

"I know."

Not saying another word, he turned on the television to catch the football highlights while opening his laptop.

Abi took her coffee and headed back upstairs to her room. Setting the cup on the side table, she sat on the bed and looked at the ceiling. "You're a horrible daughter. This is why Hell exists. It's for people who do this kinda stuff. Arrggh. God help me." She collapsed backward and reluctantly texted Shane. *Looks like I can go tonight.* Waiting for his response, she texted the same to Jade.

Of course, her friend was the first to reply. *Awesome! See you soon!*

Her phone rang.

"Hello?" she answered.

"Hey. That's good news," Shane said. "How did you manage that?"

A sinking feeling swept over her. "I, umm, told him we were going to Jade's for the housewarming party. The part about her Dad's party is true." She stopped and spouted, "I hate myself. What am I doing?"

"Yeah, that's not good."

"I know. Don't think badly of me. I just don't want him to worry."

"I get it. But promise me, after this, we're not going to any more raves. For me, I can't afford for things to go wrong. It could cost me everything. This is your first and last, okay?"

She nodded her head. "I'm good with that."

"All right. I'll see you at seven."

35 |

## Emotions

That afternoon, having finished her homework, Abi took her Dad's advice and went to sit with her Mom. Reaching the doorway, she peered inside and caught the nurse's attention.

"Is it okay if I..." Abi motioned to her, unable to finish her sentence.

The woman understood what she wanted. "Of course, dear. Come in. I'll leave you." She passed by with a sorrow-infused expression, feeling sorry for the young girl, knowing her Mother had limited time.

It made Abi feel worse for not being around more the past week. But when she was outside the house, it seemed like her world wasn't imploding. Somehow, it helped her deal with the inevitable pain and feeling of loss.

Standing at the foot of her Mother's bed, she saw her sleeping peacefully. She seemed almost angelic, positioned on her back with her hands folded over her stomach and head elevated on a few pillows. Inching towards the chair beside her, Abi had a seat, afraid to hold her hand. Despite having so much news to share, she stayed quiet. It was hard to think about anything happy. Abi sighed. How she wished she could tell her about her date with Shane and their first kiss.

Recalling their conversation when her Mother was in the tub almost a week ago, she whispered, "Things changed in a blink." She reached out and touched her Mom's hand. There was no movement and no reaction. Caressing her arm, Abi felt a tear drift down her cheek, which she quickly wiped away with her sleeve.

"I love you," she said before leaving her to rest - what she would give to hear her say it back.

Passing by the nurse standing in the hall, Abi thanked her. Upon returning to her room, she sat on her bed and cried. Burying her face in the pillow, she allowed herself to expel as much emotion as possible. Not knowing how to gather the strength to have fun tonight, she rolled over and dried her cheeks after catching a glimpse of her outfit hanging on the hook.

"If you don't pull yourself together, you will put a damper on everything. Nobody will want to be around you, just like in Boston. You are not going to let this happen." Forcing herself to get up and shower, she checked her phone. Shane was due to arrive in a couple of hours. "Now, get ready and stop feeling sorry for yourself."

# 36

# Saturday Night

After her shower, Abi quickly got dressed and snapped a pic for Jade as promised. Within seconds, her friend texted and sent a few fire emojis and the word *Perfect.* She liked the neutral flats versus the sneakers. Abi thought they suited the outfit best.

Knowing Shane would be there shortly, she texted him and warned, *Just FYI, if my Dad talks to you – remember, we are meeting up with a group of friends to attend Jade's Dad's housewarming.*

Upon reading her text, he immediately called her.

Abi answered the phone. "Hey.  Are you almost here?"

"Yeah, umm, I just turned onto Stradella." Pausing, he asked, "Shouldn't we just say we are going to a party?"

"Exactly, a housewarming party." She was not in the mood to deal with drama. "If I say anything else, he'll get mad or just worry."

"I hate lying, Abs."

"I know. After this, that's it. I'm not going out anymore. I'm not sneaking around or anything like that. But, for now, I have to keep it vague. It's what's best."

"Fine. For what it's worth, I agree with you 100%. I need to pull back, too. All I want to focus on is football, school, and us. Nothing else."

"Let's just get through the night."

"Agreed." Driving up to her gate, he said, "I'm here. Can you let me in?"

"Sure. I'll be there in a second." Abi pressed the button on the app. "The gate should be opening now." Ending the call, she grabbed what she needed and took one last look in the mirror before bounding down the stairs.

Receiving a notification that someone had arrived, her Dad walked toward the front door just as she rounded the corner. "Well, don't you look nice?"

"Thanks," she said to him.

"Make sure your ringer is on."

"It is."

Intent on meeting Shane outside, she opened the door and found him standing six feet away. He was dressed impeccably in designer jeans, sneakers, and a linen shirt with sleeves rolled up to his elbows. Abi thought he looked so handsome.

"Hello, Mr. Acardi," he said, "It's nice to see you."

"That's Dr. Acardi."

Shane's heart sank.

"Dad?" Abi was mortified.

"Sorry, Sir." The football player stood tall with his hands positioned behind his back.

"It's fine."

Hoping her father wouldn't embarrass her anymore, she caught a stern look directed her way before his eyes swayed to Shane. "I trust you will have my daughter home by midnight. I don't want a repeat of last night."

Remembering what Abi said about keeping it short, Shane replied, "Apologies, Sir. We lost track of time. Won't happen again."

"Yes, I heard you were star-gazing at Zuma Beach. Hope that is all you were doing?"

"Dad?" Stunned by his straightforwardness, Abi didn't know what to say.

Shane held Abi back. "No, Abs, it's okay." Addressing her father, Shane tactfully replied, "I will have her back by midnight, Dr. Acardi."

With a deep breath, he gathered the courage to add, "I hope you know your daughter is very responsible, caring, and considerate. I would never do anything to harm her."

Impressed with Shane's sincerity, he thought either the guy was genuinely a good kid, or he was skilled at deceiving a parent. Turning to Abi, he knew he trusted her and felt confident everything would be fine. "Go have fun. Back by midnight."

Receiving a hug, Abi replied, "We will. Thanks."

Before departing, Shane stepped forward with an outstretched hand. "Have a good evening, Sir."

Pulling the teen close with their hands still joined, he quietly clarified, "I'm trusting you with my little girl."

Not flinching an inch, Shane nodded. "I understand."

"Good." He gave Shane a pat on the back.

Joining Abi in the courtyard, he escorted her to the passenger side and opened the Jeep's door before slipping in behind the wheel.

Casually waving goodbye to the stern-looking man, she whispered, "Just look normal."

Doing that, the two inched out onto Stradella Road and drove south.

"Wow. That was intense." Abi sighed in relief.

"No, he's right, you know."

"Really?"

"Of course. You're his only daughter; in his eyes, I'm the Big Bad Wolf."

"But, you're not, though."

"You know that. But he doesn't. I've gotta prove otherwise." Shane was dead serious.

"You'd do that?"

"Absolutely. I have to win him over and earn his trust."

She laughed. "Who are you? Most guys would not even attempt it."

"I'm your first boyfriend and the best you will ever have," he teased.

"I'll hold you to that," she giggled playfully.

The handsome quarterback kept his eyes on the road and stopped at Sunset Boulevard, just outside the gates of Bel Air. Leaning her way, looking for a kiss, she gave him what he was expecting. With one eye on the light, he waited for it to turn green. Veering left, they headed to Reggie's house to pick him up.

While approaching Foothill Drive, Shane slowed down and signaled before turning onto the street lined with iconic palm trees. Each house was estate-size. Using it to loop around and reach the Mountian Drive enclave, they soon arrived at their destination.

"Reggie's place is right here."

Not seeing much of it while Shane inched toward the main gate, Abi noticed a lot of glass windows.

Pressing the intercom button, they heard their friend shout, "Hey, man! Come on in!"

The gate slowly opened, allowing them access. Moving up the incline, Abi was in awe. The massive home on the corner lot looked more like a hotel than a house. Pulling up to the front entrance, they saw Reggie exiting the door surrounded by a thirty-foot glass wall. He looked small in comparison to it.

Seeing his friend dressed in monotone Fendi from head to toe, Shane said, "This guy's style puts me to shame."

Energetically opening the back door, he jumped in. Reaching out, he tapped Shane on the shoulder. "Thanks for picking me up, man."

"No problem."

"You look great, Abi." Leaving his place, using the second driveway, Reggie remotely opened the gate for them to slip through.

"You're looking pretty good yourself." She was still captivated by his home. "Your place is amazing."

He humbly replied, "Maybe Jade and I will have you guys over to hang this week."

Knowing what was inside the mansion, Shane humorously said, "Yeah, we can go bowling?"

Abi immediately fell into the trap. "Wait? You have a bowling alley?"

Reg shot Shane a look. "Technically speaking, I own nothing. My parents, on the other hand, invested well."

Before leaving Reggie's street, Shane asked, "So, do you have Jade's Dad's new address on you? Where are we headed?"

His friend scrolled through his phone and said, "Yeah, I have it right here."

Copying the address into the GPS, Shane watched as it calculated the route. It's an hour away, dude. Is that right?"

"What are you complaining about? Thought the pick-up location was only fifteen minutes from her place. Am I wrong?"

"No. I think you're right, Reggie," Abi confirmed, showing them her phone. "It's in a corporate park off Thousand Oaks."

"That's what I thought."

Shane secured his phone in the holder.

"Come on, man. We've gotta pick up my Baby!" he laughed before tapping Abi on the shoulder. "So, ready to experience your first Black Lyon rave?"

"Guess so…" she said less enthusiastically. "A bit nervous."

"You'll love it. Just enjoy the music, dance, and stay away from the bar."

"I'll keep that in mind."

Northbound on the 405, the sun was setting along the horizon to their left. By the time they reached Jade's Dad's posh community called The Oaks, there was hardly a hint of orange left in the sky as the clouds rolled in.

Reggie texted to say they were close. "I haven't been here yet, but apparently, her Dad bought a house right beside Kourtney Kardashian's old place."

Abi turned and said, "You're kidding?"

"Nope. From what she said, hers is on the left before Jade's Dad's."

Realizing he was serious, she marveled at the cobblestone decoratively embedded in the streets and the perfectly spaced trees along the route.

Shane slowed down as they approached the newly built modern mansion. Expensive cars lined the street with three valets on hand to park the guests' vehicles.

"Wow. Looks like we're missing one hell of a party," Reggie said.

Passing the house, Shane turned his Jeep around. He stopped along the curb and got as close to the house as possible.

Black-trimmed windows stood out against the white stucco exterior. All the lights inside were ablaze to show off every beautifully designed room. The dark gray stacked-stone accent wall in front complemented the deep purple foliage and looked picture-perfect.

"She's on her way," Reggie confirmed, jumping out of the Jeep to go and meet her.

Alone, Shane turned to Abi. "Guess there's some truth to saying you were going to your friend's housewarming."

What he said made her feel horrible again. She'd lied to her Dad despite the intention of saving him from worrying about her. The bottom line was – what she was doing was wrong.

Seeing Jade lovingly greet Reggie with multiple kisses and a hug, Abi noticed she was dressed head to toe in Fendi to match Reggie. The tight white monotone midi skirt had a matching cropped halter. To offset the femininity of the outfit, she layered a cropped black leather moto jacket and edgy designer biker boots to finish the look.

Reggie opened the door for her when they reached the Jeep and helped her get in.

"Hey, guys! Ready to party?" Jade said, all hyped.

Abi tried to remain positive. "I guess so. You look amazing, Jade."

"So do you!"

"Thank you," she said humbly.

Shane pulled away and threaded them through the residential streets back to the highway. Following the GPS, it led them across Mureau Road to a corporate park with two modern glass buildings surrounded by high-end cars and tons of security everywhere.

"Guess this is the place. Black Lyon must have rented the lot from the company. That's genius. If he's on private property, the cops can't do anything about it," Shane said.

Quickly getting out to check in with security, Reggie led Jade to the Black Lyon coach bus. Having done this before, he knew the drill.

Shane found Abi out of sorts. "Having second thoughts?" he asked.

She ignored his question. "So, how does this work? We take a bus to get there?"

"Yes," he said while locking his truck. "We show our QR to security and then drive to a secret location."

"Where?"

"Nobody knows." Seeing the uncertainty on her face, he said, "Hey, Abi, listen. We don't have to do this. You say the word, and we'll do something else tonight. Maybe go to the Palisades Village if you like, then we'll pick up Reggie and Jade together if it's not too late."

Surveying the activity around them, Abi watched the partygoers, mostly admiring the expensive cars parked there. Some had gathered in groups to socialize before checking in and boarding the bus. It all seemed harmless enough. Not crazy and out of control.

"No, it's okay. Let's go."

"If you're sure?" Questioning again, Shane hesitated before taking hold of her hand.

Abi nodded. "Yeah. I'm sure."

The two walked over to the closest security guard, dressed in black. He held an iPad in his hand and refused to smile. Since his size was overly intimidating, Abi figured that was why things seemed so calm. Nobody wanted to mess with any of them.

Pulling out their phones and showing the man their QR codes for the event, he scanned each with a beep. Another screen appeared on the man's device.

"Agree to the terms of service. Place your pointer finger on the box," the burly man said without emotion.

Both of them did as he asked. Abi felt like she had just sold her soul.

"Proceed," he said before directing them toward the ominous matte black luxury coach.

Outside the door, about to board, Shane offered for Abi to go first.

"No," she immediately declined. "You go first. I'll follow you."

He climbed the stairs, still clutching Abi's hand tightly. The volume inside was intense. Everyone was hyped.

"Hey, Shane!" Reggie shouted, pointing to the empty seats adjacent to them.

The bus was packed. Shuffling down the aisle, the group chanted, "QB! QB! QB!"

Shane confidently moved to the back of the bus, where they saw Aramis sitting with Lexi. Not far from them, surrounded by his private security, Taizo had a blonde model hanging off of him, and so did Blu.

While inching past the rows, Abi happened to spot Shiri and Shiresse. Their long, bleached blonde hair was hard to miss. Knowing the twins always traveled in packs, she knew Emile wasn't far away. Right then, she found the girl seated by the window beside Mandy.

When the ex-girlfriend saw Shane, she looked at him before her eyes moved disgustingly to the two holding hands. If looks could kill, Abi would be dead.

Shane caught it.

Abi felt him squeeze her hand a couple of times to reassure her. Intent on keeping her head held high, Abi tried to act confident.

A few rows behind the posse, she spotted Adrian. To her surprise, the girl sitting beside him was Mei. Entirely focused on her pretty friend, the rugged football player looked happy. Abi could tell it was their first date since Mei bashfully giggled at everything he said while Adrian kept a safe distance from her.

Next was Laney - all over Shawn. Not surprised that the girl had moved fast with the wide receiver, Abi chuckled to herself on the way past. She didn't think he had it in him.

Seeing most of the Gilderson grade twelves helped calm her nerves.

Needing the legroom, Shane offered Abi the window seat. Immediately, she noticed the black painted glass on the inside. Running her finger over it, she turned to Shane, afraid of what she'd gotten herself into. "What is this?' she asked fearfully.

Not phased, Shane explained, "As I said, it's a secret location. This prevents people from knowing where we're going. Also, FYI, the bus jams your phone signal. None of our devices work in here or at the rave location."

While Reggie and Jade laughed and talked with Alan and Allie, Abi could tell Allie was nervous, too. Panicked, she knew her Dad wouldn't be able to see her location or contact her. An overwhelming sinking feeling took over, causing her stomach to hurt. About to tell Shane she wanted to leave, she hoped he wouldn't hate her. But just then, the bus started to move. Almost unable to breathe, she knew there was no going back now.

Cowering in her seat as the bus rocked back and forth, a security guard stood firm in the aisle. Behind him was a closed set of black drapes, which nobody could see out of.

"Are you good?" Shane asked, glancing over at her, biting the nails on her right hand.

Hesitating before answering, she tried to put on a brave face. "Yeah, umm... Can I ask you something?"

"Sure."

"So, when we get there, we can leave whenever we want?"

He nodded. "Yes. I think the shuttle runs at forty-five-minute intervals."

"Alright," she said, calming down. *It's okay,* she told herself. *Just chill out. He'll leave whenever you want to go.*

Holding her hand, giving it a few more encouraging squeezes, he said, "Don't worry. I will stay beside you the whole time. You're safe with me." Leaning over, he looked into her eyes. "Do you trust me?"

She smiled. "Yes."

When he kissed her lips, her heart melted. Cuddled beside him, she took a deep breath and tried to relax.

# 37

# Black Lyon

When the bus came to a stop, one by one, the rows emptied as people filed out. Shane stood up when it was their turn and kept Abi close. Standing behind her, wrapping his arms around her waist, they waited for the line to move.

"Ready?" he asked. His cheek was tight against hers.

Nervous, she replied, "Ready as I'll ever be."

"So, will you dance with me?"

She glimpsed up at him before bashfully lowering her head. "Normally, I don't, but I will make an exception."

"Happy to hear that," he said, hugging her tightly.

Hand in hand, they stepped off the bus. Abi was in awe of the modern mansion. Up-lit trees and strobes of light brought the grassy hillsides to life. They could see the top of a concert-worthy stage shining behind the structure. The black exterior was in contrast to the white walls scantily illuminated inside. The main door, surrounded by glass walls, was wide open and framed with gigantic real-life trees resembling a ghostly-looking forest. Above it, the hologram word Nightfall was rotating mid-air amidst the branches. Many guests stopped to take pictures with a twenty-foot-high tree trunk covered in mossy roots. With two big googly eyes and an open mouth with razor-sharp teeth, it resembled the face of an ape who had been mystically trapped inside the tree by an evil spell. Abi heard some people say that the artist Djedgepod created the set design. She wondered who he was and how he conjured up such a creature.

As everyone began moving inside, security was on high alert. The football team gathered around out front with the girls before walking through the eerie entrance as a group. In the foyer, every corner was accent-lighted. The black leather benches and custom-made furniture scattered around gave it a nightclub feel, but the place looked like a horror movie set. It was as if the darkness had taken over. DeviantArt characters hid in the shadows of each room, hauntingly. A large tree in the middle of the house had webs cascading from it while unearthly hologram creatures spied on them.

Abi peered up at the balcony riddled with climbing vines. There, flanked by security on either side, was a tall, muscular man dressed in black from head to toe. With a hood covering his head and a bandana across his face, his presence added to the ominous atmosphere as he looked down as they passed.

"Is that him?" Abi asked Shane.

"Who?"

"Black Lyon."

"Not sure," he shouted in her ear to battle the noise.

Proceeding to the back, following the flow of the crowd, Shane held onto Abi as they walked through a dark tunnel of arched, mangled trees. Scared, she saw red and yellow eyes, watching them inch past. When they reached the end, her eyes gravitated upward and panned the incredible scene unfolding, not knowing where to focus first. The one-hundred-and-eighty-degree wrap-around stage covered the enormous perimeter of the property. Draped industrial scaffolding featured LED walls on top and bottom, showcasing videos with a sinister theme. Multi-dimensional holograms of mountains, lightning flashes, storm clouds, and other-worldly moons were so real she felt like she could reach up and touch them. Snow fell intermittently from the sky while fog machines produced a thick mist that meandered across the ground, hiding their feet. The pool water danced with colorful lights. Lined by a creepy forest along the infinity edge, beyond that, she could peer through the thicket and see the hills alive with lasers, giving depth to the canyon.

Taking center stage was a Black Lyon head derived from his logo. It housed the DJ's platform accented by video screens, bringing it to life.

"This is insane," Abi yelled in Shane's ear as he looked down at her.

Smiling, he nodded as the three hologram moons of different sizes rose above them. An eclipsing star cast a beam of light over the crowd. Abi felt like she was on another planet.

To their left, three VIP areas were sectioned off and guarded by burly security guards. First was a gathering of liberal Saudi men dressed in traditional thawb and head scarves. Each had a beautiful woman draped in an intricately beaded kaftan. Sitting, lightly bobbing their heads, enjoying the show, they inhaled from a jewel-encrusted hookah on the table while immersed in their devices. Another VIP area looked to be hosting a guy's twenty-first birthday. That good-looking, testosterone-filled group kept pulling pretty girls from the crowd to join their celebration. Adjacent to them were partiers who looked like K-Pop stars. The guys and girls with picture-perfect bodies, skin, and hair were dripping in designer labels from head to toe and obsessively taking pictures. Impressed by the mix of people, Abi thought it wasn't as bad as she thought it would be.

*This was what everyone was excited about. It wasn't only the music but the magical experience that went along with it. No wonder the DJ has a lottery for tickets,* Abi thought.

She understood now why it was the place to be. This was beyond anything she could've ever expected. It was hard to fathom the scale of an event like this. Just the creative team alone used to build such elaborate sets must have cost a fortune, not to mention the tech required to build and operate the holograms, sound, lighting, and screen animations.

Gathering around the massive stage, Abi spotted Black Lyon hiding beneath his hood. Focused, thumping to the beat, he showcased his craft. The music lulled everyone into a trance, mixing songs with energetic or repetitive melodic tunes, making her forget her worries and the pain she was experiencing. Giving off an Armin Van Buuren vibe, everyone around them swayed engagingly. It was like a musical journey —an emotional ride encompassing all your senses.

Shane stood behind her. Wrapping his arms around her waist, he pulled her in tightly. As the music climaxed, five hundred people jumped rhythmically in unison with their hands in the air, cheering.

Feeling Shane's lips beside her ear, he yelled, "So, what do you think?"

Unable to shout above the noise, she gave a double thumbs up.

Happy to see all their friends dancing and having fun, Abi turned to face Shane. Reaching her arms around his neck, they moved with the beat. She could feel the ground vibrating beneath her feet as the lights and lasers flooded overhead. It was wild.

Sweating - needing a break, they ventured inside with their friends. Abi followed closely behind Shane as he carved a path. Along the way, she spotted Emile and her posse drinking with guys clinging to them. Around the elaborate bar, the servers frantically poured cocktails in droves. Some ten at a time simultaneously.

People socialized with matte black cups in hand and hung around the many modern seating areas throughout the house. Despite the rave scene, a cluster of thirty-somethings in suits and designer dresses stood out in contrast to most. The Gilderson students blended seamlessly and gravitated to an open-air room adjacent to the ghostly tree in the entry-way. Still able to hear the music, they could almost understand what each was saying.

Abi happened to look over at Reggie. His face went stoic. She followed his line of sight, wondering what prompted the intense stare, and noticed Eastwood and his goons walking through the door.

Quickly hitting Shane's chest with the back of his hand to get his attention, Reg pointed at their nemesis.

"Coop!" Eastwood's voice shouted above the music.

Right on cue, the football team created a strong barrier between them and the girls.

The suave Oligarch, accompanied by four scantily clothed young women, lifted his hands to push them away. Arrogantly approaching, Eastwood and his guys countered the football team's strategic formation.

Almost face to face, he said tauntingly, "Missed you at the party last night. You and I have unfinished business."

"Look!" Shane shouted, noticing the guy's eyes drift past him.

Locked onto Abi, he smirked creepily. "Well. Well. Well. You brought your new little tart!"

The comment fueled Shane's anger, causing him to straighten his body and drive his fist into his opposite palm. "What'd you say?"

"Oh! A little protective of this one, are we? Better hold onto her. I'm sure you don't want a repeat of last year."

Sleezily scanned by Eastwood from head to toe, Abi knew the guy's intentions. Hearing Shane tell him off vulgarly, the rest of the football team, including Blu, Taizo, and their security, joined to ward off a fight.

Outnumbered, Eastwood signaled for his group to move on. They were there to do business. Nothing more.

When they had gone to the bar, Shane turned and held onto Abi. "Are you okay?" he asked, his lips melded to her ear.

"Yeah."

"You stick close to me. Don't go anywhere by yourself."

She nodded as a stroke of fear rattled her spine.

Thankfully, their friends did not return to the stage. As the rave escalated, a stench filled the air.

"What is that smell?" Abi naively asked him.

Shane said. "It's weed."

Witnessing Eastwood exchanging goods for money, she knew he was a dealer. During a few swaps, Abi caught him intrusively staring at her. Quickly diverting her attention away, the party was now taking on a different vibe.

"Abi! Reg and I are going to dance! You coming?" Jade asked.

Shane interjected and shook his head. He figured Eastwood had probably worked the area already.

"You go ahead! Have fun!" Abi shouted before they whisked around the corner.

Seeing a seat open up, Shane offered it to Abi. Placing his arm around her, he leaned in and said, "I think we should go."

In agreement, she nodded and said, "Okay." She was happy with that.

Ready to make the rounds and say their goodbyes, Reggie appeared. Aside from the intense stare, he jarred his head to the side, signaling Shane to follow him.

Jade looked concerned.

"Wait here. Don't move. I'll be right back," Shane said.

When he left the room, she sat on the sofa amongst her classmates.

Suddenly, a change in music lured many away, cheering and shouting. A seemingly familiar set, their friends cleared out, leaving her alone. Afraid, she went in search of Shane. Sliding through countless sweaty bodies packed like sardines, she peered around the corner to her right and found him standing with Emile. The girl was hanging off him fatuously - her posse did the same to Reggie.

Constantly pulling Mandy's hands off him, Jade looked on angrily and motioned for Reg to escape them. The girls were noticeably drunk.

Abi watched Shane attempt to lean in and shout something into Emile's ear, but out of nowhere, the girl forcefully grabbed Shane's neck and pulled him toward her. Kissing him repeatedly, Abi was shocked. What was worse, he did not pull away. Flipping her body around the wall, she rested her back against it. A fight or flight response erupted. He had gone to Emile and left her alone – something he said he wouldn't do.

"You've gotta get out of here," she whispered. Heading toward the front doors, she stopped and checked her phone, remembering there was no signal.

Hearing shouts and screams from outside, Black Lyon's security urgently flew past her. The guard blocking the staircase also responded to the call on his earpiece. Leaving the area unattended, Abi looked to the second floor, hoping to find a phone. It was the only way to call a cab and have it pick her up at the corporate park. Carefully inching up the floating steps, she reached the top and sneakily veered right. Walking down the haunting, narrow hallway, hearing voices, she opened the first door on her right and turned on her phone light. Searching high and low,  she found nothing.

"Damn," she said.

About to leave, she stopped. Frozen, unable to move, she found four dark shadows standing in the doorway.

"Well, well, well," the voice said arrogantly.

Abi's heart raced.

"Look who we have here, boys?"

The three mumbled amongst themselves.

Abi fearfully said, "I need to go downstairs. Shane is waiting for me."

"What's your hurry?" the voice said.

They walked in and spread out.

Frantic, her body trembled. Shining the light on them, the guy closest to her raised his hand to shield his eyes. It was Eastwood, and there was no way out.

"So, you're Coop's new girl, huh?" With eyes fixated on her, scanning her body from top to bottom, he said, "You know, Coop and I share everything. Did he tell you that?"

The guys behind him snickered.

Eastwood slithered closer. "I don't think he'd mind sharing you?"

Moving towards her, they boxed Abi into the far corner. Barely able to breathe, taking sips of air, tears streamed down her face. She knew what they wanted. Feeling her legs give way, she stumbled backward onto the floor and recoiled in a fetal position. Crying, she closed her eyes and prayed, hoping God would hear her pleas.

The menacing crew gathered around. Eastwood knelt dangerously close. Reaching out, he gently moved a strand of hair away from her face before forcefully raising her chin upward to inflict more fear. Staring straight into her eyes, she gasped. There was nothing but evil there. Terrified, her heart hammered vigorously, making her feel faint.

"No, please..." she whispered.

The faintest light disappeared as the door closed. Abi went numb - her body heavy. Seemingly detaching from reality, a loud BANG sent her into hysterics. Eyes bulging, breathing erratically, she saw the door burst open. A flood of bodies followed. Pressed terrifyingly against the wall, her hands clinging to her head, more shadows stormed the room and violently overtook Eastwood and his friends. Hearing fists inflicting pain and profanity flying, Abi covered her eyes until a hand touched her shoulder gently, causing her to release the most blood-curdling scream as her body twitched.

Afraid to look up at the darkened silhouette, seeing a flash of his eyes, she heard, "Are you okay?"

Unable to respond, she felt him scoop her up in his arms effortlessly and carry her past the ensuing violence. Protecting her, he held her body tight to his before rushing out the door and down the hall. Swinging into another room, the man set her on a sofa. Afraid, not knowing where she was, she heard a deep voice.

"Don't worry. You're safe now."

Slowly opening her eyes, she found the dark figure sitting beside her.

"Matt, get me a blanket," he ordered.

Unable to speak a single word, she stayed silent. Trembling, she did not have strength in her arms and legs.

Given the blanket, the rescuer draped it over her shoulders. "Calm down. We don't want you going into shock."

Surrounded by walls of security monitors surveying every inch of the property, the man gave her space. Walking over to a large desk, he whispered to a security guard. With his eyes glued to the screens, he pointed at something before grabbing a bottle from a mini-fridge.

Returning, he handed it to her. "Here, drink this. It's just water. I haven't cracked the seal yet."

Abi took the bottle from him. When she did, she noticed a gold pin over his heart. It was a lion head. With her hands shaking, the water spilled as she tried to drink it. Her voice had yet to surface.

Standing in the middle of the room, the hooded man signaled to a guard at the door. "Get Martin for me," he commanded.

"Right away, Sir."

In seconds, an older gentleman dressed sharply in a tailored black suit with a white shirt and tie entered.

"Yes, Master B?" he said.

"Martin, please take our guest home." Not looking her way, he hesitated and asked, "What's your name?"

Barely able to produce a sound, she squeaked, "Abi."

The cloaked figure stopped and turned slightly to his left before he cleared his throat. "Go with Martin. He will take good care of you. I promise."

Carefully walking over, the older man kindly offered his arm. Abi was still somewhat unstable. He supported her weight when she grabbed hold.

"Right this way, Miss," he said while guiding her out. "I've got you."

In a daze, unaware of what was happening, she allowed Martin to lead them down the hallway. Descending a staircase, they reached the bottom, where a security guard dressed in dark clothing opened the door. There, she saw many matte black vehicles parked in a row.

Guided to a waiting SUV, Martin held the rear door open for her as she slowly climbed into the ample space in the back seat. Handed a blindfold, he said, "Please be a dear and put this on. It's just temporary. I promise." He ignored her reluctance and insisted, "It's just a precaution. We must protect the location."

Slipping the fabric on her head, she positioned it across her eyes. Hearing the door shut, she assumed the man seemingly got in the front seat.

That is when he asked, "So, where to, Miss?"

"Umm, Stradella Road, Bel Air."

"Ah, yes. Very good."

The music drowned out the engine's sound as they left the garage. Slowly moving, Abi swayed from side to side. Within a few minutes, she heard her phone reconnect. Receiving multiple message notifications, she asked, "Can I check my phone? My Father is probably worried."

"A few more minutes, Miss. Then, you can remove the blindfold. Apologies. It's standard procedure."

Fidgeting with her device in hand, feeling terrible that her dad was probably pacing the floor with worry, Abi felt the vehicle lean to one side. She assumed they were merging onto the freeway.

While accelerating, Martin suddenly announced, "You may remove the blindfold now."

She slipped it upward and looked at her phone. There, she saw multiple texts and missed calls from her Father. Immediately sending a reply, she typed, *So sorry, Dad. Phone reception was sketchy. I'm on my way home now. It won't be long.*

Not responding, she noticed he'd read the message. She was sure he was mad.

Full of regret, she thought, *What have I done? This is not who I am... You're not the kind of girl to sneak around and do things like this.* It was then she promised to stop it all. It was enough. She hated that she put herself in danger. Even worse, the time wasted at the rave was time she could never get back. Her mother was dying, and she had done this instead of being with her. Beating herself up, she thought it all seemed selfish and stupid in hindsight.

Twenty minutes from home, she calculated she'd arrive about ten after twelve. With tears developing, she read her Father's frantic texts. The guilt it caused was overwhelming. Hit with a mix of emotions, she cried.

"Are you okay, Miss?" Martin asked, not looking back.

She mumbled, "Umm, Martin?"

"Yes," the gentleman replied, his eyes remained straight ahead.

"Who saved me?"

He sat quietly. "I can not say."

"Was it him?"

"Was it who, Miss?"

"Black Lyon?"

"Sorry, Miss. Can't be sure."

Abi replayed the moment in her mind. Seeing Eastwood, hearing his words, she buried her face in her hands. Eyes closed, she recalled the men entering the room and when, presumably Black Lyon, carried her to safety. The glimpse she got of his eyes flashed before her. They looked kind. Compassionate, even caring.

Escaping the situation, safely held in his arms, the tears flowed. "Thank God," she whispered, knowing the unthinkable would have happened if he hadn't rescued her. Realizing she hadn't thanked her hero, she mumbled negatively, "Nice going...."

"Pardon me, Miss?" Martin said, having heard her say something.

"Oh, nothing." Thinking a minute, she said desperately, "Can you please tell him thank you? Thank you for what he did."

Not uttering a word, he nodded, then said, "Of course, Miss."

"I'd appreciate it."

"If I may. I suggest you not grace us with your presence again anytime soon."

"Umm, I won't. You can count on that."

"Very good."

From there, their conversation was sparse.

Her phone sounded. Receiving a text, Abi checked to see if it was Shane. But it wasn't. It was Jade.

*Where are you, Abi? Are you all right? We can't find you anywhere. We came back to the corporate park. Are you here?*

Her friend sounded frantic. Knowing she had to reply, she typed, *I'm okay. I went home.*

Seeing Jade's active thinking bubbles rambling, Abi was not in the mood to talk. She knew Shane was with her and probably Emile too.

*Why did you leave without telling us? We were worried, girl!*

Not ready to explain, she texted back. *I'll talk to you tomorrow. I gotta go.*

Ignoring her next message, she tucked the device in her bag.

While the driver weaved through a few unfamiliar streets, she hoped they knew where they were going. Maneuvering multiple twists and turns, they approached her house from the north side. Waiting in front of her gates, she opened it with her phone. As the barrier parted, the luxury SUV entered the courtyard and pulled up to the door. Martin immediately got out and helped her.

"Goodnight, Miss," he said warmly despite the circumstances that brought them there.

"Goodnight, Martin." Turning to see her Father in the doorway, he looked both angry and relieved. Walking over, she watched the Bentley drive away.

"I thought we had a deal, Abi? Leave your ringer and location services on at all times. I've been worried - again. Two nights in a row. I thought something happened to you."

"I know. I know. I'm sorry."

"What happened to Shane? Why didn't he drive you home? Was he drunk? Is that the reason for the limo?"

Hugging her dad like her life depended on it, she started to cry.

It caught him off guard. Wrapping his arms around his daughter, he asked, "What is it? What happened?"

Uncontrollably emotional, the tears kept falling.

"What is it, honey? Did he hurt you?" His voice went stern. "I swear if he hurt you, I'll...."

"No. No. It's not like that..." she muttered.

Holding her, he wished his wife was there. She would know what to do more than he. "Do you, umm, want to talk about it?"

Abi let go. Parting ways, she looked at him with red, puffy eyes. "No, I just want to go to bed."

"Sure, Sweetheart." Thankful she was home safe, he said, "You get some sleep. Things will seem better in the morning."

Leaving him, she ascended the stairs and went into her room. Quietly closing the door behind her, she sat on her bed before rolling over and curling up with a pillow. Not having heard from Shane confirmed her suspicions. She sobbed. The thought of things ending between them was hard to accept. They'd connected so deeply that she felt he'd etched his name upon her soul.

"Guess you were the rebound girl," she whispered through the tears. "So stupid. You got caught up and didn't see the writing on the wall." Beating herself mentally, she stripped off the fancy clothes and threw them on the floor. Before flinging the drapes closed, she saw the mansion across the canyon completely dark, but she didn't care. Her heart was breaking, and she could do nothing about it.

# 38

## The Aftermath

A ribbon of sunshine peeked through a crack in the drapes and flooded a portion of the room with light. It brightened and faded with the passing of the clouds, prompting Abi's eyes to open. Having had a restless night's sleep, she was exhausted. Waking in a sweat, hour after hour, her run-in with Eastwood was on repeat. It had become this reoccurring nightmare. Tormented, with her heart thumping violently, Abi could not stop the images from flashing through her mind.

Rolling on her back, staring at the ceiling, she buried her face in the pillows, thankful it was morning. When Shane came to mind, she knew the fairytale life she once had was now gone, just as she feared it would. He'd returned to Emile like the mean girl had warned.

Her phone chimed. Frantic, she secretly hoped it was Shane but noticed the message was from Burton. He was confirming their plans for the day.

Not sure if she would be the best company, Abi exhaled. "You can't wallow in this," she said. Thinking about what she wanted to say, she reluctantly typed, *Yes—looking forward to it.*

*I'll be there in thirty minutes,* she read out loud. "Thirty minutes?" Realizing she didn't have much time to get ready, it got her out of bed. Sending a thumbs-up emoji, Abi figured there was no time to shower. All she could do was pull her hair back in a ponytail, get dressed, and head out the door. But there was one more thing she had to do. Abi texted him back, hoping to buy time. *Can you make it forty-five instead? I need to talk to my Dad.*

Thankfully, he replied, *Yes, sure. No problem.*

Abi put the phone down and started the shower, happy not to be in a rush. As the water cascaded over her shoulders, the visions of Eastwood paralyzed her when she closed her eyes. Recalling the dark figures entering the room to save her, she fully believed Black Lyon had carried her to safety.

"Who else would have control over that many people?" she said while washing her hair. "Martin called him Master B. It had to be him."

Switching the faucet off, she remembered the gold lion pin while she dried her hair. After brushing her teeth, she got dressed and checked the time while packing her Burch crossbody bag with what she'd need that afternoon. About to leave, she looked down the hall to her Mom's room. The nurse looked at her and waved. Abi silently did the same before descending the stairs. When rounding the corner into the kitchen, she found her Dad with his laptop and briefcase on the island. Forever working, she saw that he'd made toast for himself. The scent of peanut butter filled the air.

"Morning, Dad," Abi said quietly.

Surprised to see her dressed already, he said, "Morning. Where are you off to?"

"Umm, I'm supposed to meet Burton for lunch. I wasn't gonna go, but I feel guilty if I didn't. Is it okay? I know the past couple of days have not been good. I apologize for that."

"Have to say, many scary scenarios roamed through my head last night. Do you know how it felt seeing your location was unavailable? Then, I called, and it went straight to voice mail. I mean..," he paused and shook his head disappointingly. "Once again, I thought something had happened to you. I hate being that guy – you know, the Dad that constantly badgers, but the world is not the safest these days, especially for a girl."

*You're not kidding,* she thought to herself. Aware of how this affected him, she decided to share the truth - or at least part of it. "Shane and I broke up," she said point blank.

"What?"

"Yeah. It seems he went back to his old girlfriend, so I got a limo and came home." She spared him the rest. It was a night she wanted to forget. "Now, with him out of the picture, don't worry. Things will go back to normal. I'll be home a lot more."

"I'm sorry, Sweetie." He didn't know what to do or say. Seeing the utter sadness and rejection on her face was heartbreaking.

"I just need to forget about him. Besides, talking to Burton will be good therapy for me. He's like the brother I never had."

"Okay, but I'm limiting you today to only four hours. Then I want you home. That way, I have a break from all the drama, deal?"

"Deal." Abi's phone went off. Looking at the screen, she saw it was Burton. He was at the gate. Remotely opening it for him, she said, "Dad, I've gotta go. I promise I'll be home between three and four. We're driving up the PCH to Malibu and back."

"All right," he said, following her to the front door. There, he found Burton getting out of his black McLaren.

Leaving the butterfly door open on his side, he walked over to Dr. Acardi. "Hello, Sir. Long time no see." Reaching out his hand to the man, Burton shook his confidently.

"Good to see you, Burton. You're looking well."

"I'm doing okay. Thank you, Sir."

"Abi says you attend UCLA."

"Yes, second-year Com Sci major."

"Impressive."

"Thank you."

Abi stood between them, waiting for their conversation to end. "So, I guess we should go. I have to be home between three and four."

Burton said, "Sure. No problem." Turning back to Dr. Acardi, he added, "I guess we'll see you after?"

"Yes, I will be here. Have fun, you two."

"Thanks, Dad."

Burton walked Abi over to the passenger side and raised the car door for her to slide in. Just as she got settled, her phone rang. Not recognizing the number, she ignored it and muted the ringer when Burton sat beside her. Closing his door, he started the engine. As it growled, her Dad waved goodbye as they left.

"He looks good but seems stressed." He turned onto Stradella. "Okay, Abi, what is going on? I could cut the air with a knife."

"He had a rough night because of me."

"So, you went to Black Lyon?"

"Yes, I did. But it didn't turn out the way I thought it would."

"Let me guess. You're Dad found out?"

Fidgeting, she looked down. "Not exactly. The party had no signal, so my location services didn't work. He tried to call me multiple times, and it didn't connect. He got pretty worried."

"Understandably."

"So, you're taking his side?" Abi got defensive.

"No, but I can see his point. Can't you? Come on, Abs. This isn't who you are. What's happening?"

Nervous, contemplating how much of the nightmarish encounter she was willing to share, she stayed quiet.

"So, how was your first rave experience anyway? I figured you'd be incapacitated this morning."

"Incapacitated? I didn't have a single drink, well, other than bottled water."

"Did you at least have fun?"

Abi knew she should have stayed home with her parents. Peering out the window, she said, "Life is very different here."

"What does that mean?"

She avoided eye contact with her best friend and replied, "Can I tell you something? Mostly because I need to talk about it, and no offense,

I don't have anyone else right now. You can't repeat it to anyone. Promise?"

The tone in her voice was worrisome. "Promise. What is it? Did Shane hurt you? I swear, I'll kill him if he did." Burton's protective instincts surfaced.

Abi began to sob.

Seeing this, Burton sat up straight and clung to the steering wheel with a white knuckle grip. Glancing between her and the road while he merged into the flow of traffic on Sunset Boulevard, he was afraid to hear the details. "I told you not to go to that party. I knew it would be too intense for you."

Taking a Kleenex from her bag, she tried to contain herself as she cried.

Burton reached over and placed his hand on her forearm. "What is it? Just tell me."

She pulled herself together enough to speak. "When we arrived, everything was fine - civilized. But twenty minutes later, Eastwood Korolev showed up with his goons. They confronted Shane again. Luckily, the football team was there to stand with him."

"Okay..." He listened intently.

"Outnumbered, the guys decided to move on. Later, I saw Eastwood selling drugs."

"Yes, his family is known for that." Burton hesitated before asking, "So, is that it?"

"No..." Unable to look at him, her emotions took over. Trembling, tears flowing, she couldn't stop her chest from heaving while trying to take a breath.

Burton pushed his body back into his seat, bracing for what she'd say.

"Things were okay until Jade and Reggie went dancing. In minutes, they returned. Reggie signaled for Shane to follow him. Before leaving, he instructed me to stay with the group and not move. But everyone left when a popular song played. Then, I was all alone."

"And..." Burton prompted.

"And, I decided to search for Shane. When I rounded the corner, I saw him standing with Emile. She looked drunk. So were her friends. Suddenly, I saw her kiss him, and he didn't pull away."

"What an idiot," he said, casting judgment.

"I couldn't be there anymore. I just wanted to go home, but my phone didn't work, so I snuck upstairs when a fight broke out. I hoped to find a landline and call a cab to pick me up at the corporate park. I didn't want to wait outside in the dark by myself."

"Did you find one?"

"No. The first room I went into didn't have one. When I was about to go to the next one, umm..." Abi's voice vibrated with fear.

Burton took his foot off the gas.

"There were four guys in the doorway. One of them was Eastwood. They blocked me in." Abi bowed her head. Crying, her hands shook.

Assuming what had happened, he looked out the driver's side window. His face was red with anger as he repeatedly gripped the steering wheel, wishing he had been there last night to rip those guys to shreds. Unable to look her way, he said, "Abi, please tell me they didn't...." He glanced over at her, then back at the highway.

Sobbing, she divulged, "No. But they wanted to. I was so scared, Burton."

Down-shifting on a dime, he abruptly pulled over. Stopped, he reached out and held her close. He didn't know what more to do. Feeling her body shaking, he waited for her to calm down.

Finally, she broke her silence. "When they were about to close the door, security guys broke in, and someone carried me out of the room."

"Nobody hurt you? Right?"

"No. It all happened so fast. A man rescued me and took me to the security office. One wall had a lot of monitors watching the entire property. They must have seen me enter that room and saw Eastwood follow."

He was speechless.

"The guy who saved me set me on a sofa and got me water and a blanket. He arranged for an older gentleman named Martin to drive me home. He referred to the man who saved me as Master B. I don't know. Do you think it could have been Black Lyon?"

"I have no idea. Could you see his face at all?"

"No. The guy wore a black hoodie over his head, with a bandana covering his face. I did get a quick glimpse of his eyes, though. Because I was in shock, I didn't thank him."

"Abs, you got lucky."

She knew he was right.

"What the hell was Shane thinking, leaving you alone?" Burton was furious.

"He wasn't thinking about me, that's for sure."

"Has he called to check on you this morning?"

"Nope. Not a word. Just like that, you're my only friend."

Burton felt for her. She'd been through so much before leaving Boston. Now, on top of everything, her Mom was sick, and now this. "Maybe it's for the best? You can focus on your parents and school."

Getting back on the freeway, Burton changed gears and accelerated.

"Speaking of school. How do I go back there, Burton? How do I face all those people?"

"With your head held high. If you want, I can drop you off every morning. Maybe let everyone know you are dating a college guy?"

"I can't let you do that," she said, recalling their run-in with Emile at the coffee shop and the rumor mill that followed.

He turned to her. "Well, I'd do anything for you."

"I know you would. Thank you." She rested her hand on top of his. "Now that I'm single, maybe we can hang out more."

"Yeah. I'd like that."

Checking her face in the visor's vanity mirror, she said, "Guess you got more than you bargained for today."

"It's okay. Anytime you need me, I'll be here. Don't ever think you're bothering me."

"Thank you."

Granting him a smile that melted his heart, she focused on the Pacific Ocean coming into view on the left. The sun sparkled off the waves rolling in along the shore.

"I guess you needed this drive up the coast today. I know how much you like the ocean and the beach."

"Yes, definitely." Recalling the last time she saw Burton, she asked, "Oh, I almost forgot. How was the crazy hard test?"

He turned to her and said, "Got eighty-nine percent. Not bad, but not great either."

"I think that's awesome. See, I knew you could do it. And you were worried."

"Well, the truth is, I was vying for a ninety, but the professor wouldn't give me the extra point." He wished he could explain just how challenging it truly was. There was so much on his plate.

"Can we stop somewhere? Get out and take a walk?"

"Absolutely." Burton checked the GPS. "Zuma is about ten minutes away. Wanna stop there?"

Abi stared out her window blankly and said, "Sure," remembering all the sweet things Shane had told her at the beach two nights ago. She felt stupid for believing him. Rolling down her window, she embraced the sea air as they sped along PCH. Hand out the window, cutting through the breeze, she closed her eyes and held her hair down to keep it from flying around erratically.

Burton turned into Zuma Beach. After passing through the gates, his car immediately attracted attention. Parking diagonal across a few open spots at the far end, he quickly got out and walked around to open her door for her. Offering his hand to help Abi from her seat, a few people nearby took pictures of them.

"They're probably tourists thinking we're celebrities or something," he said humorously.

She thought it was funny.

The two found a quiet stretch and had a seat on the sand. He could tell his childhood friend had a heavy heart.

"It's so pretty here," she said. "I just love it. The sights, the feel of the breeze, the smell of the air. It reminds me of home."

"Yeah. Much better than the frozen wasteland I've lived in all that time, too."

"So sorry you went through that."

He laughed. "Finally, someone who pities me." Even though he joked about it, he really hated the experience deep down. It was tough going from civilization back to the stone age. No flush toilet, just an outhouse. No hot showers - only able to boil water for sponge baths twice a week if lucky. Even rationing food before the next shipment arrived - so many Gen Zs would never have survived such conditions.

Abi sat quietly and looked out over the horizon.

Burton could tell she had drifted miles away.

Feeling her phone ringing in her bag, she checked to be sure it wasn't her Dad. Seeing that same unfamiliar number, she figured she was on a telemarketing list. Tucking it away, Abi exhaled and tilted her head toward the sun.

"What are you thinking?"

Turning to him, she said, "Strange, I feel nothing right now - like nothing. I'm numb. Guess it's part of the traumatic aftermath."

"Please tell me you won't be going to any of those raves ever again. They are no place for you."

"I know that now. Definitely not for me. I do feel indebted to the guy for what he did. I need to find him and say thank you in person. He didn't have to help me."

"I'm glad he did too. What if he hadn't?"

"I don't want to contemplate that."

"As for thanking the guy, I'm sure he knows how grateful you are."

"I could go to one more event and ask to see him, then leave."

"Given what happened, I don't think that's a good idea."

"You're probably right, but it wouldn't hurt to try. You could come with me?"

"Maybe it's best to count your blessings and leave it alone. Remember, Abs. Some girls aren't so lucky."

Abi went silent while that sank in.

He wished he could take it back.

"Look, if you don't want to take my advice, I'll go with you and keep you safe."

She nodded. "Deal."

Burton attempted to lighten the conversation. "Want to grab some lunch at Geoffrey's?"

"Sure, I'd like that."

"Okay, let's go." Getting up off the sand, Burton offered his hand to help her.

Heading back, he called the restaurant. "Yes, table for two. Ocean view in ten minutes. Reservation for Lancaster."

Close to the car, Abi felt her phone vibrate again. Quickly checking it, the number showed up in a text. To her surprise, it was Shane. He asked if they could talk. Putting the phone away, she ignored it. To her, there was nothing more to say.

Unlocking the McLaren, Burton had a strange look on his face.

"What is it?" she asked.

"Hey, remember, no sand in the car, please. Just had her detailed."

"Are you serious right now?" she froze.

"Dead. Serious."

She knew from their last drive together that he wasn't joking. His car was immaculate. Out of respect, she brushed herself off, removed her sneakers, and pounded them on the pavement to remove the sand.

Burton knelt beside her. Grabbing each of her feet, he brushed them off for her before closing the door. When he got in and started the engine, it grumbled, causing everyone around them to look. Slowly merging onto the highway, Burton suddenly gunned it. The force of the acceleration threw Abi back into the seat. Slowing down seconds later, he looked at her with a devilish grin. She, too, was smiling from ear to ear.

It wasn't long before they pulled into Geoffrey's. The Valet immediately saw them and moved two orange cones before guiding them to the spot.

"Wow. That's service," Abi said, reminded of the guys doing that for Shane on Friday night at Aramis' party.

"Sadly, I eat here often. They know me pretty well."

"It has its perks."

"Suppose so," Burton said before acknowledging the Valet. "Hey, Brian. How's it goin'?"

"Good." Brian said, "Out for a Sunday drive, Mr. Lancaster?"

"Yes, but this time, I brought company. Brian, meet Abi."

"Nice to meet you, Miss," the young man said with a smile.

"Yes, nice to meet you too."

"Believe your table is ready, Mr. Lancaster. Just see Annabell inside."

"Will do," he said while helping Abi out of the car. "Keep an eye on my baby for me." Burton passed him a hundred-dollar bill.

"Yes, Sir." The guy gave him a double thumbs up. "Enjoy your lunch."

Escorting her to the main entrance, he offered his arm. "Right, this way, Ms. Acardi." He opened the door and allowed her to walk in first. Removing his sunglasses, he greeted Annabell at the hostess desk.

"Good afternoon, Mr. Lancaster. Your table is ready. Follow me," she said without delay, grabbing two menus from the stack.

Seated outside with a view of the ocean, the two had a seat.

"You're waiter will be with you momentarily to take your orders."

"Thank you so much," Abi replied. She couldn't help but see Burton in a different light. No longer was he the unpopular boy with glasses and braces. Now, he stood out – and in a good way. "This view is incredible."

"Best seat in the house."

Their waiter arrived in minutes.

Burton made a few quick menu suggestions for Abi, and soon, they got their orders placed.

An awkward silence fell upon them briefly.

"Thank you for taking my mind off of you know who."

Looking across the table at her, he said, "Absolutely. I'm glad to be a distraction."

Curious, she had to ask, "So, how does everybody know you here? You must be more than just a regular."

"I'm here a couple of times a week, if not more."

She pondered the mystery of Burton. "Can I ask you something?"

"Sure. Shoot."

"Honestly, after today, I feel like I have no idea who you are anymore. I mean, you look so different. You attend UCLA for science...."

"Computer science," he corrected.

"Do you live around here? Everyone is so respectful of you."

"Yes, I am not far, actually. About ten minutes up the highway." There were so many things he needed to address. But he didn't know where to start. "I think they treat me well because I am respectful of them. And around here, money and courtesy are a rare combination."

"I have to say. I feel a little intimidated by you."

"Whenever we hung out in Boston, I felt that way. But now, given my situation, I feel worthy of being in your company, Abi Acardi."

She immediately tilted her head. "Awww, Burton..."

"I never felt good enough to be your friend all those years. Now, I can give you the world. Anything you want, just say the word."

"You know I'm not into material things. I'm just happy to have a smart, thoughtful friend who genuinely cares about me. That's all I truly need. Our friendship to this day means so much. You don't need to give me the world. Just your time."

The word friendship hit him like a punch in the gut. Not pushing any further, he accepted whatever she was willing to give because being around her felt familiar - like home.

At the same time, Abi looked across the table at his ridiculously handsome face. She could not deny that she was attracted to him after today, but the last thing she wanted was to ruin that friendship. It seemed it was all she had left now.

"Don't worry, Abs. I know we're just good friends. I'll take what I can get." He sipped some of his sparkling water. "So, umm, what will you do about Shane?"

"There's nothing to do. We're done. It's something I need to accept."

"If it's any consolation, he didn't deserve you anyway."

"It still hurts all the same." Her eyes began to glisten. Soon, a few droplets streamed down her cheeks.

Taking his napkin, he reached across the table and dried her tears. "It'll be okay, Abs."

Silently nodding, she turned toward the ocean so nobody else would see.

Their food arrived with perfect timing. Deciding to discuss world views and future endeavors, they swayed away from any heavy talk while finishing their lunch and sharing a dessert.

Abi checked the time. "It's almost 2:45. I guess we should get going. Don't want to be late today and stress Dad out more than I already have."

"Sure, no problem."

Pulling out her wallet to contribute to their lunch, he noticed what she was doing.

"Don't even think about it. Put your wallet away, please. I've got this. You're my guest."

"No, no. I want to chip in."

"Won't hear of it. Sorry."

When their waiter returned, Burton had cash pulled from his wallet to pay the bill. Tucking it inside the folder, he handed it back to the guy to make sure she didn't get an opportunity to intervene.

"All done. Ready to head out?" Standing, Burton pulled out her chair as Abi got up from the table. Allowing her to lead, he carefully hovered his hand around the small of her back to escort her out.

While they walked to the main doors, Abi noted how many girls stared at Burton on the way by. It made her feel special somehow.

"Thank you so much for today," she said when they exited. "This week has been tough."

"Anytime. Always here."

Burton greeted Brian and doubled the guy's tip.

"Thanks so much, Sir," he said enthusiastically.

"Appreciate the help, man. Enjoy the rest of the day."

"You too, Mr. Lancaster. We'll see you again soon."

"I'm sure you will," Burton chuckled.

Opening the butterfly door for Abi, she settled in her seat. Slowly lowering it, he swung around to his side. When he started the engine, it caused a scene.

Abi joked, "See, this is why I drive a Cooper. It draws less attention."

He laughed, "Oh, yeah?" To him, after being invisible for so long, it was nice to be noticed. But he would never tell her that. "Well, I drive this car for the speed factor." Pulling out of Geoffrey's into freeway traffic on the PCH, he peddle-shifted and stepped on the gas. Slowing down, having gotten a brief thrill, he knew the last thing he wanted was to get his car impounded, not to mention a ticket on top of that.

Speeding south, Abi gazed over the ocean, hoping the view would give her the answers to life's troubles. Sadly, reality set in while they headed home. It seemed to loom around every corner. Reminded of her Mom and Dad, school, Shane, Eastwood, and more, she wished she had the power to avoid it all.

# 39

# The Confrontation

Approaching her house along the cliffs of Stradella Road, they rounded the sharp corner and headed up the hill. Hitting the straight stretch, Abi spotted a vehicle parked on the street. Burton thought nothing of it until Abi leaned forward and focused in.

"Who's that?" he asked. "Do you know them?"

"Yeah, umm," she mumbled, "It's Shane."

"Oh, this should be interesting."

The two pulled up to the gate. Abi opened it remotely, allowing them to pass through. Slowly entering the courtyard, Abi noticed Shane following them. Immediately popping her door and pushing it upward, Abi watched the Jeep park beside her. With eyes glued to Burton, Shane got out and watched Abi's college friend walk around the car and stand firm behind her. The expression on Shane's face said it all.

"Who's he?" the football player questioned combatively.

"It's not what you think." Abi paused before making introductions. "Shane Coppersmith, meet Burton Lancaster–my neighbor from Boston."

"Is this who you went home with after the rave?" he questioned.

Moving forward, standing militarily beside Abi, Burton was about to answer him.

Shane pointed and said, "I'm not asking you. This is between her and me."

The comment made Burton's blood boil. He took a second step towards him and rubbed his fist in the opposite palm. Acting like a wall between Shane and Abi, he used a deep, commanding voice and warned, "Well, I don't like how you're talking to her. If you're not careful, this could end badly."

"Is that right?" Shane was ready to fight.

Knowing the athlete had abandoned Abi at the party, placing her in danger, Burton thought he'd taunt him a bit. "Unlike yourself, I will always protect her without fail."

"What are you saying?" Shane challenged, inching closer.

Ready to throw the first punch, Burton pointed out the obvious. "You screwed up, man, and it could have cost her everything."

Shane stood his ground but looked confused.

Abi frantically wedged between them, afraid the confrontation would escalate further. "Both of you, stop!" she yelled, pushing them apart.

"Where did you go last night? I looked everywhere. You disappeared. Do you know how worried I was?" Shane's expression softened slightly.

Abi got angry. "I didn't think you'd notice since you were too busy kissing Emile."

"Wait? What?"

"I saw the two of you, Shane. You got back together with her, didn't you? Just say it. Put me out of my misery."

"No. No, I didn't. That is not what happened." Shane looked over at Burton. "Look, can she and I talk–alone?" His sights reverted to Abi.

"That's up to her." Realizing there was a misunderstanding, Burton asked, "Abs, do you want to talk to him?"

Puzzled by what she heard, she said, "Yeah. It's okay."

"Just say the word, and I'll leave and let you hash this out." Staring Shane down, her friend added, "If I hear anything negative from her, you will deal with me. Understand."

Shane refrained from responding but didn't wince.

Moving his sights to Abi, he reached out and held her hand. "Call me later?" he said before departing.

Distracted, Abi turned to him and nodded. "Yes, I will."

Shane fumed upon hearing that.

Believing it would fuel the fire, Burton avoided hugging her goodbye. The last thing he wanted was to add more stress to the situation. He got into his car and started the engine. As it rumbled, he slowly left while giving the quarterback the eye as he passed.

At a crossroads, the two stood there alone in silence.

Needing to know, she asked bluntly, "So, why did you kiss her?"

"She was wasted, Abs."

"What was it then?"

"She kissed me. Not the other way around." The topic frustrated him.

"Same difference."

He saw the hurt in her eyes. His voice softened. "Abi…"

"Do you have any idea what I went through last night?" she stated with her hands trembling.

Lowering his chin to his chest, he wanted to clear the air. "Listen, Emile was drunk. I'm sure someone slipped something into her drink. Reggie told me that Eastwood and his goons were hovering. I didn't want anything to happen to her, so I went to get her out of there and send her home. In the midst of all that, she kissed me. It caught me off guard, but I pushed her back."

"So, then, you saved her, but not me?"

"What?" He began shifting his weight on either foot nervously. "Abi? What do you mean?"

"After seeing the two of you together, I wanted to leave. Your friend Eastwood found me when I went looking for a phone."

"What happened? Did they hurt you? If they did, I swear…." A mix of concern and anger flashed across his face.

Abi silently recalled the horrific ordeal and did not utter a word. "They said you wouldn't mind sharing me. Why would they say that?"

Unable to contain his rage, Shane went over to his Jeep and pounded his fists into the hood repeatedly. "I'm gonna kill those fuckers," he said under his breath.

She knew she'd tortured him enough. "When they were about to close the door, I thought that was it. I was trapped. There was no way out."

He leaned forward and rested his hands on the hood of the truck. Hanging his head while listening to her every word, he held his breath.

"Suddenly, the door flung open. Black Lyon and his security team pulled me out. They saved me."

Shane raised his head and turned to her. "They did?"

"Yeah, because you weren't there."

That comment stabbed him in the heart. "So, Eastwood didn't...."

Abi shook her head. "But if it weren't for Black Lyon, they would've."

The football player went silent and walked over to her. "Abi, I thought Jade stayed with you."

"No, she didn't. She followed you and Reggie. When all of you left, the rest of the group went to dance. I was alone and went searching for you. That's when I saw... Anyway, I figured you got back together with Emile like she said you would."

"Look, I was trying to do the right thing. Her life is not what you think it to be." His heart ached for Abi. "And for the record, I don't want her. I want you."

She didn't know what to say.

"Abi, please." He cautiously moved closer. "I did not mean for any of this to happen. I'm sorry."

Realizing what she thought happened - didn't - Abi had mixed feelings.

Her Father appeared at the door. "Abi, what's going on here? Are you okay?"

"Just a misunderstanding. That's all."

Trying to save face, Shane said, "Hello, Dr. Acardi."

Not saying a word to him, her Dad kept his hands in his pockets and shot Shane a disapproving look before his gaze veered to his daughter. "Are you sure everything is fine?"

"Yeah, Dad. I'll be there in a minute."

Closing the door behind him, Abi knew he would be watching on the cameras now if he hadn't been already.

Shane sighed. "Great. Now, you're Dad hates me. I guess I don't blame him."

"Don't worry. I will deal with him later," she whispered.

"Does he know?"

"Know what?"

"About last night...." He stopped himself from finishing his sentence in case he was indeed listening.

Abi lowered her voice. "No. That's not something I could ever...umm." She stopped and shook her head.

Desperate to fix things between them, believing this was his Hail Mary, he said, "The other night, I meant every word I said. You are a once-in-a-lifetime girl, and I know we've only known each other a short time, but damn, I can't imagine my life without you. I should have never left you alone. Not for a second. Please forgive me."

She took a step forward. Arms still crossed, she nervously wiped the tears from her cheek.

Not sure what to do, he reached out to her and waited.

Staring at his hand, she paused before extending hers to touch his.

Thankful, he gently pulled her in and tightly wrapped his arms around her. Holding her head against his chest, he kissed her forehead.

"How did you get home?"

"Black Lyon's butler, Martin, drove me in a private car."

Shane nodded.

Hesitating, she asked, "Why didn't you text or call me last night? Only Jade did."

"While searching the place for you, I lost my phone, or someone stole it from me—who knows. I couldn't find it anywhere. When we reached the corporate park, Jade said you replied to her text and were safe at home. I was up all night wondering what had happened to us and couldn't contact you, which made it worse. I got up early this morning, bought a new phone, and came home to upload the backup. I kept calling you, but you must have declined the calls."

"It said unknown number."

"When I texted, and you didn't respond, I drove here. Guess I hoped you'd leave the house eventually and I could follow you–maybe get a chance to talk. I wasn't expecting to find you with...."

Still upset, Abi knew the night was a series of bad decisions from beginning to end.

He slipped his hands into his pockets. "You know, you never have to worry about me cheating. My Dad cheated on my Mom. It changed my life forever. I would never put anyone through what my Dad did."

"Thank you for saying that. I would never either."

Staring at the gravel below, Shane hesitated and said, "This Burton dude? He's really just a friend?"

"Yes, I told you. He was my neighbor. I've known him for years."

"So, nothing is going on between you?"

"No. Not at all. He's like a brother," Abi said, still pondering the outcome of their drive-up PCH today.

"Okay. I trust you."

Left in strange territory, they knew they'd have to start over.

"Do you want to come in?" Abi asked.

"I'm not sure your Dad wants me around right now." Shane knew he was angry. "Can we go somewhere to talk a bit more?"

"Given last night and how I came home, he's not happy with me either. At this point, not sure I should ask to leave."

Wanting to continue their conversation, he asked, "Is there a quiet place to sit that will not bother him?"

"Sure. We can stay outside. Maybe sit by the pool?" Abi closed the main gate and led Shane to the front door. Opening it, she stepped to the left and slid the Fleetwood glass wall back before walking out onto the patio and leading him toward the pavilion rooftop.

"We can go and sit up there," she pointed along the way.

Climbing the concrete staircase to the upper level overlooking the canyon, Shane glanced back at the house and saw her Dad sitting on a sofa in front of the television. His eyes were on them.

She took a seat on a chaise. Shane did the same. Facing her, he knew he'd have to regain her trust. She'd been through a horrific ordeal, and he was to blame.

Approaching her house along the cliffs of Stradella Road, they rounded the sharp corner and headed up the hill. Hitting the straight stretch, Abi spotted a vehicle parked on the street. Burton thought nothing of it until Abi leaned forward and focused in.

"Who's that?" he asked. "Do you know them?"

"Yeah, umm," she mumbled, "It's Shane."

"Oh, this should be interesting."

The two pulled up to the gate. Abi opened it remotely, allowing them to pass through. Slowly entering the courtyard, Abi noticed Shane following them. Immediately popping her door and pushing it upward, Abi watched the Jeep park beside her. With eyes glued to Burton, Shane got out and watched Abi's college friend walk around the car and stand firm behind her. The expression on Shane's face said it all.

"Who's he?" the football player questioned combatively.

"It's not what you think." Abi paused before making introductions. "Shane Coppersmith, meet Burton Lancaster–my neighbor from Boston."

"Is this who you went home with after the rave?" he questioned.

Moving forward, standing militarily beside Abi, Burton was about to answer him.

Shane pointed and said, "I'm not asking you. This is between her and me."

The comment made Burton's blood boil. He took a second step towards him and rubbed his fist in the opposite palm. Acting like a wall between Shane and Abi, he used a deep, commanding voice and warned, "Well, I don't like how you're talking to her. If you're not careful, this could end badly."

"Is that right?" Shane was ready to fight.

Knowing the athlete had abandoned Abi at the party, placing her in danger, Burton thought he'd taunt him a bit. "Unlike yourself, I will always protect her without fail."

"What are you saying?" Shane challenged, inching closer.

Ready to throw the first punch, Burton pointed out the obvious. "You screwed up, man, and it could have cost her everything."

Shane stood his ground but looked confused.

Abi frantically wedged between them, afraid the confrontation would escalate further. "Both of you, stop!" she yelled, pushing them apart.

"Where did you go last night? I looked everywhere. You disappeared. Do you know how worried I was?" Shane's expression softened slightly.

Abi got angry. "I didn't think you'd notice since you were too busy kissing Emile."

"Wait? What?"

"I saw the two of you, Shane. You got back together with her, didn't you? Just say it. Put me out of my misery."

"No. No, I didn't. That is not what happened." Shane looked over at Burton. "Look, can she and I talk–alone?" His sights reverted to Abi.

"That's up to her." Realizing there was a misunderstanding, Burton asked, "Abs, do you want to talk to him?"

Puzzled by what she heard, she said, "Yeah. It's okay."

"Just say the word, and I'll leave and let you hash this out." Staring Shane down, her friend added, "If I hear anything negative from her, you will deal with me. Understand."

Shane refrained from responding but didn't wince.

Moving his sights to Abi, he reached out and held her hand. "Call me later?" he said before departing.

Distracted, Abi turned to him and nodded. "Yes, I will."

Shane fumed upon hearing that.

Believing it would fuel the fire, Burton avoided hugging her good-bye. The last thing he wanted was to add more stress to the situation. He got into his car and started the engine. As it rumbled, he slowly left while giving the quarterback the eye as he passed.

At a crossroads, the two stood there alone in silence.

Needing to know, she asked bluntly, "So, why did you kiss her?"

"She was wasted, Abs."

"What was it then?"

"She kissed me. Not the other way around." The topic frustrated him.

"Same difference."

He saw the hurt in her eyes. His voice softened. "Abi…"

"Do you have any idea what I went through last night?" she stated with her hands trembling.

Lowering his chin to his chest, he wanted to clear the air. "Listen, Emile was drunk. I'm sure someone slipped something into her drink. Reggie told me that Eastwood and his goons were hovering. I didn't want anything to happen to her, so I went to get her out of there and send her home. In the midst of all that, she kissed me. It caught me off guard, but I pushed her back."

"So, then, you saved her, but not me?"

"What?" He began shifting his weight on either foot nervously. "Abi? What do you mean?"

"After seeing the two of you together, I wanted to leave. Your friend Eastwood found me when I went looking for a phone."

"What happened? Did they hurt you? If they did, I swear…." A mix of concern and anger flashed across his face.

Abi silently recalled the horrific ordeal and did not utter a word. "They said you wouldn't mind sharing me. Why would they say that?"

Unable to contain his rage, Shane went over to his Jeep and pounded his fists into the hood repeatedly. "I'm gonna kill those fuckers," he said under his breath.

She knew she'd tortured him enough. "When they were about to close the door, I thought that was it. I was trapped. There was no way out."

He leaned forward and rested his hands on the hood of the truck. Hanging his head while listening to her every word, he held his breath.

"Suddenly, the door flung open. Black Lyon and his security team pulled me out. They saved me."

Shane raised his head and turned to her. "They did?"

"Yeah, because you weren't there."

That comment stabbed him in the heart. "So, Eastwood didn't...."

Abi shook her head. "But if it weren't for Black Lyon, they would've."

The football player went silent and walked over to her. "Abi, I thought Jade stayed with you."

"Yeah, well, she followed you and Reggie. When all of you left, the rest of the group went to dance. I was alone and went searching for you. That's when I saw..." she unwittingly recalled. "Anyway, I figured you got back together with Emile like she said you would."

"Look, I was trying to do the right thing. Her life is not what you think it to be." His heart ached for Abi. "And for the record, I don't want her. I want you."

She didn't know what to say.

"Abi, please." He cautiously moved closer. "I did not mean for any of this to happen. I'm sorry."

Realizing what she thought happened - didn't - Abi had mixed feelings.

Her Father appeared at the door. "Abi, what's going on here? Are you okay?"

"Just a misunderstanding. That's all."

Trying to save face, Shane said, "Hello, Dr. Acardi."

Not saying a word to him, her Dad kept his hands in his pockets and shot Shane a disapproving look before his gaze veered to his daughter. "Are you sure everything is fine?"

"Yeah, Dad. I'll be in in a minute."

Closing the door behind him, Abi knew he would be watching on the cameras now if he hadn't been already.

Shane sighed. "Great. Now, you're Dad hates me. I guess I don't blame him."

"Don't worry. I will deal with him later," she whispered.

"Does he know?"

"Know what?"

"About last night...." He stopped himself from finishing his sentence in case he was indeed listening.

Abi lowered her voice. "No. That's not something I could ever...umm." She stopped and shook her head.

Desperate to fix things between them, believing this was his Hail Mary, he said, "The other night, I meant every word I said. You are a once-in-a-lifetime girl, and I know we've only known each other a short time, but damn, I can't imagine my life without you. I should have never left you alone. Not for a second. Please forgive me."

She took a step forward. Arms still crossed, she nervously wiped the tears from her cheek.

Not sure what to do, he reached out to her and waited.

Staring at his hand, she paused before extending hers to touch his.

Thankful, he gently pulled her in and tightly wrapped his arms around her. Holding her head against his chest, he kissed her forehead.

"How did you get home?"

"Black Lyon's butler, Martin, drove me in a private car."

Shane nodded.

Hesitating, she asked, "Why didn't you text or call me last night? I only heard from Jade."

"While searching the place for you, I lost my phone, or someone stole it from me–who knows. I couldn't find it anywhere. When we reached the corporate park, Jade said you replied to her text and were safe at home. I was up all night wondering what had happened to us and couldn't contact you, which made it worse. I got up early this morning, bought a new phone, and came home to upload the backup. I kept calling you, but you must have declined the calls."

"It said unknown number."

"When I texted, and you didn't respond, I drove here. Guess I hoped you'd leave the house eventually and I could follow you and maybe get a chance to talk. I didn't expect to find you with…."

Still upset, Abi knew the night was a series of bad decisions from beginning to end.

He slipped his hands into his pockets. "You know, you never have to worry about me cheating. My Dad cheated on my Mom. It changed my life forever. I would never put anyone through what he did."

"Thank you for saying that. I would never either."

Staring at the gravel below, Shane hesitated and said, "This Burton dude? He's really just a friend?"

"Yes, I told you. He was my neighbor. I've known him for years."

"So, nothing is going on between you?"

"No. Not at all. He's like a brother," Abi said, still pondering the outcome of their drive-up PCH today.

"Okay. I trust you."

Left in strange territory, they knew they'd have to start over.

"Do you want to come in?" Abi asked.

"I'm not sure your Dad wants me around right now." Shane knew he was angry. "Can we go somewhere to talk a bit more?"

"Given last night and how I came home, he's not happy with me either. At this point, not sure I should leave."

Wanting to continue their conversation, he asked, "Is there a quiet place to sit that will not bother him?"

"Sure. We can stay outside. Maybe sit by the pool?" Abi closed the main gate and led Shane to the front door. Opening it, she stepped to the left and slid the Fleetwood glass wall back before walking out onto the patio and leading him toward the pavilion rooftop.

"We can go and sit up there," she pointed along the way.

Climbing the concrete staircase to the upper level overlooking the canyon, Shane glanced back at the house and saw her Dad sitting on a sofa in front of the television. His eyes were on them.

She took a seat on a chaise. Shane did the same. Facing her, he knew he'd have to regain her trust. She'd been through a horrific ordeal, and he was to blame.

Knees almost touching between them, Shane reached out to her. "I feel like I failed you," he whispered.

Tears streamed down her cheeks.

It made him shift to a spot beside her. Encircling Abi with his arms, he said, "I'm so sorry."

Cuddled together, Abi hoped it was the start of their healing.

"I know this will take time, but are we good?" he whispered in her ear.

Abi nodded. "Yes. I think so."

Out of nowhere, they heard her Father shout something from the back door. It startled Shane and made him quickly slide two feet away from her.

Not sure what was wrong, she peeked over the glass railing. "Yes, Dad?"

"I ordered pizza if the two of you are hungry. It should be here shortly."

"Okay. We're coming."

Nervous energy flowed through Shane.

"You don't have to stay if you don't want to."

He thought for a second. "No, I have to stay. It's the only way to fix this."

"I'll clear things up with him later. Don't worry."

He took a deep breath and said, "Yeah, but you can't fight my battles."

Walking down the stairs together, Shane respectfully kept his distance. When they got inside, her Father was already talking to the delivery guy at the front door. Abi gathered some plates, napkins, and glasses and set them out on the island.

Bringing the pizza to the kitchen, her Dad looked at Shane. It was awkward.

Abi knew she needed to clear the air but didn't want to do it in front of him.

"Dad, umm... Can I talk to you for a second?"

Not saying a word, he followed his daughter as she left the room. Climbing the staircase, they went upstairs to the library.

Abi turned to him and said, "This whole thing last night was a misunderstanding. It's a long story. I'll explain more later. But please try and be nice. He and I want to work this out."

"Are you sure that's a wise decision?"

His daughter nodded. "I misjudged him. I stand by what I said. He's not a bad guy."

"If you say so." Her Father wasn't entirely convinced.

"Please? Dad..." Abi pleaded.

"Fine."

Returning downstairs, Dr. Acardi tried to make an effort. "So, Shane? Tell me. What are your aspirations for the future?"

"Dad?" Abi said, stunned by his forwardness.

"No, Abi. If he wants to date you, he must prove to me that he has a plan for the future. A direction?"

"It's okay, Abs." Remembering how his football coach trained him to address the scouts and university coaches, Shane looked her Father in the eye. Commanding the room, he prepared his pitch. "Sir, as of Friday, I earned a spot on the NCAA Top Prospect List this year. Actually, the top spot. So far, I've had twenty-five universities reach out. That said, football is not the beat-all to end-all. I hope to work towards a business degree while playing. But if I'm lucky enough and work hard, I'll get a shot at the NFL. That has been my dream since I was a kid. Plan B is to be an athletic agent so I can guide other athletes and help them succeed one day."

The man who doubted him raised his eyebrows with a look of surprise. "You've put thought into this. Good pitch."

"Thank you, Sir. I feel like I've been working my whole life toward senior year."

"Well, what impresses me is that you want to work hard and intend to earn your future. I'm happy to hear you don't feel entitled to it."

Abi smiled at Shane when her Dad took a slice of his pizza from the first box.

"Dig in, you two. It's getting cold."

More relaxed, Shane got Abi to take a slice before he got one himself. Hoping to talk shop, he walked over to her Dad sitting on the sofa and asked, "So, Abi tells me you're a Patriots fan?"

Dr. Acardi's face brightened. "That is a subject you'd better be well versed in."

Shane laughed. "Well, as a matter of fact, I am, Sir."

# 40

# Amends

After two hours of boring football banter, Abi started cleaning the kitchen.

Seeing her, Shane walked over and said, "Here, let me help you."

Giving the two some time to talk, Dr. Acardi left the room and went upstairs to check on his wife and the medical staff.

Abi rinsed the plates before handing them to Shane to put in the dishwasher.

He asked her, "Do you think your Dad still hates me?"

"It's not a matter of whether he hates you or not. It's if he trusts you."

"I'll be honest. What I said was rehearsed."

She turned to him and said, "Hopefully, he didn't see through it. But he did say, good pitch."

The quarterback's face scrunched up. "He did say that, didn't he?" Feeling defeated and less confident, he knew he'd have to work harder to win her Dad over.

"Hey, umm, want to go out for some ice cream? Maybe meet up with Reggie and Jade? I probably need to apologize to them," Abi stated.

"Yeah, sure. If you think it's okay that you go out."

"We won't be long. Let me go and ask. I'll be right back. Just wait for me in the living room."

Shane nodded as she headed upstairs. Checking his phone, he texted Reggie to see if he was free. Before his friend could reply, Shane saw a figure out of the corner of his eye. Believing it to be Abi, he stood up but found her Dad instead.

Intimidatingly staring him down, Dr. Acardi said nothing.

"Thank you for dinner, Sir," Shane said kindly.

"Let's cut the crap, Mr. Coppersmith," the middle-aged gentleman said.

Frozen, the athlete didn't know what to say.

"Have a seat and listen carefully," he stated sternly. "You will not breathe a word of this to Abi. Is that clear?"

"Yes, Sir," the athlete nodded.

Pausing, Dr. Acardi pointed to the ceiling. "That girl has been through hell and back over the past while. She's been a rock for our family, and I'll be damned if I allow some jock to break her heart. Do you understand?"

Shane nodded, "Yes." Working up the courage, he asked, "Umm, Sir. Can I say something?"

"What could you possibly have to say?"

He thought a second and selected his words carefully. "I've known your daughter for exactly ten days. In that short time, I discovered that she appreciates nature, the sea, and the stars and has this amazing ability to make people feel included and cared for – even if they're strangers. She is above and beyond anyone I've ever met. This past week, she tutored a student in math, earning him an A-minus on the test." He pointed at himself. "That was me, by the way. When I thought I couldn't pass, she encouraged me. I am embarrassed to admit it, but she knew I was struggling. After much repetition, what I was learning finally made sense for the first time, and it was all because of her. Dr. Acardi, your daughter, is smart, caring, supportive, and thoughtful. She is kind to everyone and always looks out for her friends."

Dr. Acardi was about to speak.

Shane raised his hand to stop him from commenting. "With all due respect, Sir, please let me finish."

Surprised by that, he gave him the floor.

"I am truly sorry to hear your wife is not well, but I plan to support Abi through it. Truthfully, I've developed strong feelings for your daughter, Sir - the kind that doesn't fade over time. Now, if anyone is going to get hurt in this relationship, it will most likely be me. Unlike Abi, who is strong, resilient, and would probably have no problem kicking me to the curb, I, on the other hand, would live a lifetime of regret if I ever lost her. And I'm not afraid to say it. I'm terribly sorry for the stress I've caused the past while. It will not happen again." Having said his piece, Shane wondered how the man would respond.

Dr. Acardi stood firm before taking one hand from his pocket. He approached and presented it to Shane. "I'll hold you to everything you just said."

Right then, Abi descended the stairs and found the two men in her life standing before one another. Not sure what happened, she asked, "What is going on?"

Her Dad turned to her. "Nothing. We are good."

Thankful to hear it, Shane said to him, "I'll have Abi back by six o'clock."

The man nodded and replied, "Appreciate that."

Her sights bounced back and forth between them, not knowing what she'd missed. "Bye, Dad," she said. "The nurse says she's asleep."

"Okay, Sweetie. Thanks."

Dr. Acardi watched Shane escort his daughter to the vehicle as they walked out. He opened the door for her chivalrously. Before getting in on the driver's side, he respectfully raised a steady hand to the man. Her Dad offered him the same gesture.

Inching out the gates onto Stradella, Shane leaned back in his seat. "Wow, that was intense."

"What happened between the two of you?" She got the feeling they had words.

"Your Dad was upset with me, obviously. He said you had been through a lot with your Mom. He didn't want me coming into your life and breaking your heart."

"He said that?"

"Yes, and he's right, too. From now on, there's no bringing you home late. That can't and won't happen again."

Abi nodded in agreement.

"As of now, no more Black Lyon raves. We are staying far away from there."

When he said that, she had different views on the subject but wasn't about to share them. Driving along Sunset Boulevard, she thought about the traumatic event. Fresh in her mind, barely twenty-four hours ago, she took note of the little details and felt indebted to Black Lyon for saving her. Despite getting back together with Shane, she was determined to find the famous DJ - even if it meant attending one more rave event if that's what it took.

*Last night could've ended differently.* She thought to herself. *If it weren't for him, my life would have changed forever.*

# 41

# Ice Cream

Meeting up with their friends, Jade ran to Abi and hugged her. The two went to sit down at a table and talk after the guys took their orders.

While standing in line, they watched Jade's reaction to Abi sharing her nightmarish encounter.

Seeing them get emotional, Reggie turned his back to them and asked Shane, "So, is she really okay?"

"I don't know for sure. She's pretty shaken up. And for good reason. First, she sees Emile kiss me, and then Eastwood and his friends corner her in a room. I hate myself for leaving her alone. I never thought..." He shook his head. "Thankfully, security rescued her, but that's not the point. I should've been there."

Enraged, hearing what Shane said, Reggie wondered if Eastwood would also target Jade by association. "We need to keep a close eye on them from here on out."

"Agreed," Shane replied.

"Do you want to pay Eastwood a visit?"

"You and I both know that will make things far worse." The football captain lowered his head. "He operates on an eye for an eye. Remember?"

His friend nodded, knowing the Oligarch's son's history. Changing the subject, he asked, "Maybe we should get away tomorrow?"

"What do you mean?"

Eager to share his news, unable to hold back, he said, "I wanted to run something by you."

"What do you mean?"

"I was talkin' to Blu last night. He invited us to his annual Labor Day pool party."

"Are you serious?"

"I know, right? It seems your name being on the top prospect list has its perks. He wanted me to invite you. The girls too. What do you say? You in?"

"I don't know, man. After this weekend, things with Abi and me are on shaky ground. I just made peace with her Dad. I can't screw up again."

"You and I both know this is one of those invitations you don't turn down. If you do, it's social suicide. There's no second chance."

"Reg? Are you seriously gonna cave to that?"

"Dude, you gotta go. Come on. Humor me."

Shane knew how epic Blu's party was, but it was a tall order.

"Look, I've already spoken to Alan, Adrian, and Shawn. They're on board and bringin' the girls, too. I've arranged everything. I also wanna surprise Jade. So play along, alright?"

Shane looked away. The invitation was so tempting. He hadn't had a break all summer and didn't foresee another for months. "Okay, if you can get Abi to agree, I'll go."

"Really?" He took it as a challenge.

"Yeah.  But you've gotta convince her first."

"Don't worry. I got this."

"I don't know. Think you've got your work cut out for you."

Reg straightened his posture. "Do you even know me, my man? I have the power of persuasion." Driving his fist into Shane's shoulder, he picked up the ice cream cups from the counter. "This is gonna be awesome!" he said, loud enough that the girls overheard.

"What's awesome?" Jade asked when they returned to the table.

Sitting beside her, Reggie handed her a cup with two scoops of vanilla ice cream and chocolate drizzle. "We got invited to Blu's Pool Party tomorrow."

"Really? Like all of us? Seriously?" Her eyes danced with excitement while taking a spoonful of her icy treat. "Oh, that's so yummy," she muttered. "I can't believe we got in!"

Shane handed Abi the pistachio and matcha cup she wanted.

"Thank you," she said quietly.

"You're welcome," he said, straddling the bench to her left.

Plotting how he would convince New England, Reggie played it cool. "So, Abi? Wanna go? It's the party of the year."

"I don't think so. It's been a rough few days."

"Come on, girl. You gotta come with us," Jade begged while savoring the melted chocolate on her spoon. "It'll be fun."

Resting his hand in the middle of her back, Shane said, "It's okay if you don't want to. I understand. We can always just hang out. Do something low-key."

That comment made Reg kick Shane under the table.

The quarterback shot him a disapproving look and subtly pointed at the guy to call him out on it.

Turning to Shane, she asked, "Are you going?"

"To be honest, I'd like to. It's probably the only break I'll get between now and Christmas. Getting invited is a big deal." Not sure if she wanted to be amongst a crowd of people, Shane said, "But it's up to you. No pressure."

Thinking it through, seeing three sets of eyes staring her way, awaiting an answer, she finally said, "Okay. I'll go, but just for a little while."

"Great!" Reggie slapped his hand flat on the table, making the girls jump. "You won't regret it. Jade and I will pick you and Shane up at your house at ten."

"Like in the morning?" Abi wondered why so early.

"Yeah, umm, it's a bit of a hike. But don't worry. I've arranged for all of us to go together," he explained before throwing out the last bit of info, hoping they'd just go with it. "Bring what you need for the day and your passport."

"Passport, why?" Questioning him, Abi believed that to be strange.

Reg thought fast on his feet. "Umm, Blu's Dad has heightened security. Apparently, he's been having threats. They wanna keep tabs on people comin' and goin'. It's the only way you get in. No passport. No party." Purposefully playing on Abi's naivety, he saw her shrug her shoulders.

"Oh. Okay."

Shane locked onto Reggie's proud expression. He didn't feel right not giving Abi the whole story - surprise or not.

Opting to people-watch while they finished their ice cream, Reggie avoided discussing their Labor Day plans any further. The last thing he wanted was for the truth to surface.

While Abi quietly ate the last of her ice cream, Shane could tell she was tired. It made him wonder if the following day would be too much for her. A level of guilt settled in.

"So," Reggie paused, breaking through the awkwardness. "Guess we should head home. Tomorrow morning comes early."

"Yeah, I promised I'd have you home by six, Abi. I'm not gonna be a minute late," Shane said firmly.

Jade reached out to her friend. "I'm so sorry you went through that last night. But I'm glad you're okay." Hugging her, Abi clung tightly. "You go home and get some sleep. I'll see you in the morning."

"I'll try." Recalling the nightmares she had endured only a few hours ago, Abi dreaded the darkness looming. Secretly happy that everything was out in the open, she knew it would have been hard to keep it bottled up. Never having close friends to confide in, she felt lucky to have them.

Taking hold of Abi's hand, Shane walked her to the Jeep while Reggie and Jade left in the Ferrari. Waving to them, they, too, pulled away from the curb and into the flow of traffic.

Continuing to hold her hand, he glanced over a few times.

Abi quickly took notice. "Why are you looking at me weirdly?"

He stared straight ahead and rested his left hand on the top of the steering wheel. "Do you hate me?"

Taking a deep breath, she believed that to be a loaded question. "No, I…"

"Cause I wouldn't blame you if you did," he interrupted.

"Shane, I don't hate you. It's just, after Friday night, I thought we were in a good place."

"We were, then, all this happened."

She peered out the side window. "Look, we can't change the past."

The handsome football player did not respond, but she could tell how bad he felt.

Abi squeezed his hand gently to get his attention. "The only thing we can do is move forward. If that's what you want."

While keeping his eye on the road, he turned and drove through the Bel Air gates. "Yes. I want that, no question."

Abi could tell he was beating himself up inside. Recalling the events from the night before, she revealed, "For the record, this was my fault, also. I wandered off on my own and shouldn't have. If I had stayed close to our group, as you said, we wouldn't be here right now. What happened was the consequence of my actions." About to reply to her, Abi said, "Let's move past this and forgive each other. If we don't, it will linger."

Shane suddenly pulled over to the side of the road. Shifting into park, he rested his elbow on the center console. Gazing into her eyes silently, he leaned in, prompting her to do the same. Eyes drifting closed, soon, he touched his lips to hers, but only barely. It was like he thought of her as fragile. Delicate.

To Abi's surprise, his kisses felt different. More connected. Like souls aligning. Hesitating, he pulled back, but she could blindly tell he wasn't far. Afraid to know why he stopped, he suddenly returned for more. With it came an unexpected rush of feelings that spread warmth from head to toe-so intense it gave her goosebumps. Was this the silver lining of a night gone wrong? Had this horrific experience inadvertently brought them closer together? His kisses were appreciative. Utterly grateful.

As they parted, he smiled and answered her, "I agree on all accounts." Hugging her with a protectiveness about him, Abi melted in his arms before he gave her space. Throwing the truck in gear, he cautiously pulled onto the road.

Left with emotions swirling, she hoped any doubt was just residual trauma and nothing more. Confused, Abi's mind drifted to Emile, Eastwood, Burton, and ultimately being saved by Black Lyon. So much had happened. Approaching her house, she opened the gate and inhaled deeply, hoping time would heal all wounds.

Driving into the courtyard, Shane parked the Jeep. Turning to her, he said, "You'd better go inside. It's five minutes to six." He swung around the rear of the Jeep just as she got out.

Walking her to the door with a buffer between them, knowing her Dad was probably watching, she realized why they'd stopped along the road.

While standing there, about to go in, she said, "I guess I'll see you in the morning. If anything changes, I'll let you know."

"Sounds good." Nervously stashing his hands in his pockets, he resisted the urge to kiss her. "If you can't go tomorrow, umm, don't worry. It's fine. We can always do something else. Maybe hang out here if you want. It's up to you."

"Sure. I'll keep that in mind."

"Okay, then. I should get going." Knowing he wouldn't dare initiate anything, Abi stepped forward and wrapped her arms around his waist. Hesitant, he slowly embraced her back.

She smiled when she let go. "Night, Shane."

His hands returned to his pockets. "Night, Abs."

Standing in the doorway, she watched him get behind the wheel and slowly pull away. Once he was gone, she closed the gate and locked the front door, expecting her Dad to greet her shortly, but he didn't.

Abi rounded the corner into the kitchen. She found her Dad's laptop on the coffee table, and the game muted.

Not seeing him, she said, "Hello?"

Heading upstairs, she heard voices in her parent's bedroom. Cautiously approaching, she found her Dad conversing earnestly with the nurse. Worried, with arms crossed in front of him, he held up his chin with one hand.

Seeing his daughter standing in the hall, he walked over.

"What's going on? Is Mom okay?"

"Her bloodwork came back," he said sorrowfully.

"And?" Abi held her breath.

"Her body is weakening."

"What does that mean?" She began to panic and fidget.

"It means we need to start a few more interventions. If that doesn't work, we may have to admit her." He knew Abi hated the thought of her in the hospital.

Tears developed in his little girl's eyes.

"Don't worry. I'll do the best I can to keep her here. We have a group of doctors at our disposal now. She's in good hands." He gave her a side hug and hoped what he said would calm her down.

Holding on tightly to him, she nodded.

"You go ahead and get ready for bed if you like."

"Alright." Abi silently turned and walked to her room. Guilt settled in once again. She hated the fact that she was living life while her Mother lay lifeless. Gingerly sitting on her bed in disbelief, Abi whispered, "What are you doing? This has to stop. Your priorities are out of whack." Unexpectedly, her thoughts veered toward a world without her Mom in it. Tears streamed down her face as the future flashed before her. It made her feel angry and cheated. "Why, out of all the mothers in the world, it had to be mine? Why not someone else's?" True to her nature, she knew she would not wish this on her worst enemy. Forcefully drying her face, she muttered, "Come on. You have to be strong for Dad. Pull yourself together and gather the courage. Stop being a baby."

Standing up, she walked into the bathroom and showered before sitting with her Mom for the next hour. Sharing the details of her drive up the PCH with Burton - his confrontation with Shane and the aftermath, she left out the part about the pool party. She hoped to save that for tomorrow night.

# 42

# Labor Day

For the second night in a row, Abi restlessly tossed and turned. Haunted by countless imaginary shadows hovering over her, she couldn't get the trauma out of her head. It seemed the nightmare was still on repeat.

When her alarm went off, she saw the light of day creeping across the room. Having hardly slept in twenty-four hours, she rolled over and thought about Shane and their friends. Afraid to lose them, she was thankful they cleared the air yesterday and supported her.

"Abs, you never want to revert to how your life was in Boston. It was a lonely existence. You've got to do whatever you can to keep them close."

Unpleasant memories flooded her mind. Recalling eating lunch at home while spoon-feeding her mother in between, then rushing back to class afterward, running late most days, and never speaking to a soul. To most, she was invisible.

"Insignificant," she whispered.

Determined to stop the self-destructing thoughts rambling on, she sat on the edge of the bed and rested her feet flat on the floor. Reaching for her robe, slipping both arms into each sleeve, she stood up and headed downstairs, hoping to grab breakfast. Standing at the top of the stairs, she looked at her Mom's room. The door was partially open. Toying with the idea of going to check on her, she recalled the silence it possessed. It was almost deafening. How she wished her Mom would speak one word–just one. Sadly, there was nothing but a limp hand resting in hers most days. Her body was there, but her mother was somewhere else. It made Abi think of the in-between and heaven. Had she seen a glimpse of that already? Where was she? Sleeping? Dreaming?

Breaking from those thoughts, she continued down the stairs. Stopping partway, able to see through the trees swaying in the breeze, she noticed a black SUV parked at the side of the road.

"Huh? Why are they parked on the corner? That's dangerous." Trying to get a better look, she moved left, then right, but couldn't see into its darkened windows. Not thinking much of it, she continued down the steps to find her Dad in the kitchen. "Good morning," she said.

"Morning, Sweetheart. Sleep well?" he asked, getting up from the sofa to hug her.

Without thinking, she replied, "Not really," before offering a smile, hoping he wouldn't ask why.

"Well, it's only been a little over a week. Give it time. You'll settle in. Before long, this place will start feeling like home."

Playing along, she said, "Yes, I hope so."

Released from her father's arms, desperate for a coffee, she placed a pod in the machine. Waiting as it brewed, she saw her Dad return to his seat. He looked exhausted.

"Happy to have today off?" she asked.

"Yes and no. This is the first long weekend I've had. Since I arrived, I've only been off on Sundays. The rest of the time, I've worked. I knew it wouldn't be an easy transition for your Mom, so I decided to bank some extra days." Resting the laptop on his legs, he watched the muted news headlines and worked simultaneously.

"Is there anything more I can do for you?"

He turned to her. "No, I want you to focus on school. Besides, you have done more than your share, Sweetheart. It's time you got back to being a kid." Realizing what he said, he raised his hand. "Sorry. Young woman. Not kid. But you know what I mean."

Feeling appreciated, she nodded. "Yes, I know what you mean. And thank you."

"You're welcome."

While pouring cream into her coffee, her Dad looked across the room. "So, anything planned today?"

"Well, as a matter of fact, I was asked to go to a pool party." She took a sip from her cup. "I wasn't sure if I was going to go."

"Whose party?"

"This guy named Blu Brennan. He is a famous model and has a bodyguard twenty-four-seven."

"Really?" Her Dad was stunned. It was a far cry from when he was that age. "You should go. Even if only for an hour or two."

"I thought about staying home and just hanging out today."

"You can do whatever you like, Sweetie. I'll be spending most of the day catching up on patient files and board business, so don't worry about me. I've got a lot to do."

"If you're sure?"

"Why don't we have dinner together tonight? How does that sound? I'll order it for seven o'clock. Does that work? Then I can hear all about your afternoon."

"That sounds good." Part of Abi felt like she'd been out too much over the weekend, but she knew her friends would be happy to hear that she could join them. "Guess I'll go get ready then. They asked to pick me up at ten, but I haven't confirmed."

He smiled before returning his focus to the screen.

Heading upstairs, she went to her room and immediately grabbed her phone off the side table. Noticing Jade had called, she wondered if anything had changed, so she called her back.

The girl answered on the first ring. "Abi?"

"Hey, sorry I missed your call."

"Did you hear?" her friend said intriguingly.

"Hear what?"

"Rumor has it that three guys from the Black Lyon rave are missing."

"Who?"

"No idea. That's all I've heard. I'm sure we will learn more soon."

For Abi, the first thought that crossed her mind was – *that could've been me.*

"Hey, girl? You there?"

"Yeah. I'm here."

"Oh, thought I'd lost you a second." Jade giggled. "So, you're still coming with us, right? Reggie is on his way to get me. Then we're swinging around to pick you guys up."

"I'll be ready. What do I wear?"

"It's a pool party, girl. You gotta bring out the bikini, denim cut-offs, tank, slides, and a hoodie. Bring a change of clothes, a brush and makeup. I'm sure he'll have towels."

"Okay. Sounds good."

"BTW, it's not unusual for him to have a hundred people."

"What? Really?"

"He has an older brother. If they both invite friends, it could be more."

Abi got worried. The last thing she wanted was to be amongst a large crowd. Maybe this wasn't such a good idea after all.

"I'm going to warn you. I might only stay an hour or two. Things are a little overwhelming here."

"No problem. Whatever you can handle."

"Where does he live anyway?" Abi hoped it wasn't too far.

"You can see the school from his backyard. He's maybe five minutes from there. I don't know why Reggie said it's a hike."

Not picking up on what she said, Abi replied, "Well, guess I'll see you in a bit, then?"

"Yep."

"Perfect."

"Ciao, my friend." Jade sounded so cheerful.

"Yes. Ciao."

After ending the call, Abi quickly gathered the clothes Jade had mentioned. Placing everything on her bed, she went to get showered and ready. Thinking about the pool party, Abi felt some anxiety surfacing. Hearing more about it, she knew it was a much bigger deal than she initially thought. Everything people did around here was always elaborate and over-the-top. She was sure Blu's event would be no different.

"Okay, Abs. Go there, act the part, and blend. That's all you have to do. See. Simple." Shrugging her shoulders, she didn't fully believe it would be that easy. But with Shane by her side, she hoped he would give her the strength to walk into the place confidently. At least that, she was sure of.

# 43

## The Surprise

Minutes before ten o'clock, Abi bolted down the stairs as quietly as she could, mindful of her Mom sleeping. Dressed modestly, deciding to pack the denim cut-off shorts, she opted for the black skort instead because it made her feel pretty.

Stopping midway down the stairs, she said, "Oh. I almost forgot."

Quickly returning to her room, she opened her desk drawer and grabbed her passport. Slipping it into her Burch Merch crossbody, she heard the notification that someone was at the gate. Assuming it was Shane, she opened it with her phone and said goodbye to her Dad.

"Bye, Sweetie. You look nice."

"Thank you," she said, hugging him. "I will see you later."

"Sounds good. Have fun."

"I will. Bye." Abi hurried outside and found Shane about to knock. "Hey," she said, surprised to see him there.

"Hi. Wow, you look great. Like the skirt."

"Thanks," she blushed, spotting a black Cadillac arriving. "They're here."

Shane grabbed his bag from the back of the Jeep and locked it. When the truck came to a stop, the driver got out and politely asked to take their bags.

Handing them over to him to put in the back, Shane opened the passenger side door. "After you," he said, allowing Abi to jump in first.

Surprised by the extended seat configuration, with two captain chairs facing forward and two backward, they found Jade and Reggie reclined with their feet up, sipping mimosas.

"Good mornin', my friends."

"Wow, this is nice," Shane commented, looking around the well-appointed cabin.

"Only the best for my peeps."

Getting settled, the SUV pulled away and turned south on Stradella.

"Ready for an action-packed day?" Jade asked, raising a full glass to see if they wanted some.

"I guess I'm ready. But I'll pass on the...." Abi pointed to the champagne-infused orange juice. Rubbing her sweaty palms together, she nervously said, "So, Jade tells me there'll be a lot of people there."

"I don't know. We'll have to see. That said, the guy never does anything half-ass," Reggie laughed. "The parties he throws end up in magazines and the tabloids."

"Great, that's the last thing I need. Can you imagine my Father in line at the grocery store, seeing me on the cover?"

"I wouldn't worry. He selects what goes into the publications and what gets omitted. I think we're safe. We aren't super close to him, so the odds are slim."

"Okay. I'm banking on that."

Leaving the gates of Bel Air, headed west on Sunset, the driver suddenly merged onto the highway. Not knowing where they were going, Abi decided to sit back and enjoy the ride. Seeing Jade and Reg immersed in each other, Shane asked, "So, how'd you sleep last night?" Reaching across to her, he needed to feel connected.

She grasped hold of his hand. "Didn't have the best sleep. Maybe got three hours."

"That's not good."

Opting not to share why, she tried to fluff it off. "It'll be fine. I'll go home tonight and get to bed early. Hopefully, then, I'll catch up."

When he heard that, Shane got concerned and looked around to see where they were. He knew it would only be a few more minutes before she'd see the truth.

"Oh, did you hear? Jade said three guys went missing from Black Lyon on Saturday."

"Yeah, Reggie called to tell me earlier. Strange that nobody has gotten wind of who they are yet?"

His friend overheard their conversation and chimed in. "It hasn't made headlines. Maybe they're troublemakers giving their parents grief?"

"Possibly. I'm sure it won't be long, and word will get out," Jade said. "The elites in LA are a very well-connected group of people. Eventually, everything surfaces."

Approaching a corporate park, the driver slowed and turned into a private parking lot.

An anxiousness flooded over Shane. He believed this was all a mistake. *I should've told her. I'm such an idiot. How is she ever gonna trust me after today?* he thought.

"Where are we?" Curiously looking around, Abi leaned forward, wondering if they were close.

Jade looked left and right. "Wait a minute!"

Reggie watched to see her reaction.

The driver spoke to someone at the security console. When he did that, the gate opened, and they slowly passed through. Maneuvering the circular driveway, Abi saw where they were as the truck passed through a second checkpoint.

"Are we at an airport?" she asked.

Shane could see her mind reeling.

"Surprise!" Reggie said excitedly.

"What's going on?" Abi began to panic.

"Yeah, Reggie? What's going on?" Shane was determined for him to take the fall. He knew this was not going to go over well.

"Surprise! This year, Blu's Pool Party is at his house in Cabo."

"What do you mean?" Abi thought he heard him wrong. "Like Mexico?"

"Yep. We're flying there," he replied excitedly.

"Eeeee! OMG!" Jade hugged and kissed him.

Reggie calmly unlatched his seat belt as the truck stopped beside a private jet. "Passports, please," he said before meeting their pilot.

Abi looked at Shane as Jade got out to join him. "I can't go to Mexico? I mean… What?" Stunned, she said, "Did you know about this?"

He lowered his head.

"You knew, and you didn't tell me? What the hell, Shane?"

"I'm sorry."

"Oh, my god. I, umm, can't… No, I can't go. My Dad would have my head on a platter if he found out. All I've been doing is lying to him lately."

Reggie and Jade passed the pilot their passports as he was compiling the paperwork.

"Look, in all fairness, I thought, with all the stress you were under, that maybe it would be good for you to get away."

"What about school? We can't ditch?"

Confused, Shane said, "Nobody's ditching school. It's a day trip. One day. There and back. That's all."

Hearing that defused her anger slightly. "Just today? You can do that?"

"When you have money, you can do whatever you want." It was promising to see her calming down.

Suddenly, other SUVs pulled up. One by one, their friends emerged and joined Reggie and Jade. Each presented their passport to the pilot.

"So, everybody's going?"

"Yes." He felt terrible for putting her in this position. "Look, I'm sorry. Reggie wanted to keep it a secret for Jade. If you don't wanna go, then we won't. Plain and simple. Up to you."

Seeing all their friends boarding the aircraft, she felt torn.

"Blu's place is incredible. Like, I mean, heaven on earth. I'd love for you to see it. Only been there once before."

When she heard that, it warmed her up to the idea. Looking down at her phone, knowing her Dad would check her location, she hesitated before turning it off. "Fine. But I have to be home for seven–eight at the latest. I'm supposed to have dinner with him. Hopefully, I can push it off an hour. Will we be back by then?"

"I'll make sure of it."

She nodded. "I can't believe I'm doing this."

He got out of the SUV and offered her his hand. Taking hold, she watched him grab their bags from the driver. Walking to meet the pilot, Shane handed over their passports. Once the man had their information on the manifest, they approached the jet and climbed the stairs. Inside, she saw everyone laughing and talking.

Two flight attendants greeted, "Welcome aboard," as they passed.

"Thank you," Abi said, entirely in unfamiliar territory.

When their friends saw her, everyone shouted simultaneously, "Yeeeaahhhh!"

Timidly taking an empty seat, Abi buckled up.

Shane sat beside her. "You're sure you're okay with this?"

With nerves running at an all-time high, she was still not sure. "I guess so. Cabo, here we come."

44

# South Bound

The jet whisked down the runway and lifted off smoothly. Climbing to thirty thousand feet, the group soon moved freely about the cabin.

Abi stayed seated and looked out the window at the ocean view and the clouds. Worried about what she had done, a part of her was curious about where they were going and what the day would hold. Looking around at all her friends smiling, laughing, and having fun, she saw the flight attendants serving breakfast amongst all the chatter.

Shane reached across Abi's lap and opened a small cubby to pull out a hidden tray before the woman set her food in front of her.

"Thank you," she said to him before saying the same to the attendant.

The young woman smiled. "You're welcome, Miss."

Shane followed suit. Taking the first few bites, he looked over. "Doing okay over there?"

She nodded agreeably.

"Are you mad?" he asked.

Not answering right away, she thought that was a tricky question.

He stopped eating to give her his undivided attention.

"Look, I'm not mad. A little disappointed, maybe." She took a sip of her juice. "That said, I see what you were trying to do."

"I should've gone with my gut."

"What did it tell you?" She was curious to know.

"For us to stay home." Swiveling around enthusiastically, facing her, he said, "But, Abs, you've gotta see this place. I'm sure you'll love it once you get there. Just think about the waves crashing against the shore. The white sand and ocean breeze."

The image he was describing was enticing. She'd never been anywhere but Cape Cod and the Outer Banks. This was all new to her. Unlike them, she hadn't traveled much – especially like this.

"Who's plane is it?" she asked.

"Reggie's."

"Really?" She was impressed. In search of their friends, she saw Jade and Reg lying on a bed, chatting in the back. Just ahead of them were Adrian and Mei. They had found a quiet spot on a sofa. Seeing the rest joyful and relaxed, she could tell this was normal for them.

"Don't worry. You'll get used to it."

"To what?"

"The luxuries that come with having millionaire friends."

45

# Cabo San Lucas

Everyone took their seats when the pilot announced their descent into Cabo San Lucas. Abi saw the beautiful water as the jet circled the Baja Peninsula. Reminding herself to check her texts often throughout the day, she wanted to be sure if her Dad tried to contact her, she'd reply quickly. Afraid to miss something, she turned up the ringer volume and put it away.

Smoothly landing in the middle of the desert, the plane soon taxied toward the terminal. Reaching the private jet FBO, they saw two SUVs waiting. Each disembarked one by one while the warm Pacific gusts swirled around them. Eagerly transferring to the trucks, everyone was excited for their adventure to begin. Taking their seats while the driver loaded their baggage, the caravan was soon off to their intended destination.

Leaving the airport, Abi surveyed her surroundings. With sand everywhere, surprised at the lack of green foliage, she mostly found cacti growing in the medians between the roads. There were more abandoned buildings than homes, and the residential areas looked poverty-stricken. It was a culture shock.

*And here we arrived on a private jet,* Abi thought, noticing her friends not batting an eye at the scenery unfolding before them.

Concerned by the locked wrought iron gates over many of the residential exterior windows, Abi did not feel safe.

Feeling Shane's arm slip around her and his hand taking hold of hers, he whispered, "It's sad, isn't it?"

"Yes. I've never been anything like this."

"Here, you're either uber-wealthy or poor. There doesn't seem to be much in between."

"I can see that."

The strong winds that day riddled the air with dust. It seemed to clear a little the closer they got to the coast. After seeing so much ruin, they soon approached an area with luxurious mansions boasting beautiful landscaping—all newly constructed. This was very different from the first half of the drive. Seeing a hint of the ocean, the SUVs threaded through a narrow iron gate surrounded by security.

"Here we are," Shane said.

When they stopped, he opened the door and took hold of Abi's hand to help her out. It was sweltering hot. Getting their bags from the back, he slipped them on his shoulder and said, "Come with me."

Walking through an interior courtyard with Palm trees blowing in the breeze, Shane found the main doors. Welcomed by staff as he led her into the enormous home, they found people scattered about - some their age and some college students.

Shane said, "Looks like Blu's brother Kai also invited people." He didn't think anything of it.

She could see two distinct groups gathered in various areas. Blu's friends were the wild ones plunging into the pool while the brother's guests sipped wine in the covered seating areas.

"If you think the house looks big from this angle, wait until you see it from the beach," Shane said while gently squeezing her hand. "Don't worry. Everything will be fine. I don't plan to let you out of my sight for a second."

"Promise?" There was fear in her voice.

Kissing her, he said, "Promise."

Abi took a deep breath. About to second guess her decision, she caught sight of the ocean view beyond the colorful furniture standing out against the white plaster walls. After bypassing the living room and stepping into an outdoor seating area boasting an incredible Aztec-patterned barreled three-dimensional ceiling, they found the pool a mere twenty feet away. Abi was in awe. The infinity edge disappeared into the sea below. Miles and miles of ocean stood before them. Lined with countless chaise loungers, each with a rolled beach towel for guests, the square canvas umbrellas provided shelter from the hot sun.

Shane turned to see her reaction. "What do you think?"

Lost for words, she simply said, "Beautiful."

"Hey, Q-beee!" A commanding voice bellowed deeply.

They turned to find the pale-skinned, blonde model with ice-blue eyes coming to greet them.

"You made it! Awesome, dude!" Gripping his hand, giving him a manly pat on the back, he said, "Saw you made the prospect list! Congrats, man."

"Thanks." Shane knew the publicity would spark interest.

"Make yourselves at home. Mi casa es su casa," the guy said before greeting the rest of their group.

"Come on, let's go get changed."

Reluctantly leaving the view, she went with Shane. Passing through the living room, he turned right and opened a door. "We can change in here."

Abi entered as Shane closed and locked the door behind them. Admiring the rainbow of colors, all blending seamlessly, she turned to him and said, "This is like we are in another world."

Setting their bags on the bed, he inched closer with open arms. "I told you you'd love it."

She hugged him and said, "The view is stunning." Reminded of her Dad, she checked her texts. Thankfully, there was nothing.

"Try to enjoy your time here. It will go by fast." Kissing her, he said, "The bathroom is right through there. You go first and get changed."

"Alright. I'll be back."

Curious, she walked across the custom floor tiles with patterned inlays. Closing the door behind her, with her tote bag on her shoulder, she ran her hand along the edge of the soaker tub and noticed the white monogrammed towels and robes. Changing into her bikini, putting on sunscreen and flip flops on her feet, she tied her hair in a messy bun and put on her bucket hat. Exiting the bathroom, she found Shane lying on the bed, sleeping with his hands atop his chest. Able to see the ocean from the window on her right, she walked over and stared at the water, anxious to explore.

Hearing her, he opened one eye and jumped up. "All done?" he asked cheerfully.

"Yes."

He, too, went to change into his board shorts and emerged shirtless with his bag on his shoulder. "Ready to head out?"

She nodded.

"What do you want to do first? Pool or beach?"

"Definitely, beach."

He smiled and took her hand. "Beach it is." Sliding the doors open, they walked out onto a covered patio. Closing it behind them, he said, "This way."

Leading her down the curved concrete steps, Abi couldn't believe the color of the water. Various shades of turquoise captivated her. Smelling the aroma of food as they passed the grassy-topped cabana bar, she saw a man barbequing burgers and steak.

A woman stopped them and said, "Welcome to La Datcha. If you are hungry, Mr. Brennan has a buffet in the kitchen, and both gazebos are offering a la carte when you're ready."

"Thank you," Shane said.

Abi smiled at the woman graciously. "Yes, thank you."

She was noticeably surprised by their politeness.

They followed the stone path. Rocks towering to their right, the ocean was right there. The waves roared as they hit the shore and flooded the beach before receding repeatedly. Immersing her toes in the water, she inched a little further.

"Wait. We can't swim here. The undertow is too strong, and there's a thirty-foot drop-off right there." He pointed to the darkness close to shore. "But if you want, we can sit on the beach and let the waves roll over us."

They left their bags in the sand and walked back to the water's edge.

As a rough wave rolled toward them, Abi could feel the strength of the current tugging at her ankles. "Oh, I can feel it."

"It catches you fast. Be careful." He held her hand tightly to keep her safe.

The sun was at its peak.

"Wow, it's scorching."

"Want to go to the pool and take a swim?" he asked.

"Sure."

Picking up their things on the way by, they washed off their feet under the shower and climbed the beach stairs. About a hundred people had gathered in small groups, most talking and laughing. They were all stylishly dressed in designer swimwear and looked confident.

A voice pierced the constant hum of the crowd. "Abi! Shane! Over here!"

Seated on a chaise lounger by the pool on the far side, Jade waved them over. Reggie was with her, soaking up the sun. Seeing familiar faces scattered about that part of the house, Abi set her bag down and sat beside her best friend.

"What do you think? It's amazing, right?" Noticing Abi's nervousness, Jade hoped she was okay.

"It sure is. Never seen a house like this before."

Shane went to talk to a few people.

Abi quickly spread a towel over the chair and got comfortable. Amidst it all, she spotted Adrian and Mei cutely sitting along the pool's edge with their legs dangling in the water. Mei flirtatiously brushed her shoulder against Adrian's as he conversed with her happily. There was something so pure about their budding relationship - the innocence of it. Uncomplicated, without a care in the world, their main focus was only to learn about what made the other tick. She was happy things were going well and thought both possessed such kind souls.

Shane returned to Abi. "Do you want to swim with me?" he said.

"Sure."

She got up as he guided her into the water across the Baja shelf. Plunging into the deep end, they both surfaced. Intent on staying close to him, she wrapped her arms around his neck as he swam to the edge. Resting along the infinity ledge, the two looked out at the vastness. Reggie and Jade joined in.

"So, did you hear the latest?" Jade could hardly wait to spill.

"No. What?" Abi replied as a group of guys cannon-balled, causing Laney's swan to topple over by the infinity edge. Immediately, they saw Shawn dive in to rescue her. Watching him check to see if she was alright, Abi could tell how protective he was of her already.

"Rumor has it Eastwood and his friends are the missing guys from the rave." She had searched social media for about a half hour and only found personal accounts reporting it. No mainstream media had picked it up yet. "Can you believe it?"

Abi asked, "Are you sure?"

"No, not a hundred percent, but it's making the rounds. There are a lot of people talking about it. Most times, social is more accurate than the news. Word on the wire is someone heard a guy say that Eastwood had it coming."

Reggie hugged his girlfriend. "Keep in mind who Eastwood's Dad is. I'm sure the kid has had a target on his back since birth."

"What if it is them?" Abi fidgeted. "Do you think Black Lyon is to blame or someone else?"

"Wait. Let's not speculate until we get confirmation," Reggie said calmly.

"Agreed. It could be anyone, really," Jade said.

"Besides, I don't think the guy would ever let somethin' like that happen." Reggie seemed certain.

Notification bells suddenly infiltrated the pool area. Scanning the groups of people, each glued to their screens, Reggie let go of Jade and said, "Give me a second. I'm going to find out what's going on."

The volume around them elevated while they watched Reggie reading off someone's device.

When he returned, Shane asked, "What is it?" His friend looked concerned.

"Reg?" Jade said, trying to break his focus.

The guy dipped his head back in the water and looked at Shane and Abi. "The police just issued photos of the guys who are missing. They are Eastwood's friends."

Getting out, Shane went to view the missing person's report. With his phone in hand, he confirmed the three teens were undoubtedly Eastwood's guys. Seeing this, he lowered his head and glanced at Abi.

A million scenarios came to mind. She was in shock and whispered anxiously, "Now what?"

A few party-goers started to look their way. Knowing that their confrontation on Saturday night with Eastwood's group was witnessed by many at the rave, she wondered if some were falsely connecting the dots.

"What Eastwood did to Abi...." Reggie whispered under his breath, "...Has consequences. Maybe this is related to what happened, and maybe it's not. We gotta wait and see as more information surfaces. Let's not jump to conclusions."

"I agree with Reg," Shane voiced. "Korolev's Dad has many enemies. Who better to target than his son?"

Lost in thought, Abi saw a big guy step out of the house and onto the pool deck. Registering who it was made her do a double take. There, amidst the college crowd, was Burton with a blonde bombshell hanging off his arm.

Blu's brother greeted him enthusiastically. "Bax! Dude! You made it! Good to see you, man!" He offered a firm handshake before introducing him around.

To Abi, it was strange to see her friend in a social setting. Now, with his newfound wealth, this was the life he could enjoy on a whim.

While he mingled with a few people, he panned the pool and caught sight of Abi. Surprised to see her, he quickly made his way over.

"Hey, Abs," Burton said while the blonde model looked on.

"Hi, Burton."

Shane was not impressed.

"Wasn't expecting to see you here," he said. "Thought this was a college party."

The comment put Shane on edge.

Reggie intervened. "Yeah, well, Blu invited us."

"Didn't know Kai's kid brother invited people too."

Abi wondered why Burton was being so rude.

In an instant, Shane stepped forward with his fists clenched in front of him.

Burton could see the effect he was having on the guy. "Do you want to get a drink at the bar," he asked the pretty girl.

"Yes, that would be great," she replied.

"Guess I'll talk to you later, Abs." Smirking at Shane, they walked away.

"I think not," the football player shot back.

Wanting to stir the pot, Abi's burly friend did not miss a beat. "I think that's up to her. Don't you?" His voice was deep and threatening.

Abi stepped in, hoping a fight wouldn't break out. Standing in the pool between Shane and Burton, she shouted, "Stop, both of you!" Wading over to the steps, she got out and grabbed a towel before storming past them as the pretty girl sneered at her on the way by, reminding her of Emile.

That's when Abi overheard the girl ask him, "Who was that?" in a snooty tone.

Not skipping a beat, Burton answered, "Just an old friend."

For the first time, Abi felt a little jealous that Burton was spending time with someone other than her. Running down the beach steps, she wanted to go home.

Shane got out of the water and went after her.

Seeing what transpired, Jade was confused. When she met Burton, he hadn't come across as a prick. He seemed really nice.

*What changed?* She thought while watching Shane descend the steps. Her eyes pivoted to Burton. While Abi walked toward the shore below, he watched Shane closely as he caught up to her. A worried look flashed across the guy's face. It was like he regretted what he'd said.

Shane found his girlfriend sitting on the beach, staring at the horizon. Treading carefully, he walked over and sat beside her, close enough to graze her shoulder.

"Hey."

Sitting silently, Abi finally spoke. "I'm sorry about that."

"I'm sorry, too. I don't know what it is about that guy that irks me so much."

"Burton is harmless. I believe he was showing off or possibly wanted to get under your skin. He's not usually like that - like at all."

"Well, I'm not a fan."

She looked away.

Knowing it wasn't her fault, he reached over and said caringly, "Please don't be mad."

"I want to go home." Not responding, Abi watched the waves breaking a little ways out. This place was no longer paradise to her.

"We are scheduled to fly out at five-thirty. Guess we can't leave until then."

Knowing they didn't have a choice, she leaned over and rested her head on his shoulder, determined to make the best of it.

# 46

# Speculation

The winds picked up, causing the waves to crash against the shore with a vengeance. The humidity was rising so much that they could cut it with a knife. Sitting there, Abi hoped their run-in with Burton hadn't ruined the day. Upon returning home, she planned to confront him and ask why he acted the way he did. What he said had caused a rift between her and Shane. It was inexcusable. That is when it dawned on her - maybe it was intentional. Perhaps he was jealous. All things considered, she knew Burton hated what Shane did. If he hadn't left her alone at the rave, this whole Eastwood thing would have never happened in the first place. *Or would it?* She thought, still feeling just as much to blame. It wasn't all his fault.

"Sorry, can we go back to the pool?" he asked, wiping his brow. "It's too hot."

As the sweat rolled down her back, she agreed, "Sure."

Shane got up off the sand and brushed himself off. Helping her, they walked to the outdoor shower to hose down before returning to their friends.

Finding Jade sprawled out on her lounge chair, with phone in hand, she waved Abi over.

"Abi! I just found this online."

Showing her the post, Abi listened to her read it aloud while Shane dove in the pool.

"A frantic search is underway for a group of missing Calabasas teens last seen at an exclusive rave event in Hidden Hills. Police posted pictures moments ago and have since added a fourth unidentified male. Anyone with information on this case should contact the Los Angeles Police Department."

Abi's face went white.

"That confirms Eastwood is missing too? It has to be him. He's the fourth," Jade speculated.

Thinking a minute, Abi said, "Strange that the cops aren't announcing it happened at a Black Lyon event."

"Guess they must be certain before draggin' the DJ's name into this. Otherwise, the guy can sue for defamation." Reggie's legal knowledge surprised them.

"What are the chances that someone from the party will come forward with information?" Abi's mind reeled.

"I don't know. I believe most wouldn't. That's my thinking. It would be like committing treason amongst the elites. Snitching on Black Lyon wouldn't be the best move." Her friend knew that to be true.

"What if I don't come forward and someone implicates me? Then what?" Abi said.

"If that happens, you play dumb and say you hadn't heard the news because you're busy with your Mom being ill and all," Reg said.

Shane swam over and ran his hand through his wet hair. Seeing Abi deep in thought, he asked, "Is something wrong?" not having heard their conversation.

Jumping in beside him, Abi quietly said, "Another guy got added to the missing person list. Three of Eastwood's friends and now a fourth, quote-unquote, unidentified male teen. It's gotta be Eastwood."

Gracefully slipping into the water with them, Jade added, "Yeah, but who would report him missing? His dad would never go to the cops. So, who did?"

Unfamiliar with the guy's situation, Abi suggested, "Maybe his Mother?"

"I'm pretty sure his parents are divorced, so that is possible," Reggie said, recalling it from years back.

"I'd assume his dad would investigate and have his guys on it. He's a wanted man. There's no way he'd ever pull in the LAPD to help. They'd arrest him on site," Shane said while sitting on the edge of the Baja shelf.

"So, does that mean Black Lyon is in danger from the Korolev family?" Abi feared for her hero's safety.

Reggie floated to the middle of the pool. "I don't doubt he's involved. Actually, I'd bet money on it. If anything happens to this kid, that DJ will be number one on Korolev's hit list."

Abi was still naïve about how things worked. "You think they will kill Black Lyon?" she said, panicked.

"Well, if Eastwood and his friends are dead, hell yeah. Korolev will take an eye for an eye, for sure," Reggie stated bluntly.

"But what if he didn't do it? What if someone else attacked or kidnapped them?" Abi jumped up and sat beside Shane.

Her boyfriend introduced another angle. "But they were last seen at the rave. Who knows, maybe what happened to you has happened to other girls, and the DJ's sick of Eastwood infringing on his business. That's enough to take action against the guy."

Jade noticed Abi was upset. She gave Reggie and Shane the eye.

To change the subject of conversation, Shane slipped back into the water and treaded before reaching out his hands to Abi. She got in and slowly inched closer. His blue eyes locked to hers as he took hold of her hands. Effortlessly moving backward through the water, his legs rotated counter-clockwise like eggbeaters below. Pulling her along gently, they reached the far side. Out of Reggie and Jade's sight, he backed himself into the corner, allowing her to float straight into his arms. Comfortably encircling her legs around his torso, her arms around his neck, he held her close.

"I didn't realize you were such a good swimmer." Abi giggled nervously.

"I'll let you in on a secret. I used to lifeguard at private pools in the summers before football took off."

"Impressive. It takes a lot of work to get certified."

"Yes, but I'm no stranger to that," he proudly replied.

With a silence falling between them, Shane quietly reiterated, "Hey, umm, Abs. I am sorry for how I acted earlier."

"I don't blame you."

To a degree, he knew he'd failed her. "I don't know what it is, but that guy brings out the worst in me."

"Am I sensing a bit of jealousy?" she asked with a tilt of her head.

Defensive, he quickly replied, "Jealous? Of him? Why?"

"I don't know. Just a feeling."

He went quiet. "You might be right."

She was surprised he admitted it.

"So, we're good, right?"

Seeing him wear his heart on his sleeve, she replied, "Yes."

"Good, 'cause I want us back to where we were Friday night?" There was a desperation in his tone.

"Oh? And where were we Friday night?" She put him on the spot, hoping he'd enlighten her.

Uncomfortable with the subject, he looked away. "I don't know..." Shrugging his shoulders, he added, "How you looked at me made me feel like there was nobody else."

"On Friday, you were my knight in shining armor who was attentive when I was sad. You protected me from the fireworks at Aramis' party and knew when I needed to leave. That's when you brought me to the most peaceful spot on the beach to look at the stars and listen to the waves. Our time together there captured my heart."

"Until I screwed it up." He could not look her in the eye. "I hate myself for that."

Surveying the expression on his face, she traced his forehead with her finger. Softly resting her hand on his cheek, she drifted her thumb across his lips. She could feel his heart hammering in his chest as he tried to catch his breath. When she lightly touched her lips to his once, then twice, she paused and looked deep into his eyes.

"I've fallen in love with you, Abs," he whispered, causing a smile to spread across her face.

She was almost speechless. Able to squeak out two words, she said, "You have?"

"Yes, and I'm not afraid to say it."

"Well, I love you too."

Immersed in the moment, he wrapped her tightly in his arms and kissed her again and again. Aware of the increased intensity, he suddenly stopped. "Sorry...umm..."

Abi bit her bottom lip, knowing they got carried away.

Suddenly, Reggie and Jade cannonballed into the pool, drenching their friends.

Jade emerged from under the water about six feet away and said, "Maybe you guys need to get a room?"

Abi blushed.

"No, I think we're good," Shane stated, unable to veer away from Abi's stare.

When Reggie surfaced, he swam over to Jade. "We have two hours left." With a mischievous smile, he casually asked, "Do you wanna freshen up?"

Getting the hint, Jade replied, "Maybe."

The two left the water and dried off. Gathering their things, Reg wrapped his arms around Jade's waist and kissed her neck before she turned around to return the favor. Soon, they disappeared inside.

"So, do you think they're..."

"Yeah, pretty sure," he replied without hesitation.

Needing to know, she built up the courage and asked curiously, "Is that something you think about?" When she said it, she felt her lungs empty. Her heart beat rapidly the second the words rolled off her tongue. She could barely breathe.

"Abs, don't feel pressured because of them." He didn't know what she was thinking as she fidgeted with his hair. "Hey..." he said, getting her attention.

Acknowledging him, she nodded with an uncertain smile.

"Are you hungry? Maybe we should check out the buffet in the kitchen? Or maybe grab a burger from the pavilion before heading out."

Breaking from a million thoughts, she smiled and said, "Sure, we can do that."

"Perfect," he said, hugging her. "I really need to eat."

"Me too."

# 47

# Friction

The sun slowly descended toward the horizon, casting an orangey glow on everything it touched. Abi and Shane left the pool, dried off, and steered clear of Burton. Taking their bags along with them, they visited the beach pavilion and ordered a freshly made burger. Staying out of sight, they enjoyed their gourmet meal while soaking up what was left of the day. Sadly, they knew their time here in paradise was ending.

When they finished eating, Shane turned to her. "Wanna take a short walk before getting changed?"

"Yeah, I'd like that."

Strolling hand in hand to the water's edge, they welcomed the waves periodically hitting their feet.

"Despite everything, I'm glad I came," she said.

"See. The idea wasn't so bad after all?"

When he said that, she felt uneasy. It was the same feeling she got when she returned home from her shopping spree with Jade and had to tell her father about the enormous credit card bill. Abi knew he'd be beyond mad if he found out she had traveled to Mexico without telling him. Remembering she hadn't checked her phone in a while, she dug in her bag to find it but hesitated, knowing she couldn't turn it on yet.

Shane took his device from his bag. Holding it up to take a selfie, wrapping his arm around her, he said, "Smile."

Happy with the picture, she asked, "Can you send me that? It's a good one."

"A little something to remember our trip." Almost at the end of the beach, reaching the rocks, he said, "Guess we should head back."

Turning around, they picked up the pace. As they got closer, Shane noticed a commotion on the pool deck.

"What the hell?" he said. Seeing fists flying, a few college guys suddenly stepped in to break up the fight.

They rushed back. While washing the sand off their feet, the yelling escalated above them. Climbing the curved staircase and reaching the upper level, they found Alan, Shawn, and Adrian squaring off with another group of guys. Shane went over to them while Abi tended to Laney, who was in tears. Ming and Mei were with her.

"What happened?" Abi asked, knowing emotions were running high.

Laney couldn't speak, and Mei was mad.

"Ming?"

Comforting her friend, Ming said, "Laney's ex is here and got into it with Shawn."

Abi could tell by the state Laney was in that it was more than that. "Are you all right?" she asked.

Barely able to speak, the girl trembled and said, "No. I want to go home."

"Don't worry. We are leaving soon."

"Shane!" Abi yelled, "Get them out of here!"

Pointing at the doors to the right of the home, Shane nodded and gathered the troops. She did the same. Whisking everyone through the patio door into the room where she and Shane had started the day, they gathered around while Shane slid it closed.

"Girls, go in the bathroom and quickly shower and get changed. Once they finish, guys, you can do the same."

They listened to what she said without question.

Shutting the bathroom door for them, Abi noticed Shawn holding his hand awkwardly. On top of that, blood was running down Alan's face, and Adrian was developing an impressive shiner. Walking over, she looked at Alan first, then the other two. "These guys need ice. Can you please grab some from the kitchen along with a paper towel roll?"

"On it." Shane walked out of the room.

Quickly opening the bathroom door a crack, Abi asked Ming to pass her a hand towel. Returning to Alan, she placed it over the cut. "Hold this here," she said. "Press down to stop the bleeding."

He silently acknowledged her.

Moving on, she gingerly inspected Shawn's hand. "Can you move your fingers?"

The wide receiver winced. "Kinda. The one finger is messed up pretty good."

She saw it was already black and blue and three times its size. "I think you broke that one."

Wondering what she could use to make a split, she looked around the room. Not finding much, she knocked on the bathroom door and checked to see if the girls were decent so she could go in. Carefully slipping through a narrow crack, closing it behind her, she grabbed another towel and a ribbon she noticed decoratively holding the face cloths together. Searching under the cabinets, she found a first aid kit and two clean, folded trash bags. Returning to the guys, Abi saw Shane was back with ice in a bucket and a paper towel roll.

Doubling over a few sheets, Abi put it over the cut and told Alan, "Hold that there. Press down again," before moving on to Adrian.

Dumping some ice in a bag, she tied it off and said, "Ice that eye and cheek, twenty minutes on and twenty minutes off. Set a timer on your phone." Attending to Shawn, she said, "We need to bring down the swelling. Ice it for now, and I'll splint it before we go. You'll have to keep it elevated on the way home. Once we land, you need an x-ray done."

Switching back to Alan, she carefully took a peek at the cut. The bleeding had slowed. "I'm sorry to say, but you're gonna need stitches."

"No way? Really?" He slumped in the chair.

"Yes, it's pretty deep."

The entire time, Shane watched how calm Abi was in a crisis. He was amazed by how she took charge.

One by one, the girls walked out, freshly showered.

Seeing them changed and ready to go, Shane said, "Abi, you go next. I got this."

"Okay." Inside the bathroom, she saw what time it was. Stepping in the shower, she washed away the salt and sand and quickly dried off to get dressed. With her bag packed, she left the room. "Who's next? Gotta move people."

The guys finished in record time while Abi splinted Shawn's hand and cleaned Alan's face as best she could. Covering the cut with gauze and medical tape, she handed him extra supplies in case it started to bleed on the plane.

A knock came to the door. Ming opened it. Reggie and Jade walked in.

Seeing the guys were hurt, he said, "What the hell happened?"

"Long story," Shawn replied while comforting Laney.

"We gotta go. The plane is waitin' for us."

Abi did a sweep of the room and bathroom. "Everyone has everything? Phones? Chargers? Clothes?"

Shane laughed when each stopped to check their bags before walking out the door.

"What?" Abi asked.

"Oh, nothing," the football player said with a chuckle.

Not having time to thank Blu for the invitation, she figured they'd see him during the week anyway. Burton and that girl came to mind. Angry to a degree, she shook her head and walked out of the house. The group piled into their SUVs and tossed their bags in the back. It was a quiet ride to the airport.

When they arrived, they climbed the stairs and found their seats on the plane. It was almost six o'clock when Abi checked her phone. Her

Dad had sent two texts—one about her location services being off and the other about dinner at seven. She inhaled and typed. *Sorry, Dad. Won't be home for dinner. Two guys got hurt. Long story... We are heading to the hospital. Nothing major. Just a cut and a broken finger.*

He responded in seconds. *Need my help?*

Warding him off, she typed, *Nope. LOL. But I think I just decided to become a doctor.*

His thinking bubbles activated. *Really? Not surprised by that. LOL Always knew you would. Be safe, Sweetheart.*

*Thanks, Dad. I'll see you soon.* Abi signed off with a heart, relieved he didn't question her deactivated location a second time. Able to relax, she prepared for take-off.

The jet raced down the runway. Soon, they were in the air again.

"So," Shane whispered since everyone was so quiet. "This was a trip to remember."

Chuckling at the comment, she said, "Oh, it was memorable."

"You did an amazing job today."

"Thanks," she said. "Amidst all that, I think I decided to change my course of study next year."

"Is that right?"

"How does Dr. Acardi sit with you?"

"Really? I love it. Think that's a good decision."

"Yeah, me too."

He opened his hand and intertwined their fingers. Reclining their seats, sharing a pillow between them, she thought about everything that had transpired. Hearing Reggie laughing and Jade giggling in the back of the plane, Abi turned around and looked at them.

Thinking about their conversation earlier that day, she needed to know something but didn't know how to ask. Inexperienced when it came to relationships, not knowing what was normal and what wasn't, Abi contemplated what she'd say. "Can I ask you something?"

"Sure," he said.

She whispered in his ear. "I know you said not to feel pressured because of Jade and Reggie, umm, but…." Embarrassed, heat spread through her chest and neck.

Stunned by her statement, his eyebrows raised. "Wait? You're still not thinking about…."

"Yeah. I just need to know."

"Abs, are you asking if I'm attracted to you in that way?" he said in a softer tone, inching closer.

She nervously nodded.

"The truth?"

"Yes," she said, holding her breath.

"Every moment of every day. I thought that was obvious." Nervous, he bashfully looked away after he said that.

Exhaling, her heart melted, "Really?"

"Absolutely. Are you kidding me?" he chuckled. "Yes, without question."

Thankful to hear it, she smiled.

"Hey. There it is."

"What?"

"It's the look I've been missing since Friday. It's back." Her expression made his day. "Do you trust me?" he asked sincerely.

"Yes."

Looking into her eyes, he whispered, "Love you."

Without hesitation, she said, "Love you, too."

# 48

## Reality

Almost an hour before landing at Van Nuys, Abi found Shane sleeping. She got up and made the rounds to check on her patients before their descent. Shawn had taken her advice and kept his hand elevated on a pillow the entire flight, and Alan's cut was no longer bleeding. Instructing both to head to the hospital before heading home, Abi noticed Mei seemed angry. Adrian and her weren't sitting together.

She took the open seat beside the girl and asked, "Hey, Mei? Are you okay? What is it?"

"Nothing," she sighed, surprised that Abi was so tuned in.

"I don't believe you."

Leaning over to whisper in her ear, she said, "I saw a different side of Adrian today. The way he beat that guy up scared me. It's like something took over."

Not having seen the fight, she couldn't speak to that. "I'm sure he was defending Laney and his friends. He's a sweet guy, Mei. Don't let this paint him in a bad light." Abi straightened up and looked over at Adrian, sitting two chairs behind. He looked so sad. "Have you spoken to him since?"

She didn't answer.

"I think you should. You might discover he's very sorry for his actions and wants to make it up to you." Noticing that Adrian overheard her, he nodded in agreement and gave a thumbs up. She sneakily motioned for him to take her seat beside Mei. Soon, he walked over. Abi got up, smiled, and left them to work this out.

With everyone attended to, Abi returned to sit with Shane, who had just woken up.

"What did I miss?" he asked, seeing her hovering about.

"Oh, nothing. Just making the rounds," she chuckled to herself.

A short while later, they landed safely without incident. When the plane stopped outside the terminal, the pilot dealt with the customs agent while they waited on the plane. Given authorization to disembark, their group said their goodbyes. Abi felt like they'd developed a closer bond after this trip.

Laney stood with Shawn. He was still resting his hand on a pillow. The two hugged Abi.

"We are taking your advice," Laney said. I've called my family's private physician. We are heading to his office now. He will x-ray Shawn's hand and look at Alan's face. It's better than going to the emergency. The guys will get seen right away."

Happy to hear that, Abi replied, "Good luck. Let me know how it goes."

"We will," Laney said while tending to Shawn, visibly more uncomfortable.

"Thank you, Abi," Allie replied while hugging her goodbye. "I'll text you."

"Okay. Sounds good," she said while Shane wrapped his arm around her.

Alan approached and timidly offered Abi a side hug while bumping fists with his teammate. "Yeah, umm, thank you for helping me, Abi. Appreciate it."

"You're welcome."

Seeing them drive away in their chauffeur-driven SUVs, Abi exhaled.

"Good work, Dr. Acardi," Shane said.

"They'll be okay," Abi smiled.

"Hope so. But I'm a little worried about Shawn's hand. The team can't afford to be a man down."

"We'll have to see what the doctor says."

"Guess so," he said.

Jumping into Reggie's chauffeured truck, the driver left the tarmac en route to Abi's house.

"What are we gonna do with Shawn injured?" Reg looked concerned. "We need him this season."

"I don't know. That will take at least four to six weeks to heal. Hopefully, the break isn't a complicated one," Shane replied.

Reggie shook his head. "When Coach gets wind of this, I hate to be him."

"He can't find out it was a fight. If he does...." Shane paused, knowing their coach's stance on it.

They were so tired. Not another word was said between them. It had been a long day, and the worst part was they had school in the morning.

"So, who's ditching tomorrow?" Reg looked for a show of hands. He didn't get any from Shane and Abi—just Jade.

"No, no, no. If we got ourselves into this mess, we need to soldier on, regardless. We will get some sleep tonight, go to school and practice and catch up tomorrow night. No ditching."

Feeling guilty, they all looked at her, knowing she was right. "Fine," they said simultaneously.

Texting her Dad to tell him she was on her way home, he replied as she turned on her location services again. "Hey, any news on the Eastwood situation?" Abi asked Jade, having seen her scrolling through her phone.

"No, nothing new. Perhaps tomorrow."

Pulling into the gates of Bel Air just before nine o'clock, the SUV climbed the hillside toward Abi's place. When they got there, she opened the gate. Driving in, Shane grabbed their bags from the cargo bay behind them and handed Abi hers.

"Well, Reg. It was an adventure," Abi smiled.

"A trip you'll never forget, right?"

"Absolutely. Thank you for including me."

"No problem."

She hugged him and then Jade. "Night, you two."

"Night, Abs," Jade replied.

They waved to them as the SUV turned around and left.

Opening his truck and tossing his bag inside, he turned and reached out to Abi. Holding her tightly, he kissed her once and said, "Love you."

"Love you too."

Parting ways, he got in behind the wheel. Before leaving, he rolled down the window and started the engine. "Goodnight, Abs. See you tomorrow."

"Night. I'll see you in the morning."

Waving, she watched him leave and wistfully turned to find her Dad in the doorway. She didn't know how long he'd been standing there.

"Hey, Dad."

"Hi, Sweetheart. How are the patients?" he joked.

"I think they'll live."

He chuckled. "That's good to hear."

Abi walked inside while he closed the gate. "How's Mom?"

"Same, unfortunately."

"Okay. I'm going to head upstairs and shower."

Not looking her way, he said, "Have a seat for a second."

Afraid to know what he wanted to discuss, she nervously sat on the far end of the sofa in the living room. "Everything okay?"

"For now, yes." Her Dad hesitated and said, "I've been thinking... I may have misjudged your boyfriend."

Hit by that, Abi was stunned. "Really?"

"I noticed he was very respectful of you while leaving just now, which I am thankful to see."

"Yes, he is. I feel like he and I can talk on the same level, too."

"He certainly thinks highly of you." That made him smile.

"Thanks, Dad. He really does care about me."

"I can see that now."

Immediately, Abi wondered if he had overheard Shane tell her he loved her. Had that prompted her Father's change of heart? "So, you're not mad?"

"At him? No, not really. He'd better stay respectful of you, though."

"Don't worry. He's not a bad guy."

"Good to hear." About to walk away, he said, "Well, you go ahead and do what you need to. I ordered Thai food earlier if you are interested. It's in the fridge."

"I'm sorry I missed our dinner."

He stopped and turned around. "Somehow, I'm okay with it. I hear my daughter wants to become a doctor."

"Yeah, something clicked today."

"That's the way it happens," he smiled.

Abi got up and headed toward the stairs with him.

"I'm off to bed, Dr. Acardi," he chuckled, liking the sound of it. "Five o'clock comes early for me." Looking at her face, he said, "It looks like you got a lot of sun today."

"Yes, unfortunately," she giggled. "Night, Dad."

"Night, Sweetie."

Step by step, Abi climbed the stairs behind him. So much had happened. It was exhausting just thinking about it. A little disoriented, it all seemed like a dream now.

Walking into her room, she closed her door and went into the bathroom to turn on the faucet. Upon stepping under the rain shower, the water cascaded across her shoulders as it washed away the remnants of their adventurous afternoon. She thought about her serious conversation with Shane earlier. A part of her wondered what it would be like, while the other was afraid to know.

"If you're afraid, you're not ready, Abs."

Abi wrapped herself in a white robe. The Black Lyon rave seemed a distant memory until reality hit. Remembering that Eastwood and his friends were missing, she took out her phone and looked for updates.

Not seeing anything on the news, she turned to Twitter and Snap. While towel-drying her hair, she didn't find out anything more than she already knew. Looking out the window, the lights outlining the mansion across the canyon were fully ablaze. Too tired to spy on the lonely man, Burton came to mind. She wondered if he'd stayed in Cabo or returned home.

"He and I need to have a little chat this week," she said aloud.

Stepping into the hall, she walked to her Mom's room. There, she found her Dad just leaving.

"Everything okay?" she asked.

"Her vitals are a bit weak."

Worried, Abi walked by him. "I'll sit with her for a bit."

"Okay, Sweetheart. Then off to bed, okay?"

"Yep."

"Night, Sweetie."

"Night, Dad."

Walking in, the nurse smiled. "I'll leave you alone with her."

As she went out the door, Abi sat at her bedside. There was so much she wanted to say but couldn't. She wondered what advice she would've given her if she could share everything – all her experiences. The good and the bad. Would she be angry at her or disappointed? Rubbing her lifeless hand, she hoped to see the faintest movements, but sadly, there was nothing.

Reliving the Eastwood nightmare, she recalled how the big, strong man broke into the room flanked by four others. Amidst the commotion, how he carried her to safety was still fresh in her mind. Holding her, pressing her body against his on the way down the hall, the thought gave her chills. Unable to see his face, no matter how many times she replayed it, she couldn't get past the fact that she needed to know who he was.

"You need closure. That's what it is," she whispered.

Abi kissed her Mom on the cheek and said goodnight. Leaving the room, the nurse returned to her desk to watch over her.

"Goodnight, Miss," she said.

"Goodnight. Take good care of her."

"Don't worry. I will," she smiled pleasantly.

Wandering off to bed, she checked her phone. Seeing the heart Shane sent moments ago, she sent one in return. Abi slipped under the covers, thankful to know someone loved her.

# 49

# Nightmares

In the middle of the night, Abi woke to voices. Not knowing where they were coming from, she got up, believing something had happened. Fearful for her mom, she walked toward the door. The upper hall was darker than usual.

"Did the power go off?" she whispered, half asleep.

Hearing footsteps across the hardwood floors downstairs, she panicked and tried to shout for her Father, but nothing came out. Heart beating uncontrollably, the voices got closer and closer. Someone had broken into their house.

At the bottom of the stairs, she saw four shadows reflecting off the large glass window.

"Oh, God, no. Please help me…" she whispered.

Unable to move, frozen in fear, the dark figures started up the stairs. One by one, they caught sight of her. Abi ran into her room to hide. With nowhere to go, crouched tight to the corner, she covered her mouth, trying not to make a sound.

Crying, gasping for air, she thought, *No. No. No…*

"Well, who do we have here?" The ominous voice said. "Isn't this Coop's little tart?"

The voice was Eastwood's.

Surrounded by shadows, she closed her eyes. "No, please. No…"

Feeling their hands on her body, she screamed, "No! Don't touch me!"

Violently tossed about, she heard a sound cut through the darkness. "Abi? Abi?"

Startled, she opened her eyes as the light from her bedside table lamp brightened the room. Twitching, she turned to her left and saw someone sitting on the edge of the bed. Trying to focus, she saw her Father. Seeing his face, she reached out and clung to him.

"It's okay, Sweetheart. It was just a dream. It was just a dream. I'm here. You're okay."

# 50

# Followed

Suffering through a terrible night's sleep, waking up often, Abi heard her alarm. Barely able to raise her hand to turn it off, she finally succeeded. Not sure how she would make it through the day on such little sleep, she figured she'd make a coffee with a double espresso shot, believing it would solve the problem.

"First things first, Abs," she said, "Gotta get out of bed. Feet on the floor. Baby steps." Doing just that, she sat on the edge. Stretching her hands high above her head, she said, "Okay. Come on. Let's go."

Surprisingly dressed and ready in record time, she walked down the hall to her parent's room. The night nurse was still there. Abi could see her preparing for the staffing change in a matter of minutes. Not wanting to disturb her Mother, she signaled to the woman, offering a thumbs-up or a thumbs-down sign. Sadly, the nurse made a flat hand gesture in return, meaning nothing had changed. Waving to her, the woman did the same.

Heading downstairs to let in the day nurse, who had just arrived, Abi went into the kitchen to fuel up on caffeine. Making the strongest coffee she could, she poured it into a cup full of ice. Upon sealing the lid, she wrapped her lips around the straw and took a long sip. The taste of it filled her senses with hope. Finding a Post-it note on the counter, she read it silently.

*I hope you are doing well this morning, Sweetie. Have a good day. I will see you after school.* Ending it with a heart, he signed it - *Love Dad.*

"Well, if he can get up at five this morning after all I've put him through and be good to go, then I can too."

Out the door, saying goodbye to the night nurse, she locked up and got in her car while the gate opened. Starting the engine, she drove out of the courtyard. Glancing left and right, then left again, peering into the curved mirror to see if anyone was rounding the hidden corner, she noticed the same black SUV parked a few yards away. It was facing the traffic again.

"That's so dangerous," she said, taking another sip from her straw. "What are they doing there anyway?"

The gate closed behind her. Pulling out onto Stradella, she headed south. While driving along, she happened to look in her rearview mirror. Following her was the black SUV, noticeably speeding up. She pressed her foot on the break and slowed down, expecting them to pass. But it stayed behind her, mimicking her every move. Staring at the driver, she could not make out the face. Frantically looking back at them several times, they got so close that she could see black hoods and masks across their faces. Terrified, she fumbled with her phone and immediately called Shane.

"Hey, good morning," he said cheerfully.

"Shane!" she shouted.

"Abs? What is it?" Alarmed, he sat up straight in his seat.

"There's a black truck following me! I need help!"

"Tell me where you are!"

"I'm almost at the Bel Air gates!" She was breathing heavily. "They have black hoods and masks on! What do I do? What do I do!"

"Stay calm. Focus. Don't get in an accident. I'm on the straight stretch close to you. Hold on."

Abi swerved around each corner as she approached the intersection. Having no choice but to slow down, the SUV did the same. Stopping behind two cars, she kept looking in her rearview mirror.

"The truck is right behind me!" Hands violently shaking on the steering wheel, she feared, "What if they get out and try to take me?"

"Lock your doors. I'm coming up on the gates. I'm not far."

She stared at them while paying attention to the car ahead of her.

"If nothing happens, merge onto Sunset. I'll come up behind you."

"Okay. Okay. Oh, God. Please help me. Please help me," she mumbled.

"Abs, it's okay. Stay calm."

"Come on! Come on! Someone, please let me in." Abi noticed the older gentleman in the Mercedes from last week waving her into the space he'd created in front of him. "Oh, thank God." Moving forward, waving to the man, she turned right on Sunset with the green light, leaving the black SUV behind. "Shane!"

"I'm here!"

"I just turned on Sunset."

"I see you. I'm coming up behind you right now."

Abi looked in her mirror and found Shane's Jeep weaving in and out to get closer.

"Keep driving to school. I'll block them. They won't be able to see you in front of me."

"Okay." Focused on the road, she nodded and tried to calm down.

Shane could hear the fear in her voice as it vibrated.

"You're good, Abs. Shane is right there," she whispered.

"Keep your eyes forward. Pay attention to the road." He kept looking behind him. Seeing a black truck dodging vehicles, he figured it was them. Shane didn't tell Abi it was coming up fast. Soon, they were close enough that he could get the plate number.

"B777L," he said aloud, making a mental note. Driving across the 405 overpass, he said, "Abi, don't signal. Just make the turn and head to the school."

"Alright…"

Abi approached the intersection. Not signaling, she drove up the hill and around the corner to the school entrance. In seconds, she was waiting for the parking arm to allow her access to the grounds. When it raised, she stepped on the gas. Shane was right behind her.

"Go! Go!" he said.

Abi sped away as the parking arm closed behind her.

Shane blocked the gates to see if the SUV would show up. He was ready for a fight. Idling, he waited but saw nothing. Believing the vehicle had moved on or not seen her turn, he raced up the hillside and reached the top just as Abi flew past Gerald. Not far behind, he, too, did the same. When he rounded the corner, he found Abi sitting in her car, shaking with tears streaming down her cheeks. Driving into his space on an angle, he got out and ran to her.

"Abi? Abi!"

She shook, unable to speak.

Opening the car door, he grabbed hold of her. "It's okay. It's okay."

Trembling, he held her close. Her chest heaved through the tears.

Reggie drove in. Seeing Shane's Jeep parked across two spaces, he stopped in the middle of the aisle and got out. Jade arrived at the same time.

"Hey, man?" Hearing Abi crying, Reg rushed over. "What happened?"

Calming down, she dried her tears with her sleeve. "There was a black SUV on the street outside my house. When I left, they followed me. I saw the men inside dressed in black hoodies and masks."

"I wasn't far from the Bel Air gates when she called me," Shane explained.

His friend said, "That's crazy. Who were they? What did they want?"

Abi began to cry again. "I don't know."

"Should we report this to the police?" Jade overheard their conversation and got out her phone.

Reggie shook his head at her.

"Why not?"

He took her aside and whispered, "Did you not hear the news this morning?"

"No."

"The police have listed Black Lyon as a suspect. I think he may have done something to Eastwood and his friends. Maybe it's tied to Abi."

"What did you say?" Abi looked at Reggie.

He hated to be the bearer of bad news. "Black Lyon is a suspect in the missing person case."

"So you think those were Korolev's men?"

"No, I didn't say that."

"What should she do?" Jade found it hard to think.

"I don't know," Shane replied. "But, for now, you stay close to me."

Abi nodded, still shaken.

Shane got Jade to sit with her while he went to realign the Jeep in his spot. Reggie and Jade did the same. Together again, they locked their vehicles and headed to class.

Wrapping his arm around Abi, he could still feel her trembling. "Don't worry. I'm here now. You're gonna be alright," he said. "Once we are inside the Gilderson building, we'll be surrounded by security. It's the safest place to be."

Along the way, Reggie saw Emile walking with Mandy and the twins, Shiri and Shiresse. Tapping Shane on the back, he wanted to warn his friend.

Making eye contact with the girl, she swayed her head to the side, requesting a minute. Her face looked sincere, not the usual devilish expression she sported daily.

"Umm, Abi. Hold on one second. Don't be mad. I think she wants to talk to me. You okay with that?" Shane waited for her answer.

"Sure. I trust you."

Shane kissed her cheek and said, "Wait here. I'll be back." Looking at Jade and Reggie, he asked, "Stay with her a second."

"No problem, man."

The three watched the football player walk toward the mean girl, standing with her arms crossed.

Witnessing their conversation from afar, Jade noticed that Shane kept a six-foot buffer between them. Reading Emile's lips, she asked Abi, "Did she just say thank you to him?"

Abi replied, "It seems so."

"What does that mean?" Her friend's mind went into overdrive. "I bet she's thanking him for saving her on Saturday night."

"She should thank him. A lot could have happened to her. She's lucky Shane had her back." Abi knew he hadn't done the same for her. It was still a sore topic.

Noticing her friend felt slighted, she said, "Don't worry, Abs. He's one hundred percent invested in you."

"Yes, I know."

When Shane returned to them, he tried to act casual. "Sorry about that."

"What did she want?"

"She thanked me for watching out for her Saturday night," he stated. "I said it was the last time I was doing it."

Not sure how to respond, she simply nodded and left it at that.

Continuing on their way, Shane could tell Abi was unhappy. "Hey. Don't think twice about her."

"It's fine. Guess closure is a good thing."

"Suppose so." He presented his hand.

Without hesitation, she took hold, knowing he needed the assurance. But unlike Emile, who had Shane to save her, Abi had someone else fill those shoes. Black Lyon had heroically stepped up. Emile got to thank Shane for his noble deed. But for Abi, she still felt the need to tell the famous DJ the same thing.

51 |

# Struggles

Taizo's helicopter hovered high above the school before coming in for a landing. The sound of it reverberated off the buildings. As their group got closer to the main doors, they saw the actor walking up the staircase. Tightly surrounded by security, he looked miserable.

"Funny we didn't see him at Blu's party yesterday," Abi said, positive he wasn't there.

"No. I believe he had a press junket," Shane said.

"What's that?"

"With his new movie coming out, they do back-to-back interviews for two days to market it. So the poor guy was probably stuck in an expensive hotel room, answering reporters' questions. Don't know if I'd have the patience for that."

"I had no idea."

Shane watched a security guard speed up to open the door for the young Hollywood star. He could see Taizo was annoyed not to have the freedom to do it himself.

Following behind him and his entourage, they could see some girls staring at the actor as he passed through the halls. With his head down, he proceeded to the room where his tutor was waiting. Sadly, his agent had pulled him from regular classes and planned to isolate him for the next while.

On the second floor of the Gilderson building, Abi, Shane, Reggie, and Jade found a flurry of activity in the hallway with junior and senior students standing around glued to their phones.

Reggie stopped to talk to Adrian and Mei, who still seemed to be having problems since yesterday.

"What's going on?" he asked them, trying to take a peek at their screen.

"The Black Lyon app just disappeared, vanished. It's gone. Like - there's no trace of it," Mei revealed. "He must have had some type of kill switch embedded."

Hearing this, Reggie took out his phone and checked for the app. It was true. It was gone. Returning to Jade, Shane, and Abi, he showed them.

"Why would he do that?" Shane questioned. "Makes you wonder if he has something to hide?"

"Obviously, the guy is cleaning house and erasing every stitch of evidence they might use against him," Reg analyzed.

A conspiracist at heart, Mei interjected, "Or was he protecting his client's data from the Feds?" She raised her eyebrows curiously in a Sherlock Holmes kinda way.

Her friends looked at her, unsure what to make of the comment. Ignoring it, they moved on.

"That means no more Black Lyon raves," Jade said.

"Yeah," her boyfriend confirmed.

Overhearing this, Abi realized she would never have the opportunity to thank the DJ for what he did that night. There was no way to find him without the app and his events. It was hopeless now. She didn't know why she was so obsessed with it.

*Abi, you've gotta let it go. Get over it,* she thought. *There's a good chance the guy doesn't even remember you anyway. I bet he doesn't even care.*

Scared for her friend, Jade voiced what most were thinking. "Do you think this is connected to what happened this morning?"

"I don't know. If they are Korolev's guys, maybe he's just looking for evidence about his son's whereabouts. Or maybe they discovered Abi was the last to see him before he disappeared." As always, Reggie didn't have a filter. What he said sparked a bit of fear.

Shane gave him the eye after seeing the expression on Abi's face.

"What?" The guy said under his breath. "Just sayin'."

Walking into math and taking their seats, Shane saw Emile standing in the doorway with a blank stare. Before he knew it, she had boldly sat across the aisle from him and kept eyeing him up. Acting strangely, he knew right away she was strung out on something. He'd seen it before.

Abi tried to ignore the girl's weird behavior, but in the back of her mind, she wondered if she was making a play for Shane again. Changing her perspective, she figured the girl was the least of her problems. The reality was she'd been followed this morning by two men with hoods and masks. A thought that prompted a million scenarios to flash through her mind while analyzing it all.

Shane noticed Abi was overly preoccupied. It was unlike her not to be furiously taking notes to capture everything their teacher said. Sitting there, she was almost stoic. Doodling on her paper, deep in thought, she wasn't diving into their math questions at all.

When they got to Science, she barely participated in the prelab and offered little help. Usually, she took the lead and was well-versed in whatever topic of discussion was on the table, but not today. Shane took it upon himself to record as much as possible in light of this. He hoped to share his notes with her if she needed them.

Unbeknownst to everyone, Abi was taking inventory and trying to piece together the clues that led to this morning's incident. Was it connected to Black Lyon or Eastwood Korolev? How would it all end? What would happen to her? She compiled a series of worst-case scenarios and exit strategies just to be safe.

Glancing at Abi sitting across from him, Shane thought she was carrying the weight of the world upon her shoulders these days. With everything going on in her life, he felt guilty for adding to her stress. It made him want to protect her and be more supportive - make things less difficult because, in essence, things were complicated enough, especially after this morning.

When the bell rang, the students flooded the hallways on their way to their next class. Walking along with Abi, Shane noticed Adrian was in the dumps. Mei and Ming had gone ahead and left him behind.

"What's up, my man," Shane asked, not really needing to.

"I tried talking to Mei this morning. She's talkin' to me but keepin' me at arms' length and kinda giving me the cold shoulder. We spoke a bit on the plane home yesterday, but I think she's still mad. Suppose this doesn't help." The guy pointed to his swollen black eye. "No wonder she doesn't wanna be around me. I don't blame her."

"Give it time. She'll come around."

"I don't know…" Adrian was doubtful. "I think I've really screwed this up."

Jade and Abi overheard him.

Wanting to help, Abi suggested, "Why don't you try a grand gesture to make her feel special?"

"What do you mean?" He wanted to know more.

Jade chimed in. "Like a romantic picnic lunch in the garden? Maybe give her flowers? Or chocolates?"

They could see the wheels spinning in his head. "Like buy her some Van Cleef? My dad does that for my Mom when he screws up."

Not knowing what that was, assuming it was expensive, Abi shook her head. "No, Adrian, simple is best. You don't want to buy her off. You want to show that you like her and appreciate her. I don't think Mei is the kind that would like extravagant gifts. I could be wrong."

"A grand gesture, huh?" the big guy said. "I'll do it. Thanks, guys."

"Happy to help. Good luck." Abi hoped he'd take their advice as they saw him jog ahead and disappear around the corner while talking on the phone.

Out of the blue, Emile walked by and brushed her hand against Shane's purposefully.

Abruptly pulling away, he thought, *What is she doing?* Careful not to react because she wanted to create a scene, he ignored it like it didn't happen.

Upon seeing this, Jade quietly said, "What the hell was that?"

Signaling for Reggie to keep Abi busy, his friend stepped forward and asked her questions about their homework while Shane fell back to talk to Jade.

"I'm pretty sure she's on something. Did you see how glassy her eyes are?"

"Yes." Jade nodded in agreement. She, too, had seen this before.

"I want you to watch over Abi in art class. Make sure Emile doesn't get to her."

"For sure. No problem. I got this." She could see he was worried. "For the record, Abi is a lot stronger than you think. Believe me. The girl can hold her own." Jade seemed so sure of herself.

"Please, just keep her safe until lunch."

"I will."

Smiling, he tapped her shoulder. "Thank you."

Arriving at the Art Studio, stopping outside the door, Shane didn't see Emile around. He hoped she may have skipped out and gone home. Holding both of Abi's hands, he looked at her and said, "You're sure you're okay?"

"Yes, I'm good. I'll see you at lunch. Don't worry. I'm fine."

He nodded and rubbed the outside of her arms before kissing her in front of everyone for the first time.

Taken aback, she scanned the halls as students looked on.

"Don't worry about them," he said.

She offered a half smile.

He bent down to whisper in her ear. "I'll see you after. Love you."

"Love you too," she replied quietly.

Hating to let go of her, he released his hand at the last minute. "Bye."

"Bye," she said bashfully.

In the studio, Abi walked over to her desk. Everyone was on high alert after Jade told them the Coles Notes version of what happened that morning with the SUV. She advised on subjects to avoid in conversation, including Eastwood's disappearance, the Black Lyon investigation, and, of course, Emile.

When Abi sat down, in true Beverly Hills fashion, the girls raved about a new boutique on Rodeo opening on Saturday and their plans to attend the glitzy, star-studded evening. That is when Emile and her friends waltzed through the door.

Seeing the evil on the girl's face, Jade knew she was up to no good. The sweet person who had thanked Shane for saving her earlier was gone. This was the possessed version.

Ready to intervene, she got up as Emile approached their table. Allie saw her incoming and did the same. Standing strong beside Jade, the two created a wall to block Emile's way.

"What? Are you her bodyguards now?" Her voice sounded so snarky.

Towering over her, Jade warned, "Just walk away."

With her hands on her hips, she said, "Or what?"

"Or we will tell the teacher we suspect you're high." Jade didn't flinch. "Based on your eyes being glassy and dilated, I believe that assumption isn't far off. Don't you?"

Abi looked up from her computer, saw the confrontation, and joined her friends.

Emile's sights drifted past the blockade and zeroed in on her. It was like the devil himself was standing there. "So, you think you've won?"

"What?" Abi replied.

"You heard me." The girl's face was on fire.

"Look, Emile. I don't want to fight," Abi said, completely exhausted.

"I'm not going to let you have him. He's mine. I told you, he always comes back to me, so save yourself the trouble."

Standing firm alongside her friends, Abi stated, "Emile, he's made his choice, and it's not you." She annunciated the girl's name in a combative tone for added measure.

Jade and Allie were in awe of her reply. Both crossed their arms in front of them with attitude just as the teacher walked in.

"Do we have a problem here, ladies?" the woman asked, dropping her designer bag and briefcase on the desk to loudly announce her arrival.

Abi spoke up first. "No, Ma'am. No problem here." In an instant, she turned around and went back to her chair.

Jade and Allie followed.

"I suggest you take a seat, Ms. Raven," the teacher ordered.

Left as the only one standing, Emile looked around the class and found all eyes on her. With senses artificially on overload, seeing each expression psychedelically filled with contempt and hatred, Emile suddenly felt bombarded upon and left, slamming the door in her wake.

The teacher calmly picked up the phone receiver and called the office. "Security? Please stop Emile Raven from departing the premises. Detain her until the end of the day." Getting confirmation on the other end, she hung up and said, "All right. Everyone pull up your projects. I'm going to walk around and check on the progress you've made."

Glancing at her friend while pulling her work up on the screen, Jade found Abi with tears welling in her eyes. Reaching over to her, she placed her hand on her arm. "What is it?" she whispered.

"Have I become like her?" Abi questioned quietly.

"What do you mean?"

"You know. Rude? Angry? A mean girl?"

"No, Abs. You are far from it." She rubbed her arm. "You are nothing like her."

"Then why do I feel so awful?" Seeing the teacher heading their way, Abi quickly dried her face. Composing herself, she focused on how she would explain her design.

Put on the spot, the teacher stood beside her and asked questions. Abi answered each brilliantly before the woman moved on to Jade.

Relieved to make it through unscathed, Abi took a deep breath and looked out the window. *Don't let her get under your skin. You need to rise above it and be more mature. No cattiness. No rudeness. Remember, for every action, there is a consequence.* Giving herself a positive pep talk, she tried to think of ways to deal with Emile more constructively. How she reacted did not set an example for others. If anything, she felt cut from the same horrible cloth. Moments ago, that girl who spoke to Emile Raven was not the one Shane fell in love with.

*He loves you because you are different from all that,* she thought. Don't *fall into Emile's trap.*

# 52

# Grand Gesture

Not hearing any chatter about Eastwood or Black Lyon helped Abi concentrate on her work. No matter how bad the day had started, she felt happiest when creating. Thankfully, separating from reality for a while gave her a much-needed mental break. Ready to meet up with the guys and have lunch, she thought about what she was hungry for.

Pumped that the day was almost over, Jade leaned in and said, "Wait until the guys hear about...."

"No, please don't mention anything."

"But Abs, I was proud of how you stood up to her."

"She brings out the worst in me. I don't like who I am around her, and I'm not proud of what I said."

Jade was confused. "But..."

"No buts. This stays between you and me." Abi exhaled. "I need to find a better way of dealing with her."

"Wait? What?"

"It's obvious the girl feels threatened. Why? Because I am everything she is not, and Shane likes that. I need to be the person he sees and not sink to Emile's level. She knows what she's doing. She's not dumb."

Shocked by Abi's analysis, Jade hadn't noticed most of it. "You're right."

Abi nodded confidently. "I think so, too."

While making their way to the bistro, they found the guys already at a table.

Reg was the first to greet them. He came to hug his girl. "Missed you," he said.

"Hey, baby. Missed you too."

Shane captured Abi in his sights. "How was class?"

"It was good. We got a lot done, which was nice. I always feel better when I'm productive."

Thankful Abi seemed calm, Shane smiled. "What can I get you? Soup? Sandwich? Wrap? Pizza?"

"Just a salad would be great." She pulled out her student charge card.

Raising his hand between them, he said, "No. My treat."

Abi watched the handsome, muscular athlete leave their table and walk toward the restaurant. For her, he was the cutest guy there, and she felt lucky to be with him. This morning showed how kind, attentive, and protective he was - Saturday's incident aside.

*We all make mistakes.* She thought. *Don't lose sight of that. You'll regret it.*

Once everyone had their food, Reggie suggested they leave the public eye and head to the cactus garden terrace. Snacking a little along the way, they soon reached their destination.

"Hey?" Reggie said while leaning on the wall overlooking the garden below. "The guy took your advice."

"What advice?" Abi asked.

Jade peered over the side. "It's Adrian. Awww, look what he did."

Abi followed their line of sight. She found loads of floral baskets arranged in a heart. In the middle of it was a blanket spread out and an open picnic basket with goodies and bottled drinks. Adrian was standing beside it, looking at his phone. Texting someone, he kept his eyes peeled with anticipation.

Jade and Abi watched and waited with fleeting hearts.

Suddenly, they saw him turn around and lower his phone. Raising his hand to greet someone, they found Mei standing there with Ming.

Her sister prompted her along. She seemed to be in shock. Inching closer, Adrian extended his hand to her. The shy girl obliged, eyes locked onto his as he led her to their picnic.

"Oooohhhh...." Jade and Abi said simultaneously, clutching their chest, melting at the romantic moment.

When they walked to the picnic blanket, Adrian helped her take a seat. The two looked happy, laughing and talking. Mei was in heaven.

"Good job, my friend," Jade said, presenting a closed fist to Abi.

Getting the drift, she tapped her friend's knuckles with hers and said, "Yes, good job. Mission accomplished." Pausing a second, she asked, "Wait? How did he do that so fast?"

"It's a concierge service. We pay companies to be at our beck and call," she laughed. "He could have pulled that off in an hour if he needed. It just would've cost him a pretty penny," she said.

Surprised by the girls' reaction, Reggie and Shane decided not to pay too much attention to the grand gesture. Both thought Abi and Jade would be looking for something similar in the coming days if they weren't careful.

Giving Adrian and Mei some privacy, Abi sat beside Shane on the stone bench, glad not to see another soul around.

To change the subject, he asked, "So, are you going to tennis practice today?"

"Yes. I have to. It's the only opportunity to redeem myself after last week's fiasco." She could see he was concerned. "Don't worry. I'll be okay."

Based on her answer, he knew she would be.

Raising her face to the sun, she soaked up the rays and the peaceful sounds around them.

Reggie and Jade snuck away, leaving them alone.

Blanketed by a white haze, they could barely see the Los Angeles skyline.

"I miss the beach. Maybe we can visit again one night this week?"

"As much as I would love to, I can't. The team is away tomorrow and Thursday. I'll be back late Thursday night. We also have a third game on Friday. That one is about twenty minutes away from here. Not far."

She didn't like that he'd be gone so long.

"I think Reggie is planning to have the after-party at his place. His parents are in Europe for three weeks, so he has the place to himself."

Abi stayed quiet.

Seeing she wasn't overly enthusiastic, he figured she was worried. "Are you going to be okay while I'm gone?"

"Yes, of course." Thinking about what happened that morning, knowing how fast he came to her aid, she feared being alone but tried to be brave. "I'll miss you."

"I'll miss you too." Playfully nudging her shoulder, he wrapped his arms around her waist. "I'm just a phone call away." He kissed her gently before caressing her cheek with his thumb. Leaning back slightly, he looked into her eyes. "How did I get so lucky?"

"What do you mean?"

"You are perfect for me in every way."

"I feel the same."

Hating the thought of being apart, he sadly had no choice. This was the life he chose. Despite his priorities, football would always come first and everything else second.

He checked the time and said, "Guess we should head to study hall?"

Abi smiled. "Yes, we should."

# 53

# Unexpected

Descending the ramp into the garden, the two walked hand in hand toward the library and gave Adrian a thumbs-up on the way past. He smiled from ear to ear, and Mei was beaming with happiness. All was right with the world.

After scanning their student cards for check-in, they climbed the stairs and found their usual spot.

Shane pulled out a chair for Abi.

"Thank you," she said.

"You're welcome." Moving his chair closer, he sat beside her and rested his hand on his lap between them. Her hand gravitated to his.

While catching up on her work, she helped Shane with a few things. Able to spend the last ten minutes surfing the net and checking social media, she searched for anything new on the Black Lyon/Eastwood case. Jotting down a few notes in her journal, she tried to figure out where the missing teens could be. Again, the police posted a plea for those who attended the exclusive Saturday night rave to come forward with information. Switching to YouTube and Twitter, she noticed many people were getting involved in the search.

*Perhaps it's just a matter of time before the truth gets out,* she thought.

Writing down the theories most talked about on their channels, she hoped she wouldn't get approached by police, but more so, she prayed they wouldn't charge Black Lyon either. If they did, she knew she'd have no choice but to explain what happened.

Thinking things through, she thought, *He saved me from those guys - the ones who are now missing. That had to account for something.* Analyzing every angle, drawing a question mark on the page, she realized, *No, if anything, telling that to the police would implicate him even more. It was a motive for Black Lyon to do what he did. I need to try another approach.*

Confused, not knowing much about the law and how it works, she made a note to read as much as she could on the subject.

"What are you up to?" Shane's voice pierced the silence. At the same time, he leaned over, trying to see her notes.

Quickly closing the book, she answered, "Private thoughts."

He mischievously smiled. "What? Like a diary?"

"That's for me to know, and you..." she pushed him away playfully, "never to find out."

"Now I want to see," he said while horsing around a little, hoping the librarian wouldn't yell at him. "Is there anything about me in there?"

"No," she giggled.

The school's chimes sounded, signaling the end of the day.

"Saved by the bell," she chuckled, slipping her books into her backpack. About to loop the straps over her shoulders, Shane took it from her.

"I've got it."

She was thankful for the help. Tired, she knew her day was far from over.

While exiting the building, he asked, "So, do you think the coaches will allow you to practice today?"

"I'm hoping they will if I show up. Coach Taylor probably thinks I'm not a dependable player now."

"Personally, I believe she'll be glad to see you back. I'm sure she'll understand your situation. I can't see why she wouldn't, given the circumstances."

"Fingers crossed."

Meeting Reggie and Jade in the parking lot, Abi grabbed her gear from her car before transferring it all to Shane's Jeep.

"We will see you guys there," Jade shouted from the passenger side of Reggie's Ferarri.

Abi waved to her friend as they drove away before getting in beside Shane. They left the garage shortly after and stopped to talk to Gerald.

"Hey, Sir," Shane smiled while Abi looked on. "How was your day?"

Gerald replied, "Pretty fair. How about you two? Were you running late this morning? Is that why you sped past?"

Shane didn't want to share the details, so he replied, "Yeah, sorry about that. Won't happen again. It was a bit hectic. Abi is off to tennis practice now, and I'm hitting the field."

"Well, best of luck! Enjoy your night." He seemed upbeat and happy to be leaving soon.

"You too!" Abi said before Shane stepped on the gas and moved along.

Thinking about the black SUV from this morning, Shane cultivated contingency plans in light of it. "If something happens at practice, I want you to run into the Wasserman building. Go straight through the gym doors without stopping and find me on the field."

Not realizing what he was referring to initially, she remembered the nightmarish encounter that seemed like a lifetime ago already.

"Sorry. I didn't mean to bring it up, but I wanted us to have something in place - just in case."

"Okay. I'll do that."

"I don't expect anything crazy, but you never know. I'm on edge and don't want anything to happen to you. At school, there's security everywhere. At UCLA, it's not as safe. There are so many people coming and going."

"Jade will be with me and the coaches too."

"Yes, I realize. You just need a Plan B." Shane reached for her hand and gave it a few gentle squeezes.

"Got it."

"Love you," he said.

Upon hearing those words, her heart skipped a beat, making her wrap her arms around his waist. "Love you too," she whispered, kissing him on the cheek.

It made him happy.

When they arrived at the parking complex off Charles E. Young Drive, they drove in and found Reggie and Jade waiting. Both had a look of concern on their faces.

Shane parked in the space Reggie saved for them and got out.

"What is it, Jade?" Abi's sights bounced between her friends.

"Umm, Abs, they just issued a warrant for Black Lyon's arrest. That means they've linked him to the disappearance of Eastwood and his friends." Jade showed her the news bulletin.

Reggie debated it. "How can they issue an arrest warrant for someone who doesn't exist? He's an element of fiction. No one knows who he is. Like, nobody."

"I don't think it'll stick. I mean, unless the police have ID'd him somehow." Shane needed to state the obvious. "Maybe someone came forward with a name?"

Abi's mind was spinning a million miles an hour.

Shane could see it. "Abs?" Trying to get her attention and break her from her thoughts, he repeated, "Abi?"

"Yeah?" she said.

He rested his hands on her shoulders. "Don't worry. He'll be fine. The guy has money. And money talks."

"You really think he can buy his way out of this?" Abi panicked.

"Everyone has a price." Trying to stay grounded, he told her, "Look, you only need to worry about one thing right now. Go onto the court and secure your spot on the team. We will deal with all this after."

"You're right." Grabbing her equipment from the back, she joined Jade.

"Hey, wait for us. We are walking you to the Acosta Center and then to the courts. Not taking any chances today," Reggie said.

"But you'll be late if you do that." Jade didn't want their coach to reprimand them.

"Believe me. I don't want to be there when our coach sees Adrian and Alan's faces, not to mention Shawn sitting on the sidelines with a broken finger. It won't be good." Shane knew the team was about to get an ear full today while they strolled down the path.

The girls hoped that wouldn't be the case.

Arriving at the Acosta Center, Abi and Jade got changed quickly so the guys could be on time. Exiting minutes later, they went to the courts together.

Shane took a look around. "Remember what I said. If anything happens, get into the building." He pointed to the Wasserman doors before hugging her tightly. "Good luck. I'll see you after."

The coaches looked her way with eagle eyes. Abi took a deep breath. "Well, here goes nothing."

Walking over, she asked them for a minute of their time and explained why she had missed practice last week. It didn't take much to convince Coach Williams and Taylor to give her another chance. Understanding that her Mother was sick, they welcomed her back.

Believing that the practice was a good distraction, Abi soon found her rhythm. Point after point, serve after serve, she watched the coaches focusing on her between plays. With a nod here and there, she figured they were speaking favorably of her.

About to take a drink from her water bottle, she noticed a black figure out of the corner of her eye. Looking up along the upper bowl of the stands, she found two men watching. They were about fifty feet apart and systematically scanned the area from left to right. Unable to pull herself away from their presence, Abi started making unforced errors.

Jade followed her friend's line of sight and found the men. "Who are they?" she quietly asked during the changeover.

"I don't know." Abi's voice sounded fearful, and her hands shook.

Being strong-willed, Jade immediately told Coach Williams and pointed the men out to him. Alerting Coach Taylor, he intervened to keep the girls on the team safe.

Quickly skipping steps to reach the top, the men dressed in black casually scattered to avoid a confrontation and disappeared. Abi and Jade watched their coach return and speak with Coach Taylor.

Afraid, Abi asked, "Did they get into a black SUV?"

"Yes, how did you know?" Coach Williams replied.

Hearing that punched the air from her lungs. Had the men from this morning followed her there?

Eavesdropping on their conversation, Jade asked, "Abi? Do you want to leave?"

She refused to concede. "No," she said. "I'm staying. They're gone now. It'll be okay."

It took a while to get her head back in the game. The coaches had seen what she was capable of but now felt she lacked consistency. Once again, releasing the rest of the team from practice, Coach Taylor asked Abi to stay back a few more minutes. She and Coach Williams wanted to test her further.

The man asked, "Ms. Acardi, let's you and I play a few points before you go."

Jade sat down on the steps to watch.

On the baseline to return serve, Abi focused on her strings and controlled her breathing. Not once did her sights fall upon her opponent. Zeroing in on the ball in Coach William's hand, she swayed back and forth, ready to go. After a few challenging points, she made the coach work harder than he expected. Raising a hand, he waved her over to the net.

"I am looking for someone who will play consistently and not get distracted. It hasn't been the most stable start for you, but that's understandable, given the stress at home. That said, what I just witnessed was impressive. Make sure you are at practice on Thursday. If you play like you just did, the spot on the team is yours."

Abi nodded with a nervous smile, feeling the pressure. "Thank you. I'll be here Thursday." Turning around to pack her bag and drink some water, she found Shane and Reggie sitting with Jade. They were probably there the whole time, but she hadn't noticed.

All three rose on their feet.

"Wow, Abs. You played amazing." Shane could do nothing but smile.

She shrugged her shoulders and debated telling him what had happened earlier.

With impeccable timing, Shane said, "Did you get a look at them?"

"Who?"

"The men."

Abi realized Jade had already filled the guys in on the incident. The look on Shane's face turned worrisome. She knew this could hamper his performance over the next couple of days. He needed to keep his head in the game, not on her. Abi stared straight ahead, deep in thought.

"I can't be sure they were the men from this morning. Couldn't see that far."

"This is what I was afraid of," he said on the way back to the Acosta Center.

"I know."

He rubbed his hand along her back. "Tell me what you need, and I'll do it."

She stayed strong. "Don't worry. Really, I'm good."

The girls walked inside the building while Shane and Reggie waited outside for them to return.

"I need to protect her, but how?" Shane sat down, completely frustrated. "We are away for two days this week."

"Maybe we can ask Taizo if he can spare a bodyguard for a while." Reggie was grasping at straws.

"No. I don't want to call in favors like that."

A rogue thought then crossed Reggie's mind. "Maybe her old neighbor could help?"

"Burton? No way." Shane got defensive.

Reggie put up his hands between them when Shane reacted so negatively. "Whoa. Whoa. It was just a thought."

The more Shane contemplated it, the more it seemed like the only option. But he didn't want him around Abi, nor would he dare ask him for help. He knew the guy liked her too, and eventually, he figured there would be a battle between them to win Abi's heart. The last thing he wanted was to speed up the process. The thought of being away for the games and having her spend time with him was unbearable. To him, bringing in Burton was beyond a last resort.

Checking his notifications, Reggie saw an update on the case. "Looks like more witnesses from the rave came forward to the cops."

Shane whipped his head around. "How many?"

"The report says four."

"If I get implicated in this because of our run-in with him that night, and the scouts get wind of it, I'm done. I can kiss my scholarship goodbye. No school wants a captain with a record or bad rep." Shane ran his hand through his hair.

"What if Eastwood did this on purpose to drum up attention for himself and pin it on you to get you out of the picture?"

Shane hadn't thought of that. "I wouldn't put it past the guy."

"Dude, so many people saw our confrontation."

"I know." He put up his hand, hoping his friend would stop. "I should've never gone there or interacted with the guy."

"You couldn't have known this would happen."

Seeing the girls exit the building, Shane said, "Not a word to them about this."

"Got it."

Reggie wrapped his arm around Jade's shoulders. "Ready to go, Babe?"

"Yes, I'm exhausted," Jade said with an exaggerated sigh. "So, we will see you guys tomorrow."

"Absolutely. We will be here bright and early." As they walked away, Abi saw Shane's eyes glued to hers. "Why are you staring at me weird?" she asked curiously.

"Nothing." He chuckled to himself. "For the record, I liked seeing you kick your coach's ass."

She laughed, "Oh, you did, huh?"

"Yeah, that was awesome."

Strolling toward the parking garage, they waved to their friends as they left. Reaching his Jeep, the two got in.

"I think I should follow you home just in case. You okay with that?"

"Sure." Abi hesitated and added, "You think I'm in danger, don't you?"

He didn't want to frighten her. "No, I just want to get you there without incident. That's all."

"Okay. I guess better safe than sorry."

"Yes."

Leaving the UCLA campus, Shane kept a close eye for anything strange. While climbing the hill to the Gilderson School, he pulled into the garage and parked beside Abi's car. Getting out, he helped her with her bags and set them in the front seat before closing the passenger door. Walking around the vehicle to her side, he approached with open arms. "I'll be right behind you," he said. "Don't worry."

She nodded.

Happy to get one last hug to end the day, he kissed her. "Love you."

"Love you too."

Knowing he had to get home, he said, "We should get going. I've gotta pick up dinner for Jacob."

"Okay. No problem." She slipped into the driver's seat while Shane got in his Jeep and started the engine.

Abi pulled away.

With every turn, he followed.

She could see his eyes peeled for any sign of a black truck. It was hard to decipher what was normal or suspicious in the land of chauffeured vehicles.

Moving along Sunset to the Bel Air gates, Abi turned left and merged right onto Bellagio Way. Spying Shane in her rearview mirror, she couldn't believe he was hers. He looked so confident and strong behind the wheel. Picture perfect in more ways than one.

Almost home, her phone rang. Peering down at it in the holder, she could see it was Burton. She didn't dare pick it up with Shane's eyes on her. The last thing she wanted was for him to be jealous. Deciding to call him back later, she ignored it.

When she pulled into the driveway, the gate was already open. Inside the courtyard was an ambulance. With its engine still running, she found the first responders wheeling her Mom out on a stretcher. Screeching the car to a halt, digging into the gray stones, she opened her door and quickly raced to her Dad.

Meeting her halfway with arms outstretched to calm her down, he said, "Abi, calm down. Listen to me."

"What's happened?" In shock and on the verge of tears, she began to shake. Resting her hand on her forehead, she felt faint.

Hugging his daughter, he said, "Sweetie. Mom had a stroke."

Shane stood nearby and heard his words.

"Is she going to be okay?" Abi pleaded. "Is this it? Is this the end?"

Dividing his attention between the ambulance attendants and her, Dr. Acardi said, "It's too soon to tell. I'm going to follow the ambulance."

"I'm coming with you." Abi looked at him in desperation.

"Sweetheart, I would prefer you stayed here. I plan to assist her doctors in urgent care, and I don't want you sitting in the waiting room." As the attendant closed the doors for departure, her Dad said, "I will call you once we know more." In a rush, he looked at Shane. "Take care of her for me."

Shane nodded. "Yes, Sir."

Stepping back as her Dad got into his vehicle, Shane stood with Abi. The two watched everyone leave, including the daytime nurse, who traveled in the ambulance with her Mom.

Once they had gone, Abi turned to Shane.

Grabbing hold of her, she broke down in his arms. "She's gonna be okay. She's in good hands." Crying hysterically, he hugged her tighter and tighter. "It's okay. Don't cry."

She expelled every bit of emotion she had and soon dried her tears.

"Do you want me to stay?" he asked, moving a few strands of hair from her face.

Realizing Jacob was expecting him home, she said, "No. It's fine. You need to be there for your brother." Abi's chest caved with residual heaves.

"Are you sure? I can make other arrangements. It's not a problem."

She shook her head and tried to create a calmer façade. "It's okay. I'm good," she said.

Shane could tell she was trying to be brave. "But I don't want to leave you though…"

"Don't be silly. Go. Jacob is depending on you." Abi secretly wanted to be alone.

"Alright, but I will be here in a heartbeat if you need me." He rubbed her arms up and down to comfort her. "If you want to go to the hospital later, I can drive you."

"But you've got the game tomorrow."

"Don't worry about that." He wanted to make a suggestion. "If you go to school in the morning, I'll pick you up. I'm sure Jade can drive you home."

Secretly happy she wouldn't have to drive to and from school on her own, she replied, "That's a good idea."

"Good. I'll see you at eight unless something crops up before then."

She nodded.

"I love you." He hugged her tightly.

"Love you, too."

"Your Mom will be fine. Your Dad will make sure she gets the best care."

Tears crept into the corners of her eyes.

Hating to walk away from her, he waved before pulling out.

Standing there, she remotely closed the gate as a semblance of fear encompassed her. The sun was going down, and it would soon be dark. Grabbing her things from the car, she locked the door behind her. Reminded that Burton had called a while ago, she set her bags on the sofa in the living room and collapsed beside them.

Her hands shook as she selected his number. She heard it ring, but there was no answer. It went straight to voice mail. Not wanting to leave a message, she figured he'd see her missed call eventually. At least, she hoped he would.

Abi trudged upstairs to her room and dropped her bags on the floor before collapsing on the bed. In desperate need of a shower, she couldn't bring herself to walk to the bathroom and attempt it. Barely sleeping since Saturday night, she closed her eyes and curled up as a rogue tear crossed her cheek.

54 |

# Best Friend

Hearing a noise, Abi raised her head off the pillow. It took her a minute to realize her phone was ringing.

Locating it on her side table, she grabbed hold and sleepily answered, "Hello?"

"Hey, Abs. Sorry, I missed your call. I was in a lecture. Couldn't talk. What's up?"

She immediately broke down at the sound of his voice.

"Hey, hey, what's wrong?" His voice went from upbeat to concerned in an instant.

"It's my Mom...." Abi squeaked out before her chest heaved.

"What happened? Is she okay?"

"She had a stroke."

Without an ounce of hesitation, he asked, "Where are you? I'm coming."

Abi could hear a door slam. He was already on the move. "It's okay. Really. I'm at home. I saw you called earlier."

Burton stopped. His breathing got heavy. "Tell me what you want me to do."

"Nothing. It's just nice to hear your voice."

"Is your Dad with her?"

"Yes, he followed the ambulance. The nurse went too."

Burton felt helpless. He started pacing the floor. "Do you want company?"

"At this point, no. I'm just going to wait for him to call with an update."

Burton stayed quiet on the other end.

"Look," she paused, "I need to go. Can I call you later?"

"Please do." His mind raced.

"I will. Don't worry. Thank you for listening."

Abi said goodbye before hanging up the phone. She'd already forgotten about his rudeness in Cabo a few days back. In the great scheme of things, it didn't matter now. Her thoughts drifted to the men who followed her this morning. It prompted her to quickly go and check all the doors before setting the alarm.

Talking to herself, she encouraged, "You have to stay calm. Everything will be fine. You'll see."

Not in the mood to finish her homework, Abi ventured into the kitchen and opened the fridge. There wasn't much there. Closing it, not overly hungry, she took two slices of bread and slid them into the toaster. With a plate, knife, and peanut butter ready, she waited for the toast to pop up. Turning on the kettle, she figured a hot cup of tea would also help calm her nerves.

The house was so quiet. Placing a teabag in the mug, she thought, *Is this what life would be like if Mom passed?* Recalling everything they'd been through to date, she knew the end was near. It was just a matter of time now. She checked her phone and turned up the volume in case her Dad called. Debating whether to text him for an update, she opted to wait a bit longer, knowing he'd call when he got a chance.

Suddenly, the toaster popped. The sound startled her. Watching the butter melt, she lathered the peanut butter on each piece and poured hot water into her mug. While sitting along the island, the silence was almost deafening as she took a bite of toast. The crunching seemed louder than usual. It was hard to swallow on the verge of tears. About to take another sip of tea, she put the phone down. When she did that, a notification appeared. Someone was at the front gate. Checking the cameras, she immediately noticed who it was. Pressing the button to open it, Burton's matte black McLaren inched into the courtyard.

"How did he get here so fast?" she questioned.

Stopping in front of her, he popped the butterfly door. "Hey, hope it's okay. I knew you had to eat, so I brought burgers, fries, and your favorite - chocolate milkshakes."

Abi choked up.

Grabbing the food from the passenger side, he reached out to her. "You doin' okay?"

She crossed her arms and nodded, lost for words.

"Come on. Let's get you inside." He closed the door behind him and locked it. Before heading to the kitchen, Abi pressed the gate button.

The two gathered around the island. Burton searched the cupboards for plates. Upon finding them, he placed a burger and fries on each. The smell was heavenly.

Sitting on the bar stool beside her burly friend, Abi ate a fry. "Thank you," she said with tears falling. "Thank you for coming."

Rubbing his hand along her back, he said, "I couldn't sit back and do nothing."

Crunching on the fries, she ate them one at a time as Burton took a huge bite of his burger. He noticed she was going through the motions in disbelief.

About to change the subject to offer a distraction, Abi suddenly asked him, "So, have you been keeping up with the Black Lyon case and Eastwood Korolev and his missing friends?" She took the first bite of her burger.

"No.  Been kinda busy. What's the latest?"

"Today, they issued a warrant for Black Lyon's arrest. Apparently, a few witnesses from the rave came forward. They must have tied him to the kidnappings."

"Oh? I hadn't heard that."

"Do you think they know who he is? I mean, his identity?" She blotted the corner of her mouth with a napkin.

"I'm not sure what will happen. At one point or another, the dude's name will come out in the press or social media. Someone will leak it." Burton assumed by the look on her face her mind was reeling. "Please tell me you have given up on your quest to thank the guy for saving you?"

She went silent.

"Abi, nobody knows what his story is. It's not a good idea. It's best just to let it go and count your blessings."

"I understand. But I need to know who saved me. I just do."

"All he did was prevent you from becoming a statistic. That's all. He's probably done that a million times. You said the room he brought you to had many security screens, right? There's a reason for that."

"I know." Lowering her head, Abi felt naïve and stupid. "I should never have gone there."

"Like I told you before. That is no place for you."

"What does that even mean?"

"You are not that type of girl."

She prompted him to elaborate.

Putting down his milkshake, he said, "You're smart, and how can I say? Wholesome?" He stumbled on the word, unsure if it fit.

"Wholesome? Great. Like Little House on the Prairie?"

"Okay, maybe that wasn't the best term to use."

"Was the model you were with yesterday wholesome?" She opened her eyes wide, curious to see if he'd answer the question.

Burton turned away.

"I didn't think so," she laughed snarkily.

Addressing the elephant in the room, he said, "I'm sorry about what happened in Cabo. Not my proudest moment. End of story. So, let's just move on."

She wanted to press him further about why he said such mean things. But given that he dropped everything to be there for her tonight, she let it slide, believing he probably wanted to show off for Kai's crowd. "Well, it was very hurtful to me and Shane."

"Speaking of the jock," he zeroed in on her, wondering if he should state the obvious. "Why isn't he here with you? When I arrived, I half expected to see his Jeep in the driveway."

"After school, he is responsible for helping with his step-brother until his Dad or step-mom returns home. The day staff leaves at five, and the nanny doesn't cook. Long story. He was going to stay, but I told him to go."

"I see." Burton nodded. "Why did he follow you home, then?"

"Well, I kinda had a problem."

He wiped his mouth with his napkin. "Problem? What kind of problem?"

"This morning, I spotted a black SUV parked up the street. When I left the house and drove down Stradella, I looked back. It was following me. If I sped up, it sped up. If I slowed down, it kept a buffer between us. Luckily, Shane was en route at the same time and met me along Sunset. He got in between the SUV and me."

"He did?" Burton was impressed by this.

"Yes. He didn't leave my side all day until we both had to go to practice. There, he told me if anything happened, I was to run into the Wasserman Center and find him on the field."

"Smart. That's good."

"I really needed to impress the coaches today, which I did, by the way. But partway through, we noticed two strange guys watching us from the upper bowl. Jade told our coach, and he went to confront them. The men took off before he could do anything."

"Why didn't you call me? I was there today."

"In all fairness, it happened so fast, and I wanted to stay focused."

"We need to find out who these people are." Burton looked at her security monitor. "Do you have playback on this?"

"I don't know. I think so."

Abi got the password from her Dad's logbook in the cabinet drawer.

Pulling out the keyboard, Burton patched into the system and looked back at the history. "What time was that this morning?"

"Around ten to eight."

Quickly finding the footage, he magnified the frame on that side of the house. "Is this the SUV?"

"Yeah. That's it."

"I can't zoom in enough to get a plate number. We could've called the cops and submitted a report." He kept scrolling through the history on the cameras facing the street. He counted twelve times the strange SUV had been there since Sunday.

She hesitated before asking, "Do you think they are Black Lyon's guys?"

"Wait? Why would you think that?"

"I don't know. Maybe he likes me and wants to be sure I'm okay." When the words escaped her mouth, she thought about what she said. It sounded stupid.

"Abs, the guy is famous. He can have anybody he wants – literally. I think he'd go after someone his age, not a high school senior. No offense." He could see she was disappointed to hear that.

"Then, do you think Korolev's Dad is having me followed?" Her heart beat rapidly.

"I don't know. You were the last person to see Eastwood before he disappeared. Those teens haven't resurfaced yet, is that right?"

"No, they haven't."

"Until these guys turn up, someone always needs to be with you." Returning to the current view, Burton found a black SUV on the northeast camera. "Is that the same truck?"

She looked at the screen. "I think so."

Burton turned and walked toward the front door. Pressing the gate remote, he said, "Abs, lock it behind me. I'll be right back."

"Wait? Where are you going?" she asked, frantically following him.

"I'm going to pay them a visit." His voice sounded ominous. Stepping outside, he turned and said, "Get your phone. Watch the screen. If things get crazy, call 911."

"Burton, no!"

She couldn't stop him. Locking the door, she ran back to the monitor. Frightened, she watched Burton approach the dark SUV. About twenty feet from it, the brake lights illuminated, and the thing sped off. Seeing Burton stop in the middle of the road, she noticed something in his right hand. The blood drained from Abi's face. It was a gun.

# 55

Safe

Abi ran back to open the door and waited for him to return. Seeing him enter the gate, she pushed the button and closed it behind him. Not seeing anything in his hand now, she wondered if she had imagined it.

"Hopefully, you won't see them around for a while," he said.

On the way inside, she replied, "I hope so." Her phone rang. Picking it up, she saw it was her Dad calling. "Hello? Hello, Dad. How is Mom?"

Burton locked the door. Following Abi to the living room, he sat beside her on the sofa. Listening intently to what her Father was explaining, he waited, hoping her Mom was doing okay.

"Yeah, don't worry. I'll be fine," she said before divulging, "Umm, just in case you see on the cameras, Burton is here with me. He brought food." Abi nodded and replied to him. "Okay. Okay. Sure. I will. Thank you for the update. Night, Dad. Love you too." Ending the call, she took a deep breath. "My Mom is stable. They won't know more until tomorrow when the test results come back."

"Well, that's a piece of good news."

"My Dad is staying there tonight with her. Guess that means I'm by myself."

He could see she was worried. "Want me to stay and keep you company?"

Abi looked relieved. "You would do that?"

"Of course. It's not like we haven't done this in the past," he laughed. "Remember all the campouts in your backyard?"

"Oh, I sure do. But no telling horrible ghost stories tonight."

"I will try." He got up from the sofa and went back outside. Returning with his leather satchel and a duffle bag, he said, "I came prepared." Setting his bags down, he scanned the main floor and checked all the doors. He turned on the outside lights one by one to illuminate the property. "I've got some work to do, so I'll set up in the family room."

"Umm, sure. I need to finish some homework too. The guest room upstairs at the end of the hall is open when you want to sleep."

"I might stay down here, just in case," he said, feeling an awkwardness developed between them.

"Okay. Whatever you think." She took what was left of her food upstairs. "I'm going to go to my room then."

He nodded and gave her a thumbs-up. When she had gone, he set up his laptop. Checking the security monitor, he moved it closer to keep an eye on the street. While eating his fries, he saw the SUV return to the same spot.

# 56

## Protection

Walking into her room, Abi grabbed her computer and sat on her bed. Unable to focus on her homework, her mind drifted to the image of Burton with the gun in his hand.

*Should I ask him about it,* she thought. *If he has it in the house, shouldn't I be aware?*

Rationalizing things, unsure how to bring up the conversation, she locked her bedroom door and walked into her bathroom to start the shower. While waiting for the water to warm up, she felt like she was living someone else's life.

*So much turmoil,* she thought. *Kidnappings. Family crisis. Bullying. Peer pressure. Oligarchs. Now, a friend with a gun? This is not normal.*

After her shower, having mulled over her options, she somehow felt a little better. With her mind clear, she planned to confront Burton. Slipping on a fluffy white robe, she towel-dried her hair slightly and walked to the window. There, she found the mansion across the canyon completely dark.

"Well, that's a first," she said before getting dressed in a sweatshirt and black tights.

Unlocking her door, she descended the stairs, trying to build courage. Before entering the kitchen, she heard Burton speaking to someone. Sneakily stopping a few feet away, she listened to what he was saying, but it was hard to decipher. Then, a few words came out clearly.

"Yeah, that sounds good. Go ahead with that and send me the final price. I'll get back to you tomorrow and arrange payment," she heard him say.

Entering the room, she startled her childhood friend. His eyebrows raised after he turned on a dime.

"Look, I've gotta go. I'll talk to you tomorrow." Putting his phone down, he closed his laptop. "How are you doing? Anything more from your Dad?"

"No updates." She sat on the stool along the counter. Her heart pounded in her chest. "Umm, can I ask you something?"

Burton's sights moved to his phone screen. "Sure. What's up?"

Standing her ground, she asked, "Did you, umm…"

"Did I…." He looked over and waited for her to finish her sentence.

"Do you have a gun?" she blurted out quickly.

The expression on his face went stone cold. "Abs…"

"No, Burton. I saw a gun on the monitor. You had it in your hand when you went to confront the SUV. It looked like you knew what you were doing. What are you not telling me? Why do you have a weapon?"

He lowered his head and took a deep breath. "Abi, I am worth millions. Unfortunately, in the past year, I have been unable to keep it under wraps. I get threats every day," he revealed. "If you should know, I am certified and do not take the responsibility of owning one lightly. It is there for protection. That is it. Nothing else."

She listened intently. "Where is it now?"

He pulled the zip down on his hoodie. Under it was the holstered weapon.

"Should I be worried?"

He stood up. "Abs, you got people in black SUVs following you around." His sights veered to her left. Pointing to the security monitor, he said, "Look. They're back."

"What do we do? Should we call the police?"

"I already did that a few minutes ago when it returned."

Eyes glued to the monitor, keeping tabs on what was happening, they saw the SUV suddenly move along.

"Look, they're leaving. That's good, right?" she asked.

"What you really need to be asking yourself is, why are they leaving?" He rested his hands against the stone counter and leaned forward. Watching the monitor, he waited. Seconds later, a police cruiser drove by slowly. They hadn't seen the SUV depart.

Abi saw this. "What does that mean?"

"It means the guys in that SUV are listening to a police scanner. They knew they were coming, especially if an 11-54 was issued on your street."

"11-54?"

"Suspicious vehicle." He stood up straight and crossed his arms. "Abs, these guys are seasoned."

She immediately got scared.

"We will keep an eye out for a bit. If the truck returns, we will put in another call."

"Okay," she said nervously.

"In the meantime, I know you've got homework to finish, but do you want to watch a movie or something to keep your mind off of all this?"

"Sorry, what?" Deep in thought, it took a second for what he said to register. "Umm, yeah. I guess."

Guiding her to the sectional sofa, he took hold of the throw blanket draped along the back and covered her legs.

She looked up. "Thank you."

"No problem."

"Burton?"

"Yes?"

"Thanks for staying with me. I know you're busy. I suppose this is the last place you want to be."

"Abs, I will always be here for you. No matter what." He sat down beside her and offered a side hug. She felt safe and protected, but the gun made her uneasy.

"Can you put the…" she pointed to his chest. "…over there, away from…."

Standing up and slipping off his hood, he removed the shoulder holster and carefully placed it on the side table. "Is that better?"

She nodded. "Sorry, I'm not used to stuff like that."

"It's fine. Sadly, my life has been a series of death threats since my Father staked the claim on that property in the north. We made enemies in a short amount of time." Wanting to keep the air light, he asked, "So? What do you want to watch?" He hoped to cut through the thickness of the room.

"I don't know."

"So, no John Wick?" he laughed subtly, happy to see her crack a smile and chuckle too.

"Oh no. Please. Absolutely not." Abi remembered she hadn't called Shane. "Umm, can you give me a minute? I forgot to do something. Find us a movie. I'll be back."

"Take your time."

When she left, she saw Burton move his laptop from the island to the coffee table by the sofa. Heading upstairs, she reached the upper floor and closed her door. With her phone in hand, she Facetimed Shane. He answered in seconds.

"Hey, you. How's your Mom? You doing okay?" he asked, leaning his head against the headboard.

"She's stable. Have not heard anything more. We'll probably have an update in the morning. My Dad is staying at the hospital overnight."

"So, you're alone at the house?" he asked. "I don't like that idea, Abs, especially with these men lurking around. I should stay with you."

Freaking out, Abi composed herself. "Umm, no. You can't do that. My Dad watches the cameras, remember? If he sees you here with me alone, it will stress him out, and he'll dislike you even more. No offense.

Don't worry. I'll be okay." She wouldn't dare tell him the SUV had been sitting outside her house.

"Are you sure? I don't mind." He had a worried look on his face.

"Yes, I'm sure." Wanting to get back to Burton, hating that she wasn't telling him the whole story, she said, "I'm exhausted. Gonna try and get some sleep. I'll see you in the morning."

"I'll be there. During the night, call if you need me. I mean it, don't hesitate."

"Will do."

"Love you, Abs. Sweet dreams."

"Love you too." Hearing that, she realized he also didn't know about her nightmares. "Goodnight," she said, ending the call. Taking her phone with her in case her Dad called, Abi bounded down the stairs and walked around the corner. "So, what did you decide?"

"How about the new Top Gun? Or the series The Night Agent? Both look pretty good."

Abi sat beside him and said, "Let's go with The Night Agent. I saw the ads for that. It looks exciting, and it'll give me something to do in the evenings when Dad's not here."

"Night Agent, it is." Burton selected it on Netflix and pressed play. Watching the opening scene, they stayed quiet.

Constantly typing on his phone, she asked, "What are you doing?"

"Just work stuff."

"Like schoolwork?"

"Umm, yeah," he said before glancing at the security monitor.

With eyes on the screen, she asked, "What do we do? I can see they're back."

He turned to her and said, "Don't worry," before swaying his attention to his phone and texting someone.

Noticing that he wasn't interested in the show, she questioned, "So, you don't like romantic action suspense?"

Preoccupied, he pressed send and turned to her. "No, it's fine. I don't mind it."

"Well, for me, there is nothing like the heroine finding love in the end." She could tell the Night Agent seemed interested in the mysterious girl. "I have a pretty good feeling that this will happen here." Her heart fluttered as she watched the two actors. "It's like Shane and me. Before Saturday, I thought he was my knight in shining armor."

Burton lowered his phone. "So, he's lost the title since then?"

"Truthfully, I'm still upset that he abandoned me to help Emile."

"I don't blame you. Everything would've been fine if he had stayed by your side that night."

"You're not a fan?"

"Not exactly..." His tone deepened.

"Despite it all, he is a sweet guy." Abi thought back to their time on the beach Friday night - all the things he did and said made her smile. Cozied under the blanket, tired from not getting much sleep the past few days, she yawned.

Burton looked over at her halfway through the first episode. Her head was bobbing, so she stopped the show.

"Abs?" he said, tapping her shoulder. "I think you should go upstairs and get some sleep," he whispered to her.

Barely able to keep her eyes open, she stretched her hands high above her head. "Maybe so." Helping her off the sofa, she turned and said, "By the way, Shane is picking me up at eight. So..."

"I get it. Don't worry. I'll leave before that. No problem."

"Night, Burton," Opening her arms, she wrapped them around his waist. Resting her head against his chest, she caught him off guard.

Hesitant, he hugged her gently, then gradually a little tighter. "Night, Abs."

As she left the room, he stood there as a flood of emotions hit him. The feelings he had for her all these years had never faded. Running his hand across his forehead, he went back to the sofa.

"You can't tell her," he whispered. "The timing isn't right."

Stay

About ten after one in the morning, Burton shut down his laptop. Before heading to the guest room, he checked the monitor and saw the SUV had disappeared. Scanning all the cameras, he was confident they were safe. Eyeing his gun on the side table, he stuffed it in his duffle bag before quietly walking upstairs. As he passed Abi's room, he peered in to check on her. Happy to find her sleeping soundly, he continued down the hall. She'd left the guest room door open for him. In the sparsely decorated space, he set his bag on the bed and went into the bathroom to brush his teeth. Changing into a pair of shorts and taking off his shirt, he looked out the window. The street was clear.

"Perfect," he whispered.

Out of nowhere, blood-curdling screams emanated from Abi's room.

Grabbing his gun, he ran down the hall. There, he found her flailing around in bed.

"Abi? Abi? Wake up! Wake-up!" Setting the weapon aside, he said, "Abi?"

She fought him off and shouted, "No! No! Please...." Hysterically crying, he didn't know what to do.

Flipping on the side table lamp, he shouted, "Abi!"

In an instant, she stopped moving. In a daze, utterly confused, she looked up. "Burton?"

"You were dreaming."

Relieved, she clung to his neck and grabbed hold as if her life depended on it.

He held her close. "It's okay. I got you. You're safe. I promise." Assuming she was dreaming of the incident with Eastwood, his anger for Shane boiled over. The guy should have been there to save her from this. He failed to protect her. Now, these were the scars left behind. Her breathing was erratic. Her body trembled. Holding her as she cried, he waited for her to settle down.

When she leaned back, she noticed her hand resting on Burton's bare chest and quickly let go.

Giving her space, he took a tissue from the box on the side table when she started drying her tears with her sleeve. "Here," he said, blotting her face gingerly.

Her body heaved while a calm washed over her. But her hands hadn't stopped shaking yet.

"That was quite the nightmare..." he said.

"I can't stop them..." Veering from his muscular physique, she suddenly looked away, embarrassed.

All he could focus on was how deeply this affected her. "Don't worry. You're safe now." Pulling the covers over her when she slid back into bed, he got up and turned off the light. "Call me if you need me."

Abi sat up. "Wait, umm..."

He turned around.

"Can you just stay?"

Not sure how to respond, he knew she wouldn't get any sleep otherwise. "Umm, sure. One second." Burton went to get his phone. About to leave the room, he put on a T-shirt before setting his alarm so he wouldn't be late in the morning. Returning, he walked around to the opposite side and placed the phone on the table and the gun on the floor.

When he sat on the bed, about to lie down, Abi said, "Thank you."

"Sure."

As her eyes drifted shut, she whispered, "Good night."

"Night, Abs." Leaning back, resting his head on the pillow, he got comfortable with his hands on his stomach. The place was so quiet. Given time to think, his anger for Shane festered as he recalled Abi's nightmare. Glancing at her hair cascading beautifully, framing her angelic face, Burton had missed her being a part of his life. His best friend from Boston had always filled it with laughter and happiness. Sadly, now, her heart belonged to someone else.

# 58

# Caught

The echo of Burton's alarm filled the room in the morning. Waking to the familiar sound, he partially opened one eye and found himself on his side, cuddling Abi in his arms. She was right-tight beside him. Not making any sudden movements, he lifted one arm slowly and tried to roll over but found the other tucked under her head. Turning off his alarm, with perfect timing, he heard Abi's sound just after his. She raised herself off the pillow just enough for Burton to drift apart from her. Right then, she saw how close they were.

Left with only a foot of room on his side of the bed, she said, "I'm so sorry," and quickly slid over. "I crowded you in."

He didn't know what to say. Somehow, it felt perfect and wrong at the same time. "It's fine. No worries," he said, trying to make light of it. With his other arm free, he sat up and rested his feet on the floor. Not knowing what she was thinking, he asked, "You okay? Did you sleep well? You didn't have any more nightmares, so that's good."

"Yes. Thanks to you."

"Happy to help." Quickly getting up, he walked toward the door. With his back to her, he scrunched his face. "I'm just gonna go and grab a shower," he said, casually leaving.

"Alright," she said while slipping out from under the covers to sit on the edge of the bed.

Walking down the hall and into the guest bathroom, he closed the door. "What the hell was that?" Angry at himself, feeling he'd crossed the line, he stared in the mirror and shook his head. "That can't happen again," he solidified. Recalling her nightmare, he realized why he did it. It seemed harmless enough at the time - necessary, really.

Left alone in her room, embarrassed beyond words, Abi got up to make her bed. Seeing the indent Burton's body left in the duvet, she was thankful he was there. She would've been terrified if she'd been alone in the house all night. "I hope things won't be weird between us," she whispered before getting ready for school.

Half an hour later, she left her room, dressed in her uniform, with her backpack and Burch bag slung onto one shoulder.

At the same time, Burton emerged down the hall.

"I hate to rush you out, but Shane will be here soon. If he arrives early and sees you...."

"Don't worry. I understand." Burton's voice was calm, but as he descended the stairs, an unsettling awareness gnawed at him—something had shifted between them. "Any chance I could grab a coffee before I go?"

"Sure," Abi responded, her tone light, though a subtle tension lingered. She headed to the kitchen, and he followed.

Burton took out his stainless steel Yeti tumbler from his bag as Abi deftly pulled a mug from the cabinet and inserted a pod into the coffee machine before pressing the brew button. Silence settled over them while waiting for the cup to fill. The hum of the machine was the only sound in the house. Alone together in the quiet, Burton couldn't shake the feeling that this could be their future—moments of shared routine, simple and intimate. Despite the morning's awkwardness, his heart clung to the idea of Abi, one day, being a part of his life.

Passing him the full mug, he broke from his thoughts and poured some into this bottle above the sink. Closing it tightly, he said, "Well, guess I should head out."

"Okay. I'll call you later," she said while they walked to the foyer.

"Let me know when you get an update on your Mom."

"I will."

He opened the lock on the door as Abi pressed the button for the gate.

Turning to her, he reached out one arm for her with bags hanging off the opposite shoulder. "Bye. Have a good day."

She, in turn, wrapped her arms around his waist to hug him tightly. "You too."

About to let go, Burton saw Shane's black Jeep unexpectedly roll into the courtyard.

"Oh, no..." Abi said, immediately letting go after locking eyes with her boyfriend.

"I'm just gonna...yeah..." Knowing what it looked like, Burton quickly walked out and put his bags in on the passenger side.

Furious, Shane got out. "Abi? What is going on?" His sights bounced between the two of them.

"It's not what it looks like, man," Burton replied, trying to defuse the situation while Abi ran to him.

"Like hell, it's not." More hurt than angry, he got in his truck, slammed the door, and sped off.

Abi yelled, "No! Shane! Wait!" Hoping he'd stop. Bending forward, unable to breathe, she straightened and raised her hands to her mouth. Feeling her life spiraling out of control, she shouted, "Damn it!"

Burton went to her. "Abi, we've done nothing wrong."

"I realize, but he doesn't know that. This looks so bad." She was in shock. "I've gotta go after him. I need to explain." Hyperventilating, she shouted at the top of her lungs, "Why can't life be normal for more than a minute? The drama is constant! I hate it!"

"You need to calm down."

Almost ready to explode, she paced back and forth. "I can't!"

Wondering if she could drive in such a state, he said, "Look at me for a second."

"What?" she replied.

"If you don't bring it down a notch, I'm not letting you drive to school." Grasping at straws, he suggested, "Maybe I should drop you off?"

"No! That will only make it worse!" Realizing what she'd said and how she'd said it, Abi felt horrible. Gathering herself, she quickly backtracked, "I'm sorry. I didn't mean to... Look, I need to go. I've gotta deal with this alone." Calming herself down and breathing unevenly, she said, "Story of my life."

He rested his hands on her shoulders. "Promise me that you will pay attention and stay focused."

"I will," she replied hastily. "I'm gonna lock the door and get going."

"I'll follow you."

"Fine." Abi disappeared into the house and returned with her backpack and bag. "I'll call you later," she said while putting her stuff in the car.

"For sure."

Popping his side door, he slid behind the wheel and waved to her before leaving the courtyard. Driving slowly out the gates, he looked in his rearview mirror and stopped to wait for her. Passing him by, seeing how stressed she was, he followed closely. At that point, he decided he and Shane needed to clear the air, man to man. If she cared for the guy this much, he had no choice but to fix it.

# 59

# Truce

On her way down Stradella, her phone rang. She saw it was her Dad. Afraid of what he would say, a million scenarios rolled through her mind, including him seeing Burton on the cameras leaving this morning.

"Oh, crap. What if he saw him leave my room?" She tried to remember if there were any cameras in the upper hall. Taking a deep breath, she answered and tried to remain calm. "Morning, Dad."

"Morning." His tone sounded worried. "Was that Burton leaving this morning?" Deciding not to mention the altercation with Shane, he kept it simple.

"Umm, yeah. He didn't want me to be alone in the house, so he stayed in the guest room. Hope that's okay."

In unfamiliar territory, unsure how to react, he said, "Sure, but I hope you're not going to make a habit of this."

"I don't think I would have slept if he hadn't stayed. It was nice knowing someone else was in the house. I'm still a bit scared. It's so big."

Hearing his daughter talking casually about it was reassuring. "So, nothing, umm, happened between you two?"

"Eeww... Dad. He's like a brother, remember."

"Yes. So you say."

"How is Mom?" She hoped that would change the subject.

"Same as last night. We are awaiting the test results. Should have those within the hour."

"Okay, I'm on my way to school now. Can you text me an update when you know more?"

"Sure will."

"Love you. Tell Mom I love her too. I'll drop by the hospital after class."

"Okay. I'll send you her room information. See you then, Sweetheart. Have a good day."

"Thanks, you too."

Ending the call, Abi couldn't even take a breather. Now, she had to focus on the bottle-necked intersection before merging onto Sunset Boulevard. Burton was still behind her. The traffic was heavier than usual. Panicking, she wondered what she would say to Shane - how she would explain this. It was the second time he'd seen them together. It wasn't good.

A car between them, Abi turned right on Sunset. Burton followed and changed lanes before veering into the left turn lane leading to UCLA. Seeing him wave his hand out the window, Abi did the same. From here on out, she was on her own. It seemed to take forever to get to school.

Finally, approaching the parking garage, she stopped and said, "Good morning, Gerald."

"Good morning, Miss Abi. How are you?"

"Oh, that's a tricky question. Kinda having a rough morning. Had a bit of a misunderstanding with Shane."

"Well, he just drove in a minute ago. You'd better go find him."

"Thank you. I will," she said before passing by.

Driving around the corner, Abi found Jade, Reggie, and Shane talking.

"Oh, no," she whispered. Her heart started pounding a mile a minute. She wondered what he'd told them.

Abi parked her car, nervous about what would happen next. "Here goes nothing…"

Jade walked over.

"How mad is he?" Abi questioned. Peering past her, seeing him talking to Reggie, he wouldn't look at her.

"He's pretty hurt." Turning her back to the guys, Jade said, "I will get Reg out of here so you guys can talk."

"Thanks." Abi appreciated that.

Returning to Reggie, Jade gave him a nudge. Understanding what she wanted, he followed her and said to Shane, "We'll see you guys up there."

Cautiously moving toward her boyfriend, she stopped in front of him. He had yet to look at her. "Shane, I'm sorry," she said sincerely.

"For what? For spending the night with Burton or getting caught with him - again?"

"Oh my gosh! We've been through this so many times. Nothing is going on between Burton and me. I told you, he's like family."

"That's not the vibe I get."

The attitude made Abi mad. "How is this any different than you kissing Emile?"

"I didn't kiss her. She kissed me."

"Think what you want about this. I'm telling you the truth. I called, and I told him what happened to my Mom. Before long, he was at my door with food."

"So, was he there when you FaceTimed with me?"

Abi went silent.

"Wow," Shane said, nodding angrily.

"I didn't say anything because I knew you'd act like this."

He looked away.

"My Dad planned to be at the hospital all night. Given everything that's happened with Black Lyon and Eastwood, I was afraid to be alone in the house. So, I asked him to stay."

"Why did you ask him and not me?"

"You know the answer to that."

"So, you're telling me the two of you were all alone in the house and didn't sleep together?" He crossed his arms and stared her down.

"No!" Abi said point blank, knowing his raw definition. Flustered, she angrily added, "Furthermore, I have never been with anyone! How dare you ask me that! I'm not Emile, you know." Abi turned and hurried to the elevator.

"What's that supposed to mean?" He chased her down.

Not looking his way, she said, "Jade told me she always cheated on you." Stopping dead, she looked him in the eye and yelled, "I would never cheat!" before pressing the elevator button multiple times.

Given her anger, he could feel she was telling the truth. Calming down, he asked, "I want to be the guy you call in times like that, Abs. Not him."

"It's not that easy," she sighed. "Shane, I've known the guy since I was eight. He knows me better than I know myself, and vice versa. On top of that, my Dad trusts him."

"And he doesn't trust me, right?"

"Dad doesn't know you. Besides, in his eyes, you're the big bad wolf kissing his little girl, remember? Did you even think about how that would affect him? What would my Dad have said if you had stayed the night instead of Burton? What would he assume?"

"Yeah, but we wouldn't have..."

"He doesn't know that. I have a lot of respect for my Father, and I will not do anything to jeopardize it. Although, being around you, coming home late all those nights, going to friggin' Mexico, for crying out loud, was not a good look either."

Shane peered at the concrete ceiling as the elevator door opened. Stepping in behind her, he pressed the emergency stop button, trapping her.

"What are you doing? We are going to be late for class."

He calmly raised a hand to interrupt. "Just wait a minute. Calm down."

"What?" She was still huffing.

He slipped his hands in his pockets. "You're right."

She stopped. "I'm right about what?"

"I guess I'm jealous that the guy got to spend the night with you."

Abi rolled her eyes. "It wasn't like that."

"I believe you."

She tilted her head, relieved to hear him say it. "If it's any consolation, I debated calling you before Burton arrived. He was the safe choice. I wanted to save my Dad the stress. He's got enough on his plate right now. I've been screwing up a lot lately. I seem to be making a habit of it."

Threatened by Burton and villainized by her Father, Shane felt what she said made sense. This left him in unfamiliar territory. "I'm sorry. I know it's been a hell of a week for you. I hope we can move past this 'cause I don't wanna lose you, Abs." He held his hand out to her. "Truce?" he said with desperation in his eyes. "Please..."

Peering down at it, Abi hesitantly slipped her hand into his. "Truce."

"So, we're good?" he asked with a hint of uncertainty.

"Yes." Wanting to reassure him, she slowly wrapped her arms around his waist.

Resting his hands on Abi's hips, he shot her a sexy smirk before slowly inching her backward. Despite what happened moments ago, he looked into the eyes of the girl he loved and pressed his body against hers before flooding her with kisses.

Legs weakening, heart pumping, it left her breathless.

Stepping back, smiling brightly, he chuckled to himself. "I think we should fight more often."

She tilted her head and said, "As good as that was, umm, no. I don't like fighting."

"For the record, neither do I." Shane reached over and pushed the elevator button to start it again.

Standing hand in hand when the doors opened, they walked out to find Jade and Reggie staring at them. Both looked concerned.

"Thank god," Jade said aloud, happy to see the two had made up.

Reggie looked at his friend and secretly gave him a thumbs-up when Abi wasn't looking.

Shane did the same.

Walking along, Jade whispered to her, "Everything okay?"

"Yes," Abi nodded casually before smiling and looking up at Shane. "We are good."

Picking up the pace, the four of them got to class just in time. Taking their seats as their teacher was about to close the door, they saw Emile, the twins, and Mandy slip through at the last second. It made for an uncomfortable ninety-minute class.

Abi tried not to let her presence bother her, but it was hard. Flashes of her drunken kiss with Shane made her blood boil. Deep down, she wondered if the girl knew what she was doing the entire time. Had she done it purposefully to cause a riff between Shane and her to win him back?

Right then, Emile turned and shot her a devious look.

By the expression on her face, Abi knew she wasn't going to give up that fight.

# 60

# A Lunch to Remember

While moving on to their next class, Abi, Shane, Reggie, and Jade found most students in the hallway gossiping. They were afraid to know what had caused the stir.

Jade's notification went off on her device. The news headline in the tiny box read – *Missing Calabasas Teens Found Safe.* "OMG! Look at this!" she said, showing them her screen.

"So, Eastwood and his goons aren't dead," Reggie smirked.

"No. It says police found three of the kidnapped teens. Not four. What does that mean? Which one didn't make it?" Jade read on. "Apparently, someone dropped them in a remote part of the desert north of LA, and they had to make their way back."

Reggie laughed and said, "That's crazy."

"Wow...." Abi had mixed feelings. Thankful the boys surfaced unharmed, glad the police couldn't charge Black Lyon with murder, she prayed he'd be in the clear now. But the thought of the goon's return spread fear through her body like wildfire.

Shane could see it on Abi's face. "Don't worry. I will never let them hurt you. We will make sure of that."

Based on what happened at the rave and given the Oligarch's son's reputation, she wasn't convinced. "Maybe Eastwood is the one still missing."

"We can only hope that's the case," Shane replied.

Arriving at the Science lab, it took a while for Professor Grady to calm the class down. Everyone was still abuzz after hearing the latest news.

Abi overheard some questioning whether Black Lyon was to blame for the incident. Most threw him under the bus. Others said Eastwood had it coming.

"Take your seats, please! Phones away!" Professor Grady shouted above the roar of the class. Most listened and did as he asked, while a few rebels tucked their phone in their pocket and kept peeking at them periodically.

Handed their assignments, Abi found it challenging to concentrate. Her thoughts gravitated to the mysterious DJ who saved her. She felt he might have taught Eastwood and his friends a lesson on her behalf. It seemed too coincidental that they disappeared right after he saved her. Abi tried to piece together what came next by recalling his security, bursting into the room, wrestling the guys to the ground, and pinning them. But it was a blur. Noticeably struggling through the class, half paying attention, Jade could see something was wrong with her friend.

Nudging her, she whispered. "Hey. Are you doin' okay?"

Abi hesitated and nodded.

"You sure?" she asked silently.

Passing a note to her, it read, *Do you mind if Shane and I go out to lunch alone? We need time to talk before he leaves today.*

After reading it, Jade gave her a thumbs up, knowing more was happening than Abi was willing to share.

When the class ended, they moved on to the Art Studio. While walking down the hallway, it seemed the shock of Eastwood's guys re-surfacing was now old news. Not surprisingly, it had reduced to memes shared across social media. Amongst the posts, Black Lyon was hailed a hero for calling the teens out on their delinquent behavior. The Oli-garch's son had given the famous raves a bad reputation in LA's social circles for a while. Despite that, most attendees would still seek him out regardless. He was their connection to the *candy* supplied under the table at each event—a direct supplier that hovered about the crowd selling his goods. Abi had seen this firsthand.

Upon arriving outside her art class, Shane stood with her off to the side.

"Do you want to go out for lunch? Just you and me? I already told Jade. She and Reggie will steer clear."

"Yeah, that sounds good." He took hold of both her hands.

"Perfect. I'll see you after class then?"

He kissed her goodbye and said, "I'll meet you in the courtyard."

"I'll be there."

Walking away, holding on as long as he could, Shane finally had to let go. When Abi entered the room, she joined Jade, Allie, and Laney at their table. Mei and Ming followed shortly afterward.

Scared to know what Shane had told their friends early that morning, Abi needed to explain her side of the story. "Can I ask you something?" she said.

"Sure. What's up?" Jade was all ears.

"I wanted to set the record straight about this morning."

Jade was about to say something.

"Wait—one second. No matter what Shane said, I want you to know that nothing happened between Burton and me last night," she whispered so the others wouldn't hear. "My Dad was at the hospital. Burton didn't want me to be alone, so he stayed. That's all. Unfortunately, when he was leaving, Shane caught me hugging him goodbye."

"Oooh... That explains a lot."

"I know. I felt terrible." Abi took out her tablet from her bag and set it on the desk.

"Well, at least you guys made up. I was worried."

"Yes, me too." Pausing, she said, "So, for lunch, you're fine with us going out alone?"

"Absolutely. You both need time to talk. It's fine. Maybe we can do something after school? The guys will be gone then."

"I planned to go to the hospital and visit my Mom."

"Well, I can come with you if you want."

"Yeah? You don't mind?"

"Are you kidding? No. Not at all."

"Thank you. I appreciate that. I'm a bit scared of going."

Just then, Emile and her friends walked in. They glared at Abi.

"Ignore her," Jade prompted. "You don't need the drama today."

"Yes, I'm not in the mood."

Their teacher arrived and quieted the class. Without skipping a beat, they jumped right into their work. Happy to be creating, Abi inserted an earbud and listened to instrumental music. Time seemed to fly by. It wasn't long before they were packing up their things again.

Moving with the flow of students, Jade and Abi headed out to the courtyard. They found Shane leaning against the wall, looking at his phone.

Seeing her, he quickly put it away and greeted her with a kiss. "Hey, you," he smiled.

"Hey. Ready to go?"

"Yep." Shane gave Reggie a fist pump. "Later, man."

Letting the two be alone, their friends headed to the bistro while Shane and Abi walked to the elevator.

"I thought we could grab a couple of gourmet sandwiches at Mendocino Farms. Up for that?"

"Sure. Sounds good."

Making it to the Jeep, he unlocked the doors and set their bags in the back seat. Each got in and buckled up. Slowly passing the parking booth, they stopped and talked to Gerald quickly before heading down South Barrington to San Vincente. A strange awkwardness still loomed as Shane caressed the top of her hand with his thumb.

Abi broke the silence and said, "I am really sorry for everything. I feel pulled between you and Burton. He was there for me when I had no one else years ago. While my Mom went through treatment the first time, he was the guy who helped me out when my Dad was at work. He'd walk me home from school daily to ensure I got there safely. Just like any big brother would." Thinking about it, she added, "When he left Boston unexpectedly, it crushed me. I'd lost my best and only friend. After that, I was alone."

"I didn't know that."

"I hope the two of you can be friends one day. It would mean a lot to me."

Shane sighed.

She giggled humorously, "Okay, maybe today is too soon."

Understanding Abi and Burton's relationship a little better, Shane mellowed out. He knew now that their past wasn't what he suspected, which meant, at some point, he'd have to be civil to the guy and make an effort for Abi's sake.

"I will try my best to do that for you."

"Really?" She sounded hopeful.

"I just want you to be happy, Abs."

"Thank you."

Reaching their destination, they found an open spot on the street. Parallel parking, they got out and walked toward the restaurant. Shane swung the door open for Abi and had her lead the way.

Staring at the menu board, she opted for the chicken pesto caprese on a brioche bun while Shane decided on a chicken parm sandwich. Entering their orders on the iPad and paying the bill, they waited off to the side for them to call their names - thankful it wasn't busy.

Soon, they were on their way, with sandwiches in tow, ready to head back. Shane scanned the street while they walked to the Jeep. Noticing a black SUV across from them, he remembered the license plate from the truck following Abi the day before.

"B777L," he said.

"What is it?" she asked, not having spotted it sitting there.

"Get in the truck, Abs. Quickly." With urgency, he got behind the wheel.

By this time, Abi was scouring the street, wondering what he'd seen. His head on a swivel, he pulled away and headed north. Shane kept a sharp eye on the rearview mirror.

Abi turned around and saw the SUV. Her face went white. "Is that…"

"I'm pretty sure. It's the same plate."

Intent on losing them, Shane tried to time their arrival at each intersection, hoping to sneak through at the last minute and make them stop for the red. Failing twice, they approached the Starbucks intersection. Inching through at the last second, the men in the truck managed to stay on their tail. Then, just outside the Brentwood School, the light turned yellow. Pressing the pedal to the floor, he accelerated and raced through as it turned red, leaving the SUV stopped behind a vehicle.

Driving away, leaving them in their wake, Abi got worked up. "Who are they? Why are they following me?"

"If I had to bet, I still say they are Korolev's guys."

"But what do they want with us?"

"I don't know. Maybe Eastwood's Dad thinks we are to blame for everything that's happened to his son. The guy's still missing. That whole family is unstable. They are capable of anything. Maybe they think you submitted a report to the cops about what Eastwood did to you. Who knows."

"But I didn't."

"I know. But they don't."

They safely climbed the hill back to the Gilderson School and waved to Gerald. Shane reversed into his assigned spot.

"Do you wanna eat here or go somewhere else?" he asked.

"Here is good. I want to be away from people for a bit."

"Yeah, me too. Big game tonight. I'm sure there will be a huge crowd." He unwrapped his sandwich and took a bite.

Abi did the same. "Do you ever get nervous?" She raised the napkin to her mouth.

"Yeah, all the time. Just have to settle the nerves and focus. After that, I drown it out."

"Jade is going with me to visit my Mom. I think we'll grab something to eat afterward, then head to my place to watch the game."

He didn't want to ask her if Burton would be there, but it was eating at him. "Is your Dad staying overnight again at the hospital, or will he be home?"

"I'm not sure yet. Why?" It wasn't hard to pick up on what he was thinking.

Finally, he spit out the question. "Is Burton staying with you tonight?"

"I hadn't planned on it." A silence fell upon them. Abi leaned forward and placed her wrapped sandwich on the dash. "Do you know why I'm with you?" she said out of the blue after taking a drink of water.

"No." He shook his head. "You could be with anyone you want."

"Well, that's not true."

"I'm sure Burton would date you in a heartbeat. The guy is extremely wealthy. I can't compete with that."

Hearing his comment made her realize where this was stemming from. "I don't want Burton or anyone else. You know what I love about you?"

"What's that?"

"When you look at me, I know you accept me for who I am. I'm not the prettiest or the most popular, but you saw beyond that and found the real me."

About to refute her statement, she placed her finger over his lips to silence him.

"No, let me finish." She lowered her hand and took hold of his. "From day one, you said I was different. You made me feel special and protected. Despite the Black Lyon setback, I still feel loved. That is a big deal since I've never had a boyfriend before. What we have is full of firsts for me, so please be patient. I don't know how to do this. Not sure what's right and what's wrong? All I know is you are the nicest guy I've ever met. Your presence gives me chills. Your kisses make me melt.

So, please believe in what we've found and not think about anything or *anybody* else invading that."

Lost for words, he smiled.

"I love you, Shane Coppersmith, and fear I am in for the long haul."

"Why would that scare you?" He leaned forward.

Inches away, she gazed into his deep blue eyes, feeling her heart race. "Because life without you would be unimaginable," she whispered, her voice trembling just a little.

The space between them seemed to shrink, the air charged with a mix of excitement and anxious energy as his arms wrapped around her. Pulling her close, she could feel his warmth seeping in - calming her fluttering nerves. When he kissed her, it was gentle at first, a soft touch that made her entire body tingle. But then the kiss deepened. More intense, she found herself clinging to him, her hands gripping his shirt. Thoughts scattered as the moment sent waves through her, making her feel like she was floating. Realizing she was kissing him back, matching his intensity with a passion she hadn't known she had, for a moment, nothing else mattered—just the two of them, lost in this perfect connection.

But then, just as suddenly, Shane pulled back, his breathing heavy. He looked at her with a mix of longing and uncertainty. "Umm... Sorry if I...."

She couldn't help but smile, her lips still tingling from the kiss. "Why are you apologizing?" she asked, her voice soft.

He let out a slow breath and leaned back, his gaze never leaving hers. "I just don't want to do anything that makes you uncomfortable," he said, reaching out to take her hand.

She held it without hesitation, giving it a reassuring squeeze. "You didn't," she said, her voice steady.

His thoughts flickered back to the nightmare she endured on Saturday night. He was mindful of that and wanted to make sure she felt safe when sharing moments like this.

Right then, Reggie appeared. Walking to his car, he spotted them.

"I guess you've gotta get going?" She didn't want him to leave.

"Yes. It's about that time..." Reaching across with open arms, he hugged her tightly. "I'll miss you."

"I'll miss you too."

Feeling more confident about their relationship after their talk, he added, "I'll be back late tomorrow night. If your Dad stays at the hospital, maybe I can drop by on my way home?"

She nodded, "I'd like that. I'll let you know what happens."

"Okay. I'll call you after the game."

Abi got out of the Jeep. Shane met her at the front. Kissing her goodbye, he reluctantly let her go. "Bye," he said.

"Remember, I'll be watching." Abi winked at him before hurrying to study hall. "Love you!" she shouted across the parking lot.

"Love you, too," he said, not embarrassed for his friend to hear him say it.

When she disappeared, Reggie said, "You guys made it to the L part already?"

"Well, you and Jade have moved pretty fast yourself." Shane tilted his head to imply what he meant.

"Wait, you guys haven't...."

"No."

Confused, he said, "But doesn't the love part come after the...." He made the same gesture.

"Not for us. She's never..."

"Wow, that's impressive." Reggie was shocked by that.

"Yeah, we've decided to go slow."

Turning to his friend, Reggie replied, "Interesting. Good for you, man."

Shane tapped the guy's shoulder. "Come on. We'd better get goin'. We can't be late."

# 61

# Daydreaming

Not finding Jade anywhere, Abi headed to the spot on the second floor where she and Shane would hide out most afternoons. The space was so peaceful. There was nobody around. Flipping open her laptop and turning to the textbook page she needed to finish, she couldn't help but sway back to the passionate kiss moments ago. It was unlike anything she'd ever experienced. A chill rolled down her spine as it replayed over and over again. That got her thinking about what came next.

Amidst her daydream, Jade texted. *Hey. Where are you?*

Telling her, Abi stood up and watched for her friend. She raised her hand and waved her over.

"I should have known you'd be here," she whispered. "This is where you guys sit every day. It's a good spot."

"Yes. I like that it's away from everyone."

Jade settled in and opened her laptop.

Seeing the Study Hall Monitor about to pass them by, the two tried to look busy. Abi glanced at her friend occasionally, desperately wanting to confide in her. Embarrassed, she didn't know where to start. It was unfamiliar territory. About to ask her a question, Abi stopped and opted against it. She assumed Jade and Reggie had been together, but she wasn't a hundred percent sure since she'd never said. The last thing Abi wanted was to imply something and be wrong. Continuing to work, trying to focus, she sat back in her chair and thought about

Burton and Shane. Even Black Lyon crossed her mind. Drifting to how she had woken up beside her best friend this morning, she surprisingly didn't think anything of it despite how close they were. But was Shane right about what he said? Would Burton date her in a heartbeat if given the opportunity? Amidst that thought, the vision of waking beside Shane like that made her smile uncontrollably.

Jade caught it. "What are you thinking about?"

"Just daydreaming."

"Ooooh, about what? Do tell," she whimsically whispered while pulling her chair over.

"No, I'm not talking about it," Abi blushed.

"Hey, with a face like that, it means something happened? Please. Please, tell me," she begged her.

With the door open, Abi giggled and said, "Okay," she paused and leaned closer. "Shane and I shared this amazing kiss at lunch."

"I knew it!" Jade covered her mouth, hoping the Monitor didn't hear her. Peeking over the cubical wall, she didn't see her anywhere.

Abi lowered her head.

"Tell me more." Jade waited, ready to hang on her every word.

"Well, Shane was upset about what happened with Burton, obviously. So, I figured I'd build his confidence by sharing my feelings. I told him that he was the nicest guy I've ever met. That his presence gives me chills, and kissing him makes me melt. I told him to believe in what we've found and not think about anything or *anybody* else invading it. He told me he feels like he can't compete with Burton's wealth – that it's intimidating for him. I said there was no need to do that because I had chosen him."

"Aaaww…" She grasped her hands together and brought them to her chin.

"I don't think I told you this, but after he and I left Aramis and Lexi's party, we stopped at the beach. That is when he told me he was falling in love with me. I said it back."

"OMG... I'm dying. Shane Coppersmith told you he loves you?" She couldn't wait to hear more.

"So, getting back to what happened at lunch, Shane parked in the garage, and we decided to eat there to get some time to ourselves. Somehow, in the aftermath of all the drama this morning, our emotions kinda took over. At first, he kissed me gently, then..."

"Yeah...then...."

"Well, things escalated. It was amazing until he pulled back."

Surprised, Jade asked, "What do you mean?"

"He stopped himself because he was afraid to cross the line."

"He did?" She was melting in her chair. "He really loves you, Abs."

"I think so, too."

"So, I'm guessing you guys haven't...."

Knowing what she was referring to, Abi shook her head and said, "No."

Jade went silent, then wanted to confirm, "Have you ever?"

Nervously replying, "No," again, Abi looked away.

Jade reached out to her and said, "That's nothing to be embarrassed about. Good for you." She paused. "Does he know that?"

"Yes."

"Well, that's why he's acting that way. Now it makes sense."

"It's not that it hasn't crossed my mind." Abi waited, then asked, "So, umm, are you and Reggie...."

Jade blushed. "Yeah. I can see him being my one and only. Nobody else. Ever since he came to the school, I dreamed of being with him. Now, because of you, I am."

"It wasn't because of me. I told you, he's liked you for a while."

"How do you know that?" Jade was intrigued.

"He was just nervous to talk to you."

"Aaaww, my Baby." She leaned back in her chair. "I just love him so much. He's so good to me. Thoughtful. Kind. Everything I've ever dreamed of. This may sound naïve, but I can see a future with him. Marriage. Kids. A beautiful life. I get butterflies just thinking about it."

Abi remembered what Shane had said about Reggie's parents and their business dealings - mostly Reggie's arranged marriage to merge with another family. She hoped Reggie would stand his ground and marry for love, not family obligation.

"So, how about you? Is Shane it?"

"I can't deny there was something about him from day one when we looked at each other across the lobby at Orientation Day. That's when you told me he was off-limits - that Emile Raven owned him, remember?"

She chuckled. "Crazy how the tables turned."

"I'm a big believer that everything happens for a reason. Who knows? If he's with me versus Emile, maybe his life will venture down a more positive path."

"For sure, hands down. The relationship you two have is healthy. When he was with Emile, it wasn't."

The school bell rang.

"Wow, it's time to go already," Abi giggled.

"Time goes by fast when you're havin' fun, girl."

They packed their laptops in their bags and pushed in their chairs.

"Come on, let's get out of here. We gotta go see your Momma."

# 62

# The First Visit

The two walked to the garage while Jade perused her phone for updates on the Eastwood situation. Unfortunately, police were still searching for intel on Black Lyon.

Reading Abi the update, she added, "Don't they know nobody will reveal his identity? He has a cult following who won't betray him."

Upon debating sharing her innermost thoughts, she said, "This stays between you and me, okay? Like to the grave."

"Sure." A serious expression flashed across her friend's face. "What is it?"

"With everything that happened with Black Lyon that night, I feel indebted to him, you know. He didn't have to save me, but he did." Hesitating again, she stated, "Before the app vanished, I was thinking about attending one more rave."

"What?"

"Wait. Hear me out."

Jade quickly squashed that thought of hers. "What if Eastwood's guys are there? Or worse, Eastwood himself. You might not be so lucky the next time."

"Look, I just wanted to thank him, and who knows...."

"Who knows what? You think he'll reveal himself to you?" Jade stood with her hands on her hips, knowing her hunch was right. "I had a feeling you developed a thing for the guy. Abi, saving you was to cover his own ass. He probably did it so you wouldn't press charges or sue him. Who knows? No matter what you do or say, he will never reveal himself to anyone. That's part of his allure. Stop this fantasy thing you've got going on here and focus on what is right in front of you. And that is Shane. Nothing else. He's the one who loves you."

Hearing her take on it, Abi cowered. "You're right."

"Yes, I am. You gotta listen to me. Just be thankful you were in the right place at the right time, and he did what he did. Now, you've gotta move on."

Abi nodded. "I get it."

Arriving at their cars, done with the heavy conversation, she asked, "So, am I driving?"

"Sure. Let me just ask my Dad for directions as to where to go."

Jumping into Jade's Porsche, they headed out and said goodnight to Gerald.

Receiving the text from her Father, she told Jade the address and where they could find parking at the UCLA Medical Center. Winding their way across Sunset to Veteran Avenue, they maneuvered toward the Wasserman facility and reached the underground parking garage off of Westwood Plaza. Jade punched the button for a ticket as the arm raised in front of them, allowing access. Having to descend a few floors to find an open spot, Jade and Abi soon got on the elevator and headed toward the entrance. When the doors opened, Abi searched for the main elevators to the upper floors as her Father instructed. Finding them, she pressed the button and waited.

Nervous about seeing her Mom, Abi said, "Umm, my Dad said he would meet us there."

When the doors opened, they stepped inside. While pressing the number six, a few people got on with them. Unfortunately, they had to stop several times before the doors parted, and she spotted her Dad.

"Hi," she said, approaching with open arms.

Hugging his daughter tightly, he said, "Hi, Sweetheart." Seeing Jade with her, he asked, "Who is your friend?"

"This is Jade," she introduced. Turning to her, she said, "This is my Dad."

He held out his hand and said, "Dr. Acardi. Nice to finally meet you, Jade. I've heard a lot about you."

"Nice to meet you, too."

Abi crossed her arms. She was so nervous. She felt sick.

"This way," he said, leading them past the nurse's station to a private ICU unit. They stood outside the glass doors, where she found her Mom propped up in bed in the middle of the room with lines and tubes everywhere. Eyes closed, not awake, Abi started to shake at the sight of her.

Quickly holding his daughter to cushion the shock, Jade watched her friend and stepped back. It was an emotional moment that struck a chord. Tears developed in her eyes, and Jade hoped they wouldn't flood her face. This is what her best friend was dealing with behind closed doors. A horrific tragedy you wouldn't wish on your worst enemy.

"Do you want to go in?" her Father asked.

Brushing the tears from her face, she said, "One more minute." A rush of thoughts bombarded her. "Will she hear me? Is she responding?"

"She's in a coma, but the brain may still be able to pick up on your voice. Some studies show talking or touching a loved one's hand may help them recover."

Abi nodded. "Okay. I'm ready." She turned to Jade.

"I'll wait here," her friend said. Not prepared to see the scene unfolding before her, Jade suddenly appreciated her Mom and felt the need to text her.

With his arm around Abi, they walked into the room filled with the rhythmic hum of machines. Standing inches from her, she looked so pale.

Her Dad placed his hand on top of his wife's, hoping she knew he was there. "Hi, my love. Look who is here to see you," he said.

"Hi, Mom. It's me." She touched her arm.

"Do you want a moment alone with her?"

Afraid, she answered, "No. Don't leave."

"Okay."

Seeing Abi inside the room was too much for Jade. She needed to walk away. Finding a chair in a waiting room, she sat down and continued lovingly texting her Mother.

# 63

## Dinner & Football

During her visit, her Father sat in the chair where he'd been sleeping the past few nights. He worked on his computer while the nurses went in and out. After being there an hour, Abi kissed her Mom on the cheek and told her she would be back.

"I plan to head home to shower and change before returning for the night," he said. "Are you going to be okay at the house?" He wondered if someone would be staying with her but refrained from asking.

"Yes, I'll be fine." Abi rubbed her Mom's arm. "Love you," she whispered before walking out the door with him.

"She loves you so much, Sweetie, and so do I. Never forget that."

"I won't," she replied.

Not finding Jade in the hallway, she texted her.

In seconds, her friend appeared from around a corner. Seeing Abi upset, she greeted her with open arms. Unable to control their emotions, they both cried.

Walking back to the elevators, all three descended to the main floor.

Her Dad hugged her one last time. "I'm going to check in at the office before heading home. You're sure you'll be okay tonight without me there?"

"Yes. I'll be fine." Knowing her Dad was fishing, she said, "Don't worry. Shane's not here. He's gone to play two away games tonight and tomorrow."

"Oh?" he said. "And, Burton?"

"He's got school."

"I can stay with you, Abi, if you want." Jade smiled.

"Perfect. Thank you, Jade." Her Dad liked that idea better. "Regardless, call me if you need me, Sweetie?"

"I will."

"It was nice meeting you, Jade," he smiled. "Thank you for being here for Abi."

"I'm happy to support her in any way I can. She's been a good friend to me, too." She turned to her. "Ready to go, girl?"

Abi said, "Yes. Ready."

Parting ways, they rode the elevators to the garage. It didn't take long to pay for parking and be on their way.

"Do you still wanna grab a bite?" Jade asked, not sure what she wanted to do.

"Yes, sure. That would be nice."

"What are you in the mood for? Upscale? Casual?" She gave her a list of options before turning left on Gayley Avenue.

"Casual would be great - less fuss."

"I know this great place close by."

"Perfect."

The ride to the restaurant was short. Located a couple of blocks south of the hospital, Jade made a few turns before they found a metered parking spot on Glendon Avenue.

"This place is amazing. It's called Wolfglen. I love their food. It's fresh and made to order."

"We are still in our uniforms. Is that okay?" Abi wasn't sure.

"It's fine. I've been here with my Mom after school twice. It's got a cozy vibe."

Abi followed Jade across the street. Walking into the restaurant, a man greeted them. The space behind him was hopping.

"Ahh, Ms. Webber. Nice to see you again."

"Good to see you, Mr. Camino."

"Table for two?" he asked, seeing Abi standing with her.

"Yes, Sir."

"Very good. Follow me. Right this way." Leading the girls to a table along the right-hand side, he stepped back and said, "Here we are."

After allowing them to sit, he handed each one a menu. "Your waiter will be with you shortly. Let me know if you need anything else."

"Thank you," Abi replied.

"Yes, thank you, Mr. Camino."

"Enjoy."

As he walked away, Abi looked around. There was a mix of people.

Jade opened her menu. "Do you think the boys will win tonight?"

Perusing the entrees, Abi replied, "I think so. I have faith in them."

"After what happened this afternoon, I'm sure Shane is on cloud nine."

"Hey," Abi giggled as her cheeks turned a blushing shade of pink.

"So, what are you in the mood for? I'm getting the burger and truffle fries." Jade closed her menu.

"Well, let's make that two."

Their waiter arrived and got them set up with sparkling water and lemon. When he took their orders, the girls could sit and relax for the first time all day.

Jade wondered, "So, since your Dad's at the hospital tonight, do you want to stay at my place instead?"

Hesitating, Abi played with the napkin on the table.

"Please tell me Burton isn't coming over again."

Her friend shrugged her shoulders.

"Abi. You just fixed things with Shane. Things are good. Why would you jeopardize that?"

"I've got something to run by him." She figured saying that would justify his visit.

Jade was not happy.

"For the hundredth time, he's like a brother. There is nothing romantic going on between us."

"Whatever you say." Adding a bit of humor into the conversation, she said, "But if you did, you know, have something going on with him, I wouldn't blame you. He is kinda hunky."

"Seriously? It's not like that."

"Okay, I believe you." Thinking about the rest of their evening, she asked, "So, are we watching the football game at your place then, or what?"

"Sure. We can do that."

Their plates arrived with burgers and a bowl of truffle fries on the side.

"Wow. This looks amazing." Abi took a bite of a fry. "Oh, yeah. This is great."

Tackling the meaty main course, the girls made it through half of their burgers but couldn't resist finishing most of their fries. Given the rest to go, Abi pulled out her wallet to pay.

"Don't be silly, girl. I got this one."

"I can't let you do that."

"After what you've been through today, it's the least I can do. Hopefully, our dinner helped take your mind off of things."

"Thank you. It certainly lifted my spirits." Reality set in again, causing an unsettled feeling in the pit of her stomach. "I guess we should go. I still need to grab my car before we head home."

While Jade paid the bill, Abi glanced out the front windows. There she saw a man dressed in black. His eyes remained locked on the front door of their restaurant. Sitting up straight, she thought he looked familiar. "Hey, I know that guy from somewhere." She wracked her brain as to where she'd seen him before. Staring at his face, he suddenly turned and looked away. That is when she knew. "Hey, it's one of the men from Black Lyon's security team."

"What?" Jade pointed out the man. "Him? Are you sure?"

"Positive. I remember his side profile. He was sitting at a desk watching the monitors." Staring at him, she said, "That's definitely him. No question."

Jade was confused. "So, you think Black Lyon sent his security to follow you?"

"Well, when we leave, if this guy gets in a black SUV, then, yeah, I think so." The second Abi said that aloud, her heart skipped a beat.

"What are we waiting for? Let's find out."

Jade bid Mr. Camino a pleasant evening and thanked him for his hospitality. Abi did the same. Stopping before walking out the door, the girls noticed the man talking into a hidden mic before he walked away.

"Here we go." Abi went out first while Jade darted across the street behind her.

Both quickly got in the car before Jade started the engine and backed up. Driving down Glendon Avenue, passing the coffee house, they saw a black SUV parked to the side.

Abi looked at the license plate. "B777L," she said. "It's them."

"Did you say B and L?"

"Yes."

"That proves it. Those are Black Lyon's initials."

Turning right, Jade sped up, hoping to distance them from the SUV. Veering this way and that way, Abi had no idea where they were going. But Jade did.

"We gotta get on the freeway. I can lose them there."

"Wait. There's no point. They know where I live, so they must know what school I attend."

"What do you mean?"

"Burton and I saw the SUV parked outside my house all night last night. He tried to confront them, but they took off. A little while later, they returned."

"Tell me you're joking."

"Wish I was." Abi glanced in her rearview mirror and saw the SUV about six car lengths behind.

The traffic got thick toward the 405. Reaching the off-ramp, Jade gunned it, forcing Abi back in her seat.

"Please be careful. Please be careful," Abi repeated, more fearful of Jade's driving than being followed.

"Don't worry. I got this."

Speeding along the straight stretch, dodging in and out of the lanes, Abi could see Gilderson on the hillside up ahead.

Upon exiting onto the Sunset Boulevard ramp, Jade stopped at the lights. "Do you see them?"

Abi turned and tried to look around the vehicles behind them. "No. Not yet."

The light turned green.

"Watch as we turn to see if they're back there."

Doing that, she scanned each vehicle. "No black SUV," she said as the merging traffic stopped again.

On North Church, Jade sped along to the school gates. Waiting for it to open, they kept an eye out for anything suspicious. Continuing up the hill towards the parking garage, they entered slowly. Jade swung her car right beside Abi's.

"I will follow you closely to your place."

"Thank you."

"Well, get in! Let's get a move on."

Getting in her Mini Cooper, Abi started the engine. Driving out of the garage, Jade followed tight behind her and returned the way they came. Not seeing the strange SUV, they made their way along Sunset to the gates of Bel Air.

Within minutes, both were pulling up to her house. Abi's head was on a swivel. There was nothing on the street. As she drove in and parked, Jade stopped beside her. Fearful, she quickly closed the gate behind them.

Happy to be inside the compound, they got out.

"We made it." Jade grabbed her bag and asked, "Is it okay if I change clothes here?"

"Sure. No problem."

Abi walked into the house and turned off the alarm.

Jade looked around. "I love your house. Every time I walk in, it feels peaceful, unlike mine."

"Thanks," she said, knowing it's been far from that. "We need to hurry. The game starts in ten minutes."

Connecting the feed to the television in the family room, Abi noticed a few more social media posts about Shane. One interview, in particular, caught her attention.

Pressing play, they listened to the sportscaster. *"In truth, any of the top three QBs are worthy candidates for the QB1 mantle. We've gone back and forth throughout the NCAA Draft cycle because it genuinely is too close to call. All of the top options have their unique appeal. Youngston has the highest ceiling. Korolev has the highest floor. But Coppersmith might be the best blend of both elements. That is why he is our No. 1 pick. There's no other way to say it than this. Coppersmith's processing ability, anticipation, decision-making, accuracy, and situational placement are unmatched. His 4.43 speed and 40.5" vertical quantifies his athleticism at 6'3", 198 pounds. He also has a rocket arm and flashes key building blocks like processing capacity and pocket discipline. He can throw into insanely tight windows. Hands down, Coppersmith is the easiest QB to bank on in a draft process where risk and security exist in a delicate balance."*

Abi almost cried. She was so proud of him. He'd worked so hard to get here.

"That's your man." Jade smiled and offered a side hug. "This is awesome."

After an emotional day, Abi found it nice to have something positive to dwell on for a change.

# 64

# Home Alone

Over the next two hours, the girls sat on the edge of their seats while watching Gilderson play their game against Cate Academy. It was stressful with both teams initially tied, but when the guys pulled ahead and finally won 14 - 7, they could relax.

Switching to the post-game interviews on various websites, four players from the Gilderson team got accolades. Shane, Reggie, Alan, and Adrian were considered the athletes of the night.

Just before eight-thirty, Abi checked in with her Dad. Texting him and receiving a message in return, she was thankful that her Mom was the same and hadn't gotten worse. Wishing him goodnight, she signed off by passing along Jade's greetings.

"Well, I guess I should get going," her friend said.

Abi walked alongside her. "Thank you for being there for me today."

She couldn't help but be sympathetic to her situation. "Through good times and bad. I am here if you need me." Hugging Abi, she asked, "Are you sure you don't want me to stay?"

"No, I think I'll be good."

Assuming she'd have company shortly, she replied, "Remember what I said about you and Burton. Be careful if he drops by tonight or stays over. You don't want to have a repeat of this morning."

"I hear what you're saying."

On her way out the door, she said, "Okay. Don't say I didn't warn you."

Abi took it to heart.

Jade got in her car and waved goodbye.

Somewhat scared to be left alone, she closed the gate and texted Burton.

*Hey, it's me. Wondering if you are busy tonight. Let me know. Call me.*

When she pressed send, a certain level of guilt followed – it felt almost deceptive. Rereading the text she sent him, she realized Burton could easily misconstrue the words she used.

"You've gotta be careful what you say. The last thing you want to do is string him along." Knowing they were just friends, how they woke in each other's arms this morning could easily blur those lines. Abi looked to the sky, wishing life would give her a break from all the drama.

Locking the front door, she turned on all the outside lights. The place was glowing like the mansion across the canyon tonight. Staring at the huge home, she wondered what the guy's life was like and who he was. Still not having driven over there to check it out, she figured she'd get around to it eventually.

As time ticked by, Burton had yet to read her message, let alone respond to it.

"I wonder what he's up to. Strange," she said, looking around the main floor. The house was eerily quiet. Now, she wished she wouldn't have told Jade to go home. "Well, Abs, it looks like you are on your own tonight."

Hoping Burton would eventually text her back, she went upstairs and got ready for bed. Upon slipping under the covers, she propped her arms on a pillow over her stomach and checked her phone. Still nothing, she debated whether she should text again and stopped herself.

"He's probably busy. You don't want to bother him." Thinking about the blonde bombshell on his arm in Cabo, she figured he was with her. Not blaming him for going dark after how she treated him that morning, she felt terrible. "I was so rude and snappy. Arrghh....

You're such an idiot." The phone flopped backward when her arms went limp. She never wanted to hurt him or come across as unappreciative. "Damn, it…" Rolling over on her side, she kept the device close in case he called. About to close her eyes, it rang. Quickly picking it up, she saw Shane's face on the screen.

"Hello?"

"Hey, Abs. Hope I'm not calling too late."

"Hi. No, just got into bed."

To him, she sounded tired. "How was the rest of your day?"

"Long," she sighed. "It was sad then happy. A rollercoaster ride of emotions, really."

"Why? What happened?"

"If you don't mind, I'd rather not talk about it."

He felt she was side-stepping that for a reason or was limiting the conversation because she couldn't talk. "That's okay. No problem," he said, wondering if Burton was there. Contemplating it, he wouldn't dare ask. "We haven't left for the hotel yet. Won't be there until after midnight, I'm sure. One guy needed stitches."

"Was he hurt bad?"

"No, just a gash on his arm."

"I watched a few of your interviews and listened to the Pro Football Network analysis. Almost cried. So proud of you."

"Thanks. Appreciate that. Hopefully, all this will be worth it one day."

"It will. You'll see."

Deciding to casually fish and get her to share more about her day, he asked, "How's your Mom?"

Abi stayed quiet.

"Is everything okay?" he asked.

"Not really."

"Why?"

"I went to visit her today. My Dad neglected to inform me that she was in the ICU."

Shane could feel her sadness. "Bet it was tough to see her like that."

"It was worse than I could've ever imagined."

"Well, anytime you need me to go with you, just ask."

"I might take you up on that."

"Hope so."

Abi yawned.

"I guess I should let you get some sleep. Did your Dad make it home tonight?"

She knew what he was doing. Hoping to put his mind at ease, she said, "No. He's not here. I'm alone."

"If I were back, I'd stay and keep you company."

"You do realize that can never happen." It wasn't even in the realm of possibilities.

"I know. Your father would hate me." Shane had a solution to that. "But what if I slept on the couch downstairs?"

Abi thought that through. "Well, he would see you on the cameras. You okay being watched while you sleep?"

"If that's what it takes. Sure. I hate that you're by yourself."

"I have no other choice. I'm trying to keep the peace." Torn and pulled between Burton and Shane, she tried not to sound too negative.

Not wanting to get into it with her again, he said, "Tomorrow night, if you are still alone and you're scared, I'll swing by on my way home."

"But, my Dad...."

"I'm sure he would understand if you told him how you feel."

She knew he was right. "Don't worry. I'll be okay. This is my life now. I gotta get used to it."

Sad to hear that, he said, "Maybe so, but you don't need to go through it alone. We are all here for you, Abi."

"I know. Thank you." Hearing voices in the background, she assumed the coaches were spouting instructions.

"Look, I gotta go. We're boarding the bus. Have a good day tomorrow. I will call you after the game."

"Night. Good luck if we don't get a chance to talk beforehand."

"Thank you," he hesitated, then whispered, "Okay, love you."

"Love you too."

"Night."

"Goodnight." When Abi ended the call, she rolled over and buried her head under the pillow. He hadn't said it, but she knew he suspected Burton might be there. "Jade was right," she mumbled. "You just made up with Shane. Things are good. Don't screw it up."

# Bentley

Abi's room brightened with the rising sun. The house was so quiet she could hear the wind gusting past her window. Having hardly slept, she wished she hadn't sent Jade home. Maybe the night wouldn't have been so bad. Rolling over, dreading the day ahead, she gathered the strength to leave her bed.

Within the hour, she was on her way downstairs, dressed and somewhat prepared for the day. By eight o'clock, almost out the door, Abi stopped. Returning to the kitchen, she checked the cameras to see if the black SUV was parked there. For the first time all week, it wasn't. Unsure what that meant, she headed outside after locking the house. Settling into the driver's seat, she slowly pulled out and waited for the gate to close behind her. About to pull away, a matte black custom SUV approached. Seeing the round lights adorning the hood, she knew what it was.

"Bentley Bentayga," she whispered as the ominous-looking truck with tinted windows passed by. Eyes glued to the driver's side, she tried to see in. Flashing back to the vehicle she got into when Martin drove her home, Abi said, "Is it the same one? Can't be?" Reality set in. "Why would Black Lyon be driving past my house?" Breaking from her thoughts, as it drove around the corner out of sight, she pulled onto Stradella.

Heading south, happy to have left a few minutes early, Abi was thankful she didn't have to rush. As the rising sun flashed intermittently through the trees, she wished she had retracted the roof to enjoy the sunshine and fresh air.

"Soon, the cooler weather will be here, and you won't be able to do that," she said, assuming there would be a noticeable change.

While running through a list of tasks, Abi realized it would be a day without Shane around—the first ever. Hoping to make the best of it, she wanted to get through unscathed. Hearing a familiar song on the radio about to turn up, she happened to get a glimpse of something in her peripheral. Looking in the rearview mirror, she found the black Bentley speeding up, getting closer and closer.

"What the hell?"

On her tail, matching her turn for turn, she focused on the driver. Dressed in black, with a hood over his head, the man had two hands on the wheel. His face cloaked in shadows, Abi couldn't see his features clearly enough to identify him. Nervously shifting her sights between the driver and the road ahead, her phone rang.

With impeccable timing, she saw Burton's face on the screen.

Answering the hands-free, she shouted, "Burton!"

Immediately, the sound of her voice set him off. "Abi? Are you okay?"

Bouncing her sights between the driver and the road and hearing Burton's voice on speaker, she read the license plate under the dark, smokey plastic cover. "B111L." Easily recalling the plate of the other SUV, it was a similar pattern. Ignoring Burton's voice, she said, "Wait?"

"Wait, what? What's going on? Talk to me," he said, wishing she'd communicate.

"It's him."

"Who?"

"I think it's Black Lyon."

"What? You're kidding, right?" Burton figured she was mistaken.

"I don't know. But, this could be my last chance to…"

"What do you mean, last chance?" He looked up her location on his phone.

"If it's Black Lyon, he will stop, and I can talk to him." She felt like it was now or never.

"Abs, listen to me, okay? Do not stop the car. You don't know who that guy is."

"I've gotta know, Burton."

"Know what?"

"Why he did it. Why he saved me? Why are his guys following me everywhere?" She started to slow down. "If I don't do this now, I will always wonder." Abruptly pulling over, Abi watched the Bentley reduce its speed, but it drove right past her. With eyes on the driver, she tried to see inside. Only able to decipher the man's figure while driving past, she held her breath, hoping to see brake lights. But there was nothing.

With Burton's voice sounding more like white noise in the background, she watched the luxury truck move further and further away from her. For some reason, her heart broke.

"Abi! Abi? Answer me," Burton pleaded.

Carefully pulling back onto the road, she replied, "Don't worry. It drove right past me. He didn't stop."

Happy to hear it, he didn't say another word.

At that moment, Abi got an idea. Turning the tables, she accelerated. "I'm gonna follow him."

"What?" He sat up in his seat. Gripping the steering wheel, he thought of ways to reason with her. "No. Stop the car."

"Why? I wanna see where he goes." She sounded confident and unafraid.

"Listen to me, Abs. What are the chances it's Black Lyon? Think about it. He's got a warrant out for his arrest. Hell, he's probably fled the country by now. Why would he be driving past your house – of all places? The driver could be a criminal or worse - a pedo? What if it's a trap? Human traffickers play on your emotions and bait you. Don't fall for it."

"Seriously?" she said as his comment cast an element of doubt and fear.

"Don't be naïve."

"But..." Her mind reeled.

"But, nothing. Let it go." He felt so helpless. Too far away to rescue her, he could only talk her down and hope she'd listen.

Catching up to the Bentley, she watched it turn right on Bellagio. Faced with a decision, she thought, *Left or right?* Approaching the intersection at the Bel Air gates, she suddenly turned. Heading north, behind the Bentley, she could hear Burton pleading for information. Ignoring him, she kept driving.

"Abi! What are you doing?" He noticed her location swerve right and drive away from Sunset Boulevard. "No. You need to stop."

Uncharacteristically going against her better judgment, she sped up. Turn for turn - she stayed behind the Bentley. Hitting a straight stretch along Roscomare, she saw a Cadillac Escalade waiting to turn. As the Bentley passed by it, out of nowhere, the SUV pulled out and blocked the road.

"Aaah!" she shouted, pulling hard on the emergency brake to avoid a collision.

"What happened?" Burton shouted. "Are you okay?"

Stopped dead in the middle of the street, the SUV stayed there and did not move. Seeing the license plate, Abi whispered, "B777L. It's them."

"It's who?"

Unable to pass, she knew they'd intentionally put space between Black Lyon and her. But why? Burton's comment sparked a fear deep inside her. Quickly, looking around, there was nobody there but them.

"What's happening?" Burton pleaded before shouting, "Abi!"

"What!" she yelled back while making a tight U-turn and speeding south down the road.

Burton saw her change direction. "Keep going. Don't look back," he said.

"I am. Don't worry."

Despite him saying it, she kept an eye on her rearview mirror anyway, but nothing was there. Soon, she was coming up on Sunset. Surrounded by traffic, she felt more secure. Abi believed she could have dodged a bullet - her obsession with the DJ could have gotten her into serious trouble.

"Abs? Hello?"

She broke her silence. "Yes, I'm here," before adding, "Hey, you said you'd get to me faster than the police if I needed help."

"Kinda hard when I'm stuck on the PCH," he said before carefully asking, "Are you okay?"

"Just disappointed, really. He was right there. I could have ended this. Gotten closure."

"I realize you have this crazy connection to the guy. Maybe it's survivor's enchantment – you know, being fixated on the hero who saved you. But, Abs, nobody knows who this guy is and what he is capable of."

"I know. You're right. This was stupid."

"Yeah, it wasn't the smartest thing to do. But I get it."

"You do?"

"I do, but you need to let this go before you get yourself into something you can't find a way out of."

"I understand." Finally turning onto Sunset, she said, "I'm not far from school now."

"I see that."

"Well, I'm around if you need me. I should be at UCLA in about twenty minutes."

With dead air between them, Abi said out of the blue, "Why didn't you text me back last night?"

"I, umm, had a lot going on."

"Were you with that girl?"

"What, girl?"

"The one from Cabo."

"No."

"So, what? You couldn't text me and say, sorry, I'm busy?"

"I'm sorry...I..."

"You what?"

"See, this is the thing. If I had texted back, there's a good chance I would have come over, and if your Dad weren't there, I would've felt obligated to stay and protect you. But after what happened yesterday involving Shane, I think you and I both know it's not a good idea." He didn't tell her that being around her played on his emotions, and having to share her with someone else hurt. Not getting a response, he clarified, "Do you hear what I'm saying?"

"I get it."

"So, we're good?"

"Yes."

"Look, I gotta go. As I said, call me if you need me. I won't be far."

"I will."

He could tell she wasn't fine after what he said. But it was for the best. Eventually, he hoped she'd figure that out, too. "Is it okay if I call you later?"

"Sure. Sounds good."

"Have a good day, Abs."

"Yeah, you too."

When their call ended, she felt she'd lost her best friend. Wondering where they'd go from here, Abi was determined to make things right and get them to a place that wasn't so complicated. Amidst all that, her thoughts switched to Black Lyon as she passed through the school's main gate. If that was him driving past her house, it spoke volumes. In her mind, he wouldn't have done that unless he cared. Thinking about the famous DJ, she felt more determined than ever to find him, but it would require secrecy and a bit of luck.

66 ▌

# Secrets

Surprisingly, Abi made it to school on time after the unexpected detour. Saying hello to Gerald before parking her car, she found Jade waiting for her. The girl got out and slipped her phone into her bag. Wondering if she should tell her what happened, Abi quickly decided against it, thinking it would open a whole rash of questions - most she wasn't prepared to answer.

"So, did you hear that latest?" Jade stated, stopping in front of Abi's Cooper.

"No. What happened now?"

"Rumors are flying around that Eastwood got arrested after they found him. The police are holding him for questioning – apparently."

"Why? What for?"

Slowly making their way to the elevator, she replied, "Not sure." Immediately noticing Abi wasn't herself, she asked, "What's up? You seem off?"

Put on the spot, Abi thought quickly. "I barely got any sleep."

"See, I should have stayed with you."

"Yes, I thought that about halfway through the night."

"How will you play this afternoon if you're running on fumes?" Jade stated.

"About that..."

"Oh, no, what?"

"Honestly, I've been thinking a lot about it. I don't know if I'm gonna go today - or any other day, for that matter." Abi hoped she'd get her drift.

"Wait? Like quit the team?"

"Yes."

"Abs, you can't quit. We need you." Jade caught herself. She didn't want to put extra pressure on her friend selfishly.

"Look, after visiting my Mom yesterday, I am preparing myself for the worst. Life is about to change drastically in the coming months. It's not a matter of if but when. My Mom is going to pass away, Jade." Abi stopped. She'd never said it out loud.

"Oh, Abi, I know. I'm so sorry..."

She pulled herself together. "That said, I, umm, will need to be there for my Dad. Besides, I won't be useful to anyone when that happens. How can I focus on winning matches with my life crumbling?"

Jade understood what she was saying. "I'm sorry, Abs. Whatever you decide, it's fine. I get it."

"I just don't want any regrets. Lately, the guilt of not spending time with her haunts me."

Jade stayed quiet. She felt for her friend. "So, what are you gonna tell the coaches?"

"The truth. They'll understand."

To offer support, Jade asked, "So, do you want me to go with you to the hospital after practice?"

"No, it's fine. I'll be okay."

"Are you sure? I don't mind."

"Yes, don't worry. I am going to visit her after school, then head home. I need to get some sleep." Knowingly deceiving Jade, Abi knew she had work to do if she was ever going to find Black Lyon. At this point, time was of the essence. She was determined to locate his whereabouts.

"Just be careful if you're driving anywhere by yourself."

"I will."

Reaching their building, the two climbed to the second floor for math. Sitting down, Professor Walker arrived minutes after them. Blu was right on his heels. Slipping through before the door shut, Mr. Walker humorously said, "Glad to see you are gracing us with your presence, Mr. Brennan. Long time no see."

The class chuckled as Blu took a seat close to Abi and Jade. He didn't look as pale after being in Cabo.

"I wanted to thank you for inviting us to the pool party," Abi whispered to him. "It was nice of you."

He turned to her. "Sorry? Who are you?"

Stunned, Abi didn't know how to reply to that. "Umm, you invited Shane and me to your pool party."

"Oh, yeah, il Capitano. It's all good."

"Care to share your conversation with the class, Ms. Acardi?" their teacher said.

Embarrassed, seeing every set of eyes look her way, she could feel the heat as her face turned red. "No, Sir. Sorry."

"Very well. Turn to page two-hundred and ten in your textbooks, everyone."

Not wasting any time, they got down to business.

Partway through the class, Abi pulled out her phone and kept it hidden under the desk. Typing an email to the tennis coaches, she pressed send. Relieved to have that task off her plate, she got out her Burch book and created a plan of action to find the Black Lyon house later that afternoon. She knew it was near the corporate park – not more than a fifteen-minute drive. Pulling up google maps on her phone, she created a ten-mile radius from that spot and a twenty-mile radius as plan b.

Jade glanced over and noticed what she was doing.

When Abi caught her looking her way, she sneakily started doing her work again.

*What is she doing? I know she's up to something,* Jade thought. *But what?*

# 67

## The Search

Painful as it was, Abi made it through science and art. Having kept to herself, she continued jotting down the details she recalled from Saturday night. Recording everything from their arrival in the parking lot to the time spent traveling on the shuttle bus to the secret location - even the grassy rolling hills beyond the steel scaffolding stage held clues to finding the famous DJ.

Aware of Jade's watchful eye, Abi tried to act normal on the way to the Bistro for lunch. While waiting in line to pay for her food, she saw Jade walk ahead to find a table. Not wanting to sit and talk, needing some time to herself, Abi veered up the stairs, out of sight. Feeling bad for abandoning her friend, she couldn't ignore this overwhelming need to be alone. Something that was never a problem back in Boston.

Sitting on the stone bench across from the cactus garden, she pulled out her notebook and brainstormed while eating her turkey wrap. After study hall, she'd planned first to visit her Mom, then make the half-hour trek to the original Black Lyon pick-up location at the corporate park off the 101. From there, depending on her findings, she would search for two hours before heading home. It was then Burton crossed her mind.

"I'm sure he'll follow me," she said quietly before removing his access to her phone's location. "Sorry, Burton," she muttered under her breath. "It's just for a couple of hours. Don't worry."

"Don't worry about what?" a voice split through the air. Jade approached with her water bottle in hand.

Abi closed her book. "Umm, nothing."

Having a seat beside Abi, she looked straight ahead. "You ditched me."

"I know. I'm sorry. I just needed to be alone for a while."

"Well, you should have said that. What gives?"

Fidgeting, Abi didn't know what to say.

"Word to the wise, I suggest you tell me what you are up to because my *spidey senses* are tingling."

Unable to look her friend in the eye, she said, "I can't."

"Because you don't trust me?"

"No, it's not that."

"Then what?"

Abi was about to cave. "Promise you won't say a word to Reggie."

"Abs..."

"Jade, swear on your life and everything sacred to you." She was desperate.

Scared about what she could be hiding, Jade said, "Fine. I swear."

Hesitating, Abi thought about how to phrase what she needed to say. "Something happened this morning..."

"Oh no," Jade said, leaving the bench. "If this has anything to do with Burton, I swear..." She covered her ears. "I don't wanna know."

"No, it's not about him." Abi inhaled and said, "It's about Black Lyon."

The girl swung around and placed her hands on her hips. "Wait? What did you just say?" She looked her dead in the eye.

Abi explained in great detail, word for word, what had happened on her way to school. Jade listened in disbelief.

"So, you're telling me, you think Black Lyon went by your house and followed you?"

"Yes." Abi was serious.

"But when you pulled over, he kept going and didn't stop?"

"Right. After that, I tried to catch up to him. Suddenly, the same SUV parked outside my house came outta nowhere and blocked my path. They helped him get away. What Burton said spooked me at that moment, so I quickly turned around and left."

"Hmm." Jade was skeptical. "And you're sure it was him? Black Lyon, I mean?"

"Well, no, but the license plate was B111L. It's not a coincidence that his security has a similar plate - B777L. That's how he numbers his cars."

Jade tilted her head. "I'm with Burton on this. He wanted you to stop following the guy for a reason. It's crazy. Nobody knows his story. He could be a criminal, for all you know."

"Why does everyone go to the raves if he's involved in something sketchy? The guy is loaded. On top of that, since this whole thing went down with Eastwood, his popularity is spreading. Other DJs around the world are banning together to support him."

"Okay. Okay, one second...." She thought. "Regardless of all that, the bottom line is, you don't even know what he looks like. What if he wears the hood and the mask across his face for a reason? What if he is full of tattoos, or worse, permanently disfigured?"

"Doesn't matter. We shared a brief connection. In the end, all I want to say is thank you. If he hadn't done what he did, my life would've turned a dark corner."

"And you're sure you're not looking for anything romantic here?" She waited to hear her answer.

"No, I'm with Shane," she solidified.

"Okay. Good. I'm glad to hear that."

With silence between them, unsure if she should let her in on her afterschool project, Abi divulged, "This afternoon, after seeing my Mom, I am going to try and find Black Lyon's house."

"What? How?"

Opening her Burch book, she showed her friend all the evidence she remembered from Saturday night. "I'm going to use the time in study hall to pinpoint a few possibilities."

"There must be thousands of houses in that area, Abs. How on earth will you find the right one? It's like looking for a needle in a haystack."

"Process of elimination." Explaining her probability circle, with a ten-mile and twenty-mile radius, she said, "I am going to use Google Earth to search from an aerial view. Based on the criteria, I should be able to narrow it down."

Intrigued, Jade said, "I'll go with you."

"You will?"

"Yeah, but after practice. Meet me at the parking garage when you finish visiting your Mom."

"Alright." She stopped and made her swear again. "If you agree to do this, promise this stays between us for life."

"Deal."

They heard the bell ring.

"Come on," Jade said. "I guess we've got a house to find."

68

# Found

Climbing the stairs to the second level of the library after checking in, they went to Abi's quiet spot. Taking a seat, Jade sat beside her as she pulled out her laptop and notebook.

Locating her last entry marked by a colored ribbon, she said, "This is what I have thus far," before opening Google Maps.

Handed the notes, Jade read what her friend had recorded.

"Do you remember anything specific from that night? Like the house. Surroundings?"

"What you have written here is all I remember, too." Jade looked to the ceiling and replayed the night in her head.

"We will start at the corporate park location. The house wasn't more than a fifteen-minute drive from there, so it shouldn't be a large space to cover."

Over the next hour, the girls scoured the maps on their computers, looking for a house that matched their criteria. They targeted estate properties on large lots with very few neighbors, if any. Doing that quickly eliminated densely populated areas, businesses, and corporate parks. One after another, they came up empty. None of the houses they'd seen had black exteriors or the embedded circle in the driveway.

About to give up, Jade pointed to her screen.

"Hey, look at this place. Could this be it?"

Abi shuffled her chair closer to her. "Pull up the street view."

She tried to do that. "It doesn't have one. It's a private community. No access."

"Let's zoom in and click it to get an address."

"Okay," Jade said, doing just that. "It's Bridger Road." Pointing to the characteristics of the house, she said, "Look, it has the hillside, the pool, and the driveway circle. The house looks black."

"Switch to 3D," Abi said.

Jade brought up the image.

In disbelief, Abi leaned back in her chair and said, "Holy crap. You found it."

"Now what? Are we really gonna do this?"

"I need to. Tell me you're with me?"

Her friend hesitated. "Yeah. You can't go alone."

"Alright. After tennis practice, I'll meet you in the parking garage."

"Wow, I still can't believe we're doin' this." Jade was uncertain.

"I have to," Abi replied. "I need closure."

# 69

## Crumbling

That afternoon, the girls went their separate ways. Jade drove to the tennis center while Abi went to the hospital.

Standing at her bedside, she watched her Mother for any sign of life. With so much whizzing through her mind, Abi found it hard to concentrate. Taking advantage of the peacefulness, the white noise from the machines was somehow comforting.

"What will I say to him," she whispered aloud, unsure if her Mom could hear her. "How do you thank someone for saving your life?"

Her Dad walked in unexpectedly, startling Abi. "Hi, Sweetheart."

"Hi, Dad."

He went to the opposite side of the bed and kissed his wife on the forehead. "Hello, my Darling," he said lovingly.

Both of them had a moment of silence.

"So, how was your day?"

Abi tried to muster a smile. "It was fine."

"Everything okay?"

"Yes. I'm just tired." Wanting to know the plan that night, she asked, "Are you staying or coming home?"

"If you are okay at home, I will probably be here."

Abi looked in the corner behind him. There was a single bed with disheveled sheets. His duffle bag was on the floor, with his pajamas partially stuffed in the top.

"I'm sorry, Sweetie. I guess I'm trying to make up for lost time." A tear drifted down his cheek. "In the great scheme of things, I guess I'm not making up for anything. It's like she's already gone."

"Dad..."

He wiped the tear away. "I will try to be home more in the coming days. I hate the thought of not being here if something happens."

"I know. I understand." Abi wanted to give him peace of mind. "Jade might stay with me tonight if that's okay."

"Yes. I would prefer that you not be alone." He paused. "Let me clarify that statement. That does not mean Shane Coppersmith is welcome. You know the rules."

"Again, the football team is still away. I'm meeting Jade after tennis practice."

"Why aren't you there?"

Abi looked at her Mom. "This is all a bit overwhelming. I can't..."

He reached across and rested his hand on her forearm. "It's fine. You have lots of time to..." Biting his tongue, knowing his wife didn't have that luxury, he backtracked, "What I mean is....."

"It's okay. I know."

Nodding, he added, "If you ever need to talk, I'm always here, no matter what."

She silently acknowledged that statement before her phone alarm went off, reminding her she had to get going. Abi kissed her Mother on the forehead and raised her limp hand to her cheek. "I'll see you soon," she told her.

"I'll walk you out." Her father escorted Abi to the elevator. "Have a good night, Sweetie. I'll be home tomorrow to grab clothes and things. When Mom leaves the ICU, I'll be around more."

Thinking that was optimistic of him, she said, "Yeah. That would be good."

"Enjoy your night with Jade." He hugged her tightly.

"Thanks. I hope to."

"I'll call you later on."

She smiled and let go. Pressing the elevator button, she replied, "Okay. We'll talk then."

"Bye, Sweetie."

When the doors slid open, she said, "Bye, Dad." Waving to him as they closed, Abi felt a lump in her throat. Her family was falling apart, crumbling piece by piece. Knowing he missed his wife, she couldn't be selfish and ask him to stay home with her. If something were to happen and he wasn't close by, Abi shuttered to think what it would do to him.

"Pull yourself together, Abs. You got to remain strong." Straightening her posture, holding her head high, she said, "But for now. You need to focus. It's time to pay Black Lyon a visit."

# 70

# Closure

Leaving the hospital, Abi headed over to the Wasserman Center. She drove around the parking garage until she found Jade's car. Parked in a space nearby, she waited for her friend to surface.

When she saw her rushing along, Abi got out. "I'm here!" she said, startling her friend to death.

The girl quickly recovered from the fright. "Hey, want me to drive?"

"Sure. That's maybe better. You know that area more than me." Abi jumped into the passenger seat while Jade started the engine.

After leaving the UCLA grounds, her friend seemed pumped while merging onto the 405 North. "What are the chances we found the house today? Wow, I can't believe we are doing this, Abs."

Uncertain of what they were getting themselves into, she replied, "I want closure on this. Hopefully, he'll be there."

"What if he's not?"

"Well, then, I go back to the drawing board."

Jade glanced at her. "What does that mean?"

"Not sure yet. But I'm telling you, if I ever see his truck again, I'm following him. Next time, I won't back down."

Worried about what her friend said, Jade went silent.

"What aren't you saying?" She'd picked up on the questionable silence. "Spit it out."

Afraid to offend her, the girl kept her eyes on the road. "I don't know, girl. This is becoming an obsession."

She knew she was right but couldn't let it rest, no matter how hard she tried.

"Look, I get it. You feel indebted to him. That's understandable."

"That's an understatement." About to cry, Abi added, "I owe him so much." Shuttering to think what could have been, she wiped the tears away and plugged in the address in the GPS. "Let's just go there and get this over with so I can move on."

Jade tapped her hand. "Agreed."

Before veering west on 101, Jade and Abi followed the directions given. Instructed to take a detour to reach their destination, they maneuvered a series of turns and were only two minutes away. Slowly approaching a white gatehouse with Hidden Hills crested barriers blocking their path, Jade pulled into a school parking lot.

"How are we going to get through there? I'm sure they won't let us in." Feeling defeated, Abi exhaled, believing they came all that way for nothing.

"Wait. One second." Jade pulled out her phone and called someone.

Anxious, she hoped her friend had a solution to their problem.

"Hey, Klhoe. It's Jade Webber. How are you?" Listening to the person on the other end, she said, "So happy you like the art my Mom sent you. I bet it looks amazing." Jade nodded her head multiple times. "Yes. Yeah, for sure. That's awesome." With only silence between them, she finally asked, "As a matter of fact, I was hoping you could do me a favor." Assuming she got a positive reply, Jade asked, "I'm outside your community gates and need to visit a friend, but they aren't answering. I was hoping you could call the gatehouse and get them to grant us access. We won't be there long. Just dropping off something." Hating to lie, Jade rolled her eyes regrettably. "Really? Thanks so much. Appreciate it. Yes, for sure. Take pictures of the art and send them to my Mom. I know she will sign the release." Letting the girl on the other end talk,

Jade said before ending the call, "Good chatting with you as well. Yes. Absolutely.  Thanks a bunch. Appreciate it. Bye."

Leaning back in her seat, hating what she did, she looked at Abi and said, "You owe me big time, you hear me, Acardi?"

"Are we in?"

"We're in. Give it a few minutes, and then we will give it a go."

Seeing many luxury vehicles passing through, Jade put the car in gear and said, "Here goes nothing."

Driving up to the gatehouse, the security guard emerged and stopped them. Jade rolled down her window.

"Hello. Can I help you?" the man asked sternly.

"Yes, we are here to see Khloe K." Jade winked at the guy. "My name is Jade Webber. She is expecting us."

All he did was nod. Checking the computer screen, he returned and said, "Proceed," as the barriers lifted in front of them.

"Thanks so much."

Jade slowly passed the checkpoint and referred to the GPS.

"Wow. How do you know this Khloe person?"

"She built a new house here and bought a few pieces of artwork from my Mom. When she requested the artist deliver it, my Mom asked if I wanted to accompany her. So I did."

Abi felt a rise in her spirits as they turned onto a secluded road. Breaching the hill, seconds away from their destination, she said, "This is it," while noticing the dead-end street. Confused by the for sale sign hanging in the yard, Abi recalled getting off the Black Lyon shuttle while Jade pulled into the circular driveway. Remembering the features of the black house to a tee, they soon stopped beside the two-story glass entrance.

"Wow, this is definitely the place. But why is it for sale?"

Jade looked around. "Not sure. But with everything going down in the press, it makes sense."

"If he lives here, why was he driving past my house early this morning?"

"That, I can't answer."

Staring at the doors, Abi took a deep breath. "Wish me luck."

"Fingers crossed," Jade said.

Abi got out of the car and timidly approached the house. With hands trembling, she reached out and pressed the doorbell. Hearing the sound echo through the home, Abi could see nothing in the way of furniture or artwork inside. It was bare.

"There's nothing here," she said, turning to Jade.

Wanting to look around, the girls walked toward the garage and opened the gate to the backyard. There was not even water in the pool.

"Umm, Abs?" Jade got nervous.

"Yeah."

"I think we need to go."

Finding her staring at the outside wall, Abi asked, "Why?"

"Because someone is watching us." Jade pointed to the security camera following their every move.

Quickly jumping in the driver's seat, Jade got antsy. "Come on, Abi. I've got a bad feeling. We need to get out of here."

Upon seeing the camera interacting with them, Abi had an idea. She went and stood directly in front of it and said, "Hello. This message is for DJ Black Lyon. I don't know if you remember me from last Saturday night. You saved me from a frightening situation, so I came here to thank you. I will be forever in your debt." Not sure what else to say, she added, "Well, that's it. That's all I wanted to say." Abi turned and walked back to the car. Getting in, she waved to the camera as it followed her.

Pulling out the opposite end of the driveway, Jade slowly left the premises. "So, did you get the closure you needed?"

"Not really, but it will have to do."

"So you're going to put this to rest now?"

Abi nodded. "I hope so." Pulling her phone from her bag, she said, "We should hurry back. The football game starts in a little over an hour. Want to head to my place with take-out to watch the game?"

"Sure, that sounds perfect."

On their way to Bel Air, Jade suggested, "I'm in the mood for comfort food. You?"

"Always. What were you thinking?"

"Italian? A little Caprese salad, a couple of Calzones, and maybe a box of cannolis."

Abi gave her a thumbs up.

Immediately calling one of her favorite restaurants, she placed their order. Turning to Abi, she said, "I usually stop there and pick up food before going to my Dad's. This place is really good. You'll love it."

"I'm excited, not to mention pretty hungry," she giggled.

Double-checking the time on the dash clock, Jade said, "Hopefully, we won't miss too much of the first quarter."

# 71

# Clear the Air

Within the hour, the girls had picked up food on the fly, grabbed Abi's car from UCLA, and slowly made their way up Stradella. When they arrived, seeing the black SUV parked about fifty-five yards away wasn't surprising. Unfortunately, they'd almost missed the entire first half by the time they walked through the front door.

Entering the kitchen, Abi turned on the television and mirrored the link from her phone. Thankfully, the team was up 14 – 7. She grabbed a couple of plates and cutlery before placing a few beverage options on the counter.

Making herself at home, Jade dished out a plate and grabbed a San Pellegrino. "So, is your Dad coming home tonight or staying at the hospital with your Mom?"

"He's staying there tonight in case something happens. He doesn't want to be far."

"So, do you want me to stay with you? I don't mind."

"Umm, I should be good. Shane said he would drop by on his way home tonight."

"Oooh. So you two will be alone?" Jade was excited for her.

"Shhh…"

"What? What did I say?"

Abi got close to her ear. "My Dad could be listening."

Taking notice of the camera in the corner of the room, she gave her a subtle thumbs up. "I didn't know."

Continuing to whisper, Abi said, "Nothing like that can happen anyway. He is probably watching as we speak. I will literally have to atone for everything that goes on."

"Well, that sucks." Jade giggled. "You'd better hope Burton doesn't show up unannounced."

"I know, right? I've gotta text him. Not sure what I'll say, though. He can read me like a book."

Paying more attention to the second half while eating dinner, Abi thought about what she had done that afternoon behind Shane's back. The whole Black Lyon thing had to stop. Seeing him on the screen, focused but stressed, her heart went out to him. All he wanted was someone to love who was trustworthy and kind. In the past while, Abi knew she'd lost sight of that. He deserved better, and she needed to step it up.

*What am I doing?* She thought. *Shane's a great guy, and you are sneaking around to find an infamous DJ who doesn't even know you exist. Seriously. Even your friend believes you're obsessed. On top of that, you're plotting to lie to Burton, too.*

Given a level of clarity, she decided to let the whole Black Lyon sega die out. She needed to focus on the people that mattered. They needed her. The last thing she wanted was to fail them.

Abi noticed her phone light up. She'd forgotten to turn the ringer back on when she left the hospital.

"Hello," she said.

"Hey, Abs."

"Hi, Burton." Abi turned to Jade and raised her eyebrows.

"How was your day? Any change with your Mom?"

Stepping out, she entered the living room and sat on the sofa. "No. No change with Mom, and the day was well...."

"Not good, I take it."

"It's fine. I'll survive. Always do."

He could tell by the tone in her voice that she was feeling down. "Are you alone at the house tonight?"

"Jade's here. We are watching the football game." Abi didn't elaborate further.

"Well, I'll let you get back to it, then. Call me if you need me."

"Yes, thank you. Appreciate that."

"I know." Burton could tell something was up. "So, we'll talk tomorrow, I guess. TGIF?"

"You're not kidding. My main priority this weekend is to catch up on sleep."

"I'm guessing that hasn't improved?" Hearing that worried him.

"No, not really." Careful not to drag the conversation too long, she said, "Umm, do you mind if I go? I don't want to miss the game."

"No problem. Have a good night. Say hi to Jade for me."

"I will."

With an awkward silence between them, Abi said, "Burton?"

"Yeah?"

"Thank you for checking in."

"Anytime. You have a good night, Abs."

"Yes, you too. Night." Abi ended their call.

Returning to the TV room, Jade looked up at her friend. "So, did you tell him not to drop by later?"

"Not exactly." In an instant, she wished she had been more forthcoming about that.

"Oooh, that could be a recipe for disaster."

"Hey, why are you trying to jinx me."

"I'm not. Just sayin'," Jade laughed. "You know I'm right."

"In a roundabout way, I said you were here and left it open-ended. So, to his knowledge, you may be staying the night."

"Sneaky."

"Don't say that." The comment made her feel like a liar.

"You can't have it both ways, Abs."

"What do you mean?"

"If he is your friend, and you are as close as you say you are, then why didn't you just tell him the truth?"

"I can't tell him Shane is coming here. Are you crazy? The guy would make sure that doesn't happen."

"If I were you, I'd draw the line in the sand. Shane on one side, Burton on the other, each with boundaries clearly marked."

She listened to her friend's advice while she paid attention to the plays.

"Oh, no!" Jade shouted, seeing that Carpintenia scored a touchdown. As the ball flew through the uprights, it was now a tie game.

Over the next forty minutes, Abi seemed partially present. The stress of her Mom, her relationship with Shane, her friendship with Burton, the tennis team debacle, not to mention the Emile, Black Lyon, and Eastwood drama, was too much. For a second, she missed being alone in Boston. Thinking back on it, she thought, *No, Abi. Always be thankful for those around you.*

"This is it. Come on, guys." Jade inched to the edge of the sofa and cheered on the team.

With two minutes left in the game, Shane launched a long pass to Reggie.

Jade stood and started to bounce her feet off the floor. "Come on, Baby! Catch the ball. Please, God. Catch. The. Ball!" Her hands raised in the air! "Touchdown, Reggie Wilson!!"

The team was up 21 – 14.

"This is like déjà vu." The camera showed a replay of Shane's face when Reggie made the play. He'd turned toward the bench. Abi realized he saw an opportunity and went against the coach's game plan. Thankfully, it paid off. The coach gave Shane a nod.

As the clock dwindled, the Gilderson team gathered around and calmly celebrated.

"That was a close one." Jade fell onto the sofa limply.

"The fact that Shawn is out leaves a huge void. That will undoubtedly impact Shane's scholarship opportunities if the team doesn't make it to finals." She knew that would have crossed his mind, too.

"I've heard they are asking around for players interested in making a move. Apparently, Laney says they will be waving tuition to stack the team if they can."

"So, that means we'll get new players at Gilderson shortly?" Abi assumed.

"I wonder who will take the bait?" Jade smirked curiously. Stretching her hands over her head, she said, "Well, I guess I should get going if you're gonna have company." She grabbed her things and headed toward the door.

"I think he will get here sometime after nine-thirty."

"Okay, girl. Be good," she said while walking out the door.

"I will." Abi pointed to the cameras, making her friend laugh. "Thanks for keeping me company and for going – you know...."

"No problem. It was an adventure," she laughed. "I'll see you in the morning?"

"For sure."

"Drive safe," Abi said as Jade got into her car.

When she started the engine the purr of the Porsche was smooth as she backed up and waved to Abi while the gate slid open.

Once she had gone, Abi closed it again. Heading upstairs to change into more comfortable clothes, she left her phone on the side table and walked into her closet. Not hearing it ring while changing out of her uniform, she moved to the bathroom to take a shower.

Afterward, tying her hair back in a messy bun, she felt exhausted and had difficulty keeping her eyes open.

Her phone rang again.

"Hello," she said.

"Hey, you. We are about ten minutes away from Wasserman Field. Do you still want company tonight? I know it's late."

"Sure. If you aren't tired, you can drop by. I don't mind."

"Is your Dad at the hospital or home?" he asked.

"He's staying at the hospital."

Knowing that made things complicated, he said, "Look, I don't want to get you in trouble or betray your Dad's trust. If you'd rather I not, it's fine. Either way."

"I was looking forward to it. If anything, I can text my Dad and explain that you are visiting. If I give him a heads up, he won't be upset."

"Maybe it's better to be upfront at this point."

"Agreed."

"I'll see you in a half hour, then."

"About that. Give or take," he predicted.

Abi put her phone on the side table and walked downstairs to grab her backpack. Little did she know, but it was ringing again.

Deciding to clean up the kitchen and put the food away, she figured she had time to finish some homework before Shane arrived. Gathering some drinks and snacks and placing them all on the island, she opened her books and laptop there and wrote down the work Shane had missed that day. Taking screenshots of her notes, she emailed them to him so he would have them.

Abi happened to catch a glimpse of the security monitor. The black SUV had gone. Getting a closer look, she saw a vehicle approaching their gate. It wasn't Shane.

"Oh, my gosh. What is he doing here?" Abi panicked. Running to the front door and opening the gate, she stood in the doorway as the black McLaren slowly drove in. "What do I do?"

The driver's side popped open.

"Burton? What are you doing here?"

"I called you. Twice. You didn't answer.  Thought something was wrong, so I drove over."

"Shane's on his way here. I really can't suffer through another confrontation between you two."

When Burton heard that, he looked away.

Abi's hand melded to her forehead, realizing what she'd said. "I don't mean to be rude, but you need to go? Please. I'll text you later."

"Everything's fine otherwise, right?"

She could tell she'd hurt his feelings. "Yes – unless Shane finds you here."

He felt cast aside again. Turning around, he said, "Whatever you say, Abs."

"Thank you for checking on me. I do appreciate it."

"I'm sure you do."

By the tone of his voice, she knew he wasn't happy with her. "Wait, please don't be mad."

Sadly, he did not reply.

With her stomach in knots, she watched him get back in his car and drive out. "Damn, Abi. You're such an idiot." Stuck between them, she hated it. Closing the gate, she walked inside the house.

Feeling guilty, she wondered if she should call him. About to do that, she noticed Shane's Jeep pulling up to the gate. Opening it for him and going to the front door, she hoped he hadn't seen Burton driving down Stradella.

Seeing his face as he parked, she didn't have to guess. She was sure he had.

When Shane got out, he walked over to her straight-faced. "Was that Burton? Was he just here? Tell me the truth."

Hating herself, she lowered her head. "He was...umm... I got busy and didn't answer my phone. He got worried and stopped by to check on me. I told him you were coming and needed to leave." Sick and tired of the tension caused by their connection, she said, "No, you know what!"

Before she could say anything more, the black McLaren drove in at a clip and stopped dead in the middle of the courtyard, spraying grey stone everywhere. Burton got out and left the butterfly door open.

"Burton! What the hell!" Abi shouted in a semblance of shock.

With contempt, Shane locked eyes with the guy. "I thought she told you to leave, man."

Standing his ground, a mere six feet away, her muscular friend stared him down. "Don't tempt me…" He rubbed his fist in the palm of his opposite hand as his anger escalated.

"What are you gonna do? Hit me?" Shane challenged.

"If that's the way it has to be. I'll end it, too."

With chests puffed, standing tall to intimidate one another, Abi quickly got between the men towering above her and shouted, "That's enough! Stop!"

The guys looked down simultaneously, never having heard that tone from her.

"Back off! Both of you!" She pushed a two-foot buffer between them before walking toward the front door. "Inside! Now! Move it!"

Burton closed his car door and followed Abi and Shane. Seeing her standing in the living room with hands on her hips, she ordered. "Both of you sit!"

Finding a spot as far away from each other as possible, she was fuming. Each leaned forward with their fists clenched in front of them.

"I have had it! I really have!" She placed her hand over her forehead. "Do you have any idea how stressful this is for me?"

Nobody said a word.

"I am dealing with a lot already, and now this…." She broke down a bit. "I can't do it."

As the tears flowed, each of them looked up, wanting to be the one to comfort her.

"I visited my mother in ICU this afternoon. She's lifeless in a coma, then I come home and have to deal with this petty bullshit between you. I can't. I just…" Her hands trembled.

Both guys were about to stand up.

"No!" Abi put up her hands to stop them. "I'm not done!"

Like boys scolded by their Moms, they obeyed.

"Burton? Do you care about me?" she asked, putting him on the spot.

"Of course I do. How can you even ask that?"

She turned to Shane. "Shane? Do you care about me?"

"Yes, more than anything."

"The two of you have to come to some sort of neutral ground 'cause it's enough. Shane, I love Burton as much as I love you – it's just in a different way. He's my best friend and has been for many years. I told you, he was there for me when nobody else was. After all this time apart, he continues to support me. And I love having that person to depend on because I don't have siblings. Because of Burton, I don't feel alone."

Shane opened his mouth to speak, but Abi said, "No. Wait."

She moved her sights to Burton. "I have fallen in love with Shane. I know this is hard to hear, but it's true. It doesn't mean I love you any less. He is kind and thoughtful," she gasped, "I feel so thankful to have met him."

The room went silent.

"Please. Please," she pleaded, "Can the two of you accept your roles in my life and be civil to each other? Because I don't want to have to choose between you. I need both of you, especially now."

The guys glanced over at each other and then back to her.

Burton was the first to stand. He walked over to Shane and offered his hand to him. "Truce?" he asked.

Shane got up respectfully and nodded in agreement. "Truce."

Watching them stand there, not knowing what to do next, she walked over to Burton and hugged him before doing the same with Shane. "Thank you," she said. "I will need both of you more than ever in the next few weeks, so please...." Tears streamed down her face.

She remained in Shane's arms as Burton looked on. He knew Abi had made her choice. Forced into the big brother role, he figured it fit better anyway, especially after their awkward morning together.

"I don't know about the two of you, but I'm exhausted. I need to get some sleep."

Standing beside Abi, Shane hoped Burton would get the hint.

"If you think I'm leaving the two of you here alone, you're sorrily mistaken." He stood his ground.

"We'll be fine," the football player stated quite sternly.

Burton smirked. "And what will her Dad say to that? Not a good move, man."

Abi looked at Shane and said, "I'm sorry, but he's right."

"Well, I'm staying." The QB didn't move an inch.

"I'm too tired to argue with you. There are two open guest rooms. You decide. I'm going to bed." Abi walked upstairs, leaving the guys behind.

When she disappeared, Burton and Shane stood there in silence.

Determined to be the bigger man, Burton said, "Look, with everything going on, you and I need to tag team and support her. Whatever she needs. No question."

"Agreed," Shane said, hating the idea of having to share her. But he knew he didn't have a choice.

"That said, I am sorry, I can't leave tonight. I know her Dad would want me to stay. Inadvertently, that looks good for you, too."

Annoyed, he said, "Fine. I'm just gonna get my stuff from the truck."

They walked outside together and returned moments later. Burton secured the premises and went to check on the monitor.

"Hey, Shane," he waved him into the kitchen. "Look at this." He pointed out the black SUV sitting along the street outside. "Any idea who this is?"

"My thought was Korolev's guys."

Burton said, "She seems to think it's Black Lyon's men."

"Could be. Given what's happened with Eastwood...." Shane clammed up, not wanting to rehash that drama again.

"I know she wants to thank the guy for saving her. She mentioned it." Burton crossed his arms. "We can never let her attend another rave."

"I won't argue with that."

"Glad we agree. It's no place for her, especially with this Eastwood situation lingering." Burton's protective instinct surfaced.

"If he sees an opportunity, the guy will hurt her to get to me," Shane stated bluntly. "I know that for sure."

"Then, we both keep her safe. Create a united front."

"Absolutely."

Burton pulled out his phone. "Give me your cell number?"

"Why?"

"'Cause if something goes down, you call me and vice versa."

Shane gave it to him before Burton shared his, too.

"No matter what. We work together, deal?"

"No question. One hundred percent." Despite the agreement, Shane still hated the guy.

Burton stared at the SUV on the monitor.

Needing to clear the air, Shane stepped up and said, "Man to man, I truly love her, and there is nothing you can do that will change that."

That was the last thing Burton wanted to hear, but he needed to keep the peace. "Good to know. Figured as much."

"I will do whatever it takes to make her happy."

"I wouldn't expect anything less."

The air seemed less thick.

"Come on. Let's get some sleep," Burton suggested.

The two ascended the stairs. Abi could hear them talking on the way up. Burton showed Shane which room to use before he went to his. Tucked in her bed, smiling, she was happy they'd worked things out. Grateful to have the two watching over her, she hoped to sleep well. Tucked in, she smiled, knowing they were at least being civil to one another. She took a deep breath and closed her eyes as the fear haunting her disappeared.

# 72

## The Morning After

Abi awakened early in the morning. Not hearing a sound from the guest rooms, she quietly got ready for the day and hoped Shane and Burton were both on the ball.

Afraid to open her door just before eight, unsure what she'd find, Abi pulled it back a crack and peeked into the hallway. Funny enough, the guys left their rooms simultaneously as if waiting for her to emerge first.

"Good morning," Abi said on the way to the kitchen.

"Morning," they said in unison, somewhat annoyed by their harmonious response.

Shane walked behind her, leaving Burton to follow.

"Who wants coffee?" she cheerfully asked while standing by the machine.

Burton silently raised his hand, not saying a word.

Abi looked at Shane.

"No, thanks. I'm good."

Knowing he preferred water, Abi grabbed a bottle from the fridge and placed it on the counter.

"Thank you," he said, able to hear a pin drop otherwise.

"So, did you get some sleep?" Burton asked, hoping she had.

"Yes. Believe it or not, I didn't wake up all night. Best sleep I've had in a few days."

Understanding she'd had nightmares that week, Burton still hated that Shane's neglect had caused this.

"How about you guys?" Abi made eye contact with both of them, wondering who would answer first.

"Yeah, umm. Good." Burton mumbled.

"Me too," Shane added.

The air around them was thick, but she was happy they weren't killing each other.

Soon after, everyone was out the door.

Approaching Burton with open arms, Abi hugged him as Shane looked on. "Have a good day," she said before letting go.

"I'll call you later. Are you going to see your Mom this afternoon?" the burly guy asked.

"Yes, I'll be there after school for a bit."

"Let me know if you need some company. I'm free for a couple of hours." Burton's sights moved to Shane. He knew the comment would get under the guy's skin.

"Thank you. Appreciate that. I'll let you know."

"Sure. Sounds good." Burton stepped toward Shane. Reaching out a clenched fist, he said in a deep, commanding tone, "Later, man."

With Abi watching, Shane had no choice but to oblige. "Yeah, later," he replied, bumping his against it.

Waving to her friend while he got in his car and drove out of the courtyard, Abi turned and looked at Shane. "Ready to go?"

"Ready." Not sure what the plan was, he asked, "So, are you coming with me?"

She thought for a second. "I'll need my car to go to the hospital."

"If you feel comfortable, you can just take my truck. I'll be gone anyway."

"You trust me to drive the Jeep?" She was surprised to hear that.

"Yeah, why not?"

"Well, thank you. Maybe I'll do that, then."

"Sure."

"Should I drive it to the game or go with Jade?"

"Coach expects us to travel on the bus, so driving to the Palisades with Jade might be best."

"Okay, sounds good."

Shane unlocked the vehicle. "We'd better get a move on."

Abi jumped in the passenger side.

"So, where does Burton live anyway? Is he close by?" He asked while driving out of the gate.

"Truthfully, I have no clue. All I know is he frequents Geoffrey's on PCH and said he's close to there."

Secretly happy to hear it - Shane wanted more clarification. "So, you've never been to his house?"

"No, funny enough." That observation hit her. "I've never fully asked, and he's never said, come to think of it."

He believed that to be strange.

"Oh! With everything going on, I almost forgot to tell you. The other night, Jade and I went out for dinner. While sitting in the restaurant by the window, I noticed a man standing across the street, watching us. It turns out I recognized the guy from the Black Lyon event. He was the one who was sitting at the desk inside the security room after he rescued me."

"Are you sure it was him?"

"Yes, positive. Before we left, the black SUV with license plate B777L picked him up."

"So, you think the SUV has been Black Lyon's staff all along, not Korolev's?"

"That's my thinking."

Shane thought for a second. "Well, I guess that's both good and bad news."

"How come?"

"I'm thankful it's his guys, for obvious reasons, but we need to find out what he knows that warrants his security to follow you around twenty-four-seven?"

Reaching Sunset Boulevard, Abi turned and looked behind them. "Well, they aren't following me this morning."

"They must have known Burton and I were at the house last night. Maybe he figured you were covered and gave his guys the night off."

"How would he know that?"

"The SUV was parked on the street last night when you went to bed. They must have seen us drive in and not leave."

What he said made sense despite being speculative.

Soon, they were passing through the lower gatehouse below the school. Shane drove up the hill and turned left at the stop sign.

Abi immediately noticed Gerald wasn't at his post. Another man was.

"Stop," she told Shane while rolling down her window.

The man stepped out. "Good morning, Miss. Can I help you?"

"Good morning. I was wondering where Gerald is today?"

"I'm sorry. I don't know the man. I'm a temp. Usually, I go where I'm needed."

Worried, Abi replied, "That's okay. Just thought I'd ask." She got a sinking feeling.

"No problem at all. Enjoy your day."

"You too," Abi said.

Shane could see her mind reeling. "Do you think something is wrong?"

"I hope not," she replied as they continued underground.

Reverse parking into his spot, Shane handed Abi the keys. "Here you go."

"Are you sure you're okay with me driving it?"

"Positive. I trust you."

"That means a lot. Thank you."

He smiled and said, "Absolutely."

Abi zipped the keys into her crossbody bag's interior pouch for safekeeping.

On their way to math, life seemed almost normal. Thankfully, there wasn't any drama to contend with – yet.

Reaching their classroom, the two went and found their seats. Barely there a minute, they heard an announcement. "Would Abi Acardi please come to the office? That's Abi Acardi. To the main office, please."

Jade walked in with Reggie. "I just heard your name over the PA," she said. "Is everything okay?"

Seeing the look on Jade's face, Abi rushed out, thinking it was her Dad. Quickly checking her phone for messages, she wondered if she'd missed his call, but she found nothing. "What else could it be?" she quietly whispered.

Upon opening the door to the office, she went to speak to the secretary.

Before Abi could say anything, the woman addressed her, "Abi Acardi?"

"Yes."

"This letter arrived for you."

The woman handed her an envelope. Abi immediately noticed its signature style.

"Matte black," she whispered. Seeing no return address, Abi said, "Thank you," to the woman and turned to leave. About to head back to class, she heard a voice.

"Miss Acardi?"

Turning around, she found her tennis coach standing there. "Hello, Coach Taylor."

"I'm glad I'm running into you. Can I have a word?"

"Sure." Abi didn't want to be rude, so she followed the female coach into the boardroom.

"Have a seat," she said.

"Is everything okay?"

"Yes. I just wanted to do a wellness check."

"A wellness check? Why?" Abi was confused.

"I got you're email. I am surprised that you declined the spot on the team."

"Yes. I'm sorry. As I explained, I don't want to spread myself too thin with everything I'm dealing with at home, the hospital, and school."

"If I may – Jade told us about your Mother's situation."

Abi lowered her head.

"Look, I know you probably wanted to keep that to yourself, but your friend is worried about you, and as per protocol, we are obliged to intervene. If you need help, we are here to assist you." The expression on her face was quite sincere.

"Thank you for that, but I think I have things under control for now."

Happy to hear it, the woman added, "As for the team, the relief player spot is yours if you'd like. And whenever you feel comfortable returning to a full-time commitment, you will always be welcome. No questions asked. Sound good?"

"Yes. Thank you. I'll keep you posted."

"If you need someone to talk to in the meantime, please let me know."

Abi smiled and acknowledged the woman but knew she'd never take her up on the offer.

"You are free to return to class if there's nothing else. Make sure you pick up a slip from the secretary before you go."

"Will do."

The minute Abi walked out of the office doors, she looked at the black envelope. The label on the front had her name and the school's address. Tearing it open, she peered inside and pulled out a small piece of paper folded in half. Afraid to read it, she counted to three and held her breath. Unfolding the note, she found two words created with Scrabble game letters photocopied onto the page. The words blew the air from her lungs.

"Danger. Beware." Abi's voice waivered as each rolled off her tongue. It took a second for the shock to sink in. Immediately scouring her surroundings, she wondered if someone was watching. Needing to get back to class and be around other warm bodies, she slid the paper into the envelope and folded it twice. When she stuffed it in her pocket, she contemplated whether to call Burton but opted to text him instead.

*Can we meet at the hospital this afternoon at 1:30? I am skipping study hall because I have a big problem.*

She waited for his response. "Come on," she said impatiently. Not seeing that he'd read the message, she figured he was in a lecture and couldn't respond.

With the office slip in hand, she reluctantly walked into math, happy to see they were in the midst of a group activity. Not interrupting much, she handed the teacher the slip and took her seat.

Shane caught the look on her face. Leaning over, he whispered, "Everything okay?"

Keeping the disturbing note to herself, she said, "Yeah. All good. I'll explain later."

# 73

# The Letter

Keeping a low profile for the rest of class, Abi got up when the bell rang and exited the door. Her friends saw this and wondered what had happened earlier at the office.

"Hey, Abs. Wait up," Shane said, dodging other students crowding the hall.

Assuming Black Lyon sent the threatening letter based on its style, Abi continued making mental notes, afraid of who to trust. Deep in thought, the girl hardly noticed him walking beside her.

"Abi?" he repeated.

When she kept walking along in a daze, Shane pulled her off to the side. "Abs? What is going on?"

Breaking away, she said, "Sorry, what?"

He backed off and stared at her blankly. "What happened when you went to the office?"

With eyes locked onto his, unsure what to say, she saw the concern on his face and knew she couldn't tell him about the envelope. It would ruin his focus for the game tonight.

"The tennis coach wanted to talk to me about my email."

"What email?"

"I quit the team."

He was taken off guard. "You did? Why?"

She looked at him with a tilt of her head, expecting him to know the answer to that already.

He raised his hands between them to defuse her. "Okay, I get it. I get it."

"Coach Taylor told me whenever I feel comfortable returning to the team, the spot is mine, no questions asked."

"Well, that's good." Sure, there was more to it, he asked, "Is that all?"

"Yes."

Not entirely convinced of that, he let it slide.

Continuing down the hall, they reached the science lab and quickly took their seats. The lesson was intense, and Abi furiously wrote as many notes as possible. Thankfully, it helped her keep her mind off the warning note.

But while sneaking a look at her phone, she saw Burton still hadn't responded. It made her anxious. The envelope was burning a hole in her pocket by the minute. She contemplated sharing it with Jade for a split second but knew her friend wouldn't hesitate to tell Reggie. Always having each other's backs meant it would just be a matter of time before Shane got wind of it, too. Burton was the only one she trusted to give her sound advice.

Amidst her thoughts, the bell rang. Realizing she'd missed the last part of the lesson and hadn't recorded anything, she regretted not paying more attention. Packing up and moving on to Graphic Design in a zombie-like state, the brunette had gone through the motions all morning and was noticeably absent.

When she and Shane stopped outside the studio, he rested his hands on her shoulders. "Are you sure you're okay?"

So he wouldn't worry, she said, "Yes. I'm good." Thinking fast on her feet, she added, "It's been a crazy week."

"Understandably, so," he paused. "Look, I hope you know you can talk to me about anything."

"Yes, of course."

"I want to be here for you. Good, bad – it doesn't matter."

She nodded and reached her arms around his waist.

He clung to her tightly and rested his chin atop her head. "Guess I'll see you at the game?"

"I'll be there. Thank you for letting me borrow your truck."

"No problem. Hope your visit with your Mom goes well."

"Me too."

"If you go on Saturday, I can come with you. That's if you want me to." Like Burton, he also wanted to offer his time and support.

Abi smiled. "That would be nice."

"Saturday it is." Hugging her one last time, he said, "I should get going."

"Yes. You've got a game to win. Remember, one play at a time."

"I'll do my best."

Kissing her before he left, he walked away. She waved as he rounded the corner. Going into class, she hoped to immerse herself in her work to try and calm down. Thankfully, Emile and her posse were nowhere to be seen.

"The mean girls get their hair, nails, and make-up done on game days," Laney divulged. "Don't worry. They aren't here."

Abi released a sigh. "Perfect. I'm not in the mood for drama today." Looking to see if Burton had texted, Abi saw nothing. "Why won't you answer?" she whispered.

"Answer what?" Jade asked while taking a seat beside her.

"Oh, nothing. Just talking to myself."

Focused on her assignment, Abi kept her head down most of the class. From time to time, she checked for Burton's reply. The fact it was taking so long worried her.

First, to submit work to their teacher, Abi got antsy upon returning to her seat. She wanted to leave. Thinking about the note, she thought, *Why is Black Lyon warning me? What does he know? What am I supposed to do now? Hide under a rock? Go to the police?* Afraid to do the latter, she wondered what Burton would say.

Hearing the bell broke her train of thought. Automatically heading out the door, she heard Jade behind her.

"Hey, Abi! Wait up!"

Walking together, they headed toward the Bistro for lunch.

"What's the plan for this afternoon, then?" Her friend awaited her answer.

Intent on keeping it simple, Abi replied, "I think I might skip study hall to go home and change before driving to the hospital to see my Mom."

Disappointed to be attending study hall alone, Jade replied, "Oh. Okay."

Seeing her reaction, Abi explained, "I'm sorry. I feel a little overwhelmed and stressed. Just mentally need a break."

"I understand. No worries. Do you need a ride to the game?"

Scrunching up her face, she asked, "Do you mind?"

"Not at all. Do you want to meet at Wasserman garage at four o'clock?"

"Yes, that would be great. Thank you." Abi could tell she felt rejected. "Look, I'm sorry. I know I've been M.I.A today. Have a lot on my mind."

"I can only imagine." She rubbed Abi's arm. "Always here if you need to talk."

The two girls grabbed their salad bowls and headed to the third-level cactus garden. For Abi, it had become a favorite spot. Quiet, warm, and secluded, it was so peaceful. They took a seat on the stone bench to eat their lunch. Jade was glued to her phone while Abi soaked up some rays. Halfway through her salad, she got a notification.

Checking it, she read his message. *I'll meet you there.* A weight lifted off her.

Periodically looking over, Jade tried to figure out what Abi was doing. "What's going on?" she asked, not trying to be too nosey. Opting to be direct, she just came out with it. "Was that Burton?"

Surprised, Abi looked at her.

"Never mind. It's none of my business."

Unable to keep this to herself, Abi hesitated and said, "Can you keep a secret? Like, swear on your life secret?"

"Again?" She feared what her best friend would say next. "This is becoming a habit."

Abi interrupted the girl. "I don't want this getting back to Shane. He has enough problems and doesn't need to be burdened by more."

"Oh, my God, Abs. What is it? I give you my word."

"I'm meeting Burton to show him this." Abi pulled the envelope from her pocket and slipped the paper into Jade's hands.

She quickly flipped it open and saw the message. The blood drained from her face. "Abs, you've gotta go to the police."

"No. I can't do that. I think this was from Black Lyon. Look at the envelope. It's matte black."

"How can you be sure? It could be someone else, too. Just because they used that type of envelope means nothing. This is Hollywood-weird – like creepy-ass shit." Handing it to her as if possessed, she said nothing more.

"Burton will know how to handle it."

"How did you get it?" Jade then realized, "Wait. That's why you got called to the office this morning, right? Why you've been acting weird today?"

"Do you see why I don't want to involve Shane?"

"Truthfully, no. He should know what's happening. This could affect him too."

"How?" She needed to hear her reasoning.

"Well, if the Korolev family is after you, I'm sure Shane is also in danger. Shouldn't he be made aware?"

What she said made sense. "You're right. I was going to tell him after the game, but I can't blow his focus."

"I get that, but what if it's too late by then?"

"I'll just have to deal with it. Otherwise, I'll tell him when we drive to Reggie's."

"Make sure you do." Jade felt torn, but she gave her word.

"I promise. I will." Abi checked the time. "I'm going to sign myself out and head home to change."

"I don't think you should be going anywhere alone right now."

The comment shocked her. "I'll be fine."

"You've gotta take that note seriously."

"But what if it's Emile playing a prank? At this point, I wouldn't put it past her."

Jade thought for a second. "True, but what if it's not? I can't see her stooping this low. Are you sure you don't wanna go to the cops?"

"If I do that, they'll call my Dad. I can't bring him into this right now."

"I get it."

"If something happens to me, at least you can go to the police with evidence." Abi opened the ominous note and said, "Take a picture of it just in case."

"Now you're scaring me?" Doing as she asked, Jade snapped a pic and put her phone away.

"Don't worry. Black Lyon's guys will be on my tail when I leave the grounds. I'm quite certain of it."

"You'd better hope they are."

# 74

# Coincidence?

Leaving Jade at the library entrance, Abi went to the office to sign herself out, saying she didn't feel well. Walking into the garage minutes after seeing the strange guy sitting in the security booth, she became paranoid. After days of seeing Gerald, this guy suddenly showed up the morning the note got delivered.

*Coincidence?* She thought to herself. *Maybe not.*

Passing him by in the Jeep, she waved. He stared her down and watched as she disappeared over the hill. Fearful, she second-guessed going home. Her phone rang when she was about to turn onto Sunset.

"Burton? Where are you?" she asked without saying hello.

"I'm still at school. Why? What's up? Are we still meeting at the hospital at one-thirty?"

"Change of plans. Can you meet now?"

He knew something was wrong. "What happened?"

"I can't explain over the phone."

Greatly concerned, he said, "Alright. Meet me at the Wasserman garage."

"No. No, closed spaces."

He could hear the fear in her voice. "How about in front of the hospital?" Not hearing from her, Burton said, "Abi?"

"Okay. I'll meet you there."

Diverting toward UCLA, Abi paid close attention to her surroundings. There was no SUV following. "Where are you?" she whispered. Her fear escalated by the minute.

She quickly spotted Burton's car when she arrived at the Medical Center.

He heard a horn beep. Looking in his rearview, he was surprised to see her in Shane's Jeep. Texting him to go to the southwest lot instead of the underground, Burton acknowledged and drove around the block. Abi followed when he turned into the parking structure.

Reaching the rooftop, he found a spot along the far side and got out.

She did the same and went over and hugged him tight.

Taken off guard, he said, "You're freaking me out. What's wrong?" He hoped it wasn't her Mother.

Stepping back, she handed him the black envelope.

"What's this?"

"Open it," she said nervously, her hands trembling.

Doing as she asked, he saw the words on the page. "Where did you get this?"

"Someone sent it to school. The office called me down to pick it up this morning."

Burton examined the envelope and the note thoroughly.

"I thought someone could be pulling a prank on me – namely Emile."

"Or another girl who may be jealous of you?"

"But, based on the style of the envelope, maybe it could be from Black Lyon."

Surprised, he looked up at her. "That's what you think?"

"Yeah. It's my gut feeling."

He pondered her take on it, worried about this obsession of hers.

"What do I do, Burton? Jade says I should go to the police. But you know what that means."

"They'll call your Dad?"

"Exactly. He doesn't need the stress. I've gotta figure this out on my own."

"If you want my advice, I'd go to the cops. See if this is valid. We can ask to keep it quiet." Not sure if he should voice his thoughts - he just came out with it. "Have you told Shane?"

She shook her head. "No. I'll tell him tonight, after the game."

"Make sure you do. The guy has enemies. Maybe more now since the prospect list came out."

"You know about that?"

"Everyone knows about it. Look, whoever sent this to you is trying to warn you for a reason or wants to scare you."

"Will you go to the police station with me tomorrow?"

Burton nodded. "Sure. I'll go."

Abi took a deep breath, thankful to have a plan. "Okay, good." Ready to visit her Mom, she asked, "Can you stay with me for a bit?"

"No problem. I'm free for an hour or two."

When they arrived on the sixth floor, nothing could've prepared Burton to see Abi's Mom in the state she was in. He stopped outside the ICU glass panel door and stared at the lifeless woman. A memory of his Mom flashed through his mind. Slowly joining Abi in the room, he stood to her left.

"Hi, Mom," she said, "Look who came to visit you today. It's Burton."

# 75

# Calm before the Storm

After spending an hour there, Abi did not see her dad and assumed he was busy. Burton stepped out of the room while Abi said her goodbyes. While watching the tender moment between mother and daughter, his heart went out to them.

Joining Burton in the hall, she said, "I should probably get going. I want to go home and change clothes before heading back here to meet Jade. I'm catching a ride with her to the game."

"So that you know, I'm not letting you go alone. I'll drive you there and back. You can leave the Jeep at Wasserman garage."

Somewhat scared to hear him taking such strong precautions, Abi didn't argue. "Maybe that's best," she said while waiting for the elevator to open.

When they did, the two stepped inside and rode it to the main lobby before walking out the door to the parking garage. Returning to the cars, Abi followed Burton to Wasserman Field. Leaving the Jeep, she locked it and got into the McLaren before they sped off.

"Any sign of Black Lyon's guys today?"

"No. Not one. It's weird."

Burton went quiet. Abi could see his mind analyzing every aspect of the mysterious note she'd received - what it meant, who it was from? How it might relate to Black Lyon or the Korolev family. So many questions did not have answers.

Before long, they entered the Bel Air gates and, shortly after, arrived at Abi's house.

When she got out, Burton said, "I'll wait here."

"Alright, I won't be long."

Before she left, he asked, "Hey, can I see that note again? And the envelope?"

She handed it to him before going inside. Grabbing her backpack and crossbody bag, she opened the door and ran up the stairs to her room. Feeling a heaviness, it felt like the calm before the storm. "Stop psyching yourself out, Abi," she said.

Returning in record time, she locked the front door and got into the car with all the essentials she needed for the night.

"Ready?" he asked, handing back the ominous note.

"Yes." Abi placed it in her crossbody bag for safekeeping. "So? Anything to add?"

Carefully exiting the courtyard and allowing Abi to close the gate, he said, "No. Not really. We do need to go to the police, though."

"I promise we'll do that first thing in the morning."

"Count on it." Burton looked in his rearview mirror. The black SUV was now in its usual spot up the street. It strangely didn't follow them.

Driving back to UCLA, concerned for Abi's safety, he said, "Maybe you shouldn't go to the game?"

"Why? I have to be there." She felt she couldn't let Shane down.

"Given everything going on, do you think that's wise? Do you really want to take the chance?"

"Don't worry. I'll be okay." Tapping his arm with her hand, she smiled.

"Fine, don't say I didn't warn you. I've got a bad feeling, Abs. I think you should take this whole thing more seriously."

"You sound like Jade. I'll deal with it tomorrow." A bit frustrated, she said, "Can we drop it now."

Burton looked out his window, angry he couldn't change her mind. They didn't say another word until they entered the Wasserman garage.

Arriving just before four o'clock, Abi feared what Jade would think when Burton dropped her off.

"There's her car. The white Porsche over there."

He stopped behind it.

"I'll call you in the morning," she said.

"Okay. Until then, keep your eyes peeled."

"I will." Afraid to tell him, she said, "So that you know, we're heading to Reggie's afterward. He's hosting the after-party." She could tell he disapproved. "Why are you looking at me like that?"

Veering his sights away from her, he replied, "Nothing – just promise me you'll call if there's a problem."

"I promise."

"Where does this Reggie guy live?"

"Mountian Drive. Why?"

"No reason."

Somehow, Abi knew he'd be nearby. Hugging him, she said, "See you tomorrow."

"Yeah, bye," he said, noticing Jade's eagle eyes on them in the rearview mirror. She didn't like what she was seeing. That was obvious.

Abi got out of his car.

Burton waved and moved on.

Not saying a word when Abi got in the seat beside her, Jade suddenly skipped the pleasantries and got straight to the point. "So, what did he tell you to do?"

"Go to the police tomorrow."

"Hallelujah! Thank God. Yes, you should."

"I know...." She found it hard to breathe as Burton's concerns hit home.

Happy the guy agreed with her, Jade said, "I'm beginning to like this Burton guy more now." Backing out of her spot, they drove southwest toward the PCH.

With her head on a swivel, Abi kept an eye on her surroundings, as Burton suggested.

"So, you think the team will win tonight?"

Turning to her friend, Abi said, "They'd better. Otherwise, it will put a damper on your extravagant after-party."

Jade laughed. "You got that right. We can't have that."

# 76

## The Game

The night was cooler than expected. Abi was happy she'd brought a blanket with her. Sitting amongst the many spectators on the blue bleachers, she flipped her hood over her head to stay warm. Somehow, it made her feel safer.

Emile and her friends were cheering to excite the crowd. Intensely focused, she was happy to see Shane not paying attention to them. When he spotted her, he raised a steady hand and lowered it to cover his heart. She did the same, making him smile. The team was a man down. That meant there was a lot on the line.

Throughout the first half, it was hard for her to think about anything other than how best to tell Shane about the note. Jade was right. He needed to know what was happening. Opting to hand him the envelope and do the same as she did with Burton, she thought she'd wing it from there.

"You look deep in thought," her friend questioned.

Peeking out of her hood, she said, "I am."

"I think you made a good decision by going to the police tomorrow."

"I think so, too."

She stayed quiet, unable to concentrate on the game and shake herself from everything going on in her life.

Seeing this, Jade left her be.

By the third quarter, Gilderson was up 28 – 7. The team was doing well despite having Shawn on the sidelines.

As the game went on, Abi started taking notice of every person looking her way. Overtaken by a flood of negative thoughts, she began to feel paranoid. Suddenly, a sense of urgency made her fidget more. She should have told Shane about the note earlier. *Danger, beware,* she thought. *Couldn't that mean any day? Any hour? Any minute? Any second?* Systematically scanning the bleachers from left to right, she moved to the sidelines and beyond. The fear kept her mind alert.

Edging into the fourth, unbeknownst to Abi, Palisades had scored a touchdown. It was 28 – 14.

More and more, Jade could tell how distracted she was. Constantly rubbing her palms together, she assumed reality had hit her. "Are you looking for anything suspicious?"

Not fully paying attention, it took a second for the question to register. "Umm, yeah," Abi said. "Gotta say I'm feeling a little panicked."

"Not to scare you, but you should be. If it were me, I would be too."

Leaning forward, resting her head on her arms crossed in front of her, Abi said, "How did my life get so damn complicated?"

"Girl, popularity is not what it's cracked up to be."

"I never asked for this."

Rubbing her friend's back, she said, "I know. Hang in there."

In a blur, the game ended. On their feet, the girls cheered for their winning team.

"It was close, but we'll take it given the circumstances. Hopefully, they won't be shorthanded next week."

"Yes. They have to do something." Abi watched Shane's actions. "Did you see the stress on his face? Tonight wasn't easy."

"Reggie seemed distant, too. Shawn's absence broke their rhythm," Jade analyzed.

Sitting down, they watched the team go through the motions. Shane made the rounds and gave interviews under the sportscaster tents. Many of the scouts attending that night gathered around him afterward. She was so proud.

While checking social media, they listened to the NCAA interview, congratulating Shane on being the top pick. Other news outlets showed the clip, making it go viral and causing a stir in the college football world. Many called him *the guy to watch*.

After all the attention faded, the team loaded on the bus. The guys couldn't talk to them after the coaches rounded up the players. All Jade and Abi could do was wave as they drove away. Making it back to the car, the two left and decided to take a more leisurely route back to UCLA. That way, they wouldn't beat the bus and have to wait forever for the guys to shower. Turning onto Sunset Boulevard versus taking the main highway, Abi recalled it was the same way Shane had driven home after being at the beach last Friday.

Jade made a few phone calls along the way. Checking in with their party planner, the woman confirmed everything was going according to plan.

"It's almost showtime," Jade said excitedly. She could hardly wait for her friends to see what she and Reggie had been working on the past couple of weeks behind the scenes.

"So that means you guys went over the top, didn't you?"

"Let's just say we've arranged for some *fun things* quote, unquote. It's gonna be awesome. Wish I could do this all the time. I love hosting events."

"Maybe you should go into event planning?"

"Are you kidding? My parents would disown me if I did that."

Abi was stunned to hear they wouldn't be supportive. "It's your life, Jade. You should do what you feel passionate about."

"According to them, I should be passionate about the family business. My Mom wants me to take over her art gallery, and my Dad wants me to join his firm. Either way, I'm screwed."

"What if you sat them down and explained? Wouldn't they entertain it?"

"Nope. No choice in the matter. I've gotta continue what they started. And what's worse, I'll have to choose between them. So, you can imagine how that will end."

Feeling sorry for her friend, she was thankful to have supportive parents whose only fault was loving her too much. Her mind swayed to her Mother. How she wished she could tell her how appreciative she was of her unconditional love.

Jade rambled on, "I plan to apply to five schools for Art and Art History and five for Law. Ultimately, the acceptance letters will have the final say. I'll have to do what they want, not want I want."

Arriving at Wasserman Field, Jade went to the garage and stopped behind Shane's Jeep.

Abi got out. "Thanks for driving. I'll see you soon."

"No problem." Seeing her friend looking about, she said, "You going to be okay to wait here? I've gotta get to Reggie's to check up on things."

"Don't worry. I'll be fine."

As Jade drove away, Abi kept her eyes peeled for anything strange. Quickly jumping in the Jeep, she locked the doors. Knowing Shane would be walking across the bridge, she moved closer to it so she could see him coming. One of only a dozen cars left on the upper level, somehow, the open air didn't make her feel as claustrophobic. Texting him her location, it didn't take long to receive a response.

Within ten minutes, he was walking toward her with Reggie by his side. Freshly showered and looking so handsome, she was no longer afraid. Getting out with open arms, she greeted him.

"Hey, you," he said with a bright smile. Embracing her, he seemed tired.

"Hi."

Before they could continue their conversation, Reggie spoke up. "I'll see you guys there. I gotta go and meet Jade at the house."

"Sounds good. We'll be right behind you, man."

Reg descended the stairs and disappeared.

"So, that was a great game."

Shane sighed and shook his head. "I'm not sure what's gonna happen without Shawn. We won't be able to sustain the team the way it is right now without some stronger players." Frustrated, he stopped himself. "So, enough about that. Ready to head out?"

"Yes." Abi felt a high level of anxiety flood over her. Getting into the truck, she buckled up and said before he started the engine, "Shane, umm, there's something I need to show you."

Concerned, he said, "What is it?"

She handed him the matte black envelope. "Here."

He took hold of it and turned on the dash light. When he flipped the paper open, it stole the smile from his face. "Where did it come from?"

"The office called me down this morning. It got delivered to them."

"So, that whole thing wasn't about the tennis team? You've had this all day and didn't tell me?" He was more upset about that.

"Coach Taylor did talk to me after I picked it up from the secretary. So, really, I just left that part out. I didn't want to distract you before the game tonight. You're under enough stress. This was the last thing you needed."

Appreciating that to a degree, Shane rested his elbow along the window ledge. "Abs..."

"Please don't be mad."

"I'm not mad. I just wish you had confided in me. This is no joke." He checked over the envelope. "There's nothing but your name and the school's address on it?"

"Right. I have no idea who it's from." Hesitant to share her theory, she took a deep breath. "The only clue I have is its matte black style. It's a Black Lyon trademark."

"Yeah, you're right. Given that the guy has seemingly had you followed, it makes sense. The question still is why? Why warn you like this? Why not in person? Or some other way?"

"I don't know. With him wanted by the cops, maybe he couldn't risk it."

"Who else knows about this?" he asked.

Abi hesitated. "Well, Jade and, umm...."

"Burton?"

"Yes. He said I should go to the police station tomorrow. He is going with me."

"Well, if he's going, so am I." Shane felt slighted.

"Can I ask you something?"

"Sure."

"Would Emile do this? You know - pull a prank to freak me out?"

Shane shook his head. "She's done some stupid things in the past, but no, I don't think so."

"So, it's not a prank?"

"I can't say either way." Thinking about Burton's advice, he said, "You're right to go to the cops. If you're in danger, we must know why and by whom?" Shane placed the note inside the envelope and handed it back to her.

"Okay," she said, putting it in her bag.

Leaving the parking lot, he stayed quiet. Thinking about motives, he said, "Based on this, I'm wondering if we should skip the party."

"We can't. Jade is so excited about what they'd planned. I've gotta be there for her. Even if it's only for a little while."

"I think we should make an appearance and then head out."

"Sure. I'm okay with that."

# 77

BANG

While driving across Sunset Boulevard, Shane turned left on Foothill Road to take the back way into Reggie's street. Using Doheny to reach the Mountain Drive mansion, they approached the house and found the grounds uplit with colorful lights.

Shane's phone rang. Seeing it was Reggie, he answered, "Hey, man. We are almost there."

"Drive ahead in and park along the north wing of the house."

"Will do. See you shortly."

Slowly passing through the gates, Shane drove to the mouth of the subterranean garage. Parking on the incline, he said to Abi, "Remember, we're just making an appearance and leaving."

She nodded. "Yes. Agreed."

Locking the Jeep, they walked toward the front doors and ascended the floating steps with water trickling on either side. In a flurry of activity, the event planners, caterers, and the DJ with sound engineers on site all made last-minute preparations for the big event. Security was everywhere, keeping a watchful eye over the property.

Getting a view of the backyard through the foyer's glass walls, Abi stopped. She could see a massive stage with lights and LED screens shining brightly. "Wow, this is amazing. Look at that."

Lost for words, Jade came up behind her. "I know, right?" she said excitedly.

"Hi!" She hugged her friend. "I'm speechless. Wow!"

Reggie came up behind his girl and wrapped his arms around her waist. "This was all Jade. Her vision," he complimented. "My Baby is so talented."

"Awww…" She melted. "You're so sweet."

Kissing her, they saw the first of their guests filing in.

"It's gonna be an incredible night," Jade squealed, barely able to contain herself.

"Come on, Babe. We gotta greet our guests." Reggie took hold of her hand. "See you guys later. Grab a drink. Get some food. Enjoy!"

Abi and Shane continued through the house into the backyard to explore before the crowds invaded. Jade had food stations everywhere showcasing a variety of world-renowned flavors. They even had a candy bar. Finding five different drink cabanas scattering the grounds, it wasn't hard to select something they liked.

Spotting multiple raised platforms with seating areas resembling outdoor living rooms with lamps, side tables, sofas, and chairs, the fire bowls lining the yard's perimeter cast natural light. Sitting on the sofa by the pool, they watched the event planners give out luxury party favors to everyone arriving. From miniature Birkin bags filled with candy, Chanel lip balm, and perfume samplers for the girls to chocolate cigars and Aspinal mini flasks for the guys, she even had boxed Compartés Chocolatier delectables. It was wild.

The property soon flooded with partygoers from hedge to hedge. Surrounded by people, Abi could tell Shane was getting antsy. He could hear the distinct sounds of the exotics arriving, meaning there would be a car showcase on top of everything that night.

Music filled the air as the DJ went into action. The bass reverberated off the concrete walls and glass.

People came from far and wide. Everyone knew Reggie's event was the place to be. Some even compared it to a Black Lyon Rave. Around here, that was the highest compliment one could receive.

Cuddled beside Shane, Abi eavesdropped on a few conversations. Out of the blue, Shawn and Laney's names surfaced. From what she could gather, rumors were flying about Shawn serving jail time for assaulting Laney's ex-boyfriend in Cabo.

"Did you hear that?" Shane said.

"Yes. He won't really go to jail, will he?"

"I can't see it. Someone from Shawn's family will pull strings, pay the guy off, or threaten him to drop the charges."

Concerned about that, out of the corner of her eye, Abi spotted Adrian and Mei. After a difficult start to the week, they were now laughing and talking. She stayed close to him. It seemed they were now in a good place.

Just then, Alan approached. "Hey, Shane. Can I talk to you for a second?" he shouted over the music.

"Sure." Shane did the same and nodded.

Bending down, he shouted in the Captain's ear, "Umm, any chance it can be privately?" Turning to Abi, he said, "No offense."

"None taken," she replied loudly.

Shane leaned over and said, "Excuse me a second. Sorry."

The two guys walked a few feet away. Shane refused to be too far from Abi.

Focused on reading Alan's lips, Abi could not make heads or tails of what was said. Before parting ways, she saw Shane give him a manly pat on the back. His teammate seemed troubled.

Returning to the seat beside her, she asked him, "What was that about?"

"His parents got wind of the fight. They believe Gilderson is not strict enough for him, so they're transferring him to Westlake on Monday. He wanted to give me a heads up."

"Does Allie know?"

"He's telling her tonight. Don't say anything."

"Oh, she's gonna be heartbroken." Abi knew they'd have to be there for their friends in the aftermath.

"So, now we've got one player going to the competition and another injured, or worse. The coach told us they are actively recruiting new players. Guess that's why. The next month should be interesting." Amidst all the drama, he heard his favorite song. Wanting to be close to Abi, he offered his hand. "Dance with me?"

Nervous, she agreed. Escorting her to the dance floor, Shane twirled her once and wrapped his arm around her waist. Holding her hand, pressing her body against his, she rested her head on his chest. Hearing his heart beating, she wondered what the night would bring.

While most danced, mingled, or inhaled the food and drinks, Shane and Abi swayed with the music. It was perfect. Immersed in each other, he felt his phone vibrating in his back pocket. Checking it, he stared at the screen.

"What is it?" Abi asked.

Quickly looking up, he scanned the crowd frantically and pulled Abi close before showing her the message.

Reading it, she said, "You're dead…" A skull and crossbones were beneath the words. "Who sent that?" Seeing it ignited a sense of fear.

"I don't know," he replied, on high alert.

Within seconds, multiple notification bells sounded. One after another, screens were lighting up in mass.

"What's going on?" Abi said, watching the reaction of the mob surrounding them.

The message reached their phones. It was a link to a live feed.

The DJ on the platform above them stopped the music and mirrored the video on the LED wall. Everyone watched as flames engulfed the wall. As the camera zoomed out and the picture focused, they realized it was a house burning in the background—but not just any house.

Abi recognized it immediately. So did everyone else. Many were pointing at the images in disbelief. It was Black Lyon's Saturday night rave location - the place she'd visited in Hidden Hills yesterday.

"Why is he burning the house down?" Shane got a bad feeling.

An ominous voice announced in conjunction with the words typing across the big screen, "Sometimes, things come to an end...."

Reggie and Jade walked over, confused.

"What is this, Reg?" Shane asked.

"Dude, this is not us."

Abi's heart sank as fear engulfed her.

The Black Lyon logo digitally appeared and burned piece by piece along with the house. Stunned by the fiery scene, it caused a hum to fall upon the crowd as people watched it reduce to ash. The lights went out. Everything went dark but the jumbotron. The digitally produced swirling winds wisped past them in surround sound from speaker to speaker. On the screen, an ember appeared embedded in the dusty pile. The more the wind caught it, the more it glowed.

"But, sometimes, the end sparks a new beginning," the dark narrator explained.

A compilation of videos from DJ Black Lyon's rave events flashed and faded one by one, building up to an official announcement - Black Lyon's rebranding. Chilling music built suspense as a demonic skull ascended from the ash debris. The name Dark Demon flickered multiple times like a malfunctioning neon sign.

"Not all demons are evil," the voice announced in an other-worldly tone.

A person in the crowd shouted, "Yeeeeaaaahh! He's back!"

Cheers erupted from every angle as fireworks suddenly filled the sky in celebration. The glittery spectacle spanned from Beverly Hills to Bel Air and beyond, generating another notification to hit every phone.

Abi looked at her screen, and so did Shane. A prompt appeared with the option to download the new Dark Demon Rave app. Pressing it, they watched the promotional video. From what they could gather, the raves had now surpassed state lines. Immediately, social media erupted with the news as it spread across LA and went international.

"Dark Demon just launched worldwide," Shane said. "Wow, that's crazy. The guy's been busy."

While watching the spectacular pyrotechnics display overhead, everyone seemed more enthused about downloading and exploring the state-of-the-art app.

Assuming the text sent to him was part of the Black Lyon dramatics, Shane casually asked, "I think we should go," believing that was enough excitement for one night.

"Sure. I'm pretty tired anyway," she replied. "Besides, my Dad is at the hospital tonight. Maybe we can hang out at my place for a while?"

"That sounds like a plan." Offering her his hand, they walked up the sidehill.

"Hey! Where are you two goin'?" Jade shouted from the closest seating area. Running over to them, Reggie joined her.

"No offense, guys, but we're gonna head out."

Jade could see the football player was exhausted. "Sure, okay." Disappointed that they were leaving so early, she asked, "Hope you guys had fun?"

Knowing Abi needed to settle her mind, she said, "Yes. The party is absolutely beyond. You've outdone yourself. It's just been a tough week, you know..."

She understood what she meant. "Yes, I understand." Hugging her, she said, "Drive safe."

"We will." Shane wrapped his arm around Abi.

While waving to their friends, without warning, a loud explosion ripped through the estate, shaking the ground beneath their feet. The percussive wave hit at full force, violently leveling everything in its path. Left in darkness, the chiming sound of shattered glass filled the air as a fiery plume billowed high above the rooftop. Car alarms sounded as the foul smell of sulfur spread rapidly.

Sprawled on the grass a few feet from each other, Shane gasped, having had the wind knocked from his lungs. Groaning, he rolled over and spotted Abi. Crawling to her amidst the shards, feeling one puncture his skin, the ringing in his ears drowned out the fearful screams converging at every angle. With vision blurred, he tried to focus.

"A-b-i?" he mumbled, his chest and head aching, barely able to speak.

Hearing his muffled voice, her mind not cognitively there, she raised her head off the ground slightly, confused and disoriented.

Inching close enough to shield her with his body, he whispered, "Abs? Are you hurt?"

Unable to hear him clearly through the chaos, she saw the injured dripping in blood. Other dirt-laden ghosts seemed to wander aimlessly in a zombie-like state while many desperately ran in droves to evade the mayhem.

Spitting out her delayed response, she said, "I don't know." Attempting to sit up, she wobbled but stabilized herself. Propped against Shane, he shielded her.

"Reg?" Shane shouted to his friend, scanning the bodies moving on the ground.

The guy's voice pierced through the devastation. "Shane? Yeah, I'm good," he said. Checking on Jade beside him, still in shock, Reggie sat her up before heroically helping her. Scooping Jade into his arms, Shane did the same with Abi. They needed to get them to safety.

"This way," Reg said, pointing to the back right corner of his estate.

Against the grain, they dodged people still lying on the ground and those plowing through in fear.

Making it to the ivy wall, Reggie opened the steel door behind it. Inside was a panic room. "Stay here. You'll be safe. Shane and I have to go and meet the emergency crews." They could hear the sound of sirens and first responders in the distance.

The girls stepped inside.

"Reg, don't go. Just wait here until help arrives. Please," Jade pleaded. "What if it happens again?"

"Don't worry," Reg reassured. "I promise we'll be right back. It's okay."

The girls remained in the bunker, not given a choice. About to close the door, Reggie said, "Lock it from inside."

His girlfriend agreed to do that.

The two football players climbed the sidehill as the firetrucks pulled in front. Not wasting a minute, the brave men ran hoses and urgently spread out to assess the situation. Paramedics attended to the injured sitting along the curbs while police took statements from witnesses before allowing anyone to leave the premises.

Hit and bumped repeatedly by people fleeing in fear, Shane and Reggie finally reached the driveway. Knocked violently by a security team, desperately searching for someone, Shane assumed their client had sent a distress signal.

It was a war zone.

Finding three vehicles in flames, Shane remembered where he'd parked. "Umm, Reg. Is that my…?"

Not wanting to confirm it, Reg said, "Yeah, it's your Jeep, dude," as a police officer and fire chief approached.

"Is this your house," the chief asked.

"Yes, Sir." Reggie followed the officers and stood a safe distance from the burning vehicles. That is when he saw the full extent of the damage. The windows in the entire north wing were gone – blown out. Inside, the drapes were smoldering. Firefighters had already sprayed water on the burning shrubbery and trees below, and the concrete walls looked charred. "My parents are gonna crucify me," he whispered.

Watching his friend talking to the men, Shane couldn't believe what had happened. Rubbing his hand over his seemingly bruised ribs, he remembered the text he got seconds before the Dark Demon announcement.

"You're dead," he stammered as Jade came up behind him.

"Where's Reg?" she asked.

All Shane could do was point to him standing twenty yards away. Turning around, he expected to see Abi there but only found a group of shell-shocked people.

"Abs?" Shane said, scanning the grounds for her face. "Abi!" Locating Jade in Reggie's arms, he asked, "Where's Abs? Wasn't she with you?"

"She was right behind me."

Not sure where she'd gone, he looked left and then right and shouted, "Abi!"

"Shane!!"

Faintly hearing her frantic voice, he scoured the area in the direction it came from. "Abi! Abi?"

"Help!!"

Looking out the south gates, he saw her forced into a black Bentayga by the security team that'd bumped into him earlier. Dodging vehicles and people, he bolted toward her.

The men dressed in black shut the door before the caravan systemically sped off in formation.

Trying to chase it down, he banged on the window, but it was too fast. "Abi!" he shouted, seeing her face for a split second. "No!"

Standing in the middle of the street, feeling helpless, he saw someone getting into their Carrera 911. Grabbing the guy's key, he violently pulled him backward and slid into the driver's seat. Hearing him yelling obscenities, Shane stole the car and put it in gear before driving off at lightning speed. Approaching Sunset, the tires squealed when he came to a stop. Not knowing which direction to go, he looked east, then west. Seeing black trucks rounding the bend, almost out of sight, he said, "There you are," before stepping on the gas and fishtailing while making the turn.

Speeding along at an excessive clip, gaining ground on the SUVs, he got alongside them. Honking at the Bentley driver, the man arrogantly looked at him, ready to be challenged. Sharply veering left, the truck tried to run Shane into oncoming traffic.

"Holy shit." He held his breath and quickly jerked the wheel, barely threading between oncoming vehicles and the SUV.

Gaining control, not spinning out, he accelerated and stayed with them, neck and neck. Unable to see Abi through the tinted windows, he knew she was there and wasn't alone. There was a shadow of someone in the back seat. Willing to risk his life for her, he sped up. The world around him blurred. Focused, ready to cut off the vehicle, he glanced at the driver.

Cool and collected, the man executed an evasive maneuver and made a last-second right turn to evade the Porsche.

Losing them, Shane shouted, "Damn it!" as he bypassed the street. Thinking fast, he slammed on the brakes and cranked the wheel. Drifting, Shane made a hairpin turn as the tires squealed and smoked. Facing the opposite way, punching it, he raced through the Bel Air East gates at high speed before stopping dead at the three-way intersection. There was no sign of them.

"Which way?" Breathing erratically, his heart pumping a mile a minute, unable to catch his breath, he glimpsed at the three routes on the GPS. Not knowing where they went, he had no choice but to guess. "Straight!"

Pushing the pedal to the floor, he accelerated, shifting gears on the fly. The engine roared while speeding north on Bel Air Road. Rounding each corner, watching for them, he saw no sign of the trucks. Desperate, he kept driving and circling the area, street after street. He couldn't give up. Ten minutes went by. Then twenty, then thirty.

Not finding them, Shane slammed on the brakes. A flood of rage overtook him. Repeatedly punching the roof and gripping the steering wheel, he wanted to rip it to shreds. Reality hit. He'd lost her. She was gone. Taking his phone, he called Reggie.

"Shane? Where are you, man?" his friend said.

"Reg! These men took Abi. They forced her into a black Bentley. I went after her, but I lost 'em!"

"What?" Reggie replied as Jade listened on speaker.

Shane gasped for air. "Does Korolev have a Bentley?"

"I don't know." The guy panicked.

"The new SUV? Does he have one!" Shane shouted angrily.

The color drained from Jade's face. "Wait? What did you say?"

Shane repeated, "They were driving a...."

“Bentayga?” she interjected. “Oh my god, Shane! Listen to me! I know who it belongs to.”

“Who?”

“It’s Black Lyon!” she cried, “He took her!”

To Be Continued.....